PRAISE FOR CHRISTIAN KIEFER

THE HEART OF IT ALL

"If you want to find out the kind of novel that an offspring of Richard Russo and Alice Munro would write, look no further. Christian Kiefer is a great writer."

—**RABIH ALAMEDDINE,** author of *The Wrong End of the Telescope*

"This beautifully structured ensemble novel is Altmanesque in its complex, subtle intertwining of the lives of small-town Ohio factory workers and their families. Bringing together a diverse variety of voices, Kiefer weaves together a haunting, heartbreaking and empathetic portrait of contemporary America."

—**DAN CHAON,** author of *Sleepwalk*

"With *The Heart of It All,* the always brilliant Christian Kiefer offers readers a portrait of contemporary America that is deeply insightful, often surprising, and tenderly, beautifully observed."

—**LAUREN GROFF,** author of *Matrix*

"Kiefer deftly lulls you into his characters' lives, afloat in their isolation, before they swell into a cresting, spangled wave powered by pain and angst, that sweeps you ashore waiting to exhale."

—**MUSHARRAF ALI FAROOQI,** author of *Between Clay and Dust*

"For anyone who believes, as I do, that the best hope for our fractured country is local, not national, Christian Kiefer's new novel *The Heart of it All* will provide a welcome balm for the spirit. Here are people worth spending time with, not because they're perfect, but because they're not. What's wrong with them isn't nearly as consequential as how hard they fight for a better life, and not just for themselves. You set the book down and think, 'This is what we're made of.' Or should be."

—**RICHARD RUSSO**, author of *Somebody's Fool*

"Set in a crumbling small town in the Ohio Rust Belt, *The Heart of It All* should be required reading not only for anyone wanting to understand our country as it exists today, with all its hatred, divisiveness, and economic disparity, but also for those who wish to know how to be a decent human being even as the American Dream recedes further and further into the past. It is a truly beautiful achievement." —**DONALD RAY POLLOCK**, author of *The Devil All the Time* and *The Heavenly Table*

PHANTOMS

Kirkus Reviews • Best Historical Fiction of 2019

The Million • Most Anticipated Books of 2019

"*Phantoms* sings from its surreal beginning to its stunning end . . . Throughout, Kiefer's writing is lovely, ripe with striking figurative language, as the story unspools in a succession of devastating encounters between two American families: one white, the other Japanese American . . . This is a beautiful, relevant read."

—**JESMYN WARD**, author of *Sing, Unburied, Sing*

"*Phantoms* is a virtuosic unearthing of buried betrayals and traumas—the kind that have the force to shatter myths, both national and personal, and to breach long-held silences . . . This book hums with the pulse of poetry and the pace of a mystery. Let it draw you in and leave you changed."

—**LAURA VAN DEN BERG**, author of *The Third Hotel*

"The pacing of *Phantoms* felt like a perfect gallop into every sunset . . . *Phantoms* is a story of history, examination, and is a pleasure to read." —**NATASHIA DEÓN, author of *Grace: A Novel***

"A stunning, suspenseful, heartbreakingly gorgeous read of a book."

—**MARIE MUTSUKI MOCKETT, author of *Where the Dead Pause, and the Japanese Say Goodbye***

"In aching, earthly prose, and with resolute sincerity, Kiefer explores the savage consequences of American fear."

—**CLAIRE VAYE WATKINS, author of *Gold Fame Citrus* and *Battleborn***

THE ANIMALS

"A mesmerizing literary thriller." —***PUBLISHERS WEEKLY***

"A rare young stylist, with an abundance of vivid, engrossing stories in his brain; Christian Kiefer is a genuine find."

—**RICHARD FORD**

"Eloquent and shattering. . . . This novel embodies why we write and why we read." —***KIRKUS REVIEWS* (starred review)**

"An unusual and compelling amalgam of noir classic . . . This tough-minded thriller weaves a hot red thread through an introspective, sensuous landscape, a meditation on instinct, memory and the nature of friendship between species and between men."

—**JANET FITCH, author of *Paint it Black* and *White Oleander***

THE INFINITE TIDES

Booklist • Top Ten First Novels of 2012
Publishers Weekly • Best Books of Summer 2012
Kirkus Reviews • Best Fiction of 2012

"An astute, impressive, and ambitious debut."

—***PUBLISHERS WEEKLY*** **(starred review)**

"Smart, lyrical, deeply moving. The central character, a NASA astronaut who has touched the stars, must come to earth, as we all must. What he finds down here beneath the heavens is dizzying in its emotional complexity and pure aching beauty."

—**T.C. BOYLE, author of *When the Killing's Done***

"This is a subtle and moving novel, a re-entry and recovery story that eloquently inhabits the terrain of grief and endurance."

—**ANTONYA NELSON, author of *Bound***

THE HEART OF IT ALL

ALSO BY CHRISTIAN KIEFER

Phantoms

The Animals

The Infinite Tides

One Day Soon Time Will Have No Place Left to Hide

THE HEART OF IT ALL

A NOVEL

CHRISTIAN KIEFER

MELVILLE HOUSE
BROOKLYN • LONDON

The Heart of It All

First published in 2023 by Melville House

First Melville House Printing: July 2023

Melville House Publishing
46 John Street
Brooklyn, NY 11201
and
Melville House UK
Suite 2000
16/18 Woodford Road
London E7 0HA

mhpbooks.com
@melvillehouse

ISBN: 978-1-68589-081-0
ISBN: 978-1-68589-072-8 (eBook)

Library of Congress Control Number: 2023936563

Designed by Beste M. Doğan

Printed in the United States of America

10 9 8 7 6 5 4 3 2 1

A catalog record for this book is available from the Library of Congress

To

Michael Spurgeon and

Eleanor Jackson

for continuing to believe in me

I remember when it didn't use to be so hard
This used to be impossible
A new season has to begin
I can feel it leaning in whispering

—JASON MOLINA, "Almost Was Good Enough"

THE HEART OF IT ALL

PART 1

TOM BAILEY

Death brought casseroles and Tom took them, every one, his hands numb upon the square glass containers, many warm from the oven, others cold so that their foiled tops wept with moisture. There was nothing to be done but stand and nod and thank people for coming and answer questions about Sarah, yes, she was doing OK, considering, just tired, you know, and nodding again and nodding again and nodding again. He did not even know some of their names, people from church he had seen for years but had never really spoken to. They would tell him how sorry they were, how the Lord works in mysterious ways, how we should all have faith in times of trouble, and if there's anything I can do to help don't hesitate to call, their faces screwed into masks of concern and grief that he knew was real and yet knew also was not their grief to bear but only a mirror of his own. And Sarah's. At least you got to know him for a time before God took him away. At least there was that much. But in the deep well of his heart he wished the baby had died during the pregnancy and that they had not seen him at all, that the six months of his short life were simply erased from his memory and from his wife's memory and from the memories of his two living children. That he had to make such a distinction, to call two of his children living, made him feel a stranger to himself but then he knew that this was who he was now, that this too had been added to the scales.

His mother-in-law bustling by with the latest casserole. Pastor Mitchell in his black clerical garb, head cocked like an intently listening dog before the nearly identical shapes of Tom's neighbors, the Finns. Guests lingering, unsure of how long to stay, but surely wanting to leave, to flee. Did he not want the same? Across the small living room, Sam's head tilted toward the two other members of the bowling team, Betty and Cheryl, the three of them likely engaged in pointless strategizing. Tom desired nothing more than to tell them to grab their gear and meet him at the Bowl-O-Rama; he wanted to watch the machine rack the pins, then that moment of serenity, imperturbable and noiseless, his body simultaneously taut and loose. All there: the release, the skid, that hanging moment just before the frozen ball began to rotate upon its axis, its reflection in the waxed lane, the way it held the gutter's edge before spinning homeward. My God it was perfect. But he was not at the bowling alley. He was in his own living room on a November day in the hours after his infant son's funeral and what kind of man thought of bowling in such a moment? Sam nodded and Betty and Cheryl both opened their mouths in apparent astonishment. And sweet baby James was still in his tiny coffin under the turned soil of the cemetery. This was what was.

Sam's wife, Amy, was before him now, her hair recently recolored so that the slanting light from the window lit its outline in shades of maroon. "You tell her to call me," she said. "Whatever you need. And I know people say that all the time but really, Tom, whatever you need, you just pick up the phone."

"I appreciate that." He nodded for emphasis.

Amy patting his shoulder as if he were a pet of some kind. "Oh, honey, I can't imagine what you're all going through," and when he said nothing in response, for what could he say, she said: "Well, you just call us if you need anything. Really, Tom. Friends and family. We're both, aren't we?"

"Sure, Amy," he said.

"And make sure Sarah knows that too. I went back there to the bedroom, you know, just to see her, but she's sleeping now and thank God for that. I mean, God knows she needs her rest. So you make sure she knows I'm here for her."

"I'm sure she already knows that, Amy."

"I know she does but tell her anyway."

He told her he would. He knew she meant well, that she was—despite what Sam sometimes said about her—a good person, or was trying to be a good person, was trying, that is, in the way we all try and fail to be what we are not, to be better than who we actually are.

From somewhere toward the kitchen: his mother-in-law's voice. She had driven down from Wisconsin a week before, had set up the funeral arrangements and had insisted on this reception, or whatever it was. He did not know what he wanted except that it was not this but Sarah had said nothing, nothing at all, and so, in the end, he had acquiesced, meeting her silence with his own, his mother-in-law's bustling energy both welcome and unwelcome, achieving things that he simply did not have the heart to do himself. Yes there was to be a funeral. For a baby. For his baby. James. How strange to think of such a thing. The coffin had been so small. Like a toy. Sarah like crushed paper. Her mother stood beside her and Tom stood flanked by Charlie and Janey, his daughter, his eldest, nearly as tall as himself, his son, at fourteen, only a few inches below that. Janey wept quietly during the service but Charlie only looked on, his face blank and pale in the shifting November light, staring out through the flap of hair ever-covering his eyes. Dry oak leaves rustled yellow and orange above them. It occurred to him now, in the aftermath of that horror, in his own cramped living room, that he did not know where either of his living children were. Only the dead child.

The door again and his mother-in-law's voice: "And who are you now? What's that? And who's this?" and finally a kind of halting assurance, "Oh, oh, of course, please yes, please come in," and when she stepped back the figure that entered the room was Mr. Marwat, the man's wife and teenaged children filing in behind and the door swinging closed again. "Tom? Tom?" his mother-in-law said, spinning around to find him. She looked, to Tom, somehow deranged: a woman shaped like a loaf of bread, her face a porcelain rictus of smiling agitation and concern. "Here he is, mister . . . what did you say your name was again?"

Around them, a brief lull, a change in register which was the sound of people noticing and commenting but putting effort into seeming like they were not noticing or commenting. A cluster of dark skin and white eyes. Marwat's suit the color of polished armor, his wife and children dressed—all of them dressed—as if they had just come from church. But from what church could they have come?

And he knew he would have to speak now, knew it and dreaded it even as the words escaped his lips. "Mr. Marwat," he said. "Thanks for coming by." He glanced to Mrs. Marwat. "All of you," he said.

"Tom," Marwat said, "I'm so sorry for your loss."

His hand was smooth and soft and the feel of it brought a flush of unwarranted anger racing through Tom's chest. But he said nothing, only nodded yet again at words he had heard a hundred times, three or four times each from everyone in the house. He had been nodding all day. He would nod, it seemed, forever now.

Marwat reintroduced his children, Saroya and Rashid, in age a mirror of his own, both appearing utterly terrified at having been brought to this house of death and sadness.

Marwat leaned close. He smelled of cologne. "Can I have a moment?" he said in his familiar, lilting accent. His face fleshy. His black hair shone as if oiled. Perhaps it was.

"Sure," Tom said.

"Maybe outside?"

Tom looked to Mrs. Marwat, who only nodded, a motion so subtle that it might not have occurred at all. Beside her the two children looked utterly lost, glancing at each other and then at their mother and then around the room as if to locate something by which to anchor themselves. Gawky, awkward teens.

"Charlie and Janey are around here somewhere," Tom said to them. "Maybe check the back."

"That's OK," the girl, Saroya, said.

"Well," Tom said, "I'd appreciate it if you'd check in on them. It'd be a help."

"They'll do that," their mother said, nodding seriously. "Absolutely."

The girl rolled her eyes, the boy only continuing to stare about the house, perhaps searching for an exit.

Marwat went to the door and Tom opened it and together they stepped outside. The change in the air was welcome, a kind of brightness that flooded into his chest as he followed the sharkskin into the bite of autumn, the lowering sun casting shadows out across a road that seemed, in the coming darkness, to match the suit color perfectly. The grass crunching underfoot. From the west: an occasional gust of shivering wind. Early yet for snow, but there was no doubt that it was coming.

"Listen, Tom," Marwat said, turning to face him. He looked over Tom's shoulder to the house then reached out and took his arm and directed him farther away. Marwat was not wearing a coat, only the shiny gray jacket. He was Tom's own age although in truth Tom thought of him as much older, as if the relative darkness of the man's complexion added some undefinable span of years to his life, this despite the fact that their children were the same age, went to the same school, as his own. How strange the world had become. And all of us caught spinning upon its still, unmoving surface.

Marwat stopped and turned, glancing toward the silence of the house. The light around them stretched low and carried with it the faintest tinge of orange. "I wanted you to have this," Marwat said. In his hand was a thin envelope marked with the logo of the factory. "It's just to help a bit. Just for . . . expenses and such."

"Oh," Tom said. His eyes were on the envelope and then he realized that he was supposed to take it, that it was for him, and his hand reached for it and he said thank you and held it in his hands, looking at its shape. It was a check, he was sure, although how much he did not know. He wondered if he was supposed to have tried to refuse it once or twice before giving in and accepting but the truth was he needed the money and was glad to have it, however much it was or was not.

"It's not an advance, you understand," Marwat said. "It's a gift. To help you in this difficult time."

"I appreciate it," Tom said.

"It's from both of us. Rafia and myself."

"You'll thank her for me, won't you?"

"Of course."

Tom looked at the envelope in his hand. "I'd better—we'd—I mean, I should probably go back inside. Thank you again." He folded the envelope and slipped it into his coat pocket. "I appreciate it. Really."

"I'm glad to be of some help," Marwat said.

They both turned back toward the house but Tom did not step forward. Marwat opened his mouth to speak, but then closed it again. He reached out one thin-fingered hand and set it upon Tom's shoulder in the same place so many others already had. The language of grief apparently identical for all. A faint squeeze. Then Marwat moved back toward the house, up the thin cold stairs, and disappeared inside.

Sam emerged soon after, huffing down into the yard, his breath blowing steam. "Shit, it's freezing out here," he said, tugging his coat around the great swell of his belly, his cheeks pink with cold. "What'd Marwat want?"

"Just condolences, same as everyone."

"Couldn't have done that in the living room like everyone else?"

Tom shrugged. "What's happening in there?"

"Same. I think we're getting ready to head out, if that's OK."

"Why wouldn't it be?"

"Just that, you know, I can hang. If you need me to, I mean. Not that you'd need me to. Shit. Just sayin', you know . . ."

Tom could not help but smile, faint though it was. "I'm all right, Sam," he said.

"Well, Amy's in there talking to your mother-in-law so really we might never leave."

"My mother-in-law can talk," Tom said.

"Both of them," Sam said. "You wanna smoke?"

Tom took one and Sam lit them both. For a long while, only the silence of the coming night. On the street, the white oaks had gone black in the last blazing light of the setting sun. The whole of that part of the world entering its slow plunge toward night.

When the door opened again it was Marwat once more, this time his family in a line behind him. A few words then. Yes he'd be taking some time off. Good good. Thanking Mrs. Marwat for coming. Finally the gray SUV started up in a low hum and pulled off the gravel and into the road. A small flock of grackles flooded up from some distant tree and settled once more. The sky so bright and the world so dark, an endless silhouette of trees and houses running in angles slightly off square, the sidewalks darkly shattered by root and frost, the streetlights above them winking now into muted brilliance. From where he stood, Tom could feel the whole of the drift plain—its kettles and kames, its hills and valleys and tillage—spreading out in a similar hush, a sound to match the buffeted silence of his heart.

"I guess I won't see you Tuesday night."

"Probably not. Maybe not for a while."

"Just me and Hardiman in a duel to the death," Sam said. Then he shook his head, "Aw shit, I shouldn't have said that."

"Said what?"

"Never mind."

"Don't get all weird on me," Tom said.

"I can't help it," Sam said.

Again the quiet of the coming night. Last birds in the sky, unknown, unknowable in their black silhouettes. The maples and oaks along the road shook in some high hidden breeze and then the same breeze rushed down across the grass, stinging their faces and bringing water to their eyes. Sam took a final drag and dropped the cigarette to the grass and crushed it with his heel. "Gonna try to extract the wife," he said.

Tom nodded. And then he was alone again. The sky still bright. The landscape all around plunging into irresolute shadow and then darkness and then night. He dreaded what that would mean. For himself. For his wife. For all the days to come.

KHALID

Ohio in the gloaming. A plane of lakewater hardens to pewter and slate. Upon its bank: lit asphalt and concrete and neon and shadow, a tangle and fade and resurgence and fade again, southward, southward flow the tangled streets until, all at once, there are streets no more, no streets and no city, as if there never had been, so wide and empty is the raw, dark country beyond, the whole of that tumult funneled to a single thin ribbon of isolated highway cutting the coming eventide. It is here, between towns huddling in the new darkness and in the stubble of harvested corn and soybeans and the dusk-shadows of grain silos and red-board barns, that comes a quietude in descent: upon field and forest, upon deer and bobcat, otter and marten, squirrel and mole, the world of flesh and blood and bone, of tooth and claw going to ground. In shadowed oaks and beech and maple, the coming winter's first finches twitter the failing day. Grosbeak. Siskin. Crossbill. Nuthatch. Shovelers tuck into the marshy darkness while, high above, Canada geese cross the last light of the southward-leaning sky and under which, in the rolling hills beyond the outskirts of electricity, Amish families glow with oil flame, their windows abloom with muted golden light. From the road: the garish, flat coruscation of an automobile. In its headlights the growing night is cast in black shadow, angular, turning, the bracken gone berserk, stretching even in the failing light, and then racking back to its true shape once more. An owl's wings flash against the windshield. A shrew disappears into its hole.

At the edge of town, square-cut windows float, amber and adrift in the coming night, the families within mostly hidden from roadside traffic but for an ephemeral glimpse: a woman passing the window, a child, a man, the warbling glow of a television. Fugitives in brief. The town itself folds in upon the dusk. In the best of times it is, truth to be told, a haggard place, once a center of modest industry but that time is a century gone and what remains struggles for simple continuance, its citizens surviving paycheck to paycheck, on loan, on credit, on faith, a small town growing smaller as the years pass and the hard winters continue. Structures of brick and clapboard, a history of additive architecture: American four square, Queen Anne, Greek revival, neoclassical, ranch homes on streets which were once the newest part of town, and, of course, homes of no description at all: peak-roofed boxes with railed patios, storm doors rattling. Upon many, one might envision the clean bright lines of another era, a time of prosperity that has the feeling, now, of myth. Placards indicating the homes of high school football and basketball players and a few yet remaining for the previous year's presidential election. MAKE AMERICA GREAT AGAIN. All of this amidst the darkness of meltwater stains, missing shingles patched with plywood or plastic sheeting, broken windowglass with duct-taped cardboard, between which are those who are just able to maintain and repair and hold together the tenuous shamble of their lives. Dead lawns mowed clean to bare bristle.

And yet to Khalid the place was a kind of earthly paradise, not in comparison with Lahore but only in comparison to the quality of his own heart. Even now, driving away from Tom Bailey's, he could not help but feel that he had arrived in exactly the place he was always meant to be. What a feeling it was that he could help a man in need, an employee to whom he had entrusted certain aspects of the factory's operations, his foreman, and which he, Khalid Marwat, was now in a position to aid.

He wanted to chatter away to his family, at least to Rafia, but his wife and two children were utterly silent in the car, enwrapped in a dire quietude that had descended the moment they had left their home for the Baileys', Rafia staring out the windshield at the unrolling street, the children, just behind, on their phones, each illumed in a dim halo of blue light. His thoughts were of the ice-cream shop but when he pulled into the little parking lot, it was to find the building dark and empty.

"What are you doing?" Saroya whined from the back seat. "It's Sunday. It closes at four."

"Tone," Khalid said, turning the wheel so that the little SUV rocked over the asphalt in a loop, back toward the street. "Kroger will be open."

"Why are we going to Kroger's? Can't we just go home?"

"There's no ice cream at home."

"Who wants ice cream?"

"Everyone."

She scoffed petulantly. "I don't."

"You will."

"You're obsessed."

"Probably true."

Rafia said nothing beside him. It had been she who had insisted they attend, all of them together, although he assured her that he was perfectly willing to go alone, to make an appearance and to hand over the envelope, an amount, five hundred, which he at first had thought a bit extravagant but which his wife had convinced him was more likely barely adequate. "They lost their child," she said to him, repeating it again and again. "I understand that," he said. She had advocated for a thousand dollars, but he knew that the factory could not readily justify such an added expense, even in these circumstances, and, in any case, he did not understand how a thousand dollars would change the fact of what had happened. And yet now he wondered why he had not given Tom Bailey more.

He parked near the cart return at the market. "Come on," he said to the interior. "Everyone gets to choose their own flavor."

"Just get me Chunky Monkey," Rashid said from the back seat.

And then Saroya: "I'll take Cherry Garcia."

"Oh my," he said. "And I thought you didn't want any."

"Fine," Saroya said. "I do, OK. You happy?"

"Very. Now you can come inside and pick it out yourself."

"Can't you do it?"

"Am I your servant?" Khalid said.

And the children, together: "Yes."

"No," Khalid said. "If you want ice cream, you come inside with your father."

Saroya moaned but then she whipped off her seat belt and opened the door. Rashid a moment afterward.

"Come on, my love," he said then.

"I'll wait here."

"Come on," he said again. "We'll go inside together. All of us."

"I can't imagine what they're going through," she said. "His poor wife—"

"It's a tragedy but we've done what we can."

"I know," Rafia said. She turned to look at him. Her eyes were steady and bright and beautiful even in the greasy lamplight of the parking lot.

"You know what will also be a tragedy?" he said. "If they're out of Half Baked."

"Stop, jaan," she said. "It's not something to joke about."

“I’m not joking,” he said, raising his hands before him. “I’m very serious. I’m likely to cause a scene. You might have to bail me out of jail. How would that look?”

“You’re impossible,” she said, but he could sense the slightest turn of a smile in her voice.

“Come on,” Khalid said. “Cookie dough awaits.”

“Chubby Hubby,” she said.

“Yes, I know. That’s how you like me,” he said.

This time she batted a hand at his shoulder and opened the door.

Inside, the market was bright and quiet and mostly empty. The two children were not visible as they moved to the ice-cream aisle and he picked his pint and she stood looking. “Do we need anything else?” he asked.

“Not tonight,” she said. “I’ll come back later this week with the list.”

He nodded. “We’ll need to run to Columbus too.”

“I know, jaan,” she said. “You’ve told me that exactly one million times.”

“Right,” he said. “So you almost remember.”

She rolled her eyes. “I’ll get everything on the list. Mother and father will be satisfied.”

“You know, you might also need to go to Cleveland if they don’t have what we need in Columbus.”

“Stop worrying,” Rafia said. “I’ll get everything. It will be fine.”

“Especially lamb,” he said. “There’s never lamb here. I don’t know what my parents will think if there’s no lamb.”

“They’ll be fine.” She sighed. “Are we done here?”

“You didn’t pick a flavor.”

“I don’t want ice cream,” she said. “I just came inside so you’d stop bothering me.”

"Did it work?"

"Not really," she said.

They found the children in the magazine aisle. Saroya was becoming a beautiful young woman, a fact that astonished Khalid as much as it troubled him, and Rashid, two years younger than his sister, had gone from being a carefree child to a sullen, self-absorbed teen in what seemed the span of a single afternoon. He wondered anew what his father would think of the two of them and how the elder Marwat's observations might ultimately result in some dire judgment of Khalid's role as parent or, even worse, on Rafia's, his mother being, if he were honest, the more judgmental of the two. They were, he tried to remind himself, of a different generation and, at least in comparison with the children, a different culture, for as much as they were Pakistani, he knew that ultimately Saroya and Rashid were American, more American than he or Rafia would ever be.

Their cashier was, as far as Khalid knew, the only Black woman in town. She rang them up without extraneous conversation and soon they were in the car again. Khalid had hoped that the ice cream would lighten their mood some and it seemed that even the short trip to the grocery had done so, for Saroya and Rafia were engaged in a conversation about some new and rather absurdly named drink at the local coffeeshop. Khalid wondered what day Rafia would be going to Columbus. The idea of his parents' impending arrival filled him, yet again, with that combination of dread and excitement. How he wanted them here at last and how he feared they would pick apart the small, beautiful life he had made.

The road they took wound back through the battered neighborhood streets that constituted the town. Through the window came the shadowed declivity at the choked base of which ran the river, its burbling flow draining southward into country gone equally black and beside which stood the empty park, deserted now of children and appearing, in the early hours of the autumnal night, as a macabre wasteland out of one of the horror movies he sometimes caught his son watching on his laptop when he was supposed to be doing his homework. In the rearview, he could see Rashid's face doubled, the landscape of gray trees and rough-worn houses reflecting across his features like an ever-changing mask.

He had a sudden urge to ask his son how he was doing in his algebra class. At midsemester, Rashid's report card had revealed a failing grade and yet Khalid knew that were he to ask the boy about the class, his son would say, I'm doing fine. A lie. And right to his father's face. As if Khalid's position of authority as the boy's father was of little consequence. And all the while what he wanted, at least where it came to the children, was to interact with them about anything other than their own failures but it had increasingly come to feel as if their failures had made, of all their lives, a kind of pattern. There were standards, there had to be, and they were reasonable enough. His own education in Pakistan had been marked by teachers who would beat him if and when he failed in his lessons. Avoidance of that punishment had been an obvious and clear motivator and while it was true that he balked at the idea of some teacher beating his own children, he could not help but wonder why they regarded their own self-improvement as such an utterly casual concern. For Rashid it was, and had ever been, lackluster grades. Saroya, at least, excelled in school but hers was to break the house's very reasonable midnight curfew on every possible occasion. It was as if the basic boundaries he and Rafia had set for the children were thought of not as rules but as casual suggestions. What would his father say when he arrived in Ohio? What would his mother? He shuddered to think.

Their own neighborhood now: the road's path beginning its quiet loops across the small grassy hills that ran against the edge of the river, the homes here larger, more sturdy, fronted by manicured lawns and flower beds, although now such features were mostly shriveled, no income sufficient enough to maintain against the coming winter. Theirs was a two-story block of brickwork shaped into a kind of arc upon a small hill. A few other similar-sized homes but not many, and the road a thin ribbon of asphalt that snaked through the grass between them, curved driveways disappearing through the trees.

The garage door slid open and his children were out of the car before he had even come to a full stop. "Don't let the door slam," his wife said to their retreating forms but already the door that led into the house had crashed closed. She let out a brief groan of frustration even as she opened the door herself and disappeared inside, the grocery bag dangling from one arm.

And then Khalid, alone in the garage, the car's heat ticking in the cool of the night, behind him the black driveway and the street. No stars as of yet but soon. In the summer months, he would sometimes stand in the yard in the hour after twilight and listen to the sounds of crickets, that overlapping sine wave drifting to him from somewhere down the hill. He had read that it was a love song of sorts, a way in which to attract a mate. Now though, in the autumn cold, only a faint, lethargic rustling: eventide rolling across the great sweep of Ohio. A breeze he could not feel but which sifted through the elm's yellow leaves. The distant hollow bark of a dog. He wondered where the crickets went in the winter months, if they lived, somehow, under the snow, or simply perished when the weather turned, their love song there one day and just as suddenly gone.

PAULA

The closing shift an endless stretch of hours, the night so hesitant in coming that there were moments in which she wondered if it ever would, some internal clock telling her that it had to be night, that it just had to be night, and happening to pass a window to find that the sun still hung bright and hard in the late afternoon sky. Break for Shelly. Break for Laura. Black leaves on the butter lettuce. Spill in the milk aisle. She was not officially the night manager, not in title nor in pay, but for nearly a year it had been her the others had looked to for guidance when anything went amiss. Tonight the whole store was understaffed on account of the funeral and Sarah Bailey gone for so long now that it was unclear if she would ever return, although the store manager had done nothing to fill her vacant position in the deli department. Of course Paula knew she should have attended the service as well, and while she had found ways to justify her own absence—someone had to run the store that Sunday, after all—the real truth of it was that she felt she had long ago fulfilled her life's measure of funerals and when at last the store's front windows revealed darkness, her relief came not because she had been counting the minutes toward the end of her shift but because the close of that day meant that the service for Sarah's child was over, her relief temporarily banished by the appearance of the Pakistani family who owned the electronics factory, their clothing enough to inform her from whence they had come. She rang up their ice cream without comment, after which she prayed that the pall of ghosts that had fallen over her day would release her, although of course she knew that would not be the case, and that what she truly awaited was not the end of that sad funeral at all.

She was nearly finished closing when her phone buzzed at last. She said her sister's name.

"We're here," came Franny's reply.

"Just about done."

"How long?"

"Ten minutes maybe. I got lasagna we can microwave."

"I can't stay," she said. "Eddie's waiting up."

"He can wait. I haven't seen you since last Christmas."

"Wish I could," she said. "I'm gonna need a little gas money."

"Eddie don't give you enough for gas?"

"Don't make me beg," her sister said quietly.

"Franny," Paula said into the phone. She sighed then. "All right but it's gonna take me a minute."

"I can't wait too long. Can't I send Anthony to the door?"

"No," she said simply. "Just wait, Franny. Drive around back by the garbage bins."

"Can't you come out the front?"

"Come to the back," she said again.

She finished up as quickly as she could, totaling out the day's registers and putting the thick leather envelope into the safe's slot and turning out of the office at last, the door closed and locked behind her.

She went through the store one final time then, its silent aisles clean and shining, packages aligned in antiseptic brightness, orange and yellow and red, the front door locked and the parking lot empty of cars, pools of pale light adrift out there in that endless night at the outer edge of which she could just see the flickering of a truck passing on the distant highway. She rounded to the back now, past the office, checking the handle a final time before finally pushing open the security door and stepping into the cold.

Franny's car was the same as it had been for many years, a smoking, dilapidated Chrysler, once gold in color, mirrors duct-taped into position, one rear brake light covered by a sheet of red plastic. How it continued to run year after year, Paula did not know. She thought her sister would appear to greet her but the only motion that came from the car was the passenger door squeaking open and her nephew stepping outside. "Hey, Auntie," he said. He was, in the dark, but a slip of a boy, nineteen and underdressed for the cold, his eyes points of pale light, the rest of him mostly a silhouette. A sock hat over his hair.

"Hey Anthony," Paula said. "You OK?"

"I'm fine," he said quickly. He returned to the inside of the car, leaning into the door, perhaps speaking briefly to his mother behind the wheel. When he stepped free again it was to pull the seat forward and extract a battered duffel from the back. Then the door closed altogether.

"She coming out to say hello?"

"She don't feel good," he said simply.

"She high?"

He shrugged.

Neither moved and Paula descended at last to the car. Her sister sat behind the wheel, staring forward, turning only when Paula knocked her knuckle against the glass. Her sister's gaze offered no recognition at all. Then something released and she cranked the glass down.

"You plan on just driving off without saying anything to me?" Paula said.

"Like I said, I gotta get back to Eddie," Franny said quietly. There was, Paula recognized, a heaviness in her voice. Her eyes held within them the faintest tinge of yellow, dark skin ashen and tight in the dim glow of the dashlights. She looked, to Paula, terribly thin, a starved, feral creature.

"You come over and have some coffee before you get on the road," Paula said.

"I can't."

"Can you drive?" She looked then to Anthony, a few feet away at the back of the car, the taillights and exhaust cloud enveloping him, a bright shadow-washed blur. "Can she drive?"

"I can drive, goddammit," Franny said.

"So there's some life in you after all," Paula said.

"I can drive better than you."

"Don't be like that," Paula said, an edge in her voice. "I'm doing you a favor, not the other way around."

"Fine," Franny said, and in the next moment she was yelling: "Anthony! Anthony! Get back in the car!"

"Oh, stop," Paula said. She reached for her purse, fumbled with the clasp and finally had a twenty-dollar bill in her hand, which she held in the air close enough to her that her sister had to reach her hand out the window to retrieve it, a hand which, as Paula watched, trembled slightly in the cold, shadowed air. "What do you say now?" Paula said.

"Thank you," her sister said, eyes downcast.

"You come over and have a plate," Paula said. "Eddie can wait a minute."

"I gotta go," she said.

"You don't gotta go. No man's worth dying on the highway for."

"I gotta go," she said again. "Take care of my boy."

And then, before Paula could say another word, the sedan jumped forward, Paula stumbling and leaping away and finally standing there in the aftermath of her sister's life, the Chrysler's mismatched brake lights dipping and wobbling and finally winking out of sight as the car rounded the edge of the building and was gone.

There had been a time when she would have screamed something in the wake of that departure, some stream of curses to follow her sister into the darkness but now she only stood, hands on hips, exhaling steam into the black air. Her back ached. In the sudden stillness behind the grocery she could hear Anthony shuffling against the weight of his duffel.

"You got what you need?" she said, her eyes still focused on the vacancy of her sister's departure. Kroger was on the edge of town and beyond it ran the fields and farms and tangled forestlands of North Central Ohio, a landscape of gentle hills that eventually crumbled into Cleveland and the great cold gray sweep of Lake Erie. She had almost never seen that lake, despite having grown up just a few miles from its shoreline. After all these years, she still thought it a place people who looked like her did not go.

"Yeah," Anthony said.

"She gonna make it back OK?"

"She always does," he said simply.

"All right," she said. "My car's out there. Let's go."

She turned now and watched him as he looked in the direction she had gestured, the car in its pool of light, cold and clear and empty, the boy standing in his thin jacket, duffel over his arm, thick headphones slung around his neck. She knew almost nothing about him but when her sister had called to ask her if he could come stay with her for a time she agreed almost wholly without thought. Since that conversation, she had oft wondered at her own reaction as it seemed utterly out of keeping with what she had always known and how she had always behaved toward Franny, at least since they had become adults and had diverged along such different paths, or rather after she had diverged, Franny having remained behind as if to satisfy a measure of abject suffering known only to her. She knew her sister to be alternately manipulative and broken, depending on what man she was with and where she was in her ongoing cycle of sobriety and addiction, a cycle that was, Paula knew, more tied to economics than any desire to live clean. She should have asked Franny what the boy had done to make him want to come out here to the countryside, to this little town in which Paula had lived for nearly two decades, a town of blue-collar whites which had, even during the years in which Paula had been here, begun to crumble in on itself. The laboratory her then-husband had worked at was gone, of course, and so was the bottling plant and the wool factory, that history marked by the empty husks of great brick buildings, their windows boarded long before Paula's arrival as a young bride.

That she had come here at all, that she had braved this foreign place, a place wholly devoid of people who looked like her, who came from whence she had come, could be wholly accounted for by her adherence to the man who had been her husband. That she had remained in the wake of that failed marriage, remained, that is, in a town for which she did not feel much affinity, if any, was, perhaps, more a reflection of her own sense of stubbornness than of action. She had not chosen to stay here so much as she had chosen not to return to Kinsman, the idea that she might have traveled elsewhere never entering her thoughts at all. And so she remained and had, across two decades, managed to build a small quiet life here, a life the exact opposite of Franny's, joining a local church and making the best of her job at the grocery, rising to the position of head cashier and performing the tasks and duties of management during those periods when the actual store manager was absent, and while she had no friends to speak of, no real friends, she at least knew that she would survive. Most of the time, that felt like all she could really ask.

"Hungry?"

"Yeah," Anthony said.

"Let's get on then," she said. "I've got some leftovers in the fridge."

"OK," he said.

They stepped forward as one, their feet sharp against the asphalt. The loading dock was a great pale wedge in the night. "Don't be thinking I'm gonna be waiting on you," she said now. "I'm not your momma. You're nineteen and that's plenty old enough to take care of yourself."

"OK," he said.

"Just want to make that clear."

"OK."

"You don't talk much, I guess."

He stood hunched in on himself as if embarrassed by his own skin. Something in that posture pulled at her. Only a boy, she thought.

They were at the car now and she unlocked the doors and he slung his duffel inside. When he turned again she caught his arm and he froze, his eyes blinking. "I'm glad to see you, Anthony," she said. "You know that, right?"

"Sure," he said.

"Let's get on home now," she said finally. "Got a room ready for you."

And at last they clambered into the little car and wound their way out from behind the store and to the road and the town beyond.

JANEY

She was up and out of the house before the sun had fully broken from the horizon, her progress accomplished in quietude, the house around her ticking and groaning as if it were similarly enkindling toward the day. The door to her parents' room was closed and dark and quiet. In the bathroom she did not even turn on the light, brushing her teeth in darkness, hoping the fan provided enough ambient noise to hide the toilet's flush, the sink's gurgle, her careful opening and closing of cabinets and drawers.

When she was ready, or ready enough, she slunk into Charlie's room and shook him gently until he opened his eyes. "What are you doing?" he mumbled.

"Going to school. Tell Mom and Dad when they come out."

"Dad said we didn't have to go."

"I know. I want to."

"Why?"

"I just do," she said.

"You're crazy," Charlie said.

"Just tell Mom and Dad when they wake up."

"Right," he said. Already he was returning to the sleep from which she had roused him.

Outside, the sun a low blinding haze that blasted the trees to spindly black outlines along the street. She looked up and down that strip of asphalt, first one way and then the other, but the cars that trundled in the near distance were unfamiliar and so she turned in the general direction of the school, phone in hand, texting until she received a response, frozen gravel and stones crunching under her feet all the while. Ice in the thin puddles along the road. The houses she passed were worn boxes arranged along a loose grid of streets, yards browning into winter, paint peeling, roofed in patches of slanting asphalt tile in which gaps appeared here and there like mouths missing teeth. Some held within the faint light of waking. A shadow across a kitchen window as some mother or father started breakfast for children perhaps still asleep within. Lives that had not been blown apart. The thought of it, of what had happened to her, to her own mother and father, to all of them, once more brought that feeling into her chest, not sadness but a kind of prickling that threatened to rush all through her at once.

As a balm, she raised the phone and used its camera to look upon her face. She had readied herself in the darkness, so worried she had been that either of her parents would see the light or hear her motion and would come to investigate and would then tell her to remain home. What she saw in the screen was exhaustion. She seldom wore makeup but she wished she had some with her now.

From behind her, the rumble of a car, the muffled thump of music from within. She waited for the customary intrusion of Shannon's voice upon the air but it did not come and when she turned it was to find her friend merely sitting behind the wheel, phone in hand, waiting for her to enter.

"What's up, buttercup?" Shannon said when Janey had slid into the passenger seat and closed the door. The car: a ragged Impala with patches of gray Bondo along one side.

"Another day in paradise," Janey said.

"Seriously, how are things?"

"Weird," Janey said. And then, after a pause, "Super quiet."

"I should've been there, I guess."

"I didn't want anyone there."

"Yeah, I know."

"So what's happening at school?"

There was a brief pause as Shannon pulled the car across a small intersection. Janey could have walked to school—she had done so many times—but it felt as if she had been alone with her family for too long, although now, sitting in the passenger seat, she wanted only to return to that dark nest.

"Oh. My. God," Shannon said now. "You don't even know about Samantha and Chris Phillips." The words came in a rush and it took only a brief mumble from Janey for Shannon to launch into the most recent gossip and controversy.

"In the skate park?"

"I don't know," Shannon said, impatient. "Near it, I guess. Not in it. Well, maybe in it. Is that even important?"

"Well, I mean, yeah, it's kinda skeezy."

"Oh my God, right? Totally skeezy. That's so, like, gross."

Shannon continued as the car turned into the parking lot and they found a space amidst the other poorly parked vehicles, students drifting across Janey's vision like ghosts of some life she could hardly recall, although she had only been out of school for two weeks. Who were these people? Who had they ever been to her?

She did not know what she had expected. Perhaps the impossible: that no one would even know what had befallen her family and so she could simply reenter the routines she had vacated those weeks before. There were times during the day when she wondered if the worried gazes that crossed her vision were simply reflections of her own imagination but no no no they knew and they watched as if she had transformed from the familiar person they had grown up with into some exotic creature, feathered in grief, their eyes flitting across hers so quickly that it was as if they harbored some secret knowledge, their voices hushing in the hallways, in the classrooms. The worst of it was that she felt, already, as if her grief was over, or rather that she would survive it, the baby's presence in her life, James's presence, amounting to six months of anxious terror ending, of course, in the worst day of her life, the worst day in any of their lives, her parents' grief, especially her mother's, incandescent in its fury, the effect of which was, to Janey, as if the actual physical world, the immutable facts of gravity and light and air, had, all at once, been rendered not just false but fraudulent, counterfeit. Even now her mother was a ruin in the back bedroom. She wondered when that much of it would be over, when they could stop lurking in silences, when that dark, malevolent bird that roosted now upon their roof would flap away once more. She wanted that more than anything, for all of it to simply be over. When would it be over? For her. For any of us.

At lunch Shannon waved her over to their table and she crossed the cafeteria automatically and slipped into her customary seat upon the bench. The conversation there did not falter, although she was sure others around them quieted, whispering to their lunch companions briefly before returning to whatever conversations had ensued before her appearance. She wanted to shout at them to leave her alone but of course that was exactly what they were doing.

Talk of the upcoming basketball game, Shannon's eyes meeting Janey's own for a moment. "I might just stay home," Shannon said.

"God, why?" Kimmy Wiest said from across the table. "It's, like, the only thing to do."

"Sounds like fun," Janey said. Her voice sounded odd to her ears, unused.

"Yeah?" Shannon said. "Well, maybe we go then if you want to."

"Yeah," Janey said. "Let's."

"Right on," another of them said. A swell of chatter then. The ringing bell of a new message on someone's phone.

"So, like, you're OK, right?" This was Kimmy Weist again, razor-thin, her frizzed hair the color of lemon rind.

Janey thought Shannon might say something to deflect the question but her friend was on her phone now, tapping away at the little screen in feigned concentration. The table had quieted at this question, although all of them were trying hard to look as if they were mostly unconcerned with her reply. "I'm OK," Janey said at last.

"If you, you know, need anything," another girl said. "I know people say that stuff but, you know, if you do."

"Sure," Janey said. "Thanks."

"Yeah any of us, really," Kimmy Wiest said.

And then a chorus of for sures and absolutelys and yesses and whatever you needs, Janey nodding until the conversation shifted again to other concerns. She listened in silence, understanding that this was how it had been when she had been absent for those weeks: their pointless talk continuing without her and on the same topics that had occupied them all year. The cute boys. The occasional party. The upcoming winter formal. Some girl none of them knew particularly well had received a car for her sixteenth birthday, used but functional. Basketball, yes, but can't make the football game. Friday night shift at the pizza place. We'll come after for a milkshake. Cool. I'll be the one shackled to the deep fryer. And on and on.

The room filled with similar conversations across identical tables. Greasy kids with their role-playing games and books and computers on the outskirts. Aggies in their clutch across the room. Smart kids from the AP classes in their clusters. Others arranged by type or interest or ability or inability or style, self-parsed into similar units. As she watched, her brother's friends, the small coterie of skater kids that hung out at the park near her house and were generally thought of as causing whatever mischief cropped up in the town, wandered through the center of the room, clothes baggy, sock hats pulled over shaggy hair. Everything a kind of disguise. And here she was at her own table, with a gaggle of girls that in truth she did not even like very much. She did not like her brother's friends much either but she liked them more than she liked her present company, an idea that struck her with such force that she sucked in her breath in alarm.

"You OK?" Shannon said.

"Yeah you look, like, weird," Kimmy Wiest said.

She shook her head. "Yeah, yeah, fine. I just—uh—I just remembered something. Be back in a bit." And with that she was up from the table, her heart beating wild in her chest. She crossed the room nearly at a run and although she had felt, all day, the eyes of the school upon her, their hushed silences marking her passage, she knew now that this had not been the case at all, for as she moved through the room the conversations at the tables she passed simply continued, not unaware of her passage but manifestly indifferent to it, to her, in the same way she was indifferent to the nerds and geeks and aggies and all the rest, an emotion that did not feel negative so much as it felt like vacancy, like emptiness.

"Hey, Janey," a voice said. She thought it might have been one of her brother's friends, perhaps Kent, the tall lanky one, but she did not stop to look, her momentum pulling her out of that cavernous room and into the empty hallway beyond.

MARY LOU

In the final hour of Monday's workday, Mr. Marwat told Mary Lou that his parents would soon be arriving from Pakistan, a fact that she already knew from Mrs. Marwat, who had likewise told her a week earlier during one of the few conversations they had ever had that were not directly related to the administrative workflow of the factory. Why each of them had chosen, independently, to repeatedly inform her of this future event she could not guess, although she had begun to wonder if it was meant as a subtle forecast of things to come. Mrs. Marwat had come to work in the office and so was it not possible that Mr. Marwat's parents would be similarly employed? If so, where did that leave Mary Lou?

Of course she asked no questions when Mr. Marwat informed her, once more, of his parents' impending arrival, instead only commenting, banally, on the length of the flight.

"Oh yes," Mr. Marwat said. "Twenty hours in the air, not including stopovers in Istanbul and Chicago."

"Holy moly," Mary Lou said.

"Holy moly, indeed. You've flown overseas, yes?"

"Oh no," Mary Lou said. "I've only been on an airplane once and it was a long time ago."

"And where you did you fly to?"

"Phoenix but I don't really remember. I was a little girl."

"Phoenix, Arizona." He nodded. "I've never been there."

"You're not missing much," she said. "It's desert and shopping malls."

"Sounds like Pakistan," he said, "except for the shopping malls."

It was never wholly quiet in the upstairs office, the various noises from the factory rattling up through the poorly insulated floor: hissing and clanking and crackling and popping sounds that Mary Lou did not even hear anymore but which were, she knew, ever-present upon the air. The upstairs office was a kind of cube that floated above the welding and assembly areas, a long metal staircase running from the concrete to their little administrative aerie. Through the office window, one could peer down at the rows of workbenches and the small figures that stood at their stations going through the endless repetitions of clamping and welding and turning and stacking. Sometimes, when she returned from her lunch break, she would find Mr. Marwat standing in that window, watching as the empty stations were once more filled with his employees and the process resumed.

"Well, we'll both be in the same boat soon enough," Mr. Marwat said now.

"What's that?"

"Parents. Your mother still lives with you, yes?"

"She does," Mary Lou said.

"And soon we'll have both my parents with us as well. Full houses all around."

"How long will they be here?"

"Permanently," he said. "They're moving in with us."

This information was new. "Gosh," Mary Lou said. "I hope that's . . . well . . . That'll be good, then, right?"

"Oh yes, yes, of course. And I'm sure it's good for you having your mother at home. You get to spend some time with her."

"Yes, it's good," said Mary Lou.

"But does she drive you a little crazy? Don't answer. I don't want to know."

"A little."

"To be expected," Mr. Marwat said. "We made them crazy and now they get their revenge. Tell me, if you don't mind my asking, what do you and your mother do together? I mean, what is entertaining to her?"

"I don't know. What do you mean?"

"Do you play card games or go to the movie theater or something like that?"

"Oh, I don't know, she mostly just watches television in her room."

"Ah I see," Mr. Marwat said. "What does she like to watch?"

"Oh, she's pretty crazy for political stuff these days," Mary Lou said.

"You mean like CNN news and such?"

"That kind of stuff, yeah," Mary Lou lied.

"As long as it's not those maniacs on Fox, right?" This in an undertone.

"Right," Mary Lou said.

Mr. Marwat gazed at her thoughtfully as if awaiting some further comment. She did not know what this conversation was about but it was not unlike her employer to drift out of his office at some odd moment of the day to engage her in conversation the topic of which was invariably specific and yet seemingly obtuse as the same time. His sudden interest in her mother's television viewing habits was on par with other seemingly random conversational turns. Once he had asked her in detail about the menu choices at the local Buffalo Wild Wings. Another time it was automobile tires, a subject upon which she knew virtually nothing. And another: the differences between softball and baseball, to which he had added a bewildering knowledge of cricket, a word she did not even freely associate with a sport at all.

She had been somewhat confused by such conversations early on in her employment at the factory but she had grown accustomed to Mr. Marwat over the five years she had been in his employ. Occasionally he would call her into his office simply to tell her a joke he had read on the internet, jokes that she always tried to laugh at and which were sometimes funny in a groaning sort of way. The most recent had been, "I spent a lot of time, money, and effort childproofing my house but the kids still get in," this delivered in so casual a way that she had not even understood it to be a joke until Mr. Marwat had burst out laughing and said, "Is that not funny? The kids still get in?" What was funny was watching him laugh at his own terrible joke. That, at least, brought a smile to her face.

"It's good when we're able to take care of our parents," Mr. Marwat said now.

"I guess that's right," Mary Lou said.

"Oh it is," Mr. Marwat said. "Where I come from it's an expectation to do so. The children take care of their parents. It's shocking here that they put their old people into homes and ignore them."

"It's sort of the normal thing to do, I guess."

"But it's not normal," Mr. Marwat said. "Your parents raise you and then you repay them by sending them away. I'll tell you, Mary Lou, there are some things in this culture that I just do not understand."

"Me neither," she said.

"Well, I guess I just wanted to say that I'm glad you are taking care of your mother," Mr. Marwat said. "When my parents arrive, I hope I do as good a job as you're doing."

"Oh I don't know if I'm doing a good job."

"You've always done a good job here," Mr. Marwat said. "I don't see how you'd do a good job here and a bad job at home. That doesn't make any sense at all."

An hour later, on the drive home, she stopped at a traffic light and happened to focus on her hands, held at ten and two upon the steering wheel, the knuckles gone white. She released her grip but the tightness remained. She knew Mr. Marwat meant well, and his comment that it was the duty of the adult child to take care of the parent was something she thought she believed as well—she had to believe that, didn't she?—but God that comment at the end; what a comparison to make, her job at work and her job at home serving masters as different as any that could be invented. She sometimes wanted to mash the gas pedal down against the red light but the light always turned green before she was able to screw up her courage and anyway she knew she could not leave her mother unattended for much longer.

"What do you even do there?" her mother asked her that night as they ate the Stouffer's lasagna Mary Lou had baked.

"I do the invoicing and talk to the customers."

"Which customers?"

"Oh, they're, you know, companies that use the transformers we make."

"But what are they used for?"

"They move energy from one circuit to another."

"How do you know all that?"

"Just learned it on the job." Mary Lou picked at her lasagna. Orange grease pooled upon the plastic plates. "Anyway," she said, "I don't do the electronics part. Just the paperwork part. I run the office."

"Well, that's something, I guess," her mother said.

After dinner, she helped her mother back to the room Mary Lou had organized for her and lowered her to the BarcaLounger and handed her the remote. Her mother's body was the opposite of her own: like handling a starving bird, a creature of sinew and bone. "You need anything?" she asked, but her mother only shooed her away from the screen.

In the kitchen once more, she sat at the table, the grease-smeared plates remaining where they had been abandoned, and ate a pint of ice cream, alone. Already her mother's voice was raised in outrage, the sound a high wheeze: "Lock her up! Lock her up!"

Those maniacs on Fox, as Mr. Marwat had joked, but it was no joke at all. If her mother somehow discovered that she, Mary Lou, had secretly cast her vote for the woman her mother called Crooked Hillary, she likely would demand to move out. Or no, she would demand that Mary Lou move out, move out, that is, of her own home, so that she might have the run of the place without the irritation of Mary Lou's constant presence. In truth, Mary Lou did not follow politics closely enough to know much more than the barest of Clinton's policies; what she saw was a group of bullies calling a woman names and trying to drag her through the mud and that, quite simply, she could not abide. And yet her act of familial defiance still pained her, as if she had done something secret and awful. That she felt this way about voting her own conscience made her understand anew just how deeply her mother had burrowed into her heart.

"Are you going to be here all the time?" her mother had asked soon after Mary Lou had installed her in the spare room.

"I live here," is all Mary Lou could think to say in response.

"If you got in shape you could get yourself a man, you know. I got your father that way. A woman's got to use her assets."

But what assets Mary Lou had, exactly, she did not know.

"A crook!" her mother yelled from the other room now. And once again the phrase that she had come to repeat over and over again like a parrot who had learned but three words of English—"Lock her up!"—a slogan that did not even seem relevant since the bullies had won. A full year had passed since the election; why continue to rant about the loser?

Mary Lou had finished the ice cream and opened the cabinet under the sink and dropped the container into the plastic bin. The clock read seven. So many hours yet to fill. In some ways she wished she had a man, as her mother had said, if only to have something to do, somewhere to go, some other, different energy in the house besides her own and, now, that of her mother. She knew if she went to bed she would only lie awake, listening to the television voices, her mother's unrestrained shouting, at some point finally rising to see if her mother had fallen asleep and she could, at last, silence the constant stream of noise that had come to dominate her hours at home. She almost wished she could work longer at the factory, although of course she knew that Mr. Marwat would gently remind her that he could not pay her overtime; instead he would no doubt suggest that his wife work additional hours to help alleviate Mary Lou's workload and while Mary Lou had nothing against Rafia Marwat, she missed the total autonomy she had once enjoyed in running the office. Mr. Marwat had told her that she, Mary Lou, was to be his wife's supervisor and that, in all things relating to the running of the factory's office, Mrs. Marwat would defer to her judgment. Of course, Mary Lou was smart enough to understand that this would be, and was, far from the case.

Sometimes, especially in the early days of Mrs. Marwat's coming to work in the factory office, Mary Lou would find herself staring at her almost without thought, for Rafia Marwat, while not exactly beautiful, comported herself with a variety of elegance that Mary Lou found utterly fascinating. She wore clothes that must have come from Columbus or even Cleveland, for Mary Lou had never seen their like for sale, certainly not at Walmart, where Mary Lou purchased her own clothes, clothes that, by her own preference, draped over her like a kind of tent. Mrs. Marwat's clothes were shaped like she was: like a stout hourglass. Mary Lou watched her dark eyes and black hair, wondered at the fact that she had come from Pakistan, a place Mary Lou could hardly imagine. She thought of sultans and camels, even though she knew, or thought she knew, this to be a kind of fantasy. Sultans and camels were from India. Or maybe Arabia.

In those exceedingly rare moments when Mary Lou looked at her reflected self, what she saw was a woman shaped not like an hourglass but like an apple, an apple with pale, blotchy skin and dust-colored hair. In varying degrees, it was effectively the same reflection that Mary Lou had seen since she was a child. The fat girl had become a fat woman. That was what she saw, especially with her mother here to remind her of all she was not.

Then her mother's voice came again and this time Mary Lou paused and listened, thinking at first she might have heard incorrectly. But then her mother yelled the name again: "Margaret!" It was the name of Mary Lou's aunt, her mother's sister, and it was enough to rouse Mary Lou from her ice-cream stupor. She struggled out of the sofa and stumped her way into the spare room, the television's volume growing as she moved, not a talk show now but apparently the news. Twenty killed in a shooting in Texas. That was what she heard. This was the world in which she lived.

"What do you need, Mom?" she said when she had reached the doorway.

Her mother was in the same position she always occupied, the big lounge chair tipped back, slippered feet up in the direction of the television, its volume so loud that Mary Lou winced. "Did you take the remote?" her mother shouted over the noise.

"It's right there," Mary Lou said, gesturing toward the arm of the BarcaLounger where the remote rested.

"It is not, Margaret. You took it. You know you did."

Her mother was looking directly at her. Mary Lou looked nothing like her mother's sister, a thin woman with a wild thatch of wiry blonde hair fringing a face as stern and unforgiving as a barrister's. Mary Lou felt a shiver run down the straight line of her vertebrae. "Mom?" she said. And then, as if talking to her mother through the long-distance line of a telephone: "It's Mary Lou."

Her mother seemed to waver then, shifting almost as if the entire woman appeared not in the flesh but as an image on the television that continued to pour forth its political commentary across from her, that image clicking away for a moment, clicking, perhaps, to an adjacent station that nonetheless held the same image as the channel before only slightly delayed, as if real and unreal at the same time. "Well of course you're Mary Lou," her mother said now, her brow furrowing. "Who else would you be?"

"You said Margaret, Mom."

"I did no such thing."

Mary Lou watched her for a moment, her mother's gaze turning in on itself, becoming steel once more. "Your remote's right there on the arm of the chair," Mary Lou said.

"Of course it is," she said. "Just leave me alone. You're interrupting the news."

"OK Mom," Mary Lou said. She turned and walked back down the hall to the little living room, where she sat on the couch in the darkness, staring at the cold empty table where that same television had once stood. Before her mother had arrived she might have turned it on there, flipped through the channels from the comfort of the same chair her mother now occupied around the clock, searching for a travel show or a movie set somewhere in Europe—Paris or London or Berlin—places she had never been and knew now, had even accepted, that she never would. Twenty hours on a plane. This time tomorrow she could be in Istanbul. Sultans and camels again. The one thing she knew for certain was that her life had not turned out the way she hoped. Not by a long shot.

TOM BAILEY

His mother-in-law would have stayed forever had Tom not finally asked her, as kindly as possible, to return to Wisconsin. "Are you sure, Tom?" she asked. "I can help out with the kids." She had helped out a great deal, truth be told, but there had come a point in which he felt that the only way to move forward was to try to reclaim the structures of their lives before and so he thought he would feel relief when at last her silver Buick turned out onto the road and drove away, spirals of dead leaves spinning in the eddies of her wake, but when he turned to face the house once more what he felt was dread and confusion. His wife had emerged briefly when her mother was leaving, had hugged her and thanked her before returning to the bedroom. A week had passed since the baby's funeral and Sarah had hardly been out of that shadowy den, had hardly even been out of bed, showering only when Tom convinced her that she needed to, that it would make her feel better, that it always had in the past.

"I just don't feel good," she said one night as he sat on the edge of the mattress staring at the wall. A wooden cross she had hung there. Nothing else.

"I know," he said.

"It's not what you think," she told him. "There's something wrong."

"You just need some rest."

"I don't know what to do, Tom."

"You'll be all right," he said. "Just give it some time."

He did not know how much time she would need or if it was even time that she required. He felt profoundly sad at what had happened, not an accident but a defect of the baby's heart that had not been fixed in time, an act of God's will, such as it was, but he also felt, knew, that life continued, that the relative stability of their lives had to resume, in some way, in the wake of what had happened. There was no guilt as there was nothing any of them could have done. This is what the doctor had told them. Sarah's inability to return from their shared grief was something he could understand, at least to a point, but he did not know what to do about it other than to give her the space he thought she needed, to encourage her to shower from time to time, to make sure she was fed, although she ate very little, and to try to talk her through whatever it was she was feeling, which was, in some profound way, deeper or harder or more jagged than his own grief and which spindled against the hard limit of language. What forgotten dialect articulated the depths of the human heart he did not know. Sarah was, or had been, the child's mother and such bonds are writ in blood. If nothing else, her incapacitation had showed him that. She could not rise from it. She simply could not rise.

And yet he knew, too, that life—such as it was—would continue, especially for their children. Janey had returned to school the Monday after the funeral. He did not actually know if Charlie had gone to school or not and in thinking this he also realized that he had hardly spoken to either of them since well before James had been born, so focused had he and Sarah been on the end of the complicated pregnancy, then on the birth, the new baby, and finally, of course, on what had happened. Charlie had passed him briefly on the Monday after the funeral, blazing through the front door without a word, the screen banging shut behind him despite Tom having told him to be as quiet as possible. Tom had caught a brief glimpse of his son's face and was reminded that despite his son's serious nature, his quiet, his reserve, he was still only a boy of fourteen, a boy with too-long hair that covered his eyes, skateboard always at hand, even in the dead of winter. The truth was, Tom could hardly remember seeing his son at all since that moment, although he had a vague idea that the boy had been present—in his room, on the cheap mobile phone Sarah had talked Tom into buying for him, or on the old, out-of-date PlayStation Tom had bought secondhand from Cheryl at the factory. That both of his children, his living children, had answered his call that dinner was ready was a miracle in itself but there they both sat in their customary places, waiting for him. Waiting for them both.

Sarah was awake—at least there was that—her body leaning against the headboard, eyes on the television and then, as he stood in the doorway, on him. "Dinner," he said.

"Can't you make me a plate?"

"Sure," he said. "It'll be on the table."

"I think I'll eat in here."

He sat on the edge of the bed. It sometimes felt as if all he did with his wife now was to sit on the edge of the bed. She had always been thin but now he felt as if she were wasting away. Her cheekbones sharp. Her throat in cords. "Honey," he said, "come eat with us."

"I can't," she said.

"Why not?"

"I hurt."

"I know you do."

"No, I mean I hurt. Physically. My body hurts."

"Maybe you'll feel better if you come out."

She looked, in that moment, so bereft that he could feel her sadness in his chest, solid, stonelike, and very cold.

"Maybe for Janey and Charlie?" he said then.

"Don't do that."

"They miss you."

"Don't guilt me about it," she said.

"I'm not guilting you."

"Yes you are, Tom. Yes you are. That's what you're doing."

"That's not what I mean," he said. "They haven't seen you in weeks, Sarah."

"I talk to them."

"They need you. So do I."

For a long time she did not speak and finally he said, once more, "It'll be on the table waiting for you," and then he stood and returned to the kitchen, the eyes of the two children watching him as he emerged from the hall.

"Is she coming out?" Janey said.

"Let's eat," Tom said.

"Dad," Janey said.

"Let's just eat," he said again.

Charlie did not hesitate, reaching across for the casserole dish Tom had defrosted, the instructions written in Sharpie on the aluminum foil cover by their neighbors, and spooning a great glop onto his plate.

"Jesus Charlie," Janey said to him. "Don't you even care?"

"About what?" he mumbled through his hair, through the forkful of tuna and noodles that already filled his mouth.

"About Mom, idiot."

"Dad said to eat."

"We can wait for her. We should. We should wait for her." Her voice had started to spiral up in pitch even as it screwed down in volume. At the end of it was a kind of silent squeak.

"I'm eating," Charlie said.

"You're . . ." Janey began, her voice catching in her throat. Then a whisper: "You're an asshole."

"Janey," Tom said.

And then his daughter was up from the table, her hands balled into tight, pale fists. In the overhead light, her knuckles shadowed into knifeblades.

He thought she would turn and charge down the little hall to her room. He would wait a few minutes and then would go to find her there and to try to comfort her, but instead she stood unmoving and when he followed her gaze it was to see Sarah's arms wrap around her.

"Oh," he said, standing so quickly that his scraping chair sent up a wail from the floor.

Sarah waved him back, her eyes closed, her arms around her daughter. The girl was weeping now, her shoulders the mirror of her knifeblade knuckles, those hard, sharp wingbones jerking in rhythm with her tears. Charlie sat looking at them both, then looking at Tom, his fork moving mechanically back to his plate. "Mom," he said simply, as if in confirmation. She had donned Tom's sweatpants and a T-shirt and had pulled her hair into a loose ponytail and although she looked exhausted, depleted, he could not help but smile at the sight of her standing in the little dining room.

"Don't squeeze too hard, honey," she whispered.

Tom did not hear if his daughter answered.

They remained like that until Janey's tears lessened and finally Sarah opened her eyes. "Looks like I got here just in time," she said.

"Come and eat," Charlie said.

"Yeah, yeah," Tom said, a note of frantic desperation in his voice, the sound so absurd that he let out a sharp weird bark of laughter at the end of it. He had already risen and had pulled out Sarah's chair, awkwardly leaning across the table. Charlie finished the job for him.

"Very polite," she said to him as she sat down, lowering herself slowly into the seat, wincing. "Haircut," she said to her son. And her hand reached out and touched the long flap cascading down just past the tip of his nose.

Charlie shrugged. "I like it," he said.

"Good thing I'm the mom and you're not," Sarah said. She looked across the table at the casserole dish and then at Tom. Oh my love, he wanted to say, to shout. How I've missed you. How we all missed you. How incapable we are when you're not with us. "I got up for tuna casserole?" she said.

"From the Finns."

"Figures," Sarah said.

"It was either this or something gray and lumpy."

"This is gray and lumpy."

"Grayer and lumpier."

"Who from?"

"The other one? I don't know. Laurie Silva, maybe?"

"That's her stew. It's probably super good."

"Well," Tom said, "then we'll have that tomorrow."

"Dad's going back to work tomorrow," Janey said.

Tom could feel, could sense, Charlie looking up through his hair, an act that irritated him, his son's lack of interest in anything Tom wanted or needed him to do—his chores, his homework—and then his sudden complete focus when there was the potential for chaos. Tom looked over at him but Charlie glanced away at the last moment, returning his attention to the noodles and peas and tuna on his plate. Gray sauce from a box.

"Oh," Sarah said. "I guess—do they want you back so soon?"

"It's been nearly a month."

"Yeah, OK," Sarah said.

"I need to make a paycheck," Tom said.

"You've got sick time saved up."

"We can talk about it later."

"No, it's fine," she said. "It's good. You should go back to work. You should."

"Well," Tom said. He forked some of the casserole into his mouth. Viscous salt pressed into a wet, semi-solid shape.

"So how are things with you two?" Sarah said softly. She had not lifted her fork but did so now, staring down at the steaming heap that Tom had spooned upon her plate.

"OK," Janey said.

"That's all I get?"

"Yeah, it's just, you know, school."

"What's the drama these days?"

"Nothing much, I guess."

"How about you, Charlie?"

"Charlie hasn't been back to school yet," Janey said.

Tom watched as Charlie shot his sister a look through that curtain of hair but Sarah only said, "Oh," and then, "So what have you been up to?"

"Not much," he said.

"I'm not sure I can handle all this outpouring of detail."

Charlie grinned. "Yeah, OK, so I'm mostly, you know, like, skating around with Kent."

"Working on a trick?"

"Not really. Just skating."

"How's Kent?"

"OK I guess. He's just, you know, Kent."

"I do know," she said. "So tomorrow."

"What about it?"

"School?"

"Ugh, gross," Charlie said.

"Yeah, buddy," Tom said then. "It's time."

And to Tom's relief, his son nodded. He did not know what his son's grades looked like but he could not imagine there would be any good news from that quarter. With Janey they had wondered which college they might be able to afford. With Charlie they wondered if he would even make it through high school.

They had, each of them, tucked into their meals. At some point Janey tried to tell her mother something that had happened at school, perhaps some of the drama her mother had asked about, but Sarah had stopped looking up from her plate, eating almost mechanically, and Tom could feel her waning, her body, her consciousness, once more folding in on itself. "Sarah," he said. And when she did not look up he said it again. "Sarah. Hey."

"What?" she said, and now her eyes were on his own. Tired and darkly circled but still brown and dark and deep, rivers upon rivers.

"You OK?" he said.

"I'm just so tired," she said. "I'm sorry guys. I don't know what's going on with me."

"Maybe you've got the flu," Janey said tentatively.

"Or mono," Charlie said.

"Yeah, maybe it's mono," Janey said. "That lasts for, like, ever."

"Maybe," Sarah said. "Listen, you guys, I gotta go lie down."

"OK," Janey said.

Tom was already out of his seat, hovering beside her, pulling her chair back as she struggled to rise. "You sure? Maybe you should eat more."

"I'm just so tired."

"You've been in bed for weeks."

"Dad, she's tired," Janey said. "She said she's tired."

He looked across the table at his daughter, her face a mixture of anger and concern, and then back to his wife, struggling to rise until he reached for her and pulled her to her feet. Her reaction was to cry out in pain.

"What?" he said. "What did I do?"

"Hurts," she said, her breath catching.

"What does?"

"I don't know," she said, then she exhaled. "I don't know. It's gone now. You just hit some nerve, I guess."

"Dad," Janey said.

Sarah was on her feet, unsteady, and when he touched her he could feel her body pull away from him, her skin seeming to writhe under his touch.

"Dad," Janey said again.

"What?" His voice hard and cold.

"You're hurting her."

He did not respond now, Sarah hovering there as if she did not know what to do. How frail she looked. And how tired.

"Dad," Janey said again.

And now when he spoke his voice was loud, too loud, and he knew it even as the words escaped his lips: "Shut up! Just shut the hell up! Please!"

She was gone from the table then, his daughter, her flight a pale blur and then the bang of the bedroom door closing.

Charlie looked up at him from across the table, one eye clear and bright, the other hidden behind that curtain of hair.

"You got something to say?" Tom said to him.

"Nope," Charlie said.

Sarah was stepping back from the table now. "I'm all right," she said.

"You sure?"

She nodded and waved away his hands when he tried to steer her, to steady her, her motion halting at first, some antediluvian creature on spindly, ancient legs. "I need to lie down for a while," she said absently.

"All right," Tom said. "Good. You get some rest."

If she said something further he did not hear her. She was moving down the hall and he watched her as she passed the doors that led to their children's rooms, both of them closed, and then reached their own bedroom, his and hers, opening that door, and slipping inside, and then closing it again. The bright quiet click. He watched all of that from the end of the hall, watched, too, his daughter's closed door, hoping it would open once more even though he knew that it would not.

"Well, champ," he said to the table. "I guess it's just you and me."

Charlie shrugged.

"Probably could've done that better," Tom said, staring at the table, the uneaten plates of food.

"You think?" Charlie said through his hair.

"Don't start," Tom said. "Let's just eat."

"I'm done," Charlie said.

And Tom: "Of course you are."

And a moment later, with his whole family in the house, he found himself eating the Finns' cold tuna casserole alone.

ANTHONY SHAW

His auntie stood in the attitude of every adult woman he had ever known, hands on hips, brow drawn sharp, her whole expression stern and disapproving. She was taller than he was, although he was of middling height for a man, her body thick but in a way that suggested power and solidity rather than sloth. She was, Anthony thought, the exact opposite of his mother, at least physically, and he wondered at the bare fact that they were sisters.

"You know how to tie a tie?" she asked him now.

He might have cracked some kind of joke or said something sarcastic but instead he only shook his head and she wrapped the blue striped necktie around him and worked the knot and slid it up to his throat. When it was done, she stepped back and stood appraising him.

"Ain't you gonna say nothin'?" he said at last.

"About what?"

"How do I look?"

"You'll do."

"That's great," he said. "Thanks a lot."

"Oh you look handsome," she said, waving her hands at him as if to dust him off from afar. "Just know that you're not fooling anyone."

"Why'm I doing this then? They're not gonna give me a job."

"Point isn't wearing a disguise. It's showing that you care enough to come to them with respect."

"All right," he said. "Come at them with respect."

"To them not at them," she said. "There's a difference."

"Sure," he said.

"You understand me, Anthony?"

"Sure," he said again.

"Tell me then."

"I'll come to them with respect, Aunt Paula," he said slowly, exhaling. "I will."

"Good," she said. "Good boy."

He had told her already what had happened in East Cleveland, what had happened and what had not, and tried to explain why he had fled that broken place, that he had not been in trouble, not really, or not specifically, had not joined a gang or become a trapper or been arrested or any of the things his auntie apparently feared. In fact, his problem was, in essence, that he was not a gang member or a trapper or a felon and did not want to be any of those things. He was simply Anthony. He had not been particularly good in school, although he had finished and had graduated, unlike many of his peers, and now he simply did not know what to do next, the calendar a great and terrible sweep of empty days.

He had told her, too, about he and Rudy, their coming up together on those streets, in those schools, two skinny teens in ragged secondhand coats too insubstantial to protect them against the freezing wind blowing endlessly off the lake, hair shorn to stubble, identical headphones slung around their thin, shivering necks. Their bond had been tighter and closer than if they had been brothers of the flesh because that bond was based not on biology but on choice, their lives similar in ways that many of their lives were similar, raised by single parents on the verge of utter ruin, their families fraught by prison time and addiction narratives that had become so prevalent, so common, that they had come to feel like clichés even though they were the lived reality of their days and nights.

It was the music he thought of now, the secret soundtrack that had come to dominate and define them, a soundtrack which seemed, to everyone but he and Rudy alone, so utterly bizarre as to be an in-joke that only the two of them understood. "The Devil's music," Rudy's mother had called it, after which Anthony made sure that his own mother never heard what sounds poured from his headphones, a music which had come to them as if by providence from a college radio station the signal of which fluttered in and out of range, the music itself so harsh and decayed that Anthony could not determine when what he listened to was static and when it was the music itself. At first they had held the station in unbelieving wonder at the sheer absurd intensity of the sound: a sonic assault that felt not simply devoid of melody but actually opposed to its very existence. "Cookie Monster hit the pipe," Rudy said and they both laughed. And yet they also continued to listen, that track morphing into some other, or perhaps it was all the same long cut, crashing guitars and huge droning chords and vocals whispered and screeched and shouted, voices of men and sometimes of women and other times of creatures they could not imagine or identify, all of it finally dying out in a wave of fuzz and feedback and gasping breath.

At last the DJ's mumbling voice came through the speaker: "That's . . . uh . . . Burning Witch from their record *Crippled Lucifer*. And before that Eagle Twin. And coming up after a PSA block we'll hear from an English band I really like called Teeth of Lions Rule the Divine. Pretty solid smoking music if you know what I mean."

"What was it called?" Rudy said.

"Teeth of Lions Rule the Divine," Anthony said.

"Man, that's funny. They got jokes."

"You want me to switch it?"

"No way, man," Rudy said. "I gotta hear it now."

They did hear it, a seemingly endless soundscape like a hundred guitars playing a single note, drums skittering across wasteland. When the vocals finally began they sounded as if they were being shouted from some bottomless well, nearly wordless, like syllables loosed of language. Rudy began laughing midway through and then they both were, banging their heads in the air in some slow-motion semblance of what they had seen heavy metal bands do on the internet but once that was done, the shock of it over, they settled in and continued to listen and when the radio show cycled back around the following week they listened again. Rudy found some tracks on the internet, at first as a kind of joke, handing Anthony his headphones. "Listen to these crazy-ass motherfuckers," he told him, eyes wide, mouth curving into a half grin. And Anthony did listen. To Wolves in the Throne Room and Khanate and finally, once again, to Teeth of Lions Rule the Divine.

"What are they even doing?" Rudy said to him, eyes shining. "They're just totally crazy. Right? Right?"

"I don't know," Anthony said. "What's this band called?"

"Gnaw Their Tongues," Rudy said, and laughed.

Again the drums roared—hardly a rhythm at all—against the huge drone note, the vocals a rumbling screech, a cry of such terrible anguish that Anthony's heart raced in his chest. How often had he felt just this way in the years of his childhood. How often did he feel just this way now. He closed his eyes.

Like everyone they knew, they had been raised on hip-hop and occasional pop music and the sounds that pumped from computer speakers and car stereos in the high school parking lot consisted of Kanye and

Kendrick and Pusha T and Drake. This had been the soundtrack of their lives, the sounds of their neighborhood, delineating and demarcating the very boundaries of their desire, of what dreams they could have and to what they might aspire. That was what music was, what music was for, and yet in the sonic wash of Mizmor and KTL and Wolves in the Throne Room it felt as if they had, for once, been afforded a view into some other reality entirely, not the vacuous rapacity of a lifestyle Anthony knew he would never achieve but instead a grim acknowledgment of the fierce terror of life's essential fagility, not only brittle but actively aflame.

"I'm feelin' that stuff you downloaded," he admitted to Rudy one afternoon as they walked back from school.

"Boy's got jokes," Rudy said.

"I'm not joking."

"No?"

He shook his head.

"What's your favorite then?"

"Burning Witch. That Khanate track. Moss."

"For real?" Rudy said, and Anthony could see his friend's eyes watching him from the periphery. "No jokes?"

"Naw. No jokes."

"Same," Rudy said, smiling. "I been listening to it on repeat for, like, days. I thought you'd think I'd lost my brains."

"We probably both have."

He had left the music out of the story he told his aunt except in the most general terms, instead focusing on what he knew she would understand: the day Rudy had been shot, trying to express just how random it had all felt, as if God himself had reached down from the sky and had punched two holes in Rudy's chest and had extracted his soul, all of it with such expediency that Anthony had hardly time to flinch at the sound of the gunfire before his friend was gone.

"Was he in trouble?" his aunt had asked him. "Were you two in trouble?"

"It wasn't like that," Anthony told her. "It was someone else. They were shooting at someone else. We were just in the way."

"Christ almighty," she said. "You poor boy."

His voice sounded thick. Rudy was dead before he hit the sidewalk, one of the two bullets having passed directly through his heart. That night, in his room, Anthony pulled his headphones over his ears and turned the music up so loud that the guitars and drums and screeching vocals distorted somewhere in the center of his skull. It was still not loud enough. It would never be loud enough again. And yet the pain of that sound ran through him like a blade of pure, unadulterated truth. This was exactly how he felt and he did not know if he would ever feel any different.

"That's why," he told his aunt. "It's not, you know, because of my mom. It's just because I couldn't . . . you know . . ."

"That's a good enough reason for me," she said in response. "God knows. That's a good enough reason for me."

His aunt helped him assemble a rudimentary résumé and drove him a few miles out of town, into the broken fields of corn, to a steel building the size of a small warehouse. This was, she told him, only the first stop among many, the other businesses occupying what had once been the town's center, that battered collection of small, locally owned storefronts, following which she would take him to the newer fast-food restaurants and gas stations catering to those passing through on the way to Cleveland or Columbus.

Now he looked up at the corrugated steel wall, the door's bleak silence. "What do I say?"

"Just introduce yourself. Tell them you're looking for work and hand them your résumé."

"They're hiring though?"

"I don't know if they are or not."

"So we're just guessing?"

"Looking for opportunity, and don't take that tone."

"Sorry."

"Go on now."

He had expected to be turned away at the door but instead a man pointed up a flight of stairs which he followed bewilderingly to an office that floated above the factory floor. There, a heavyset white woman took the paper from his hand and after a few moments he was ushered into a small office where a brown-skinned man in a pale-blue suit asked him questions about his lack of work history, about his time in the city, about who he was living with in the town.

"Where does she work?" the man asked him.

"My aunt Paula? She works at the Kroger's."

"Oh yes," the man said, "I think I know who you mean." His accent was so musical that it felt almost like something being acted out, as was his physical presence: cleaned and pressed and manicured with precision, his face slightly jowly, soft, even his fingernails polished to a sheen.

There were more questions, of course, and Anthony mumbled responses. He did not understand what was happening until it suddenly occurred to him that he was being interviewed for a job he did not even know existed, still did not. Now it felt, in almost the same moment of his understanding, that the whole thing was slipping away. "Look," he blurted, "I—I need this. I'll be here. And I'll do it right. I will. I know I don't have anything on paper to speak of for jobs and stuff but I need this."

The man who sat across from him simply stared, his eyes wide. Then he called through the door behind him. "Mary Lou?" he said.

The big woman appeared in the doorway, saying nothing but peering into the room with an expression of earnest interest.

"We'll be adding this young man to the assembly floor," he said.

"Starting when?" the woman said, glancing at Anthony and, much to his surprise, briefly smiling and nodding in his direction.

"When can you start?" the man asked.

"Now," Anthony said.

"Now?" The man glanced back to the door again. "The young man wants to start immediately."

"Tom's not here to train him."

"Oh yes," the man said. "That presents a small obstacle."

This is where they change their mind, Anthony thought. Here's where it ends. And yet the woman in the door suggested another name, someone called Cheryl, and the man nodded and they discussed Cheryl's availability and then called the woman up from the floor, Anthony waiting with his hands in his lap, trying not to jog his sneakers against the carpet.

He did indeed start that very afternoon, running outside to the parking lot briefly to tell his aunt to pick him up at 5:30. "You don't even have a lunch or anything," she said. "Can't you start tomorrow?"

"Don't wanna," Anthony said, turning around again.

"Oh, honey," his aunt said. She shook her head, her face screwed into a beautiful confusion of pride and concern all at once. "Your auntie'll bring you a sack lunch before noon."

He did not understand his own abrupt need and yet there was

something undeniable, an understanding or assumption which bordered on abject and manifest terror, as if to lose this opportunity would be akin to closing off a future he had not even begun to imagine, still had not. And to think that an hour ago he had not wanted a job at all.

That first week he learned the rudiments of the labor for which he was employed, standing at a designated spot at a long workbench between others who sometimes held shouted conversations into which he was not invited, performing a simple task that he repeated and repeated and repeated, the small metal block upon which he worked passed down the line and through the whole floor until it reached the end and was stacked and crated and shipped out to whatever company or industry or individual had ordered such a thing to be manufactured at all. He did not really even understand what it was he was making, although he supposed that this was ultimately of little concern.

During breaks he smoked alone out at the edge of the parking lot, seated at a worn picnic table under an enormous tree upon which great orange leaves clacked in response to the slightest breeze. There he rested his aching feet and burned a single cigarette down to ash, always careful to be gone before the other smokers filed out of the factory door, moving to his customary spot at the far side of the steel enclosure, away from the eyes of his coworkers, for he had already decided that it would be easier for him if he simply did not engage, if he merely kept his head down and did his work and smoked his cigarettes in solitude and talked to no one. And that much was true until the Wednesday that the factory's door opened earlier than it usually did, at least in Anthony's limited experience, and Tom Bailey walked through it and into the cold bright November afternoon.

TOM BAILEY

His lunch was a turkey sandwich on white bread, upon which slid a slice of American cheese greased with mayonnaise. A bruised apple. A handful of stale chips in a Ziploc. He wondered briefly what Janey and Charlie had brought for their lunches, if it was better or worse fare than what he had been able to uncover in the kitchen, the casseroles gone now and the refrigerator and cabinets a match of his dwindling bank account: both shockingly empty.

The men and women he worked with had greeted him warmly when he had first appeared in the doorway, their bodies huddled around the coffeepot and the machine that stamped their timecards. Now they had gone through the first four hours of the day, his motions flooding back to familiarity once more, first some attention to the paperwork, Marwat and later Hardiman getting him up to speed on the most recent schematic, then onto the line, for although he was foreman he was not excluded from the physicality of the work that needed completing and in some ways he welcomed that labor, its repetition, the way his muscles remembered what to do: the block of metal placed into the machine, the buttons pressed, the hot spark of electricity, and then the rotation and the buttons again and then placing it on the cart, his, by choice, the last station in the row, the electrical transformer complete and added to the stack. That he was in his forties and this was how he spent his days was a kind of horror to him and yet it was the job he had and he lived now in a time and place when he was lucky enough to have it. He knew this much, knew it in the pith of his heart. After the bottling plant had closed, jobs had been hard to come by, the whole of the county stumbling into some period of privation from which it had never recovered and perhaps never would. What he knew was that he had failed in many ways and had been unlucky in many ways and yet there was this small success of having a job and keeping it.

His daughter had said something to him a few nights before, that her friends at school seemed somehow less intelligent now, and when he asked her what she meant she told him that she did not really mean less intelligent but maybe less interesting to her, their gossip and their stories holding a central pointlessness into which she could place no meaning or purpose. Now, sitting at the row of tables, he understood exactly what she meant. Around him, his coworkers carried on about the same subjects they had talked about for all the years that had preceded them. There had been times in the past when he would have joined in and yet now it all felt like chatter that held no function, purpose, or interest. And yet these were his friends—his work friends, but also the only friends he had—and so he did his best to nod and to smile and to mumble some stock response when it was required of him: "Oh yeah" and "That's great" or just a soft chuckle at a joke or comment he had not really even heard. They talked of the coming winter, of snow tires and of the league season at the Bowl-O-Rama, repeated hunting and fishing stories, and then the sideways shift to talk of the distant spring.

He ate quickly, as was his habit, glancing from time to time to where Rachel Denker was seated a few dozen yards across the beaten linoleum. She had burst into laughter at one point and he had looked at her and in that moment they had locked eyes and she had winked at him. He felt his face rush with heat and was relieved, when he glanced around his own table, that no one had noticed the exchange. God knows he had not thought of her at all during the days he had been home but it seemed the old flirtation would resume now that he had returned. It had been something he had looked forward to at work, the small pleasure of that spark; now, though, he did not know what he felt. Maybe he would never feel anything again. And yet he looked to her again, hoping her eyes might once more search out his own and when that did not happen he mumbled something about heading outside for a smoke and stood, tucking the empty paper sack into his coat pocket and pushing through the steel doors into the cold.

Before him, the old oak at the edge of the parking lot stood against a gunmetal sky, its fire-colored leaves atremble in the faint frozen breeze. Winter coming hard upon the season. Under the tree: the worn picnic table at which Tom sat for a quick cigarette every afternoon, weather permitting. He was not always the first of the factory's smokers to descend upon the table's worn planks but he was nonetheless surprised to find that someone was already seated there, the smoke of his exhale slipping sideways across the gravel of the parking lot. Tom had seen him when he had first come on the floor but the newcomer had worked at the far bench, the position to which all new employees were relegated, and Tom had not even had an opportunity to introduce himself during the morning hours. Even at that distance the figure was so wholly out of place at the factory that Tom had to wonder what situation had brought a young Black man to the countryside of North Central Ohio.

Tom did not register so much as a brief glance in his direction as he crossed the gravel of the parking lot but the man looked up warily after Tom reached the table. Not much older than a boy. Twenty at the outside.

"Hey I'm Tom."

"Hey," the boy said in response. Hardly a glance.

"Got a name?"

"Anthony," the boy said.

"New here, yeah?"

The boy nodded.

"I'm the foreman," Tom said.

The boy put his cigarette in his mouth and they shook. "Isn't the foreman the other guy?"

Tom nodded. "Yeah I was out so Hardiman was filling in."

"Gotcha."

"How long you been on?"

"Week and a half."

"Hardiman's got you on Station 1?"

"Yeah, that's right," Anthony said.

"How is it?"

"OK."

"It'll get less boring. Let me know if you want to try another station."

"Won't someone get mad if I take their spot?"

"No one cares. Well, Hardiman might. And Sam. But no one else will."

"He the guy with the Trump hat?"

"That's Sam, yeah."

"I guess I'll stay where I'm at," the boy said.

Tom nodded.

They sat together in silence then, alternately puffing on their cigarettes.

In the distance, across the swell of low hills, a small flock of birds rose from a chaos of yellow and orange and spindly black branches and spun in the air like kites loosed of their strings. Tom could sense Anthony watching them, that despite his attitude of casual disinterest, the birds had somehow captured him with their looping and turning, the distant throaty squawking across green hills drifting to winter brown.

"Grackles," Tom said.

"What's that?"

"That's what they're called. Those birds. Grackles."

This elicited a brief grunt from the boy. Then: "Sounds like something you'd buy from a gas station."

"Like a chip or something?"

"Yeah, like 'Cool Ranch Grackles.'"

Tom paused a moment and then said, "They could be shaped like little birds."

Another grunt from the boy. "You, like, a bird guy or something?"

"Not at all. Just lived here a long time." An exhale of smoke.

"How long?"

"Pretty much my whole life. You?"

"Cleveland."

Tom nodded.

"You been?"

"Once or twice to the airport. Cleveland: Home of Duck Tape."

"Duck Tape?" the boy said.

"Yeah there's a sign on the way out of the airport."

"Duck Tape," the boy said again.

"Containing ten percent real ducks. Now in the grackle aisle at your local Walmart."

This time the boy smiled for the briefest moment, his teeth bright white in the cold. Then that expression was gone and the boy stared out once more toward the metal siding of the factory. "I've never been to the airport," he said.

"No?"

"Where'm I gonna fly to?"

Tom shrugged. "Only place I've ever flown is Wisconsin."

"What's there?"

"Cheese. Cows."

"You flew to Wisconsin for cheese?"

"Naw," Tom said, "mother-in-law."

Both looked up when the bang of the steel door came to them from across the parking lot. Sam was crossing the gravel toward them, the assembly plant's huge blank shape like an iceberg surrounded incongruously by filthy and dilapidated cars and trucks, Tom's own among them and Sam's as well, and of course by the network of fields and the stubble of harvested cornland and copses of fall trees in the draws and along the hilltops.

"I'll catch you," Anthony said. Then he slid off the edge of the table and stalked away, flipping his hood over the black fuzz of his hair, shoulders hunched against the cold.

Tom continued to sit at the edge of the table, his feet on the bench, but Sam settled onto the bench itself, saying nothing, the two of them puffing smoke that swirled around their heads like halos.

"Hey," Sam said.

Tom nodded.

"You met the new guy?"

"I did."

He expected Sam to offer some further comment now and Tom would shake his head and tell him not to say shit like that, at least not at work, and Sam would act like he had said nothing untoward but to his surprise Sam did not speak about Anthony at all, instead mentioning something about the cold and they both looked up into the gray sky through the clapping leaves of the oak.

"League's up tomorrow," Sam said then.

"I'm aware of that," he said.

"I been working on my cutter. Trying it as a gutter shot."

"Yeah? How's that working out?"

"So far not good," Sam said. "Shit, I'd just love to wipe that smile off Hardiman's face."

"I wouldn't get your hopes up," Tom said.

"That guy pisses me off."

"No way!" Tom said, feigning surprise.

"Shut the fuck up," Sam muttered.

From across the parking lot, the steel door opened again and Mary Lou appeared, moving toward them through the gravel, her breath puffing audibly. Her baffled down jacket came down past her skirt line and below it her feet looked too small, like doll's feet or like twin clappers swinging beneath a bell.

"How much you think she weighs?" Sam said in a low voice. "I mean as a theoretical question."

"I have no idea."

"Two fifty? Three hundred?"

"Enough, Sam."

"How much."

"Two seventy-five," Tom said quickly. "Now shut the fuck up."

Tom could feel the cut of the breeze as it lifted. Mary Lou glanced briefly in his direction as she passed but did not stop or say anything to him until he said her name and then she paused briefly and smiled for a moment. "How you been, Mary Lou?" Tom asked her.

"Oh all right. You know." She smiled grimly. "I'm glad you're back," she said.

"I never thought I'd say it, but so am I."

"How are Sarah and the kids?"

He shrugged. "We're managing."

"Tell her I said hello, OK?"

"I will."

"I'll pray for you guys on Sunday if it's OK."

"I'll take it," he said.

For a moment she stood there, awkward, Sam and Tom both looking at her. Then she said, "Well, welcome back," and nodded and turned and began shuffling out into the parking lot again, her breath spiraling into the air as a white cloud, a vapor trail. They watched her open the door to her car and slump into the passenger seat, her thick hand and wrist appearing once more to pull it closed behind her.

"Can't she even sit out here with us for lunch?" Sam said.

"Why would she wanna do that?"

"Just to be friendly," Sam said. "I think she's sleeping with the enemy."

"Hardiman?"

"There's a thought. Like the mating of whales."

"Who'd you mean if not Hardiman?"

"I meant our lord and master, Mr. Camel Humper."

"Jesus, Sam. You're gonna get fired for that shit."

"Well, why else does she get to run the whole office while we're all down on the floor."

"You think you can run the office?"

"That's not the point," Sam said.

"She's about the nicest person either of us know," Tom said. "You oughta remember that before you start talking shit about someone."

"You know I don't mean nothing by it," Sam said. "I just run my mouth. It's what I do best."

"You sure do."

"Christ almighty you know how to bust a guy's balls," Sam said.

Tom smiled. The laugh that rolled out of him was long and soft and felt like a much-needed exhale after holding his breath. He could not remember the last time he had laughed.

"Hey, you ever been to the airport?" Tom said now.

"Which one?"

"Cleveland," Tom said, "home of Duck Tape."

"Duct tape?"

"Duck. D-U-C-K. There's a sign in the airport. Welcome to Cleveland. Home of Duck Tape."

"Duck Tape," Sam said. "That's a stupid thing to be proud of."

"Not if you're a duck," Tom said.

Across the parking lot, the other smokers were headed out across the gravel toward them now, already in their tight groups, cigarettes lit or being lit, lighters in the air, smoke disappearing in the wind. He did not know where the new kid, Anthony, had gone to finish his cigarette but Tom could not find him in the view of the parking lot, the cars, the factory, the long stretch of hills and trees and grackles beyond.

CHARLIE

Kent Westin did not come to school on Monday or Tuesday or Wednesday and did not respond to Charlie's texts, the latter event not necessarily having any particularly dire implications as Charlie knew that Kent's mother sometimes took his friend's phone away so as to punish him for minor transgressions, doing so, in fact, with enough frequency that Charlie had come to expect Kent's lack of response.

Charlie's parents had, the year before, forbidden him from entering the small, battered house in which Kent lived with his mother and, more rarely, his father, the latter of whom, according to Kent, was employed in some vague capacity that often put him on the road. Charlie's parents had not adequately explained why this sudden rule had come to be and would not discuss it with him in any detail other than to say that it was nonnegotiable and had nothing whatsoever to do with Kent himself.

"What the heck then?" Charlie had said in response. "This is a bunch of crap."

"Language, bud," his father had said.

"Well it is," Charlie said.

"I know, bud," his father had said. "We don't like it either but it is what it is."

"What does that mean? You're not telling me anything."

His mother sat on the sofa, just pregnant enough that her shape was different, softer but not better. "Kent's mom is going through some stuff," she said now.

"What kind of stuff?"

His parents looked at each other, that infuriating, self-righteous glance.

"Well, honey," his mother said now. "She's had some problems with drugs. Did you know that?"

"No," he said simply.

"Well we think, I mean your father and I think, that she's got those problems again. That's why you're not allowed to go over there."

"Well that's just great," he said.

"He can come over here anytime," his father said now. "Whenever."

"Yeah, absolutely," his mother said. "Whenever. And you can tell him that, OK?"

Charlie was trying not to cry. He was too old to cry, or at least this is what he told himself as he sat across from them. He wanted nothing more than to hit something or someone. The wall. The car. His sister. Even Kent.

"This sucks," he said instead.

"Yes it does," his father said. "It certainly does."

It made some sense to him later, of course, remembering how Kent's mother would sleep through most of the day, or how, when she was awake, she seemed only barely present, as if a ghost occupying a woman's frail figure. Once she had come into the kitchen wearing only a thin T-shirt, her nipples clearly visible. When she reached up to retrieve a box of cereal from atop the refrigerator, Charlie could see that she was wearing nothing under the T-shirt, nothing at all. Her body was so pale, the color of bone. Between her legs: a darkness of hair and pink flesh, fascinating and horrifying in equal measure.

Now he wondered just how different his own household was from Kent's. He knew his mother was taking OxyContin, among a hundred other pills. Perhaps then his own homelife and Kent's were no longer quite as different as they had once been, both their mothers adrift in their separate boats on some immeasurable glassy sea.

Now he swung his skateboard around the corner onto the street upon which Kent's battered house huddled in disrepair. Paula, the woman who lived across the street and with whom his own mother had once worked at Kroger, was just in the process of locking her front door and as Charlie kicked up the street she turned and stepped down to the sidewalk. He waved a hand at her.

"Hey," he said.

"Hey there," Paula answered. "Haven't seen you around much."

"Yeah, things are weird," Charlie said. He had stopped skating and stood in the middle of the street, Paula continuing down the cracked walkway to her car.

"I'll bet they are," she said. "You tell your momma I've been thinking about you guys. Praying for you at church on Sundays too."

"OK," Charlie said. "I'll let her know."

"You going to see your friend?" she said now. She nodded in the direction of Kent's house and he nodded in reply.

"Yeah," he said.

She seemed to consider something, glancing once more at Kent's house. "Well, you be careful," she said at last.

"I am," he said.

She reached her car and opened the door and slid inside without another word, the door clicking closed and the vehicle starting up, its tailpipe blowing white smoke into the freezing air.

Charlie pulled his scarf tighter around his throat, lifted the skateboard, and entered the house's ragged side yard, dipping below the edge of the window when he saw Kent's mother standing at the kitchen sink, her hair in tangles and her dress hanging on the sharp edges of her shoulders like a shroud. The image of her terrible nakedness came unbidden to his mind.

At Kent's window he tapped the glass with his knuckle. The pane almost immediately slid aside. Already came the skateboard—Charlie took it by its trucks—and then Kent himself, long and lanky like his father, unfolding through the open window and landing lightly on the ruined grass.

They knew well enough not to speak, not yet, instead Kent taking the board and waving Charlie forward, not toward the street that fronted the house but in a straight line away from it, through the neighbor's backyard and down the choked draw to the banks of the river, its shape gray and sluggish amidst the brambles and the flooded shapes of black alders and birch, their leaves gone pale yellow and brown and some of which were ringed with decay, the banks blanketed with that panoply of color, wet and thick and slippery underfoot. Kent reached into his back pocket and produced a pack of cigarettes. Marlboros.

"You got a full pack?" Charlie said.

"Stole 'em from my dad." Kent smacked the pack against his palm a few times and then pulled the plastic string around its lid, the clear cellophane drifting into the fallen leaves at his feet. The foil next and finally he removed a cigarette and passed the open pack to Charlie who took one and waited for Kent to be done with the lighter and then lit his own and the two boys stood there in the leaves with their skateboards, smoking in silence.

"When did he come back?"

"Couple days ago."

"How is it?"

Kent shrugged. "Cool," he said. "It's good he's back. It's been, like, a couple years."

"Yeah seems like a while. He's been working?"

"Driving trucks and stuff. He's got a million stories. Some are pretty funny."

"Cool," Charlie said. "I've got a little weed."

"Me too," Kent said, "but mine's mostly stems and shake."

"Same."

"We could see what Dyl has."

"I'm fine with this." He waved the cigarette in the air.

Kent extracted his pipe and then the baggie and packed a small bowl and lit it and drew in a long breath, the cherry glowing red against his face in the shadows of that cold riverbank. "You want?" he said now, proffering the pipe.

Charlie took it, inhaled, held, and then breathed out in a gust. They passed the pipe back and forth in relative silence. "Maybe we hit the park before it's too dark to see?" Charlie said.

Kent nodded. "Finish this first."

"For sure." Charlie tipped the hair back from his eyes.

They smoked the pipe to ash and Kent tapped it into the wet leaves and returned it to his pocket. "Let's hit it," he said. Then they clambered up the grade to the street and crossed the little bridge and pushed off in the direction of the skate park, their wheels a faint roar against the asphalt. The bleak house that was Kent's home receded behind them until Charlie could no longer feel its lurking presence. Then it was just he and Kent, the two of them kicking away under trees gone raucous with the bright blaze of some season Charlie could no longer understand.

MARY LOU

The heat struck her with the solidity of a wall.

"Mom?" she called.

And to her relief, a response: "What?"

"Why is it so hot?"

"Open a window," her mother called in response.

She dropped her purse by the door and hung up her coat. Already she was sweating through her clothes, the few snowflakes that had settled upon her shoulders bursting into steam. The thermostat switch was set simply to HEAT. She turned the switch back to AUTO. "Mom you can't just do this," she called.

She turned toward the bedroom, where she knew she would find her mother in the BarcaLounger as always—she could already hear the muffled sound of the television—but there was something else amiss, not just temperature but a smell of something burning which she thought for a moment might have simply been dust from the overheated vents but then her eyes went to the kitchen and a brief strangled, "Oh!" escaped her lips. On the stovetop stood a single pot, its shape a bright, blazing orange, the burner under it licking up its luminous sides.

Later, at the hospital, she explained to the doctor how stupid she had been to grab the pot handle but she was afraid the whole house would burn down at any moment and did not know what else to do, the pot's glowing shape crashing into the glasses even as her opposite hand flung the faucet handle up. A great explosion of steam burst across her hands, her face, her neck.

"That's probably worse than what the pot handle did," the doctor had told her.

"Really?" she said.

"Superheated water vapor. That can be really dangerous. You might have burnt your lungs."

"Did I?"

"Are you having trouble breathing?"

"I don't think so."

"I wouldn't worry about it then. But we should talk about your mother."

"My mother?"

"If you hadn't gotten home when you did, it might have been a lot worse."

"It'll be fine," she said, her voice not much more than a whisper.

When she had gone to her mother, her hand wrapped in a wet towel, her face wet with tears, the woman's first response had been to look at her incredulously and say, "Don't you have the sense to use a potholder?" But then she rose from the BarcaLounger to look at the wound and took Mary Lou into the bathroom to see what kinds of medical supplies were available.

"Mom, you left a pot on the stove."

"I did not."

Mary Lou pursed her lips and nodded. "You did, though. You've gotta be more careful. You could've burned the house down."

"I've never left a pot on the stove in my life," she said.

"Mom," Mary Lou said to her, but her mother only shook her head again and began to shuffle back toward the BarcaLounger. "You'd best get to the doctor," she said without turning, waving one hand behind her as she reached the end of the hall and disappeared out of view.

"Does your mother often forget things?" the doctor asked her now. He was a handsome man, beautiful, the kind of man who would never even look at Mary Lou in ordinary circumstances, of this she was certain, a lesson she had learned at an early age. She was only what her mother called chunky then.

"Sometimes," she told him.

"Important things?"

"I guess. Why? Is it Alzheimer's or something?"

"Well, that's kind of what I was getting at. I mean people forget things all the time. I can't remember where I put my keys most mornings."

"She forgot my name," Mary Lou said quickly. "She called me by my aunt's name."

The doctor looked at her closely, his gaze sending a frisson of pleasure through her. "Even that could be nothing. Sometimes I call my dog by one of the kids' names."

"Maybe you have Alzheimer's," Mary Lou said.

"Ha!" the doctor said, his perfect teeth a white arc in his mouth. "You should have been a doctor!" He smiled again and shook his finger at her. "Who's her primary care physician?"

"She hates doctors."

"You should have her take some tests. Could be it's nothing."

"What if she has it?"

"Let's get her tested first," he said.

He had already bandaged her hand and wrote her a prescription for some antibiotics and supplied her with a handful of sample-sized rip-top plastic tubes of topical ointment with a prescription for more. "Is one more important than the other?" she asked him.

"What do you mean?"

She blushed, could feel the heat of it in her face. "If there's a choice to get one or the other, should I get the pills or the ointment."

He sat back now, his white coat as immaculate as his teeth. "Hang on a minute," he said then. He rose and left the room and she sat confused and embarrassed until he reappeared with a paper lunch sack. "This oughta do it," he said. "Enough for three or four weeks. Maybe a little extra."

The bag was filled with more of the little sample tubes. "What's your copay?" he asked her. "For seeing me, I mean."

"Fifty," she said. "Twenty-five for the regular doctor. Urgent care's more."

He nodded. "I wish I could help with that part."

"You've been fine," she said. And she meant it. When she rose to leave, after the paperwork had been signed, he put a hand on her shoulder. "Don't forget to get your mom into the doctor," he said. "It's important."

"OK," she said, feeling the warmth of that touch.

"Hey now," he said. "It's gonna be all right. But get her in for the tests."

"I will," she said. "I promise. I'll do it. I will."

"Good girl," he said quietly.

In some life other than this one, his words might have been condescending, but what she knew, beyond his touch, beyond the warmth of it, the feeling of his hand so gentle upon her, was that he had just said two words her mother had never said to her and never would. And it was all she had ever wanted to hear. Nothing less. Nothing more.

KHALID

Khalid stood at the base of the escalator, craning his head for any glimpse of his parents, wondering if he should have worn his kurta after all. Rafia had found it for him in the very back of his closet, wrinkled and limp but otherwise intact despite not having been worn in seven years; he might have asked the local drycleaner to revitalize the garment but in the end he had gone with his favorite suit, dark olive, a suit that nearly always elicited a positive response from his wife.

He was therefore relieved when he saw his father—at last his father!—in similar Western dress, a suit of lightweight fabric in dark blue, its cut not unlike that which Khalid wore and surprisingly unwrinkled despite the many hours of air travel. And yet how old his father looked, his hair gone gray and his eyes betraying a sense of confusion as he seemed to search for his wife despite the fact that the woman stood just behind his shoulder and was clearly speaking to him, his father nodding even as he stepped gingerly onto the escalator to begin his descent. And now Khalid could see his mother, hair covered by a black hijab, the kurti she wore modern enough that it likely appeared, to American eyes, as simply a long, blousy shirt. She saw him almost the moment that he saw her, their eyes meeting and his mother's face brightening at the sight of him, one hand raising to wave.

He greeted them both, shaking his father's hand before embracing him, his father clapping him twice on the back, smiling. "You look older," his father said in Urdu, his voice upturned as if he had asked a question.

Khalid embraced his mother. Her hand patted his face gently, as if he were a child.

"It's been a long time," Khalid said, smiling.

"Too long," his mother said. "Where's my daughter-in-law and my grandchildren?"

"Rafia's busy preparing the house for you, Ami-ji."

"She should have done that days ago," his mother said, waving a hand in the air. "I was looking forward to seeing her."

"She's been preparing for days."

"And my grandchildren?"

"Still in school," Khalid said. "Everyone will be at the house when we get there."

"The lake is very big from the air," his father said. Again, Khalid could not help but notice just how old his father appeared. He had been in his early sixties when Khalid had left Lahore for Ohio and now his father was seventy. Those years away had wrought a change that could not be reversed or altered. It seemed impossible that the vibrant, sometimes bull-headed patriarch of Khalid's life had become this old man and yet here was the evidence in the flesh before him.

"Lake Erie," he said. "We'll go there in the summer. There's a big water park on the shore."

They had both climbed into the back seat of the SUV, leaving Khalid alone in the front. Small talk about the flight and the length of the drive, the city draining back to graying fields. Khalid had awakened to a few tattered snowflakes but the snow had since stopped and what remained was a biting cold, not quite the hard snap of winter but certainly near freezing. He had wondered if either of his parents would comment on the temperature but neither had.

"Have you been keeping up with the children's Urdu?" his mother asked from the back seat.

"I've tried to," Khalid said.

"Good," she said.

In truth Khalid doubted any of them could coax his children into speaking Urdu, if they even recalled how to do so. They had both been born in Pakistan, of course, but for seven years they had spoken their home language only sporadically and now answered both he and Rafia in English even if addressed in their native tongue. It was hard to believe now but Rashid had just turned seven when they departed Lahore, Saroya nine—small children and their mother traveling across the world.

In the rearview mirror, his father sat in silence looking out the window at the passing trees and fields. "Most of the state is farming," Khalid said into the mirror.

"It looks that way," his father said now. His voice was the same, at least. "And what do they farm?"

"Soybeans and corn, mostly," Khalid said.

"Soybeans," his father said. "An ingredient in many foods these days."

"Yes, and corn too."

"Sugar," his father said, the word upturned like a kind of querulous announcement. And then, in his heavily accented English: "High-fructose corn syrup."

"That's right," Khalid said, smiling and nodding, although his father's eyes did not shift from the window. "You've been practicing your English?"

"Not enough," his father said.

"It'll come quickly. Full immersion."

"Yes, it's too easy to go back to Urdu at home."

"How is it there?"

"Crowded and hot."

"So the same?"

"More crowded. More hot. Not like here."

"Cold, yes?" Khalid said.

"Very cold." There was a pause now, the road unfurling, the flat gray of the sky rolling on above them. But then, quietly, came his father's voice: "Also very . . ." his father began now, pausing as if to find the right word. Then he said: "Alive."

"Yes, very alive."

"The trees are beautiful," his mother said.

"The first time I saw the fall colors I almost crashed my car I was so busy looking out the window."

"I can see why," his mother said. "It's beautiful."

And then his father's voice once more: "How are things at your factory?"

"Moving along."

"I'd like to see it."

"Of course. I'll take you there whenever you'd like."

"Your father should rest first." This had come from his mother, quickly, as if she were interjecting in an effort to keep her husband from committing his time.

"Of course," Khalid said. "Of course you should. Both of you. We've got a comfortable room prepared."

The road continued onward, cars around them changing lanes and passing them or being passed. Khalid glanced at the speedometer, adjusted slightly, glanced into the mirror once more. His father continued to stare out the window at the rolling hills and bright copses of trees.

Khalid had been waiting nearly two years for their arrival and it felt impossible that they were actually here, in Ohio, at long last.

"I look forward to discussing the business with you," he said now, and when his father did not respond he added: "I could use your expertise."

"I'm not well-versed in American business practices."

"All business is business," Khalid said.

"My time in that world is over." In its reflection from the glass the sound seemed to come from outside, a disembodied voice from the stubbled fields themselves. And now his father's eyes met his in the mirror. "I'm glad to see you, Khalid," he said, his eyebrows rising and lowering briefly.

"I'm glad to see you too, Abu-ji," Khalid said. "Both of you. I can hardly believe you're here."

"Neither can we," his father said. "There was a moment on the plane when I wasn't sure we'd ever make it."

"Oh stop," his mother said, her voice mirthful. "You've always been so impatient."

"Impatient? It was an eight-hundred-hour flight!"

They all laughed then, briefly. His father's face in the rearview: a fading senescence in the reflected sky's endless afternoon dusk. He wondered what his father would see when he first lay eyes upon the little manufacturing plant with its staff of twenty souls. His father's career in Lahore had been with a major chemical manufacturer; twenty employees—twenty-one with the newest hire—was unlikely to make much impact and yet Khalid hoped the man would be proud and that he, Khalid, would appear successful in his eyes. He had been, was, aware that his attending Ohio State rather than Harvard or Oxford had been a disappointment to his father's pride but perhaps his life here might offer a way toward revision, although now, with the ever-wintering hills flowing across his view, he wondered anew at the bare geography of his life and his choices. Behind them ran the great concrete-and-steel complex of Cleveland, a locale at least analogous to Lahore—in size, in industry, in commerce. He wondered if his father would view the quaint, beautiful town in which he, Khalid, had settled as some backwater village. The man was unlikely to voice such an opinion but Khalid would know, of course he would, the judgment apparent in every gesture, in every unspoken word. And yet Khalid also had pride in his accomplishment. He owned something here, had worked out the details of banking and immigration, the attendant complexities of paperwork and finance, the legalities an endless maze. The factory, when he had first contemplated its purchase, was an entity on the cusp of collapse. That he had resuscitated it, that his tenacity had actually worked, was a vindication of that struggle. He had done it. He had succeeded.

What he wanted most of all was to show his father, to show them both, that he was successful, not only in business but with his home, his wife, his children. The house was of brick and the yard clean and clear and beautiful. The whole place was beautiful: rolling hills and pastureland and cornfields and soybeans and red barns and silos as if every scene that passed by the windows was but an image from a picture postcard. Not Lahore, not even Cleveland, but something cleaner, brighter, more beautiful. Look! he wanted to shout. Look at where I live! Look at the paradise your son has brought you to!

But when his gaze returned to the rearview it was to find his mother's eyes staring back at his across that reflection and what he saw in them was an expression that he had not often seen in his mother's gaze: not the strength and vitality of her unflagging devotion to her husband but rather something else, a sense of fatigue, of wariness, perhaps even of fear. He smiled at her and she smiled back. "I'll let Rafia know when we're close so she can put some tea on," he said to her reflection.

She nodded. "I'm looking forward to seeing her," she said. "And my grandchildren."

"Not as much as they're looking forward to seeing their grand-mamma." He used the English word here as he thought it might elicit a smile and she did smile, although it was with such a profound look of sadness that it nearly took her son's breath away.

ANTHONY SHAW

Anthony had taken to walking in the early evenings, at first because it reminded him of Rudy and then because he could think of no other way to occupy the hours between work and dinner and, finally, sleep. Sometimes he would feel himself moving through some simulacra of their old haunts in the city—the ruins of the old observatory, the bleak encapsulated wilderness of Forest Hill, the strip of fast-food restaurants that lined Euclid—those images so distant as to be imaginary, as if his mind had constructed them out of adherence to some reality that no longer existed and perhaps never had. But no, of course it had, for he had lifted Rudy's shoulders from the street, had felt that slack wet weight in his arms.

He had begun with a quick stroll from his auntie's to the coffeeshop in town, ordering a decaf and sometimes sitting in the warmth for a while, thumbing the paperback he kept in his pocket, perhaps reading for a bit, perhaps not, and finally returning to the cold, his motion, across many such nights, increasingly divested of direction or purpose, his passage looping down unknown streets and his understanding of the geography around him increasing night after night. He knew, of course, this was an activity not without a certain measure of risk, that he was an oddity in that place, in that town. He could feel eyes watching him as he moved, his gait slow, steady, hands in his coat pockets, hood up, headphones clamped over his ears, eyes forward on the sidewalk. "Good evening," he would say, nodding and making direct eye contact if anyone happened to pass on the sidewalk. "Oh, good evening," the answer would come. And then a brief smile, this, perhaps, no different from how anyone else would be greeted and yet he could sense his own strangeness, his own difference. Oh, good evening.

The first few times he had entered the coffeeshop, the girl at the counter had smiled like a lunatic and spoke in a loud, weirdly ingratiating voice, but that effect had quieted some over the subsequent visits. "Welcome back," she said now. She no longer asked his name and yet he would find it written in Sharpie upon the paper cup when it appeared at the end of the bar, a fact which he found not so much surprising as shocking, as if his anonymity, not in shape but in name, had been assumed with such depth of feeling that it had achieved the solidity of a fact and now, with the surety of a girl's hand scribbling seven letters on a paper cup, that anonymity had not simply been obliterated but had been revealed as a lie. He did not know if he felt relieved or terrified.

When he first arrived he had wondered why his auntie would choose to live in such a place but already he had come to feel a certain slow rhythm in the days, a quietude that seemed to rise from the earth itself which was, he thought, manifestly different from anything he had ever experienced in his life, although that was also untrue, for he could hear, had heard, the shadow of just such a place in the music. What he thought of, and what he now drew upon from his headphones, was a great undifferentiated sheet of droning guitars. Some of the music he and Rudy had clung to reminded him of East Cleveland but this, SUNN O))) at present, felt of this landscape or something similar, a topography of grackles and old oaks and the bleak darkness of the season.

A creek ran below the road and he skipped off the sidewalk and came down the embankment now, still clutching the paper cup that bore his name. A passing car caught him in its swinging headlights just as he went out of sight, the shadows rotating crazily and then winking out again. In the headphones, the drums had just kicked in, a slow, heavy throb, slower than any human heart and which, as he slipped under the black trees and his feet found the gravel walking path that wound along the waterline, pounded against the lowest frequencies. Already cold enough that his sweatshirt was inadequate protection, his skin all in gooseflesh under the layers. There would come a time soon enough when it would be difficult or impossible to linger out of doors and when that happened he would be effectively trapped in the bare garret that was his auntie's spare room, a space containing nothing but Anthony's clothes, a few paperbacks he had bought from the junk store, and a wooden cross mounted on the wall above the bed.

His auntie would have dinner ready soon and she would expect him to be there for that meal, for where else would he be? What he did not know, what he did not want to ask, not even of himself, was how long he was to remain in this place. At what point would he return home, home to East Cleveland? He knew no one here, no one who would miss him were he to vanish, although he supposed such a reckoning did not include his auntie. Perhaps, being family, she did not count for such a measure. Some of the people he worked with knew his name and he theirs—Cheryl, Tom, Mary Lou, Mr. Marwat—but what consequence did that have? He temporarily worked at that place, knowing all the while that most of the others had been employed there for many years and would continue for many more. He did not know what his life would bring, but he could not fathom the idea that he had survived to spend it assembling objects he still did not understand. Transformers, of all things. And yet what did they transform?

That the place from which he had come still existed just an hour's drive to the northeast seemed some impossible geography. The place where Rudy had been killed. Where Rudy was dead. Where Rudy had been alive. But Rudy had not been the only person he had known back home; there were others, some of whom he might have even called friends. Chuck. Benno. Benno's sister Shanice, for whom he had held a wild lustful crush. Perhaps he still did or perhaps such a thing could be kindled were he to return. And yet, despite everything, he did not think he could go back there, not yet, and not because he had been banned from the place or because he feared for his life in any way that was tangible but because he knew, not in a way that he would have been able to articulate but simply in the blood and bone of his being, that the timeline there was not measured in years but in months or days or weeks or hours. Rudy had taught him that. He had no choices in the place to which he had come and yet that lack was still greater than that of the place he had fled.

The river level was low. Even in the dark, he could see where the bank had been undercut during previous seasons, exposed roots entangled through dirt and stone and plunging down the brown current upon the surface of which an image of the black sky was reflected, tatters of brightness sometimes shining back at him from what source he did not know. He wondered what Rudy would think of this place, of where he was, of what he was doing, of what his life had suddenly become.

The wash of low guitars faded in his ears and was replaced by the muffled susurration of night sounds. He pulled down the headphones. The quiet burble of water. The distant hiss of a car from the road. Then a crunch of dry leaves somewhere ahead of him. He looked up, startled, to find a figure a few dozen feet away. Ahead of him the path opened into the local park, its play structures angular and insectoid in the night, and the pooling yellow light under the streetlamps cast the figure in a black, sharp silhouette.

He turned back toward the road, the action no decision at all but merely instinct, and in that moment came a bright wash of light. He might have run had he not glanced back to see the girl upon whom the light had affixed like a beacon: her body half turned, her heavy coat in sharp relief, a twist of long brown hair blowing backward from around the edge of the fur-lined hood. He could not see her face but something in the way she stood spoke of fragility, like a figure of glass teetering there in the night. Her hand came up to shield her face, its shadow a dark streak crossing her hood.

"You all right, miss?" This voice had come from the source of the light and now he realized what he should have known already: not a flashlight but the mounted searchlight of a police cruiser.

"What?" she called.

"Are you all right? Are you in any trouble?"

"I'm just, you know, walking."

"Are you in any trouble?"

"No," she said.

"We got a call," the voice returned.

The officer had not turned the spotlight from her face and she continued to stand with one arm outstretched to block the full force of that light. She looked, to Anthony, as if she were casting some wild spell from her outstretched palm.

"Do you . . . want me to do something?" she said then. Her voice was hard and crisp. Anthony still could not see her face, only that long twist of hair and the bare fingers outspread in the light.

"You live around here?"

"Back there," she said, thumbing away from the river, behind her, into the battered houses that made up most of the town.

"Maybe time to head home."

"It's only, like, six o'clock," she said.

"It's for your own safety," the officer said. "We got a call about a prowler."

"A prowler?" she said.

Anthony took a step back and then another and to his horror the leaves under his feet crackled at a volume that seemed utterly impossible and then the light was on him and what he thought was run run run but instead he stood there, removing his hand from his sweatshirt pockets and holding it aloft, the coffee cup clutched in the other.

"Who's that there?" someone said—perhaps the other officer, the partner.

"You there," the first voice came. "Don't move."

"Just walking," Anthony said. "Same as her."

"You know this man?" the officer shouted and when the girl did not respond, the officer yelled, "You, miss. Yes, I'm talking to you. Do you know this man?"

"What? No," she said, gasping.

He knew she faced him now but he could not see her, could not see anything in the glare of the light. "I'm just out walking. Just going for a walk."

"What's in your hand?" the officer shouted.

"Nothing," Anthony said. But then he realized this was not entirely true. "Coffee," he said. "From the Perk."

"Drop it," the officer said.

He opened his hand, let the cup drop. The sound was low and wet.

"Miss, go home," the officer said. And then, a moment later, "Now!"

He could hear her footsteps moving across the grass and dry leaves, could hear them for a few brief moments before there was nothing but his blood pumping and his breath steaming the air.

"Just stay like that," the officer said now. "Don't move." And then the officer was before him, a man who looked not much older than himself, uniformed and panting, a faint haze of perspiration upon his upper lip despite the cold.

"I'm not moving," Anthony said. "I . . . I live here."

"In the park?"

"No, no," Anthony said, the lump in his chest blossoming into panic. "With my aunt."

"Who's your aunt?"

"Paula Chapman. She work at the Kroger's."

A slow blinking. Anthony did not know if the look was contemplation or erasure.

"You got ID?" one of the officers said.

"Sure," Anthony said. "It's in my pocket. My back pocket." He moved to reach for it and the officer's hand went to his gun and Anthony felt his stomach flip, his mouth going dry. "Just my wallet," he said. "Don't shoot me now."

"Don't give me a reason to."

"I'm not."

"Let's just calm down." This from the other officer.

"All right," Anthony said. "All right." He could see neither of them, only a great white halo that obliterated everything. "What do you want me to do?" he said. His voice was a dry whisper.

There was no sound out there in the night. Not even the water. Nor the leaves. Nor the trees. Grackles in their nests. Dreaming obscure and lightless dreams.

PART
2

SARAH

Let us talk of absence and the great gutting silence to come after.

Each doctor spoke as if into a glass well, the first nodding and nodding and asking a few perfunctory questions and prescribing a retinue of painkillers and muscle relaxants and finally telling her to come see him again in a month or two. The second asked if she had ever suffered from depression and Sarah had burst into tears as Tom told the doctor about James. What she wanted to say, what she wanted to tell them, to tell them both, was that she could not stop thinking of that moment. There must have been something she could have done. Instead she had screamed as the baby went limp and turned blue, holding him and squeezing him and shaking him but doing nothing that might have pulled him back from the dark heaven to which he had already traveled. The cardiologist told her she was not to blame, but he had not been there. Only she had; only she had felt his little body go limp in her arms. The sound in her skull was the sound of her own screaming, its echo across all the days that followed.

His weight, his warmth, his cooing babble, all of it had been for her alone and no one else, for she had given him her blood. To hold such a body, helpless, to be given that responsibility, that blessing, and then for all that weight and warmth and babble to become a blunt and physical terror. A hole in his heart, the doctor had told them, had told them too that they would need to hold off on the operation for some months. He was so small, his tiny face with its dark, luminous eyes. He saw her, his expression that of recognition, but of course he recognized her, even in the darkness of her womb he knew his mother.

But he had not made it through the delay and the months after had been a rasping blade running through her bones, her muscles, the sinewed places of connection, a reality that she knew Tom did not understand and which, perhaps, he did not even believe, his expression moving from concern to something placating, patient, as if she were but one of the children narrating a long story the subject of which he did not understand and ultimately about which he did not even care.

The second doctor had prescribed antidepressants, which Sarah took regularly but which further drew down the thick blanket of dry cottony fog that had already come to feel as if it were the permanent weather of her mind. She knew she was depressed, for how could she not be, but the doctor's words about emotional and mental health suggested that the pain she described was ultimately a construct of her mind rather than her body. How she wished this were true. The pain continued through all of it, the only recourse the heaviness of the painkillers prescribed by the first doctor, the effects of which included constant lethargy and a constipation so severe she felt as if her colon had been filled with concrete.

She slept fitfully, always half awake, dozing through days and nights without end, a fact which, she knew, had turned her home into a kind of museum, the children and her husband tiptoeing around the place so as to not disturb her rest. How she loved them for their quietude but how guilty it also made her feel that she had so changed the very character of their home.

All of this she related to Amy at the kitchen table. They had been friends since high school and had been through everything together, from boys and parties and school events to first jobs and their marriages and the birth of their children. And now this.

"I need to be better for my kids," she said now.

"You need to be better for yourself, honey," her friend replied. "I got some leftover Oxy if you want me to bring it over. It's the heavy stuff from when Sam had his dental surgery. You'd need to be careful. It'll knock you out."

"I already have that. I swear, Aim, it's like I'm a drug czar."

Amy fingered the edge of her paper coffee cup. She looked just as she had in high school, older but physically the same: thickset, ruddy cheeked, hair dyed a somewhat unnatural shade of red—this, at least, was different—freckles by the end of summer but now, just past the start of the new year, her skin was pale and flushed, worry lines creasing the edges of her mouth, her brow.

Outside the disheveled warmth of the house, Ohio had hardened into winter, leafless trees blackly reaching into skies drifting with snow.

"You remember my cousin Emily?" Amy said now. "She had a weird pain thing. Went to a specialist in Cleveland."

"Did he help her?"

"I think so. I can find out who the doctor was."

"I don't know if we can afford it," Sarah said.

"That's what credit cards are for," Amy said.

Sarah smiled. "I'm not sure Tom would agree."

"Tom wants you to feel better too," Amy said, "probably more than anyone."

"He's worried about money."

"Everyone's worried about money."

"I know but we're really behind," Sarah said.

"We'll get you all through. Don't you worry."

"It's like I'm going crazy. That's how it feels. But there's something wrong. I know there is."

"I know, honey," Amy said. "We'll figure it out."

"I'm scared, Aim."

Amy reached a hand across the table and squeezed Sarah's briefly, the sensation warm and soft and loving and Sarah's heart welled with the contact.

"And Tom's so patient but Lord knows I'm not being a very good wife."

Amy scoffed at this. "OK now you've gone too far."

"It's true though."

"Yeah let's not start acting like we're bad wives after what our husbands put us through."

"I'm just back there all day," Sarah said, thumbing toward the bedroom.

"So fucking what," Amy said. "You're trying to get well. And if Tom gives you any grief about that you just let me know and I'll knock his ass into next Tuesday."

Sarah laughed. Then she asked about the doctor who helped her cousin.

"He said it was lupus," Amy said. "You ever heard of that?"

"I think so."

"Her body's basically attacking itself."

"Jesus," Sarah said. "What do you do about that?"

"I don't know too much about it," Amy said. "She was over at Christmas. Seemed tired but she was there."

"That's good at least," Sarah said. She could not hide the sadness in her voice. She knew she had become someone she herself did not recognize, not the person Amy had befriended but some other, dark, dour figure in a bathrobe in the middle of the day, a ghost of who she had been. But maybe now this was all there was. Maybe she had shriveled to some essential self and this was what it looked like: pale and haggard and sunken-eyed like some witch woman of old. God she could still feel James like a ghost in her arms. How she just wanted to squeeze him to her neck, her chest. He was so warm. So soft. His eyes crinkled when he smiled. Oh God. Oh God.

"Just breathe, honey," Amy was saying now. "Come on." A hand on her shoulder. "It'll be all right. It will. You'll figure it out. I'll call my cousin and get that name. And hell, if Tom won't take you I'll do it myself."

"Tom will," Sarah said. A tremble in her voice.

"I know he will," Amy said, "but he'd better do it nice otherwise I'm coming over here to kick his ass."

A bark of raw laughter. She wished Amy could be there always, sitting at the table, waiting for her, ready to kick the crap out of anything or anyone foolish enough to get in her way. What she wanted, what she needed, was a champion. A dragonslayer. But she was a wife and a mother and what dragon pursued her through the dark forests could not be seen, not by her husband or her children or even by her doctors, not by Amy, not even by herself, and yet she could feel its fire deep inside her body, twisting in blackened flesh. She had sometimes wished—feared and wished—that there would be some evidence of pain visible upon her skin: a path of redness, a bruise, a mark of charred ash. But there was no evidence of how she felt, her agony held ever inside like a secret she could not release no matter how many people she told.

JANEY

She had seen him several times in the months after, on the street by the pizza place once, walking with his hands in his pockets and his hood up, head down, and another time not far from where she had first seen him, by the frozen skate park, this time his head craning upward as if he had lost something in the boughs of the trees and sought to regain it once more. Each time she wanted to stop and talk to him, to tell him she was sorry that she had walked away that night in the park when the police had come but that she had been scared, which she knew was no excuse at all but which was the truth; and yet each time she saw him she felt frozen in inaction, convincing herself that the bundled figure might be someone else or that he was simply too far away to make speaking with him seem casual, although why this would be a criterion of her making contact was something she herself did not understand. Perhaps it was simply a manifestation of her own cowardice.

In the low stress and struggle of the holidays, she had stopped thinking much about him at all. But then, in January, she entered the coffeeshop one evening and there he was, seated at a small table near the window, staring down at a ragged paperback, thick black headphones clamped over his ears. It took her a long moment to screw up the courage to speak to him but at last she stood beside his table. She could not see the book's title but he seemed intent upon it and he did not look up at her for a long while, finally sensing her there, his eyes rising to take her in. His gaze sent her skin into a prickling heat that was both embarrassment and something else she could not name. He pulled the headphones from his ears and she could hear a brief tinny screech before he tapped his phone and the music fell silent.

"I . . . uh . . . I wanted to say hello," she said.

"OK," he said. "Um . . . hello?" He was, she realized, quite handsome, his eyes a deep brown that looked up at her with frank curiosity. When she did not say anything more he said, "Something you need?"

"Oh, no," she said. "I just . . . uh . . . I saw you before and I thought . . ."

And again the long pause. "You thought what?" he said. There was no animosity in his voice. Just a wary sense of politeness.

"I was . . ." Janey began, stopped again, looked at him there, his book, his coffee, and then said, "I'm not doing this very well."

"I'm not sure what you're doing at all," he said simply.

"Can I sit down?"

"Are you gonna try to sell me something or get me to come to your church or something like that?"

"No," she said, smiling for a moment and exhaling loudly, too loudly, she thought.

"OK then," he said. He nodded at the empty chair across from him and she took it, setting her book bag on the floor and then her mocha upon the table and slipping at last into the chair. He closed the book and slid it to the side. *Dune*. She had never heard of it and thought for a moment that she might start by asking him about the book but instead she said, "I was at the park," the words coming in a quick, breathless burst.

"OK," he said.

"No I mean the night the police came. Back before Thanksgiving. You know?"

He was looking at her, staring, and then he nodded. "Wait—you're that girl?"

"Yeah. I didn't know what was happening. It freaked me out."

"Well at least they were looking out for you." He shrugged. "I'm Anthony," he said.

She said her name and he put out his hand and she shook it. Warm from the coffee cup and dry. "Pleased to meet you," he said.

"Yeah," she said. "Same. So look I just wanted to, you know, apologize."

"What for?"

"For leaving you there. Well, I mean, I didn't really leave. I watched what happened. They took you away in the police car."

"It's what they do," he said.

"Did you do something wrong?"

"You mean illegal?"

She nodded.

"Naw," he said. "Just walking."

"Same as me," she said.

"I guess."

"What did they do? I mean, where did they take you?"

"Nowhere, really. They called my auntie. Then they took me home. Told me to be careful."

"I should've done something."

"You should have done what you did," he said.

"I could've stayed and at least made sure they knew I was there. Watching them. I could've taken a video with my phone. I didn't even do that."

He shrugged and sipped at his coffee.

"They're not allowed to just take you away. Not without cause."

"Says who?"

"Says my civics teacher," she said and then blushed, looking down at her coffee cup in embarrassment.

He shrugged. She had said to him what she had wanted to say, what she had thought about saying for weeks and weeks, and yet now that she had said it she did not want to leave the table. Her options for conversation were Shannon and Kimmy and the other girls, their vacuous texts, their pointlessness. She had gone to a party just before Thanksgiving. Keg stands and weed and beer in red plastic cups. She was seventeen. She had been drunk three times and had been high twice and somehow that felt like enough. She knew what she did not want but that was all. She had had the same friends since first grade. And yet she suddenly felt as if there was nothing to say to them. Everything was the same. Everything in the whole town was the same.

She did not know what to say now and the table fell once more to silence. Anthony brought his coffee to his lips and when he brought it back to the table his eyes found hers. A throb of heat. Say something, she thought, but nothing would come and finally, her voice a rush of exasperation and irritation, not at him but at herself, for her failure to keep the conversation aloft, she said, "Well, I guess I'll head out."

"I was just gonna ask, uh, what you're into," he said quickly.

"Oh," she said. Relief now. Relief. But what could she say? "Um, I don't know."

"All right," he said.

"No, I mean, I really don't know. I'm trying to figure that out. Lately it doesn't seem like I'm into anything."

"Yeah, I get that."

"Do you?"

"Sure."

The espresso machine sent up a gout of hissing steam. From the counter came a brash, loud voice. She half turned. The mayor in a basketball boosters sweatshirt, his thinning hair swept back across his pate. She turned back to Anthony. "That's the mayor," she said.

"Don't dress like a mayor."

"Yeah that's because of basketball. We almost made it to state last year."

"High school?"

"Yeah," she said.

"So he's, like, the basketball mayor?"

"Pretty much. Everyone's into basketball around here."

"You into basketball?"

"I don't know. It's just a thing."

"I got you."

Outside, the earth was a frozen mass, cold enough that she could sense it even inside, as if the coffeeshop had been built upon a glacier that cracked and shifted under them. The snow had been heavy and then an ice storm and then the sky had cleared and had remained bright and blue for weeks on end, a rarity for January, when often snowstorms came one after another. Now the crust of the snow was everywhere, so hard that it was like a shell encasing the earth itself.

The mayor had disappeared once more, the room quieting.

"So those cops," Janey said. "That kind of thing . . ."

He waited for her to speak and when she did not he raised his cup to his lips and sipped and returned it to the table again. "Happens," he said.

"But it shouldn't."

He shrugged.

"It's just, you know, this is where I live."

For a long moment he did not understand what she meant. The implication seemed to be that she was somehow claiming the place for her own and thereby excluding him from it. And yet he did not think, looking at her there—a pale white girl, a teenager, her face marred by the red swell of an occasional pimple, eyes wide and troubled but not unkind—that she was capable of such honesty. But no, not honesty, for it was not honesty that she would have reached but a kind of banal cruelty that was, he knew, everywhere, geography demarcated by lines of inclusion and exclusion. That is what it would have been: a pointing out that this was her home and was, therefore, not his. And yet she did not seem so bold as to sit at his table and remind him of his place in what she thought of as her world. "Yeah, well, it's where I live too," he said simply.

"That's what I mean," she said and now her eyes were bright and contained within them, all at once, a kind of flame. "It's bullshit. We both live here. It just, you know, sucks."

"Sure," he said. "Maybe we can talk about . . . something else?" He rotated the coffee cup between his hands. Her eyes, when she looked at him, were the color of ice.

"OK," she said. She felt a wave of heat come to her face. She nodded to the headphones. "Um . . . so . . . what are you listening to?"

Now he shook his head, smiled. "What do you think I'm listening to?"

"I have no idea," she said.

"Take a guess."

"Taylor Swift," she said, and smiled.

"Tay-Tay." He was smiling now too. He slung the headphones from around his neck and handed them to her and then fiddled with the controls on his player. "Close your eyes," he said.

"What?"

"It's better that way."

And so she did. The room black. And what came to her, the diminished volume lower than what she heard when he had first removed the phones from his ears, was a rising, tortured wail, drums and guitars and a vocal so pained that it seemed almost otherworldly. It was metal of some kind, this much she knew, but beyond that what she heard felt like the stuff of nightmares.

"OK," she said, lifting one from her ear. "Not what I expected."

"Not Taylor Swift," he said.

"That would be kind of amazing if it was," she said.

"Taylor's metal phase. It could be her F-You Kanye album."

"Totally," she said, smiling now. "Turn it on again."

He did so. She closed her eyes and he sat staring at her. She looked peaceful, as if asleep. She was not strikingly beautiful but there was a plain kindness there that he was drawn to. It was strange to sit watching her.

Then she pulled the headphones off once more. "I'm sorry," she said.

"Sorry for what?"

"For what I'm gonna say." She winced. "OK so that is literally the worst thing I've ever heard in my entire life."

"Bold statement."

"Yeah sorry sorry. I shouldn't have said that."

"No it's fine. You're not wrong. You're not wrong."

"What do you like about that? It's just, like, noise."

"It's hard to explain. There's a story behind it. And it's not all that, you know, harsh."

"I'd like to hear it. The story, not the music. Is that even music?"

"Yeah, it's music. It's a band."

"Wow, yeah, so . . ."

"Sometime maybe I'll tell you about it," he said. "But now you."

"Now me what?"

He nodded to her phone.

"Oh," she said. "I'm not really a music person. I just listen to whatever. You know? Pop music or country or whatever's on the radio."

"You gotta pick one," he said. "I mean, if you want. You don't gotta do anything."

"Oh jeez," she said. She looked down at the table. The paperback was worn and old. On its cover was an orange desert. In the bottom corner, a few small figures dressed in white. "I guess . . ." she said. Then paused. "I've been listening to this dumb song my mom likes."

"Excellent," Anthony said. "I love dumb songs from moms."

She thought he was mocking her but when she glanced up she saw he was smiling, his hand held out for the phone. "Come on now," he said.

"Don't laugh."

"Don't laugh? You heard what I'm listening to."

She tapped the screen and then lay her phone in his hand. The flesh there was pink and lined. He took it and held the tiny speaker to his ear. She could not hear it at all but after a moment he smiled and closed his eyes, his head moving in a slow rhythm.

"All right, all right," he said.

She thought he would hand the phone back after a few seconds but he continued to hold it to his ear until the song was done.

"Who's that?" he said.

"Garth Brooks. Did you hate it?"

"I did not."

"You're lying."

"Now why would I lie?"

"I don't know," Janey said. "Just to be polite?"

"Hmm . . ." he said. "I don't think I'd lie. Not about that anyway."

"What would you lie about?"

"Oh, we getting deep now?"

"Maybe," she said.

He smiled again. His teeth were so white. Already she wondered if she would see him again, here or elsewhere, for although she had only been at the table for a few minutes, already she knew she did not want to leave.

Her phone vibrated on the table. A text from her father: Are u home? "Oh, hang on," she said.

"No worries."

At perk, she texted.

Ive got 2nd shift. Need you to check mom. She's not answering.

"Shit," she said.

"What?"

"It's just . . . it's . . ." She looked at him and then at her phone again. It was only four thirty and yet the sun was already deep in its gloaming. "I gotta go help my dad with something," she said.

"Got things to do. No worries," he said again. "It was nice to meet you, Jane."

She almost corrected him, almost told him that her name was Janey and yet she liked the way it sounded when he said it, as if she were an adult and he was her friend, another adult, and they were having coffee together the way adults might. And yet when she spoke again it was to blurt out her age: "I'm seventeen," she said.

"Um . . . OK," he said, his eyes widening.

"I just thought, you know, you should know."

"Yeah, I don't think I need to. Do I?"

"No, I guess—I mean, I didn't mean anything by it." She shook her head, put the phone in her pocket, reached for her bag. "Jeez, I don't know why I said that," she said. She was up then, the bag on her shoulder, paper coffee cup in her hand.

He shrugged. "I turned twenty last month."

"Twenty?" she said.

"Two zero."

"What's that like?"

"Kinda sucks," he said. Then he smiled at her again. His eyes met hers somewhere above the table, the battered paperback, the paper cup that was his.

"See you around?"

"For sure."

She nodded, waited a beat too long, and turned and headed for the door, already texting her father. Home in 20, she typed.

And again: She's not answering the phone.

On the way.

She texted Charlie then. You home? Already she was on the wooden stairs that led in a short flight to the sidewalk, its surface outlined by snow and ice. The cold shot through the seams of her coat like tiny knives. She texted again: Hey. Text me back.

Then she slipped her phone into her jacket pocket once more and slid her hands into her gloves.

"Shit," she said. "Shit shit shit." Her breath a steam cloud in the clear frozen air.

CHARLIE

He had been headed home until he had seen his father's text, a text which he ignored because he knew if he did not answer Janey surely would and then it would not be his problem and he would not need to rush home to confirm that his mother was asleep in the back bedroom as she always was. Despite this, he checked his phone a few times as he continued along the broken sidewalk, checked just to make sure his father did not text him again and when sufficient time had passed—a minute, two—and he was satisfied that Janey stepped in, he turned in the general direction of the coffeeshop, dropping his skateboard and kicking off down the street. He had hoped that Kent might meet him there but Kent had not answered his earlier texts. He had briefly considered crossing town to tap upon his friend's window but the thought that he might come upon Kent's father was enough to keep him away.

The sun had dropped behind the trees now and with it the air hardened to crystal, biting against Charlie's cheeks and the exposed part of his neck where his coat collar left a small gap. Maybe he would just go home after all. Too cold to skate. Too cold to do much of anything.

The streetlights began to click on all up and down the street, the sidewalk between them going black. Alone but for a single figure across the asphalt. He might not have noticed her at all but for her garb: an old woman moving through a pale circle of incandescent light in nothing more than a bathrobe and slippers. Even as he watched, he expected, at any moment, for her to shuffle toward one of the houses and disappear inside, but she stood mostly still upon the sidewalk, only her head in motion, craning this way and that as if she were looking for someone or something she had lost, an oddity that Charlie could not shake.

He had gone another ten yards or so before stopping and turning to look once more and finally popping his skateboard into his hand and crossing the street, stopping where a small berm of dirty, ice-covered snow separated the asphalt from the sidewalk. "Hi," he said, "uh, are you OK?"

"It's really cold," the woman said, a quaver in her voice.

He saw now that she was at least as old as his grandmother, although how old that was he did not know. Seventy? Older? Her hair a tangle atop her head, protuberant eyes looking to him and then to the sidewalk and back to him again. "Yeah, you should go inside," he said.

"Good idea," she said, but she did not move, only continued to stand there, her pale, white hands clutching at the front hem of her bathrobe. Her legs like bare bones, so white they were, so thin.

"Do you . . . um . . . do you need some help or something?"

"Do I look like I need help?" And now there was an edge in her voice even through the shivering. Annoyance. Irritation.

"Kinda," he said.

"You people," she muttered.

He almost departed again then and yet remained there, watching her. "Is there someone I can call or something?" he asked.

For a moment she said nothing, only continuing to stare all about her with those wide, bright eyes. "My sister." Her teeth chattered in her head so loudly that Charlie could hear the sound from where he stood upon in the street.

"OK, I've got a phone. What's her number?"

"Seven . . . um . . . seven . . . and . . . ah . . . I can't quite . . . uh," and she fell silent again.

"Do you live here?"

"Where?"

"In one of these houses?"

"No," she said simply.

"Nearby?"

She looked, to Charlie, as though she might shriek in terror, her eyes looking about her in a panic. "Where am I?" she said. "How did I get here?"

"I don't know," he said.

"Who are you?"

"Charlie," he said. "My name's Charlie."

"Do I know you?"

"No, I just saw you walking."

"Saw me doing what?"

He thought of calling his father and then his sister. His phone was out of his pocket and in his hand again. "I'm calling 911," he said, more to himself than to her.

"Why?" she said. She looked suddenly frightened.

"You need some help."

"Can you help me?"

"I am," he said. "I'm trying to."

"Why don't you just call Mary Lou. She'll come and get me."

"Who's Mary Lou?"

"My daughter," she said. And then she said a phone number, the prefix of which was familiar enough to Charlie that he knew it must have been local. He asked her to repeat it and to his relief she was able to. When a woman's voice answered he asked her if she was Mary Lou and when she said that she was he told her that he had her mother with him.

"What?" the woman said through the tiny speaker. "Who is this?"

"Charlie," he said. "Charlie Bailey."

"Tom's boy?"

He was surprised at this recognition but he nodded and then told her that yes, Tom Bailey was his father, and then that he had found her mother walking in a bathrobe and that she was out on the sidewalk with him. "She's really cold," he said into the phone.

"Oh my God," the voice said. Desperation. Fear. "Where are you?"

He told her the street name and then read the number off the nearest house. "She doesn't know where she is," he said.

"OK, OK," the voice said. "I'll be there in five minutes. Stay with her. Please stay with her."

"Sure," he said.

He slipped his phone back in his pocket and clambered over the little berm of snow so that he stood before her on the sidewalk. The old woman watched his movement curiously. "You need a haircut," she said to him.

"That's what my mom says," he told her.

"She's right."

"Mary Lou's coming to pick you up," he told her.

"Mary Lou?" she said. "Mary Lou can't drive."

"Why not?"

"She's not old enough. How old are you?"

"Fourteen," Charlie said, confused. The woman he had spoken to on the phone sounded like an adult. "She said she was coming to get you," he said. Something was wrong with her, this much was obvious enough, but right now what he was worried about was the cold. "Put my gloves on," he said. When she did not take them he lifted her frail hands and slipped them over the thin, wrinkled skin.

"Who are you?" she said.

"Charlie," he told her. "My name's Charlie. What's your name?"

"Ginger," she said, her tone seeming to indicate that she was exasperated that he did not already know this piece of information. "Why are we outside?" she said now. "I'm so cold."

He put his sock hat on her next and then stripped off his coat and placed it over her shoulders. The cold seemed to strip him of all his warmth immediately, but there was adrenaline now, a rush that ran through him all at once. He looked up and down the sidewalk, thought of knocking on some random door for a blanket but then a car appeared, rounding the corner and coming to an awkward diagonal stop in the street.

Charlie recognized the woman who exited the car as someone he had met once or twice at the bowling alley or elsewhere, someone who worked at the same place as his father. "Mom," she said. Her breath, coming from the car, was a great explosion of steam in the dark air.

"Oh, Mary Lou," the old woman said. There was a catch in her voice, the cold or a brief, strangled sob.

"Mom, Mom, you're freezing. What are you doing out here?"

Her mother did not answer her. The old woman's face was drawn into a rictus of cold, her lips tight, her eyes staring everywhere.

"Let's get you into the car," Mary Lou said. She turned to Charlie now. "Can you help me?"

Mary Lou took one arm and Charlie the other and when they reached the car, Charlie darted to the door and pulled it open and then moved out of the way as Mary Lou positioned her mother in the passenger seat.

Charlie could feel the heat from within and his body seemed to cry out for it all at once. Then the door was closed again. Inside the car, the old woman looked forward through the windshield, her expression one of confusion. His hat remained on her head, his coat across her shoulders. He knew she still wore his gloves as well but he could not see them from where he stood.

"Thank you so much, Charlie," Mary Lou said. "Thank you so, so much."

"Sure," Charlie said. "No problem."

"You saved her life," she said. "Thank you."

"Jeez," he said. "You're welcome."

"Hop in. I'll drive you."

It was strange being in the back seat of some woman's car, some woman who he recognized but did not know, not really, the radio playing a hushed country music station that faded in and out of range, its sound, when it fell to static, merging with the engine hum and the hiss of the road outside so that it seemed simply to disappear, a strain of guitars or drums rising occasionally from that emptiness to regain its rhythm once more before fading again.

The moment the doors had closed, Mary Lou had turned the heater on full and already it was stiflingly hot in the car; nonetheless, the old woman trembled with cold, her teeth audibly chattering and Mary Lou asking repeatedly if she felt all right, if she needed to go to the hospital, her words tumbling on and on and the old woman continuing to tremble.

Charlie leaned forward and lay his bare hand upon the old woman's shoulder. He could feel the thin bones through his coat. "Hey, you're OK now," he said simply.

She did not answer him but her trembling quieted. It was strange to see her in his hat, in his coat. He sat back in the seat once more.

"Where are we going again?" the old woman said.

"Home," Mary Lou answered.

"Why is it so hot in here?"

Mary Lou flicked the heater switch, the vent's roar diminishing to a gentle hiss.

In the new quiet, Mary Lou asked him the kinds of questions adults asked when they did not know what else to say: What grade are you in now? How are things at school? Do you have a girlfriend? He answered them all truthfully. Ninth grade. Things at school were fine. No girlfriend. She paused sometimes to check with the old woman who was her mother but now that she was out of the cold and had stopped trembling there was apparently no danger and the woman's responses were relegated to asking, repeatedly, where they were going and why she was wearing her robe and slippers. Mary Lou told her mother the truth the first two times she asked but the last time she told her that they were going to a slumber party and this was what everyone would be wearing. The old woman was silent then, perhaps in contemplation of the party to come.

When they reached Charlie's house she half turned in the driver's seat. "I really appreciate what you did," she told him.

"I didn't really do anything," he told her.

"Thank him, Mom," she said to her mother.

"What for?" the old woman said.

"For saving your life."

"He didn't save my life."

"Uh . . . I'd better go in," Charlie said.

"OK," Mary Lou said. "Tell your dad I said hello."

"Will do," Charlie said, and then, to the old woman, "Have fun at the party."

After he shut the door he realized, yet again, that the old woman still had his coat, his hat, and his gloves, but stopping the car seemed impossible. Tomorrow's walk to school would be freezing but he would deal with that problem when it came. For now, he turned to the house. He did not know if Janey was yet home but he could not remain outside without his coat and so he mounted the stairs at last and entered to find his sister and his mother both present and visible, his sister in the kitchen with a couple of pans sizzling on the stovetop, his mother not in the back bedroom this time but actually on the sofa in the living room, watching television. "Hey, honey," his mother said as he came through the door.

She wore her bathrobe and slippers, much as the old lady had outside, and Charlie's thought was to wonder, standing there, shivering in the doorway, if his mother would share the old woman's fate, to wander through an ever-encroaching darkness, her mind empty of all but the sharp bite of the freezing endless dusk.

"Where's your coat?" she asked him.

KHALID

Rafia did not seem to be listening to him, or perhaps was listening but did not hear him, or perhaps simply did not understand the level of concern that Khalid truly felt for the situation.

"Golf? Golf?" he was saying now. "Can you imagine my father playing golf?"

"Of course I can," Rafia said. "That's what men of your father's age do. That's what men of your age do."

"Golf," he said again, a statement this time rather than a question.

"Something then," Rafia said. "It doesn't need to be golf. Just something."

There were times, even after all these years, when he simply did not understand the woman he had married. That Rafia would take what he had said and process it and come up with golf—golf of all things!—as a solution was so utterly foreign to everything he thought he was saying that he could not even determine how to round back to the topic at hand, his entire linguistic reserve reduced to that single syllable, which now he repeated for the fourth time: "Golf."

The problem he had been describing, or trying to describe, failing to describe it seemed to him now, was that his parents had never actually arrived in Ohio or rather that the elderly couple he had retrieved from the airport, while indisputably and obviously his parents in fact, could not be reconciled with the version of his parents that lived in his memory. Wasim Marwat had been respected in Lahore, had risen from nothing to a position in management, an achievement that Khalid had been reminded of repeatedly for the entirety of his young life. Indeed, Khalid had assumed that immediately upon his arrival in Ohio, his father would begin to nitpick Khalid's own more modest business success, assuming, that is, that Wasim Marwat would behave much as he had when Khalid had been a younger man, offering his opinions on virtually all aspects of his son's life, in particular his business affairs; his mother, meanwhile, mostly silent except when she felt Khalid was not paying sufficient attention to his father's various edicts.

This was not just what Khalid expected but what he assumed, the fact of it so incontrovertible and inevitable that it felt, to Khalid, as sure as the sun rising in the sky, the changing of the seasons, the reality of gravity. And he and Rafia had discussed these facts at length in the years leading up to his parents' arrival and so Rafia, too, had been ready—as ready as one can be—for her mother-in-law to insinuate herself into all aspects of the governance of their home and yet Khalid's mother had been mostly quiet and deferential when it came to the day-to-day operation of the household. And yet when he brought this up, this in concert with his father's serious lack of meddling, Rafia's response was neither relief nor resignation but simply acceptance, as if his mother's watching television much of the day was part of the natural order of things rather than a repudiation of everything Khalid had ever known.

"Why are you so troubled?" Rafia had asked him. "He's retired, jaan. Just let him watch TV and relax. You didn't want him to be poking around in your business anyway."

This was true of course and yet now that his father had shown no real interest, he found himself longing for exactly what he had been dreading. He had even gone so far as to ask his father for particular advice on subjects upon which, in truth, he did not actually need any input whatsoever. "Abu-ji," he asked one night during their evening meal, "I wondered if you might take a look at the average pay rates for assembly workers in this region."

"I don't know anything about the pay rates in this region," his father had replied.

"I know," Khalid continued. "I have some data collected. I thought you might be able to give me your advice."

"On pay rates?"

"On whether or not we're paying our workers in keeping with local trends."

"I'm not expert in local trends," his father said simply.

"Just as a favor to me."

A pause and then, finally: "I suppose."

"Wonderful," Khalid said. "I'm very grateful."

The patriarch looked across the table and nodded but in truth he did not look particularly enthused by the request. There was, at times, Khalid thought, a barely perceptible sense of ennui in his father, of deflation, a condition which was beyond Khalid's understanding. After all, he had spent much of his childhood trying to gain his father's attentions despite the fact that Wasim Marwat was, in the context of his parenting, a man who judged his son's behavior by the stiff yardstick of his own adult life, that is when he was present at all, for the patriarch was concerned with business first and family a more distant second and was, therefore, and perhaps understandably, simply absent from much of his son's day-to-day life. That his father had, much later of course, given Khalid the initial investment which had allowed him to buy the factory had been, in a sense, a real surprise, for by that point he had more or less relegated himself to the understanding that his father did not ultimately have much interest in him at all, although his mother assured him that this was not the case, that indeed his father paid quite close attention to his progress through the world. How this manifested itself, at least when Khalid was younger, was as a sporadic thread of criticism of this progress. He had failed to gain admission to any of the Ivy League schools to which he had applied, finally choosing Ohio State only because it offered, at the very least, an American university education. His father's response had been profound disappointment, perhaps even embarrassment. Indeed what his mother had defined as his father's interest in him had been, in Khalid's actual lived experience, something quite different. This was what he had dreaded upon hearing the news that his parents would be joining he and Rafia and the children in America. And of course while he knew, in his heart, that, yes, he should have been grateful that his father's presence here had been exactly the opposite of what he had feared, he could not help but be baffled and concerned by the conspicuous absence of the lionlike man of his childhood.

At some point during their first months in America, Khalid had even asked his mother if there was something wrong with his father, if he was suffering some illness.

"Illness?" his mother said, shock and alarm in her voice. "Why would you say such a thing?"

"I'm sure it's nothing. Abu-ji just seems . . . I don't know . . . very quiet."

"Bacha, your father is seventy years old," his mother told him. "He's a right to rest."

"I'm not suggesting otherwise," Khalid said, eyes downturned. "I'm just concerned."

"You don't need to be concerned," his mother said sternly. "We're all together again and your father and I are both very happy to be here with you and Rafia and the children."

And yet he continued to feel that something was amiss. "I don't know what to do about him," he told Rafia now. She lay in bed, a novel open on her lap.

"You worry too much," she said. "Have you talked to him about getting started on converting the rumpus room?"

"I brought it up but he didn't seem like he wanted to talk about it."

"Maybe it's time to bring it up again," she said.

"I will."

She peered over him now. "It's what they wanted," she said.

"I know, I know," Khalid said. He shook his head as if to dislodge an aberrant idea. "And I'll talk with him about it."

Their first Christmas season with his parents had been surprisingly enjoyable. Khalid loved the brightness of those days and had even taken to putting up colored lights on their own home as a gesture to the neighbors and the community, as if to suggest that they were not so different from anyone else after all. Rafia made homemade eggnog, a particular favorite of Khalid's, although Rafia herself did not much enjoy it, and they spent Christmas itself as a long leisurely day in front of the fireplace. He had wondered if his parents might criticize them for involving the family, however obliquely, in a Christian holiday but neither his mother nor his father said a word about it, drinking Rafia's eggnog and watching a marathon of *Yakeem Ka Safar* on one of the satellite television stations.

"It's been almost three months," his wife said now from the bed, apparently holding fast to the idea of converting the downstairs into proper living quarters. "I thought we'd have their apartment done by now and they'd be moved in downstairs."

From the bathroom, Khalid shook his head. "Do you remember how he was in Lahore? Do you remember the first time you met him?"

"Of course I do, jaan," she said. "Now you're just being ridiculous."

"But he was a lion," Khalid said to himself in the mirror. "A tiger."

"Yes and you came all the way to America to be away from all that."

"No," he said in response, shaking his head vehemently.

"To get out from under his shadow then," she said now.

"All right, fine, fine," he said. "But now he just seems so . . . unoccupied. He watches television of all things. Television!"

"We all watch television."

"That's not the point." A pause and then: "Wait."

She looked at up when he emerged from the bathroom. "Oh no, no," she said from the bed. "I know that look. You're having a terrible idea."

"I'm certainly not," Khalid said.

"Oh yes you are. Just tell me. What is it? I'm ready."

"It's not a terrible idea," he said now. "It's a brilliant idea. You'll see."

"That look only means terrible things."

"Shush," he said. "I've figured it out."

"I don't even want to hear it."

"Fine then," Khalid said. "I will say nothing more."

She waited, her fingertips light upon the book's blue cover.

"Right, so here's what we'll do," Khalid said, his own finger outstretched and stabbing at the air.

"Here it comes," she said.

"It's so simple," he said, pausing for effect. "I'll employ him at the factory. In an official capacity."

"Employ him to do . . . what exactly?"

"I'll make him vice president. Or chairman of the board."

"There is no board. What are you talking about?"

"Then we'll make a board."

"He's retired. The whole point of retirement is that he's not working anymore. He needs a hobby."

"Oh and now I suppose we're back to golfing. Where does this thing about golfing come from?"

"You've got a thing about golfing."

"You keep bringing it up."

"Did I bring it up? Or did you?"

"You did."

"I did not."

"Fine, then I did, but it's the same thing."

"You are an impossible man."

"You are a golfing fanatic."

"Come to bed."

"My father. Hitting those little balls. Walking around with a little hat on his head. Wearing those funny pants."

"Yes all of that," she said. "Especially the hat and the funny pants."

SARAH

The first two doctors had required a fifty-dollar copay but the doctor who had diagnosed Amy's cousin was out of network and so that appointment would be entirely out of her own pocket. She knew they could not afford such a bill, not ever but particularly not now, with all of Tom's missed work, her own inability to return to Kroger, the funeral expenses, the copays and prescriptions from the previous doctors; the calendar had become a great funnel sucking ever downward upon their bankbook. But of course this was only part of the reason she did not tell him. The other was more complicated and more painful for she had begun to sense that he did not much believe that her symptoms were anything more than a prolonged state of grief. He would never admit to such a thing but she was almost certain it was true. There had been a time, years before, when they might have been honest with each other and there might yet be a return to such a time but what they had entered, what they had lived within for many months, was a bubble filled only with hushed vapidity offering little more than the simplest of observations, as if, after all these years together, they could only talk about weather, light politics, television programs, and, in the most basic terms, the children.

How she longed for someone to point to her and say, definitively, that there was, indeed, something wrong, something physical that could be seen on an X-ray or in blood work or in a CAT scan, after which a treatment plan could be developed that was, would be, should be, more than swallowing painkillers in her dark bedroom for days on end. What a feeble strand to hold to and yet this was all she had. She would have drained all the bank accounts in the world if she could only find the right person, the right doctor, who could see inside her body in whatever way was required. She felt like she had become a person without skin, her nerves exposed to the slightest breath. Why then could no one find the reason for her pain? Every doctor palliated and the amber bottles of pills multiplied in the bathroom. What she wanted was her life back. What pill offered that? She would take it by the bottle.

And, God, when she saw this doctor, this third doctor, she had not even realized how strongly she had begun to hope, how she had managed, somehow, to engender the possibility that there might be an end to whatever illness had come to roost upon her enflamed skeleton, not until she felt that bright strand snap all at once, for the person who sat before her upon the chrome stool in his white shirt and slacks was not even a man but a boy who looked not much older than her own daughter, although of course he would have to be, would need to be to have finished medical school. Wouldn't he? Wouldn't he?

She did not realize she had begun to weep until she felt Amy's warm hand come into her own. Sarah grasped it in desperation.

The doctor sat before them on his little stool, pen in hand, blinking like a baby turtle. "I haven't even started yet," he said lamely.

"Yeah, um, can you just give us a minute," Amy said.

"Of course." And the doctor rose and stepped out of the room as if fleeing a burning building and they were alone.

An hour later, they were back in the car again, Amy at the wheel. The edges of the city fell away quickly and the wasteland of midwinter North Central Ohio unfolded around them: low hills and black trees scoured by the weather. The snows had come in mid-December and then a long pause in which the earth huddled into its hard-shelled carapace, a freezing that stretched across a holiday season that felt, to Sarah, as if it had never actually come, although she knew Tom and the children had done their best to cheer her, the radio playing Christmas music all day and Janey sitting next to her on the couch for as long as Sarah would remain there, hours and hours if her body could stand it. What a wreck she had become, watching vapid home-improvement shows while her own home drifted to ruin.

"We won't give up, honey," Amy said. "We'll figure this out. We will."

"I thought he'd know," Sarah said. "Your cousin and, you know, I mean . . ."

"We'll figure it out."

"It's not just in my head, you know. It's real."

"I know it is," Amy said. "Next time we'll find a doctor who's gone through puberty, OK? Doogie Howser can kiss my cha-cha."

Sarah could feel her friend watching from the driver's seat and so she tried to smile at this.

"Now the real question is, where are we gonna eat?"

"I should get home."

"Baloney you should get home," Amy said. "I've got you and I'm not letting you go."

"But the kids will come home and I won't be there."

"So what? Let 'em fend for themselves. Really we should've just stayed in Cleveland. Who knows what we're gonna get out here on the highway.

So what are you hungry for? I say we find somewhere comfortable and have a real meal together. It's been a while since we've done that."

"I don't know," she said. "That appointment was expensive."

"Oh no you don't," Amy said now. "I'm buying."

"You've already done a lot."

"And I'm doing more."

Outside, the road curved southward in a black loop. The landscape scoured. A kind of tundra interrupted by trees reduced to bracken.

"What's happening at work?" Sarah said.

"Oh man," Amy said. "The suits are in town."

"From corporate?"

"Yep. A bunch of fuckers, those guys."

"What are they doing?"

"The usual," Amy said. "Walking around with their little clipboards and making marks and then disappearing into Tim's office. And if you talk to them at all, it's like *Stepford Wives* shit. You know? Like they're all, 'Oh how's your day? How long have you been working for the Kroger family?' Makes me want to puke."

"Be careful," Sarah said.

"Oh, you know me. I don't fuck around with that stuff. Just smile and keep smiling. But boy howdy, I'd really just like to tell them all where to stick it, you know?"

"Who's running night shift?"

"No one," Amy said. "Paula's there but she doesn't do anything. I mean there's really no one on night. Everyone just has to fend for themselves. It's weird. It's like the lunatics running the asylum. Not that Tim does anything for us but at least there's someone you can go to. At night it's just kinda like good luck."

"They should just make Paula the night manager."

Amy swiveled in her seat to look at her, the landscape whipping by outside the window. "Paula?" she said. "Or how about your old friend Amy Simmons?"

"My old friend Amy Simmons would burn the store down."

"But I'd get paid more while I'm doing it," Amy said. "Seriously, though, Paula?"

"Who else?"

"I don't know but not her. She's just a busybody. Has to be up in everyone's business all the time."

"That's pretty much what a manager is supposed to do," Sarah said.

"I'd prefer a manager like Tim. Someone who hides in his office all day."

"Someone you can boss around without actually having to be the boss."

"Bingo!" Amy said. "Here." She handed Sarah her phone. "Find us somewhere to eat."

She held the thing in her hand, the screen blank now, black, shining only with the dim outline of her own haggard reflection. How exhausted she was and yet, sitting there in the passenger seat of Amy's car, she knew she did not want to return to that dim stale bedroom in the home she shared with her husband and children. When she really thought about it, she did not, in fact, want to return home at all.

TOM BAILEY

At ten the break bell rang and he set down his welding and stood and stretched his back. The cart at the end of the row was almost full and in confirmation he heard Joey call out, "Ninety-nine."

"Goddamn," Sam said. "No wonder I'm tired. Our foreman is a slave driver."

"That's the truth," Tom said. "Someone should fire that guy."

From behind him came a musically accented voice: "Good morning." The man who stood there could only have been Marwat's father. In appearance he was, perhaps unsurprisingly, an older version of his son, this man's hair salt-and-pepper gray rather than black but otherwise nearly identical. The fleshiness of his face, his lips, was the same. Even now he stared back at them with his son's wide, frankly curious eyes.

"Morning, Mr. Marwat," Tom said. Then he said his name and extended his hand. The man took it and they shook. He wore a suit coat and slacks but his white shirt was unbuttoned at the throat, exposing a triangle of brown skin.

"You are shop foreman," the old man said, his accent thick and his words, his English words, slow and careful.

Tom told him that he was.

"Why does everyone stop work?"

"Ah right," Tom said. "It's break time. Ten o'clock and then lunch at noon for an hour and then another break at three in the afternoon."

"Very many breaks," Mr. Marwat said.

"No breaks in Pakistan?" Tom asked.

"Not so many," Mr. Marwat said.

"Gotta have a break to smoke our cigarettes," Tom said now.

"You go outside?" Mr. Marwat said.

"Can't smoke inside on account of the equipment," Tom said. "Flammable oil. Things like that."

"What about the cold?"

"If it's cold we just smoke faster," Tom said. He smiled to indicate that this was meant as a kind of joke and after a moment Mr. Marwat smiled back, although it was not clear to Tom if he understood it as such.

"Making buddy-buddy with the senior raghead?" Sam said to him at bit later at the coffeepot, his voice half hushed.

"Christ, Sam, shut the fuck up."

Sam laughed.

Rachel Denker was in the queue off to the side of them. Her work shirt was pulled tight and tucked into the front of her jeans. "My eyes are up here, Tom Bailey," she shouted to him, smiling.

His coworkers around him all laughed and Tom could feel himself blush with mortified embarrassment. When he glanced back at her, she was still smiling and when he made eye contact she winked.

"Well, gentlemen," Hardiman's voice came from behind them. "Ready to have your asses handed to you again on Tuesday night?"

They both looked. There stood Hardiman, piggy eyed, his mouth turned in a wry grin.

"Like hell we are," Sam said.

"You willing to put money on that?"

"Sure I am," Sam said.

And then Hardiman: "Yeah? Twenty says I take you in points."

"At the end of the night?"

Hardiman nodded.

"You're on," Sam said.

Hardiman clapped his hands together. "You might as well just give me the money right now, Simmons."

"Fat chance."

Hardiman laughed as he turned toward the long tables they used for lunch.

"He's got you beat by at least fifty points even with your handicap," Tom said once Hardiman was out of earshot. "You know that, right?"

"It's the principle of it," Sam said.

"What principle is that?"

"Calling me out at work like that."

"That's because he knows you'll empty your wallet, you dumbfuck."

"What else am I supposed to do?"

"Smarter man would walk away."

"Shit," Sam said, "I don't walk away from nothin'. That's not how I was raised."

"Don't matter how you were raised anymore, does it?"

"Does to me," Sam said.

"Well, then I guess you're gonna owe John Hardiman twenty dollars on Tuesday night."

"Maybe so," Sam said. "But I got my pride."

"You do," Tom said. "You do have that."

They had each poured a Styrofoam cup of coffee while they spoke and Tom sweetened his with fake sugar and powdered cream and now they exited the dismal breakroom, their talk continuing in low tones as they reached the outside door and Tom pulled it open.

Rachel Denker stood on the other side, hair tousled, breath steaming the air.

"Whoops," Tom said. He stepped back, bumping into Sam who stood just behind him, and she entered the relative warmth of the assembly plant, the door swinging closed again and with it the outside blast of frozen air clipping away. "Morning," he said.

"Morning, Tom."

"Gettin' cold."

"Too cold for me." She stood there looking at him. "See you Tuesday night?"

"Hope so," he said. "All depends on Sarah."

She pouted. "She's still not feeling well?"

"She has good days," he said. "And less good days."

"Well, I hope you make it. If you do, I'm gonna be watching you."

"Why's that?"

"Gotta learn your secrets."

"You should be watching Hardiman if you want to learn secrets. I haven't taken the league trophy since he joined."

"John Hardiman doesn't have any secrets I'm interested in."

"Well, at least he has some. I don't have any."

"Everyone has secrets."

"Not me."

"Especially you," she said. "Tell him, Sam."

Sam spluttered out a few disconnected syllables.

"See," she said, "Sam knows what I'm talking about." Then she turned away from them and her body was all sway and motion and curve.

"Goddamn," Sam said after she was gone and they were crunching across the snowed-over gravel outside.

Tom did not respond but his thoughts were much the same. Goddamn. Above them, the sky was gray, the clouds heavy with new snow to add to the old.

"I wish you'd tap that so you could tell your buddy all about it," Sam said, and when Tom did not respond: "Sarah's still sick?"

"Pretty much. Doctors can't figure out what's wrong, though, so there's that."

"Doctors are fucking idiots," Sam said. "They just want to take your money and do whatever big pharma says they should do."

Tom shrugged. "It's what we have," he said.

"I guess she's not coming back to league any time soon."

"Well, Christ, Sam. Yeah I guess that's probably the last fucking thing she's thinking about right now."

"I'm just saying we've been holding a space open. Doesn't do anyone any good if no one's playing in it."

"Christ almighty. Just shut the fuck up."

Mary Lou was behind them and passed as they fumbled in their pockets for their cigarettes, Tom mumbling a good morning and Mary Lou replying in kind. "I've got something for you," she said.

"What's that?"

"Hang on." She moved to the car and opened the door and returned with a small stack of clothes: a jacket, a hat, some gloves.

"What's this?" Tom said.

"They're Charlie's."

"Charlie's?"

"He didn't tell you about my mom? He found my mom wandering around in the dark last week."

"Oh jeez," Tom said. "She all right?"

"She's fine. Well, she's not fine but she's fine from that night. Charlie saved her life."

"No shit?"

"Yeah, if he hadn't been there, she would've froze to death. Anyway, these are his things. He put them all on her while they waited for me to get there."

"Wow, he didn't say a word."

"Well, that's teenagers, I guess."

"I guess so."

Sam had taken his seat on the bench, adjusted the red hat which had become, since the election, part of his daily uniform.

"So," Tom said now, "you said she was fine but not fine or something like that?"

"Oh yeah, well, she's got that Alzheimer's."

"Oh shit, Mary Lou," Tom said. "I'm sorry to hear that. That's awful."

"Yeah, so, it's been pretty hard. She keeps trying to burn down the kitchen. Wanders outside. That kind of thing. I've got an appointment with that retirement home out on Keene. See what it's all gonna cost. You know."

"You know what?" Tom's finger wagged in the air, pointing to Mary Lou and then nodding to Sam and then to Mary Lou again. "You do any bowling?"

"Bowling?" Mary Lou said. "Oh jeez, no. Not me."

"Ever want to?"

"I don't know. I'm not really one for sports."

"Thing is," Tom said now, "we've got an opening on the league team. We could use someone. I mean, it doesn't have to be right now. When that stuff with your mom is settled maybe."

"I'm sure I'd just drag your score down."

"Not really," Tom said. "It works on a handicap. So you're really just trying to beat your previous score."

She blushed now, her face, in that moment, achieving something girlish, something young, and Tom could almost see the child she had once been, the children they all had been before life had become so complicated. "I don't even know what a handicap is," she said to him. She glanced over at Sam briefly, then back to Tom again.

"Well," Tom said now, "think about it, OK."

"She's telling you she doesn't want to," Sam said.

"Just think about," Tom said, ignoring Sam. "It's really more a way to hang out with some friends on a weeknight. Forget about things for an hour or two. Have a beer and throw some balls around."

She blushed again. "I'll give it some thought, I guess," she said.

"Good," Tom said now. "Good good."

For a long moment, no one spoke, and then Mary Lou said, "I've gotta go back in. Lots to do."

"For raghead senior or raghead junior?" Sam said.

"Jesus, Sam," Tom said. "Will you cut that shit out?"

"I'm just making a goddamn joke," Sam said.

"It's only a joke if it's funny," Tom said. He turned to Mary Lou. The expression on her face was one of horror. "Sorry, Mary Lou," he said. "Sam's an idiot. As well you know."

Mary Lou's eyes flitted between his face and Sam's. "Well then," she said finally, nodding once more and then turning toward the factory door again.

"Jesus, Sam," Tom said. "You can't be saying that shit."

"When did you become such a goddamn snowflake?"

As if to make Sam's point, Anthony Shaw appeared from just beyond the steel wall of the factory, his own cigarette flicking through the air in a brief arc.

"Speak of the devil," Sam said.

"Don't be an asshole."

"Whatever," Sam said.

From what seemed like a great distance came the sound of the whistle indicating break time was over. Tom had never been so glad to hear that lonesome mechanical howl.

CHARLIE

Kent silent all day, sullen, his eyes dark and downcast and even when Charlie or one of the others—Beaver or Josh or Dyl-Dog—cracked a joke or found a funny video on their phone, even when they all laughed together, Kent hardly looked up. When he pulled his sweater up and over his head and his long-sleeve T-shirt ran up with it, Charlie could see the bruise running across his stomach, black and purple and swollen and he hoped that no one else had seen it but then Dyl barked at him from across the table:

"What the heck, K-mart? What's with the hematoma?"

Kent dropped his arms to cover himself, worked his way out of his sweater so that it lay in front of him in his lap. "Yeah, bruised myself up good," he said simply.

"Doing what? Rodeo?"

"Skating."

"Jeez, let me see," Dyl said.

"Naw," Kent said.

And now it was Beaver: "Come on, let's see."

He shook his head again. "Just me being stupid on my board," he said. And then announced that he needed to go to the bathroom—"Gotta shit," is what he said—and then disappeared. Charlie and the others sat there watching him go. "That was weird," Tommy said.

"He's got some stuff going on," Charlie told them.

"What kind of stuff?"

"Stuff at home."

"What kind of stuff at home?"

"I don't know. Private stuff, I guess."

Dylan shrugged, scratched absently at a cluster of pimples on his forehead. "You get my text earlier?"

Charlie nodded.

"You coming?"

"I don't know. I gotta check something first."

"K," Dyl said. "Make sure Kent knows. He didn't answer either."

"I don't think he has his phone," Charlie said.

"We've probably got until five thirty until my folks get home. This dildo's bringing the new *Call of Duty*." He tossed a french fry at Beaver directly across from him at the table.

"Mr. Dildo, if you please," Beaver said importantly.

"Mr. Beaver Dildo. Got it," Dyl said.

He thought he would catch Kent sometime between classes and when he did not he wondered if his friend had skipped and once again texted him and once again received no response. But then after school, in the crowd of students and cars and buses and parents, he saw, through that tumult, Kent's back as his friend cut through the crowd of milling students in the direction of his battered, unkempt home on the edge of town.

Dyl-Dog was there again, sock hat pulled low over his hair. "Hey, so you guys coming over?" he said.

"Yeah yeah, I'll meet you there," Charlie said absently.

"Righto," came the reply.

There was, even at this distance, a clear sense of both direction and purpose in Kent's pace and so, when Charlie set off in pursuit, he did so at a jog which, after a momentary pause to let a car pass—Rashid and his older sister and their mother—accelerated into a run when it became clear he would not catch up with Kent any other way. By the time he reached him, Charlie was wholly out of breath, heaving and panting so that Kent had to stop and wait for him to recover, cigarette burning in his fingers. "What's up?" Kent said simply.

When he could, Charlie said, "Nothing."

"You ran all this way for nothing?"

He nodded. "You headed home?"

And now Kent's turn to nod.

"Bunch of guys are headed to Dyl's for *Call of Duty*."

"New one?"

"I guess," Charlie said.

They had not taken another step and Kent puffed once more on his cigarette. "Can't," he said. "I gotta get home."

"OK," Charlie said. "Bum a smoke?"

"This is my last one," Kent said.

"Shoot," Charlie said.

He had experienced this version of his friend before, this sullen, quiet version, but he was not sure he had seen Kent look so colorless, so afraid, so bereft, the eyes that stared back at him hollow and exhausted.

"What?" Kent said now.

"Nothing."

"Right," Kent said. "I gotta get." Then he turned and stalked away. Charlie ran to catch up. Around them, various cars passed: parents picking up their kids from school and teen drivers returning home of their own accord. Someone waved out the window as they passed but Charlie could not see who it was.

"So what's up with the bruise?" Charlie said now.

"Hit the edge of the ramp." Kent clapped his hands together to emphasize the contact.

"At the park?"

"Yeah."

"Is the park even—I mean, like, isn't it all snowed over still?"

"Yeah, well, you know, I cleared a path and stuff."

"How?"

"Just did."

"You cleared a path?"

"Yeah I cleared a path," Kent said, an edge in his voice now. "What the fuck?"

"Sorry," Charlie said, looking away now, out across the beaten and winter-scoured houses around them. And then, because he was already talking, because he could not stop himself, he said, "It's just that, you know, I didn't think there was anywhere to skate out there."

They had crossed one street and were moving up the broken, ice-coated sidewalk under spindly, spiderlike branches that reached endlessly into a sky the color of gunmetal. The houses around them were small boxes separated from the street by lawns of snow and ice and dead grass, their porches hanging with rows of crystalline icicles that sometimes reflected the low light of the cold winter sun. One of their classmates stared back at them from a plastic yard sign: HOME OF PHILLIP FILSON. PROUD TO BE AN OWL, the "o" an orange basketball.

The street upon which Kent lived dead-ended into a patch of frozen grass. After heavy snows, the city's plow would create a great hill of snow there. Years before, when they had all been younger, he and Kent would spend days and days sliding around on that hill, building forts and tunnels until the whole thing was a half-collapsed warren. Then another storm and a fresh load of snow and they would start anew. Those days seemed another era now. Impossible that anything like that had ever happened at all.

The sound of some metal band from a tinny speaker and then a tight, drawling voice from the collapsing porch: "My wayward."

Kent's father sat in a ragged padded chair, a beer in one hand, several empty cans lined along the broken porch rail. He looked exactly as Charlie remembered him: a gaunt figure in a thick Carhartt coat the color of freshly turned earth, eyes burning with some inner heat, tattered goatlike beard upon his chin. When he smiled it was to reveal a sweep of pale teeth gapped by absence.

"Who's your friend?" Kent's father said from the porch.

"Charlie," Kent said. "He's been over before."

"Hell, I remember you," Kent's father said.

"Hello, Mr. Westin," Charlie said.

"Tell your friend he can come up if he wants," Kent's father said. "We're just gonna watch some TV."

"I've gotta go home," Charlie said. "Homework."

"Suit yourself," Kent's father said now. He stood from the chair, guzzled the end of his beer, and then lifted a lit cigarette from somewhere out of Charlie's sight. Behind him blazed the starry cross of a Confederate flag. Charlie had seen it hanging in the garage—"The rebel flag," Kent had called it—but now its shape blocked the front window like a drawn curtain. Kent's father nodded to it now. "What do you think, buddy?"

"Good," Kent said simply, his feet on the rotting stairs that led up to the porch.

"Hell yeah," his father said.

Charlie had just turned away but the hollow-cheeked, angular visage of Kent's father seemed to swing in front of him, overlaying the snowed-over street, the bleak, leafless trees. Charlie turned back to the house from the edge of the sidewalk.

"Hey . . . uh . . . we were gonna go over to our friend's house and play some videogames." The words had come in a rush. He saw Kent's hands curl into pale, sharp fists.

Kent's father turned back from the door and peered out into the gloaming. "We who?" he said.

"What?"

"You said we. Who's we?"

"Oh, uh, you know, me and Kent if he wants to go. Or if he can, I guess."

Kent's father stood in silence for a moment, his bead-like eyes shooting across the landscape without expression. And then, abruptly, his entire face transformed into a weird grimace, his voice rising in a bizarre high-pitched whine: "Oh uh can Kent come out and uh play? Uh we want to go uh jack each other off."

Charlie stood paralyzed.

Kent's father's face had returned to normal immediately after the outburst: gray and weathered and strangely lifeless once more. "You wanna go play with your friends?" the man said. "Go ahead."

"No, it's cool," Kent said, his voice trembling.

"No fucking go on. I don't fucking want you here anyway."

"Come on," Charlie said now. His chest felt light and cold and sharp all at once.

"No, it's cool," Kent said. "I'll . . . I'll hang out here."

His father stood for a moment, utterly still, and then guffawed as if the whole strange scene had been nothing more than an inscrutable joke. He slapped Kent's shoulder hard enough that the boy staggered. "Goddamn, boy," he said, "you look like you're about to shit your pants. And you," he pointed to Charlie, "I'm pretty damn sure you did shit your pants." Another peal of laughter that felt, to Charlie, as if purposefully bad acting. Haw haw haw. And then to Kent again, "Come on now. Your momma's making some grilled cheese."

"OK," Kent said, a wan, tentative smile upon his face.

He swung the boy through the door and then paused upon the threshold to look back at Charlie, the blazing gaze of those hot, bead-like eyes searing through the bitter cold of that failing day. "Just jerking your chain, little man," he said now, his mouth stretching to a leering grin. "You want some grilled cheese? Come on up."

"No . . . um . . . thanks though," Charlie said, mumbled.

"Suit yourself." He continued to stand there, holding the screen open with one hand.

It seemed a long while before Charlie was out from under the shadows of the leafless elms and into the greater light of the street beyond. He glanced back at the house, expecting Mr. Westin to be there, for he had not heard the screen clack shut, but the porch was empty, the house seeming, in that moment, the same as any other: worn and haggard and secreting within mysteries that no one else would ever know.

MARY LOU

"I know it seems like a lot," the woman told her, "but you're paying for the quality of the care."

"I understand," Mary Lou said.

"I know how you feel," the woman said. There was a box of Kleenex on the desk. The woman had leaned forward several times during their conversation to nudge the box in Mary Lou's direction but Mary Lou was not crying.

"Is there paperwork to be filled out?"

"Not as much as you might think," the woman said. She rummaged under the desk. A thick sheaf of papers in a white folder. On the cover read the name of the facility and the tagline We Care About What You Care About. Mary Lou sat reading those seven words for a long while, the phrase swimming into all possible configurations but still failing to make any logical sense.

She signed and signed and signed and in the end was told that her mother could move in the following week. "We can have someone talk to your mother about what we have to offer here," the woman said. "Sometimes families like it when someone else helps break the news."

"That's all right," Mary Lou said. "I'll do it myself." But when she returned to the lounge she wished desperately that she had agreed to the woman's offer, so much so that she nearly turned to flee back to her desk to tell her yes yes please have someone talk to my mother please for I am a coward and cannot do it on my own.

Her mother sat in a wingback armchair, alone in a room filled with the quiet chatter of a dozen ancient men and women. In one corner sat a television, its volume muted so that the figures there moved and gesticulated without sound, and it was at that glowing box that her mother stared.

"You ready to go, Mom?" Mary Lou asked, approaching the chair.

"I don't even know what we're doing here," her mother said.

"This is where your new apartment is," Mary Lou said. And then, because that was not really the truth of it, she said: "This is where you'll be living for a while."

"But I'm living with you."

"We've already talked about this."

"No we haven't," her mother said. "If we'd talked about it, I'd remember. You're not making any sense." Her mother had not made any movement to leave, eyes wide and wet, hair rising thinly like some heap of twisted spidersilk.

"Listen, Mom," Mary Lou said now. She looked about her for a chair but there were only similar wingbacks set at some distance. "You need more help than I can give you at my place."

"I don't need help."

"You do, though." Around her, Mary Lou could sense that the others in the room were listening although she could not be sure and did not know if she even cared. She had chosen this moment to talk to her mother because the alternative would be to discuss things at home. And of course they had already had this discussion, the fact of which only served to underscore why they were here at all. "Do you remember wandering outside?"

"What do you mean wandering?" her mother said. "I don't wander."

"OK, OK," Mary Lou said. "So maybe you thought you were going somewhere then. Do you remember going outside, Mom? To maybe check the mailbox or something like that."

"When?"

"Last week."

She scoffed now, a dry, hard sound. "You're asking me if I remembered going outside at some point last week? Don't be stupid, Mary Lou."

"Well, Mom," Mary Lou said, "you did."

"So what?"

"You might have frozen to death out there. That's what. Tom Bailey's son found you on the sidewalk in your robe and slippers. It was twenty-five degrees. If he hadn't found you and called me I don't know what would've happened." But of course she did know what would have happened: her mother's heart would have stopped beating and she would have been found, as people sometimes were in the great swath of geography that was the Midwestern winter, cold and dead, their skin, her mother's skin, pale blue and dusted with bright white frost. "You scared me," she said.

The doctor had told Mary Lou that her mother's disease was progressing more quickly than he had anticipated and she might be considered to be at the start of Stage 6. He handed her a sheet of paper and told her she should read it in case she had any questions to ask him. "There's only one more stage," she said. Because there are moments in all our lives in which there are no questions.

"That's right," the doctor said.

"How much longer then?"

"There's really no way to tell. Everyone goes through the stages at a different rate." This doctor was a thin man of about her own age. She had felt a measure of pride when she had been made office manager at the factory but now she wondered if she had settled for what had presented itself rather than pursuing something she actually might have wanted. She no longer even knew what such a want, such a goal or desire, could look like. Then she thought of her mother and for a moment understood that the man she faced, the doctor, had been raised by someone else, someone who might have told him that he could do whatever he wanted, that he could follow his dreams out into the world and return—or not return—better than he had been before.

She had found the retirement home in the phone book and was told that they had an opening but that she would need to get her paperwork in quickly if she were to secure the spot. Her mother had a meager amount in the bank but Mary Lou spent very little from month to month and between the two of them there was enough for the room and care, at least for now. It was not an insubstantial sum and would drain Mary Lou's bank account to zero if it went on for longer than a few years but for now it was possible and what other option did she have but to put her mother in a situation where there was someone to watch over her, to make sure she was healthy and took her pills and did not wander outside into the snow.

Now her mother returned to the distant silent television. Mary Lou wondered if she had forgotten she was there, had forgotten everything but that glowing box. "Mom?" she said tentatively.

"What?"

"Are you hungry? Maybe we should go out to dinner tonight. You know. To celebrate."

"To celebrate what?"

"Your new apartment," Mary Lou said.

For a moment there was no response and Mary Lou wondered if her mother had forgotten her again. At what point did Stage 6 turn into Stage 7? But then her mother said, "Where is my new apartment?"

"It's here in this building."

"Is Theo here?"

"No, Mom. Dad's not here."

"Where is he?"

"He's been gone for a while."

"Oh, that's right," she said. "But you're here."

In other circumstances, her mother's tone might have been accusatory or angry or vengeful—certainly she had displayed all these qualities over the recent months—but this time the statement was gentle, as if a kind of acknowledgment. A strange shivering wave ran through her.

"Do you want to go out to dinner tonight?"

"Where would we go?"

"We could go back to that pizza place. You liked that pizza place."

"That's fine," she said. And then a great, wild sob escaped her. "You're trying to get rid of me. That's what this is. You're trying to get rid of me."

Mary Lou could not easily kneel but she managed now, her knees and hips aching from the effort. "Oh Mom," she said, taking the old woman's papery hand in her own and stroking it softly, "I'm trying to take care of you, but I can't do that all day."

"I don't need anyone to look after me all day," she said. "I just need a little help now and then."

"And here there'll be someone to help you whenever you want. And won't that be nice?"

"No," her mother said. "It won't. All I want is to sit and watch my shows. That's all."

"And you can do that here all day long."

"What about my chair?"

"Well, it's my chair but I can have it brought over."

"I don't like any of this, Mary Lou. I don't. And I won't agree to it."

"Oh Mom," Mary Lou said. "It's already done."

Her mother's face swung about to look at her now and in her eyes, not wet with tears but dry, Mary Lou saw only desolation and fear.

"We're going to dinner," Mary Lou said.

"Where are we going?"

"I thought we could go that pizza place you liked."

And her mother finally allowed herself to be helped to her feet.

"Is Theo coming?" her mother said.

"Dad's not here, Mom. He's been gone for a few years now."

"Gone where?"

In the glass doors, they could both see their reflections—two women, together and yet alone—beyond which, beyond the glass, lay twinkling starlit pools of darkness, black fields bleeding endlessly into night.

TOM BAILEY

Tuesdays had always been bowling night although he had not been to the lanes since September, when baby James's heart defect had begun to spin them all out of control. He had missed those nights, that moment of escape from the regularity of his days, although of course even the bowling had been regular, an early dinner and then the two of them, he and Sarah, spending a few hours together away from home. A beer or two as they bowled. The crash of pins. The occasional whoop or holler as someone nailed a strike farther down the lanes.

He had tried to talk her into coming to the Bowl-O-Rama with him, although he knew, even as he made the attempt, that she would not. "You could just sit," Tom told her. "Have a beer. I'm sure the girls would be happy to see you. Everybody would. You don't have to bowl."

"I just can't," she said. "Tell them all I said hi, OK?"

That she had managed to get back and forth to Cleveland to the doctor's appointment—an appointment he had not known about and which had cost them nearly two hundred dollars—and had spent the afternoon with Amy—a fact he had learned not from Sarah but from Sam—was a subject they did not discuss, although he sometimes could feel it rising in him like a kind of heat. He had not touched her with any sense of intimacy for too many months to count, his fingers upon her skin eliciting a shiver not of pleasure but of discomfort. He knew that his inability to truly understand what she was going through, how she felt, was a failure on his part but knowing this did little to assuage his frustration and his loneliness. Suddenly his wife had become a ghost in his house, as if she had gone with the baby, not to heaven but to some murky underworld, and there was nothing he could do to bring her back to the world of the living.

They did not talk about it again but on Tuesday night after work he showered and shaved and dressed in a button shirt and his jeans and retrieved his ball from the floor of the closet. Sarah had moved from their bedroom to the living room. As he entered, all three—Sarah and Janey and Charlie too—looked at him, wide-eyed, as if surprised to find him at home at all.

"So I'm headed out," he said.

For a moment there was no response from any of them. Then Janey said simply: "You're bowling?"

"It's Tuesday."

"Is it?" Sarah asked. Her face was illuminated by the shifting light of the television, an afghan pulled up around her. You didn't tell me this was superglue! the voice on the television shouted, followed by a wave of laughter from the studio audience.

"You can come with, you know," he said.

"I'm fine here," Sarah said. She had half turned to the television now, where two people were pulling at a third, a thin, dark-haired man who had been apparently glued to a table.

"You guys look pretty cozy," he said, trying to lighten things.

"We're good, Dad," Janey said.

"Hey, maybe we can all go to the lanes on Saturday, if the weather's not too bad," Tom said.

"Sure," Janey said, a note of dismissal in her voice.

"All right then." He stood for a moment by the door. None of the three bodies on the couch moved. "Take care of your mom, you two," he said.

Charlie's hand came up now. Thumbs-up.

He thought Sarah might turn her head once to look at him, to say something when he opened the door, but she did not, and he closed it upon that scene: the three people he cared for most of all, all seated with their backs to him in that warm, glowing room.

He tried not to watch Rachel Denker as she bowled, but in not watching her he watched her always, his body adrift from too many beers with Sam and the others, too many beers and too many chicken wings, the overall effect of which was a leaden buoyancy, as if he were both floating and sinking to the bottom all at once.

Her jeans so tight they were like a second skin. Hair pulled back.

He bowled well below his average, missing all the spares and ending at 148, still feeling his long fallow days away from the lanes, that and the drifting of his concentration, an effect, he knew, of the five MGDs he had swilled during the course of the evening. "Slow down there, champ," John Hardiman said to him midway through their first round.

"What for?" he said.

"Suit yourself." Hardiman stepped up to the line, drew the ball back and bowled a perfect strike, his sixth in a row, the ball curving in a wide arc that nearly tipped into the gutter, the pins exploding everywhere in their dark alcove.

"Shit," Tom said.

"We'll get 'em," Sam said.

"Yeah, we'll catch 'em yet," Betty Lucero said. Next to her on the bench, the fourth of their team, Cheryl Briggs, clapped and emitted a short, brief, "Yay," into the general cacophony of the lanes.

But John Hardiman's strikes continued and when he entered his eighth frame, they all stopped playing and stood on the raised carpet and watched him. Even the Bowl-O-Rama's owner came out from behind the counter and stood with them as Hardiman threw another perfect ball in a sharp curve down the lane, the pins exploding into his eighth strike in a row.

Tom stood by, watching with the rest of them, his hands loose at his sides. In his ever-increasing drunkenness, the lanes seemed to waver and roll as if upon some fluorescent-lit ocean through which John Hardiman moved like a sharp-bladed skiff, the ball coming off his hand and curving over those waves and cracking into the pins once more. Across from him stood Rachel Denker, smiling, her hands rising in a flurry of applause as Hardiman finished another throw and the people around him clapped and cheered. He too clapped. Sam pounded him on the shoulder in a brief explosion of excitement.

"Holy shit," Sam said. "Holy shit, two more frames. Holy shit."

Tom looked over to his sweating, smiling face.

"Hey, if I gotta lose, why not lose to a perfect game," Sam said.

Tom laughed briefly, not at the words but at the whole situation in which he found himself, drunk with all his coworkers watching a guy none of them liked bowl strike after strike, all of them following the ball down the lane, its arc, that explosion of pins. That repeated explosion of pins.

He was slow in removing his shoes, in toweling off his swirled blue ball and returning it to the leather bag, slow and purposeful, thinking that he might get another beer but also thinking that doing so would be a terrible mistake, that the whole of the night had already, somehow, been a terrible mistake. And yet he had watched John Hardiman bowl a perfect game, which meant that the secret misery he felt was likely his alone.

And then there she was.

"Tom Bailey," she said to him, coming across the lanes to where he sat by his now empty beer bottle.

"Rachel Denker," he said.

"How'd your team do?"

"Not too good."

"Distracted by John?"

"Ha," he said. He could not help but smile. "Just moving a little slow tonight."

"How many beers did you drink?"

"I don't know. Some."

"You think you're OK to drive?"

"Do I think what? Of course I'm OK to drive."

"Maybe I should drive you home?"

"No, I'm good," he said.

In the parking lot: patches of black ice, a situation he registered at the same moment he found himself struggling to keep his balance, his feet slipping in all directions at once. "Christ almighty," he said. He stepped more carefully now, coming to the truck and unlocking it and sliding inside, the ball bag on the seat next to him, and then sitting there in the car for a moment while the engine warmed, the heater vents trickling frozen air into the cold interior.

He saw her when he had the pickup turned toward the exit and she waved him toward her and he followed that motion, curving in toward the lit glass doors and pulling to a stop and cranking the window down.

"So I was thinking I might go get something to eat," she said. "You feel like coming along?"

He looked out the front of the windshield and then the side. The parking lot empty but for himself and Rachel Denker. "I don't know," he said.

"Just friends having a bite after league."

"I guess that might be OK."

"Can I drive your truck?"

"What?"

"I wanna try it out," she said. "I'm in the market."

"Shit," he said. "All right."

He opened the driver's door and stepped out and immediately went down on the ice, his legs shooting forward so he fell, ass first, onto the frozen asphalt. "Fucking hell," he said.

Her hands were on his shoulders, trying to help him up although her own footing was not much better than his own, her small frame inadequate to support his weight and size. "Oh jeez," she said. "You all right?"

"Yeah," he mumbled, sliding his feet under himself and using the open door to pull himself up, aware of her hands on him, their pressure through his jacket.

When he stood at last, her arms were around him in a kind of embrace. "You steady?" she said. Her eyes were wide and beautiful, staring up into his.

"Yeah, I think so."

She released him then and he stood confused, momentarily forgetting what was happening, why she was climbing into the driver's side, then remembering and leaning on the truck's grille as he circumnavigated its long expanse and at last clambered into the passenger seat and swung the door closed.

"I've never sat on this side," he said. A long crack in the windshield glass bifurcating the icy parking lot.

"First time for everything."

"I guess so. Where are we going?"

"Slocum's is probably the only place open."

She shifted into gear and the pickup began to roll forward over the frozen asphalt and then swung out into the road. He closed his eyes for a moment and then opened them again.

"Don't pass out on me, Tom Bailey," she said.

"I'm not. I'm all right. I'm fine."

"We'll get some food in you and then we'll get you home."

"My wife's home," he said.

"Well, good, then she can take care of you."

"I don't think she's going to take care of me much," he said and the loneliness that gripped his heart in that moment nearly made him cry out in agony and in shame.

"I'm sure you'll be fine," Rachel said.

But he was much less sure.

The road before them was a solid sheet of ice reflecting the lights of the homes that lined that black surface on either side, the car moving forward in a straight line until the ice fell back to salted asphalt again.

The meal did indeed flatten the world some, the low waves of alcohol rolling from some distance. He could feel their approach.

"Say that again?" A butterfly shrimp clutched in his fingers.

"I was asking what the doctors say."

He scoffed. "They don't say anything except here's the bill."

"That's so hard."

He shrugged. "Sometimes I wish it was something like cancer. I know that sounds terrible."

"What do you mean?"

"If it was cancer you'd be able to see it on an MRI or something. But with this, you can't see anything."

"Just because you can't see it doesn't mean it's not there."

"I know," he said. "It'd just be a little easier if it was, I don't know, clear or something."

"I guess that puts a lot of the day-to-day stuff back on you then."

"I guess so."

"That's why it's for better or for worse."

"Sure."

"She'd do the same for you."

"She'd do a better job than I'm doing," he said, and as he said it he knew it was true. Sarah would not even be in the situation he was currently in, trying to sober up after a drinking binge at the bowling alley with the coworker he had a secret crush on. He knew then that he was behaving like a teenager and the heat that flooded through him all at once was shame. He looked up at Rachel Denker, seated across from him in the booth, and she returned his gaze.

"What?" she said.

"You know I used to be pretty good," he said. "Not like perfect-game good but pretty close sometimes. I don't know what happened. I'm actually getting worse, not better."

"You've got a lot going on, Tom," she said. "No one expects you to bowl a perfect game."

"I do," he said. "Once in a while, anyway."

"Have you ever?"

"No," he said, chuckling slightly despite his darkening mood. He almost said, Has anyone? but of course such a response no longer made any sense at all.

"You're beating yourself up for something you haven't ever done," she said.

"That's about the size of it."

"Does that make any sense?"

He took the final butterfly shrimp into his mouth and bit down. The woman across from him had worked at the factory for two years and lived in the next town to the west. He knew she had a daughter but he could not now recall her name.

"Rachel Denker," he said.

"Tom Bailey."

"I don't know the first thing about you."

"What do you want to know?"

"I don't even know how to answer that," he said.

She smiled at him then, her face a warm beaming light across the table. "Things'll get better, Tom," she said. "You'll see. Just hang in there."

"Oh, I'm hanging," he said.

He paid the bill and they stepped into the night once more. It had begun to snow. Tom was driving now, leaning toward the windshield and piloting the truck down the center of the street, the snow an onrushing infinite spiral.

When they reached the bowling alley once more, she started her car and then returned to the relative warmth of his own. They watched as a yellow snowplow moved slowly down the street, its plume a bleak shadow, the street behind a hazy black stripe.

"It was nice hanging out," she said.

And when she turned toward him, he was already so close that his lips were almost touching hers. When he kissed her she did not move at first. He could smell her hair: a tropical scent like coconuts. He reached for her and it was then that she jerked away. "Whoa, hang on," she said.

He pulled her toward him once more and his stomach was a wild bird thrashing through cold corn. His tongue against her teeth.

"Tom, stop."

"Why?"

From some distance: a hard, sharpness against his chest and then, as she pulled free of him, the slap of her palm across his face. Her voice was a distant muffled echo. "Stop," she said again.

He sat back into his own bewilderment, one hand upon the steering wheel, the other upon his numb, warm cheek. "Ah God," he mumbled. "I'm sorry."

"Go home," she said. "Fuck."

"Wait," he said. But already she was gone. A cloud of cold air hovered in the cab.

Snow everywhere and her own car smoking into the blizzard. He rolled the window down to call to her but she had already disappeared inside and then her car lurched forward through the falling snow and was gone.

In the dim dome-lit interior of the cab his face looked yellow and weary. What remained was most of an entire night spread upon the hills and plains, the stubbled fields, and under which slumbered people lost in dreams they would not remember upon waking. And Tom Bailey: awake and alone in the parking lot of the bowling alley. What a confusion that each decision leads to the next, that our lives become our lives and no other. And what disappointment to be reminded, again and again, how many of those decisions are wrong.

ANTHONY SHAW

A text soon after he had emerged from the shower and had pulled on his jeans, his phone dinging and his reaction surprising even to himself, wondering immediately if it might be Jane again. There had been that first encounter at the coffeeshop and then, a few days later, a second, when they had talked for nearly two hours and had exchanged numbers although even in that moment he wondered if he should be giving his phone number to a young white girl, seventeen. Surely to do so was a mistake. And yet he had and now felt a twinge of excitement upon seeing her name on the phone's lit screen.

u up?

He sent her an emoji: thumbs-up.

me too. A frowny face. too early.

very. need coffee.

cu at the perk maybe?

He paused a moment before answering, wondering what he should write, what was possible to write and what was permissible and finally sent a thumbs-up. He had not intended to stop at the coffeeshop that morning, or any morning, and yet now he knew he would and would probably sit there acting like he was reading his paperback so as to appear casual, as if he might have been there regardless of her text. And there he would remain for as long as he could and still make it to work on time. That was what he would do.

He could hear his Aunt Paula in the kitchen, the clank of pots and pans. Most often Anthony ate cold cereal and drank a quick cup of coffee before walking the half mile to the factory, his aunt occasionally driving him if she felt adequately presentable. Occasionally, if she had the day off and did not plan on using her car, he would drive himself. Sometimes she would be awake even before he was and there might be promise of a real breakfast then, eggs and bacon and toast if he was lucky, and it appeared, from the smell of it, that on this morning he was indeed.

"Morning, Auntie," he said, stepping into the kitchen.

"Morning." She stood before a sizzling pan in her bathrobe and slippers, spatula in one hand.

"You want me to put some toast in?"

She grunted an assent. "Who's texting you this early?" she said.

"A friend," he said. He pulled the loaf down off the top of the refrigerator and set to opening the bag and removing two pieces.

"A friend?"

"Yeah someone I met at the coffeeshop. You know."

"Male or female?"

"Female."

She turned to look at him, briefly, and then plated the food. When she spoke again it was to ask him not about Jane but about work, a subject upon which he had nothing much to report—he did his job and spoke to no one, and that was all—but his aunt was not satisfied with his dismissal of the subject and poked and prodded him until he gave her some idea of the place and the people.

"You'll need to make do," she told him.

"What do you mean?"

"This is where you live now. People should know you. They should see you enough that they don't see you. And I don't mean wandering around in the dark by the river."

He shook his head, still embarrassed, perpetually so, by his brief encounter with the local police, embarrassed and frustrated and angry. "I don't do that anymore," he said. "That's why I go to the Perk."

"That's good. What do you do there?"

"Just sit and read and play on my phone. You know."

"What are you reading?"

He set the yellowing paperback on the table.

"Ooh thick one. What's it about?"

"A desert planet," he said. "There are these giant sand worms that live underground. Like so big that they'd, like, eat this whole town in one bite."

"Sounds pretty out there to me."

"It is, I guess."

"You're enjoying it, though?"

"I don't even know," he said honestly. She raised her eyebrows and he smiled in return. "I gotta get to work," he said.

"I don't need the car today. Keys are on the hook there."

"I appreciate it," he said.

"I know you do."

He stood from the table, took his plate to the sink, and then stepped into the entryway.

His aunt called to him as he slid into his coat and pulled his sock hat down over his hair. "Hey Anthony," she said.

The hall was dark but beyond it his aunt stood in a pool of warm kitchen light, coffee mug in one hand, robe cinched tight around her waist.

"You're doing a good job," she said.

He smiled again. "I'm trying," he said.

"Be careful out there."

"Always am."

The phone into his pocket against the worn paperback, then the key to the front door, and finally the car keys on their hook.

At the Perk he sat at the table he favored and set the book on its surface next to his mocha and clamped his headphones over his ears and then removed them so that they lay around his neck. He had never visited the coffeeshop in the morning, only after work, but it was, of course, the same: a small room, walls lined with nostalgic tin signs advertising agricultural implements long since made obsolete. During his first visits, he had felt as if he were being watched and perhaps that was true: the milling figures of working men and women and high school students, all of them white, wondering briefly at the Black man at the table in the corner; he never caught them in the act of watching but he knew they were, not with malice or even ill will but only with a variety of guarded curiosity, wondering—and of this he had no doubt—who he was and from where he had come, that surreptitious communal gaze seeming, over time, to fade some, his presence there, quietly reading or just as quietly thumbing his phone's tiny screen, becoming, in less time than he might have guessed, merely part of the topography of that place.

The book was, he supposed, part of that topography as well, for his feeling of being conspicuous was not only because of his skin but because he had come to understand that people at the Perk did not simply sit and do nothing: they worked on their laptops or read books or did their homework. He had never been much of a reader, but he had come upon a dingy secondhand bookstore on one of his solitary walks and had bought a few paperbacks, choosing them based on their cover art and thinking, as he did so, of Rudy, who would have chosen the same.

The first time he brought a book with him to the coffeeshop was the evening that Jane appeared at his table, stammering and confused, and it was not until after she left that he began to read, at first not understanding anything of the story, the names awash in his mind: House This and House That and words that were, he thought, completely manufactured, and discussions of something called spice, which at least he understood to mean drugs of some kind, that fact beginning to bring the rest of it into focus: that this was a trap house the size of a planet, and these men and women were essentially drug lords. Or so he thought. He did not know if any of it interested him at all, but what was he to do but keep reading. At least it was different from where he was, from who he was. At some point, days later, he lifted his head from the book and realized that a full hour had passed and in that hour he not been in that small Ohio town at all but had stood in the desert and had felt the dust and sand and sun of an alien world, a familiar otherness that he recognized not from reading but from listening to music, to Deafheaven and King Woman and Converge and a hundred other bands that both brought him to himself and pushed him into some black emptiness that felt like home. He wished he could tell his friend about what he was reading, about the planet Arrakis, about the enormous sand worms that tunneled underground, about Paul Atreides and his loneliness. But there was no Rudy. Not anymore. And so there was no one to talk to at all.

Until Jane.

And, as if the thought had manifested the person, there she was.

"Hey," she said.

She looked windblown, hair tangled in the wool of her scarf, her gloves. Her cheeks flushed with cold.

"Hey yourself," he said. "Off to school?"

"Yeah, got a quiz today. You?"

"Someone's gotta be making money," he said.

She dumped her bag in the chair across from him and then moved to the counter. He was surprised and unsurprised by her sense of propriety, her understanding, after only meeting him twice, that the chair across from him was hers. But maybe she felt that way about the whole of the room, the whole of the town, for surely there had never been a moment in her life when she might have been made to feel otherwise. He watched her as she ordered, could not stop watching her. Even in the coat and hat and scarf she was a thin slip of a girl.

A moment later she had removed her bag and slid into the chair.

"What's your order?" he asked.

"Oh I got a mocha."

"Same as me," he said.

She smiled. "I kinda thought you'd get a black coffee or something." And then, "Oh jeez that probably sounded pretty dumb."

"No, it's cool. All Black people drink black coffee."

"Wait, really?"

"Got you," he said. And then he smiled. And she smiled.

"How's the book?"

"I have no idea," he said. "Sometimes I really like it and sometimes it's pretty boring. A lot of politics, only it's all, you know, fake politics. I mean made up or whatever. So sometimes I'm like, who cares?"

"Yeah I haven't read too much science fiction stuff."

"What do you read?"

"I don't know. I'm not much of a reader."

"Yeah neither am I."

She looked down at the book.

"Well, look, boredom will make a guy do some pretty strange things," he said.

"Even reading about space worms?"

"Exactly. What's this test or whatever you've got today?"

A voice from behind called her name, called Janey, and she said, "Hang on," and went to the counter. Anthony watched her there. A trio of tall, pale boys stood at the counter, each wearing a white button-up shirts and green-and-gold neckties, waiting for whatever beverages they had ordered. One of them glanced briefly to where Anthony sat, his eyes making contact, flitting away, returning, flitting away once more.

"Basketball again?" Anthony said when she had returned.

"Yeah. Playoff tonight."

"You going?"

"To the game? I don't know. I kind of stay home lately."

"Why's that?"

"My mom kinda needs me around."

"Yeah," he said. He thought of asking her more about the subject but then understood that she would have said more if she had wanted to. "So what's this quiz about?" he said instead.

"Econ," she said.

"Econ," he repeated. "How to buy and sell things."

"Pretty much," she said. "We've been talking about statistics and prediction models. Stuff like that."

"Hold on now," he said. "This conversation got deep fast."

She smiled. "Did you take econ?"

"I'm not even sure we had econ at Shaw."

"That's where you went to high school?"

He nodded.

"How was it?"

"It was East Cleveland."

"I've never been there."

"You wouldn't like it."

"Is that why you left?"

"Pretty much," he said. "There was some other stuff. Just got, you know, kind of intense."

"I'm sorry," she said. "That sounds hard."

"Yeah, well, it's a lot more mellow around here. I'm still trying to figure this place out, you know?"

"There's not much to figure out," she said. "What you see is what you get."

"I'm not so sure you're right about that."

She paused and then said, "Yeah, OK, I get it. I know what you mean."

"Aw shoot," he said now. "I didn't mean to drop the heavy."

"Yeah it's all right," she said. Her voice was a bit breathless, as if somewhere, inside her own body, she had run to this table, this moment.

"All right now. Enough about all that. Tell me about econ and the whoop-de-doos and whatever you said before."

She laughed.

"I'm serious. I've got about . . ." He looked at his phone. "Five minutes before I gotta split to work. Full econ knowledge drop. Wait, wait." He raised his hands to his temples, closed his eyes as if settling into some meditative state, and then said, "All right. Give it me."

"Oh jeez," she said. "I suddenly realized I'm gonna fail this test."

"Oh no you're not," he said. "You're gonna do fine. Come on now. I'm waiting for the deep econ knowledge. Let's go."

He found himself smiling again, grinning, and for the first time in so long he could not recall, he realized that what he felt was some variety of happiness and then, coming right on the heels of that experience, a second thought, that he wished he could call Rudy and tell him about this strange, thin girl he had met in this strange, small town, strange not because she was odd or different but because he was. How different his life had become in just a few scant months. He wondered if he had changed, if Rudy would even recognize him now. But Jane had begun speaking and he pulled himself to concentration again. Whoop-de-doos. Great heavings of wealth and disparity rolling across oceans of digital cable. And in three minutes he would stand and say goodbye and head to the car and drive to the factory, where he would earn $8.30 an hour to assemble metal objects he would never understand. By his way of thinking, this was the only economics that mattered at all.

TOM BAILEY

Sarah had been asleep when he reached home and was still asleep in the morning as he rose, groggy, head throbbing. Over cereal, Janey asked him if he was sick. "Just had a few too many," he said. "You guys had better get a move on."

He called home at ten o'clock from his pickup, during his first cigarette break of the morning, but there was no answer. The interior of the cab appeared utterly filthy in the bright slant of morning light: a mold-like growth of dust on the dashboard, stains on the seat, fast-food wrappers crumpled on the floor. The night before was a blur from which he could pull only the vaguest details. Hardiman had bowled a perfect game. Then he had gone out with Rachel afterward. Had that happened? Yes, he had been out with Rachel Denker. They had eaten and then something in the car. My God. What had he done?

Rachel did not say a word to him all day, would not even look at him. At lunch he asked if he could talk with her alone and her look was withering but she stood from the table and they moved a few dozen yards away to the empty workstations.

"Look," he said, "I don't totally remember what happened last night—"

"That's convenient," she said.

"You're right, you're right." He looked down at the floor. Dark grease worn into concrete. "I just wanted to say I'm sorry for how I behaved."

"But also you don't remember?"

"I remember enough."

"Great," she said. "Are we done here?"

"I guess so."

She turned and was back at the table a moment later. Cheryl looked across to him. He did not know if her gaze indicated some knowledge of what had happened, but he thought he saw pity there. Pity or disdain. "Fuck," he muttered. And what did he think his feeble apology would accomplish? What do any of us? Our actions remain unchanged, our embarrassing histories, language a poor mediator between that world and this. Rachel Denker sat next to Bob Sharp now, the senior tester, and her white teeth shone in the air when she laughed. Old Man Marwat, as they had come to call Mr. Marwat's father, wove silently through the empty workbenches like a ghost. Anthony Shaw at another table, the conversation swirling all around him as if he were not there at all.

"You want to try again next Tuesday?" Hardiman said when he passed Tom and Sam sitting on the bench in the cold with the other smokers at the end of the lunch break.

"Sam's not interested," Tom said.

Sam shifted next to him uneasily.

"You talking for him now too?"

"What's your average, Hardiman? Two thirty?"

"Forty-two. Two forty-two."

"Yeah, so how about you and I take a run next Tuesday. Twenty bucks says I beat you in overall points."

Hardiman stood there for a long time thinking.

"Shit, I'd do forty," Tom said.

"Twenty's good," Hardiman said. "It's on."

The other smokers at the table applauded feebly.

"Let's hope you bowl better than you did yesterday," Hardiman said.

"You just worry about yourself," Tom said. "I'll worry about what I'm gonna do."

"Fair enough," Hardiman said. He stood awkwardly for another moment and then turned and stepped off across the gravel toward the gray box of the factory.

"Asshole," Sam said.

"Asshole still bowled a perfect game," someone at the table said.

"Still an asshole," Sam said. "I hope you wipe that damn grin off his fat face."

"We'll see," Tom said. "Last night I was nearly a hundred points low."

"Oh yeah? Is that why we lost?"

"Very funny," Tom said.

Out beyond the parking lot, the landscape ran as an undifferentiated icefield, its horizon disappearing beyond a low curve of hills.

"You going to the game tomorrow?" Sam said.

"Isn't tomorrow Thursday?"

"Basketball," Sam said. "Big game against Grange."

"Shit, that's right."

"You all right?"

"Yeah, I'm good."

"Just seem weird."

"I am weird," Tom said. "Feel like I'm living in *Groundhog Day*."

"We all are," Sam said.

"No shit." Tom felt a sudden and nearly overpowering urge to vomit, his mouth flooding with saliva, eyes watering. Then the moment passed. He looked around briefly to see if there had been any reaction from his coworkers. Cheryl and a couple of the other women looked at him curiously, their faces lost in some thought he could not read.

CHARLIE

Trinity Methodist stood midway down the block, a compound composed of an old manor house with a newer wing attaching it to a squat modern rectangle in brick beside which rose the monolith of the bell tower, all of it overlaid by a thick blanket of midwinter snow. It had been months since Charlie had been there but the sense of familiarity, of sameness, remained, even the flyers posted on the corkboards that lined the walls seeming identical to those that had been present before.

Faces familiar too, although he could not find the names. One woman stopped him and asked about his family and told him she hoped they would return to the Sunday service when they were ready and he told her that they would, he was sure they would, and she smiled and called him a good boy, as if he were a child, and then moved down the hall again, the scent of mothballs following like some unsettling perfume.

When he and Kent reached the after-school room at last it was just as frenetic and colorful as they both remembered from their days within its confines: children building or destroying, reading or dragging books about by their torn and ragged pages, some laughing, some screeching, some simply quiet amidst the tumult. Mrs. Simmons stood in a cluster of leaping children, holding a book aloft. "If we get cleaned up, we can start storytime," she yelled above the noise and to Charlie's surprise the children quieted and began the process of tidying the room.

"Charlie," she called.

"Hey Mrs. Simmons," he said.

"Is that you Kent Westin?"

"Hey," Kent said as they stepped through the waist-high gate that separated the children from the exit door.

"My mom said you wanted me to come by," Charlie said.

"I did, I did," Amy said. "I've got something for her. But first—" She pulled him into a hug, squeezing his shoulders against her. She smelled, to him, like flowers. "How are things?"

"Things are OK."

"And you, Kent Westin," she said, reaching out a hand and swatting him lightly on the shoulder. "How come I don't ever get to see you anymore?"

"Just busy, I guess," he said.

"Your mom good?"

"Yeah," he said. And then, "My dad's home right now, so . . ." He trailed off.

"So that's good, right?"

"Sure," he said. "I mean, yeah."

Her nose wrinkled at Kent's tone but Charlie did not think his friend noticed. "So, boys," she said now. "Since you're here, I wondered if you could do me a favor."

"Sure," Charlie said.

"Could you take this stool over to the corner there? It's where we do the reading."

"Sure," Charlie said again, but it was Kent who took the stool and lifted it above his head and stepped gingerly through the frenetic industry of crisscrossing children.

"Listen, kiddo," Amy said now, to Charlie this time. "I could use some help around here."

"What do you mean?"

"I mean some help," she said. "Don't you remember when you and Kent were kids how there were always a couple teenagers who came in and helped out?"

"I don't know," he said. "Maybe."

"You had a crush on one of them. What was her name? Marcia maybe?"

"Mandy Dell," he said, the syllables flooding out of him before he could stop them, nor could he halt the grin that came after.

"Oh my goodness," she said, smiling. "You still remember. Mandy Dell. That's right. She was a cutie, wasn't she?"

"I guess," he said. He could feel the heat in his cheeks.

Kent had settled the stool into its location in the corner and Amy called to him now, "Stay there," and he looked up at her through the flap of curling hair that cascaded, like Charlie's own, across his eyes. "I got something else you can do," she said to Charlie.

"What?" Charlie said.

She moved to where Kent stood, Charlie just behind. "You remember this book?" she said, holding it up for Kent to see.

"I love that book. That was, like, my favorite."

"Good," she said. "Why don't you read it to the kids."

"What? I don't think . . ." he began but she cut him off.

"Sure you do," she said. "Just hold the book up so they can see the pictures. They like it if you do the voices."

"What does that mean?"

"You'll figure it out," she said. She turned to Charlie now. "And you. You can act out the story."

"You want me to do what?"

"You'll figure it out. Just don't be boring. If you're boring they'll eat you alive."

"Uh . . . OK," he mumbled.

She clapped her hands then, clapped them in a rhythm that Charlie remembered from when he was a child in the same room: clap, clap, clap-clap. And all the children quieted and began to gather around where he and Kent now stood.

"Kids, we've got some special guests today," Amy said, stepping through the children until she stood next to the two boys. "Charlie and Kent are going to do our story. They were kids in this room just like you and now they're all grown up and go to high school."

Blinking silence. Charlie looked at Kent, expecting to see some expression of terror or at least veiled disgust at the situation Charlie had unwittingly brought him to, but Kent's face instead carried some measure of calm pride. "Hey-o," he said, waving to the tiny faces upturned toward him, toward them both. "I'm Kent. This is Charlie."

Amy: "Say hi, everyone."

And the children, their voices overlapping and mumbly: "Hi, Kent and Charlie."

"OK," Kent said now. "This is, uh . . ." He looked at the book in his hands. "This is called *Stick Man*. It's about a man who is also a stick."

"What's a stick?" a little girl asked in the front.

"You'll find out," Kent said. He turned to Charlie. "Ready?" he said.

"I have no idea what I'm supposed to do," Charlie said.

"Be a stick, Stick Man," Kent said.

So Charlie did his best, stiffening his body and moving not so much like a stick as like a robot and yet the children laughed and Kent began to read about Stick Man and his adventures, the dog that picked up him and carried him and dropped him again, Charlie saying, "Oh no!" and thumping to the carpet and all the children laughing anew. It was the laughter that spurred him on, the laughter and Mrs. Simmons's watchful eye and Kent's reading, miraculous in ways that Charlie could not have guessed, although he remembered now that Kent had been the best reader whenever he had been called upon in the English classes they had shared. But this was something else, a kind of emotional release, a kind of drama that Charlie had never before seen in his friend and what Charlie felt, more than anything, was that he could not let Kent down, not now, not in front of Mrs. Simmons and these expectant, rapturous, laughing children, their dewy eyes staring up at him, pulses quickening during those dire moments in Stick Man's ongoing story. When Kent read the book's refrain, a kind of existential cry the likes of which was perhaps only truly possible in the pages of a children's book—"I'm not a stick! Why can't you see, I'm Stick Man, I'm Stick Man, I'M STICK MAN, that's me, And I want to go home to the family tree!"—Charlie dropped to his knees and mouthed the same words, hands in the air, hands over his heart, like a desperate mime calling out for his own salvation, Kent rising to his feet and the children shouting wordlessly in concert with these moments of existential grandeur before stilling once more to await whatever would come next. Identity itself hung suspended over a world filled with mundane terrors. Would Stick Man survive it? Would any of them? In that moment, at least, he thought that they would, all of them together, and the children too.

JANEY

They met again and then again, quickly entering into the ease of a friendship that felt as if it had been a part of her life for a long, long while. Most often they shared the same small round table that marked the location of their first meeting, talking quietly and laughing. She could feel that they were being watched, the eyes—especially—of her classmates pausing to wonder at them together in conversation. Had Shannon or Kimmy appeared, Janey had no doubt they would have come to sit at the table as well, uninvited, unbidden, would have said something like, "Hey who's your friend?" and in some ways Janey almost wished that would happen as it would have felt like the moment after the blister is popped and the fluid runs clear and that sharp painful ache bleeds away all at once, their curiosity about him, about Anthony, managing to press away, in a moment, the strange feeling of secrecy that had crept over her and perhaps had crept over them both.

Later they would take their twin mochas into the night, ambling side by side through the long rows of winter-blown trees and decaying storefronts that made up the center of the town. She had never much contemplated the street, its ubiquity merely part of her lived experience, unconsidered and unanalyzed, and yet, walking with Anthony, she wondered at the scene and how it did or did not compare to his own experiences of the world. She had been nowhere, the cartography of her body ranging no farther than Cleveland to the north and Columbus to the south, her grandmother's home in Wisconsin once, a circumscription of the world which had suddenly come to feel as a great limitation and now, on the street, beside Anthony, took on the further character of a terrible aching absence, as if the geography to which she had been exposed represented not the current temporal boundary of her experience but rather its absolute and breachless limit. There was no way out. And now she recognized, for the first time, that nothing on the streets around them differentiated this town from any other, the neighboring towns the same faltering shells of lost industry, the small shops that lined the main street now cut off from the more active highway traffic served by newer chain gas stations and fast-food establishments, their perpetually lit signs ever aglow. Were Anthony to be dropped in the next quaint midwestern village or the one after that or after that, in any direction, how could he differentiate between where he was and where he had been, the towns all repeating an American dream the wick of which lay guttering in the acrid, smoking candlewax. My God. How could it be that she had never seen this place for what it truly was? And yet of all the places in all the world: Here was Anthony at her side. No one on the sidewalk but them, the cars on the street shushing through a haze of snow that had just started to fall.

She had asked him before how he ended up in her town but he had avoided answering, giving her only the vaguest response or turning it into a kind of joke. "I'm in witness protection," he would say. Or, "I killed my sensei and have to wander the world without a master." Or simply, "Who knows?"

"You do," she said.

"Do I though?"

"Um . . . yeah?"

"Right," he said, nodding. "It's hard to get anything past you, Jane Bailey. What's your middle name?"

"You're changing the subject again."

"Or am I?"

"Stop," she said, tilting herself so that her shoulder collided with his. Then she said, "Stephanie."

"Jane Stephanie Bailey," he said. "That is the whitest name I've ever heard in my life."

"Hello," she said, pointing her gloved hands to her face.

"I like it. Jane Stephanie Bailey."

"You can thank my dad next time you see him."

"Yeah, I don't think I'll be mentioning . . . really, any of this."

She knew he had meant it as a kind of joke but it hurt her nonetheless, hurt her and gave her a strange sense of excitement.

"Hey," he said and when she did not answer he swung his own shoulder into hers.

"What?"

"You asked me why I came here," he said. "It's because of a friend of mine."

"What's his name?"

"His name was Rudy," Anthony said.

"Was?"

"Like I said, nothing gets past you, Jane Stephanie Bailey."

He told her then of his friend, friend in reality but more like a twin brother to him, the two of them joined ever at the hip, getting into whatever trouble they could whenever they could, the kind of trouble boys might have gotten into anywhere and at any time, but this was not anywhere or any time, this was East Cleveland in the first decades of the new millennium and so there could be no sense of innocent trouble, of boys being boys.

"I had to get out of there," he told her.

"And so you came here."

"Yeah, well, because my auntie's here so . . ."

"So that's good."

"It's all right."

"You'd rather go back to Cleveland?"

"Yeah I wouldn't say that exactly."

"What then?"

"I guess that's just it, right? I don't really know where I'm supposed to be."

"Yeah that's how I feel all the time too. Like maybe I'm supposed to be somewhere else."

"Maybe that's all right. Maybe it means we'll both go do something else."

"That's pretty much what I dream about."

"Where would you go? Like, if you could go anywhere."

"I don't know," she said. "Los Angeles, maybe. It's not like I will though. Not really."

"Why not?"

"Girls like me don't get to do that kind of stuff."

"Girls like you means what exactly?"

"Just that, you know, not everything's really possible like they tell you in school. Like they say you can do whatever you put your mind to. But really that's, like, you know, bullshit."

"At least they told you that," Anthony said.

"About the limits, you mean?"

"Naw, that you can do whatever you put your mind to."

"They didn't tell you that in school?"

"Ha," he said, deadpan. "My high school was a joke."

"But in elementary school?"

"Caledonia," he said then. "Right around the corner from the high school so it was easy for the high school kids to come over and shake us down for pocket change before school or after school or whenever they wanted. So, yeah, we learned pretty quick what the rules were and who made them."

"That's awful," she said.

"Yeah what's more awful is I did the same when I was in high school. Went over and scared the crap out of some little kids and took their lunch money like it was mine."

"But then you didn't?" she said.

"What d'you mean?"

"I mean you stopped? You felt bad about it and you stopped?"

"No, we didn't stop. I mean we did, at some point, when we were, like, seventeen or something, but only because the money wasn't worth the hassle. That was for, like, freshmen and sophomores, you know—going over to the elementary school and making the collection."

"God," she said. "That's just, like, super mean."

"I guess it sounds like that," he said. "It's just the way things were done. EC rules."

"What's EC?"

He looked at her out of the corner of his eye. "East Cleveland," he said simply.

"Oh right," she said. "Sorry."

For a time they walked on in silence, the streetlights illuming the falling snow so that faint pinpoint shadows blurred around the pooled frozen light of the sidewalk. They moved side by side as if piloting some current only they could feel, their coats occasionally brushing each other as they moved.

"What's your aunt like?" Janey said after a time.

"She all right. Kinda intense but she takes care of me. Looks out. You know."

"That's good."

"Yeah. She works at the Kroger's."

"I guess I've probably seen her there."

"Only Black lady works there," Anthony said.

"Yeah so then I've definitely seen her. My mom worked there for a couple years. I wonder if they know each other."

"Probably," Anthony said.

"Funny to think about," Janey said now. "My mom and your aunt knowing each other. And then us knowing each other."

"I guess so."

"Where's your uncle?"

"Don't know. He split. I didn't know him real well. I didn't know my auntie much either until I moved out here. But she's all right. Got me these headphones for Christmas." He tapped the phones draped around his neck.

Cars shushing through the falling snow. The police cruiser did not even slow but she could feel its passage like a great stiffening under her flesh. Even when it had turned the corner and disappeared from sight, she could still feel that hardness. She had never thought of the police at all. They were simply a presence, there to protect them, to protect her, and yet now she knew that this was not true for everyone and if it was not true for everyone then it was not even true for her.

"I hate this place," she said quietly.

"You what now?"

"I do," she said. "I hate this place. I wish I could just walk away from it. Go do something else."

"Los Angeles, I guess?"

"Anything. Could be something super stupid. Like washing dishes at a diner or something."

"No college or whatever?"

"I don't know," she said. "Last year I would've said yeah for sure but now I don't know."

She told him that she felt she did not have any friends anymore, that the death of her baby brother, her mother's sudden incapacitation, her father's long shifts at work, that these things had changed something in her, in the way in which she viewed the world, her friends at school seeming to become, in the course of just a few days, utterly empty and vacuous.

"I get you," he said simply, "but you gotta do something. You can't waste it."

"Waste what though?"

"You," he said. "You're smart. You look, you know, like you do. You can't just go work at a diner."

She felt a heat in her chest. "What do you mean? How do I look?"

"Oh you know how you look." He looked at her askance, his eyes squinting. "Come on now," he said.

She raised her eyebrows. "You think I'm ugly," she said, smiling but trying not to.

"Let's not get all weird now," he said. "You know you're pretty."

"You think I'm pretty?"

"Jane-Jane," he said now, shaking his head. It was a kind of nickname he had bestowed upon her, this hyphenated doubling of what still felt as an adult version of her childhood name. "You are a tricky one, aren't you."

She smiled again, ducking her head into her scarf in hopes he did not see it. She felt as if she were walking in Paris on some winter night. She wanted to wrap her arm through Anthony's, to feel the warm of him against her.

"Anyway, you don't really hate this place."

"Sometimes I do," she said now. And then, so quietly he could hardly hear her: "It's racist."

"Racist?" he said, smiling again. "That's just like saying there's air."

"I know," she said. "I mean, I don't. I know I don't. I just, you know, like, this is my town. You know? I just never thought that, you know, that kind of thing would happen here." She knew it was a topic that she continued to bring up, continued to even though she could sense that it was something he did not much want to dwell on, and yet it was, remained, at the front of her consciousness such that she could not let it go, especially not when she was walking the dark street with Anthony, watching cars pass, wondering which would stop and which would shine its floodlight upon him, upon them both.

He shook his head, stopped walking for a moment. "Jane-Jane," he said. He stood in the cold, blowing steam, his head shaking from side to side. "Come on now."

She had taken a step past and now turned to look at him, darkness flooding out behind, his body outlined in the last streetlight before that side of town came to an abrupt end, the street continuing into a black void swirling with falling snow and through which glowed faintly the spectral branches of bare winter trees.

"I know," she said. The cup in her hand was empty and she waved it briefly through the air before her. "It's just, I don't know, I worry."

"I know you do, but you got nothing to worry about."

"You," she said. "That's what I'm worried about."

"I can take care of myself," Anthony said. "Don't fret about that."

"I can't help it. Every time I see a cop car now I just feel like they're the bad guys."

"No one got shot," Anthony said.

"That's not funny."

"Not supposed to be."

"It's just, you know, I like you," Jane said.

They had turned automatically and had begun to walk again, side by side, their breath twin bursts of steam upon the air.

"You don't have anything to say at all?" Jane said.

"I'm thinking."

"About what?"

"All kinds of things."

"Like what?"

"Like I'm wondering what that means."

"What what means?"

"Come on now."

"Yeah?" she said. "So?"

"So . . . sure . . . but you mean that like friends right?"

"Oh yeah, yeah, of course, I mean, duh, yeah."

"OK because this," he said, his hands out before him in the darkness. "Us out here, walking around in the dark . . . I mean, it'd be easy to, you know . . ."

"Misconstrue?"

"Exactly," he said. "Also, good word. Ten points."

"Thank you."

"So we're just friends."

"Friends," she said.

The night was soft around them, soft and very cold. When she bumped her elbow against his arm he removed his hand from his jacket pocket and took her gloved wrist and threaded her arm through his. Neither spoke. Not a word. And in that way they moved: a single shape, anonymous in the night.

TOM BAILEY

He did not call home for the rest of the workday and when it was clear there would be overtime needed to finish the day's order, he took the shift himself rather than offering it to the line, relieved to have the opportunity to clock the extra hours but more relieved to have a reason to stay away from home. The plant was empty, even the blaring radio silent, and he welded as if in a daze.

When he was done he removed his goggles and set them on his locker and clocked out and then stood for a long time staring at his phone. At last he tapped the screen.

Her voice seemed strained and small, like a distant bird.

"There you are," he said.

"Here I am," she said. "Where are you?"

"They had an overtime shift to get this order done. I told Charlie to tell you."

"Maybe he did," she said. "I've been sleeping."

"New pills still knock you out?"

"I don't think it's the pills," she said.

He could see her there in his mind, her tousled hair. In bed all day. It hardly seemed possible but then he had seen the medicine cabinet, the pill bottles going empty.

They talked for a few minutes more and then the phone call ended. He texted Janey next, asking her to check on her mother and telling her that he would be home in an hour. Still at work? she texted back.

Almost done, he wrote. He thought of calling Sam then to see if he could get away from home long enough to meet him for a beer. He had not spoken to his friend since lunch and he wondered now if Sam had avoided him for the rest of the day, although he could think of no reason why. Sam had been on the phone during their afternoon break—a rare event—but that did not mean anything.

He stepped into the early dark, pulled his collar tight around his chin, his exhaled breath a pillar of smoke. Beyond the single dull light of the parking lot the darkness shifted through falling snow, the effect of which was to render the landscape into an obscure and tenuous blur muffled by quietude. A few empty spaces away from Tom's pickup stood Mary Lou's sedan and he pondered this in a bleary, exhausted way as he moved forward, almost falling twice on the various frozen surfaces of the parking lot and finally making it to the door and then nearly falling a third time as he fished in his pocket for his keys. A shiver ran through him. At last he sat behind the wheel, listening as the engine lethargically sputtered, catching finally into lazy fire.

"Fuck," he said. He thought he should shout it, should hammer his fists against the dash until he broke through, but such actions seemed only stupid and futile and instead he sat there mutely as the engine warmed, at last putting the car into gear and moving forward.

He did not see Mary Lou until he was pulling onto the street. She was huddled near the factory's sign, wearing the same baffled down coat she wore every day, her shape like that of a great tan bell, her feet poking out from beneath and planted in the drift. He braked;

the pickup loosed from the earth for a moment and then slid to a stop. He leaned over, rolled down the passenger side window. "Mary Lou," he said.

She looked up at him, her face a pale orb in a wash of shadows. "My car won't start," she said, her voice on the verge of tears. "And the fucking tow truck won't come."

"Get in," he said. "It's freezing out there."

The truck's cab shifted as she clambered into the passenger seat, the door crashing closed behind her.

"Fuck, fuck, fuck," she said now, her words crumbling into tears. "There's only so much I can fucking take."

He had never heard her swear before, never heard her speak in anything but the calmest, most considerate terms, and now he sat looking at her curiously. "Jeez, Mary Lou," he said. He could not keep the mirth from his voice.

"Well, goddammit, Tom. Goddammit the whole goddamn thing."

"That's about right," he said.

For a moment they were silent, watching the endless swirl of winter snow in the flat hard light of the headlamps.

"Why does everything have to be so hard?" she said now, her voice a long exhale into the night.

"I wish I knew," he said.

"I'm freezing," she said.

He flipped the heater switch on full and they sat in the cab, the engine running, exhaust pluming out across the windshield. "When's this tow truck gonna be here?"

"I have no idea," she said. "I called him an hour ago." She turned to him now. "I'm sure you're ready to get home. I can wait inside."

"I was going to go get a brandy at Ted's, actually," he said. "Or a whiskey. Maybe both."

"Yeah it's been one of those days, right?"

"They all seem like that lately," he said. "You're welcome to join me."

"At Ted's? I don't know."

"Friendly place," Tom said. He knew she would not come, although he was sincere in inviting her, wanting someone to be there, wanting not to be alone.

For a long moment she did not speak, the only sound that of the hissing heater vents. Then finally: "OK," she said. "Let's go."

"Yeah?" Tom said, smiling now. "What about your car?"

"What about my car?" Mary Lou said. "They've got my number. Bunch of dang . . ."

He waited and then said, "Shit heels? Fuck faces? Motherfuckers?"

"Yeah all of it. Shit-heel-faced motherfuckers."

"Well, all right then," Tom said and he shifted the pickup into gear and they were off into the night, sliding and careening and sailing through those dark ice-covered streets.

KHALID

His father had taken to writing down English-language words and phrases in a small notebook he had purchased specifically for that purpose, a notebook which would appear, each night, the moment the dinner dishes were whisked away. Then would begin the linguistic review, the senior Marwat reciting each collected word or phrase, asking for clarification and occasionally arguing with his son if the definition did not make sense to him, as if Khalid might somehow smooth out the oddities of the language. But there were so many phrases the origins of which Khalid did not know and did not care to know. He kicked the bucket. We're flying by the seat of our pants. It's raining cats and dogs. Or, the oddest of all: it's colder than a witch's tit in a brass bra on the shady side of an iceberg. Rashid had burst out laughing at this. "Where did you hear that, Daada-ji?" he said.

"Yes, where did you hear that?" Khalid said, unsmiling.

"I don't know," his father answered in Urdu. "Someone at the factory. They're always talking and talking as if I can't hear them."

"That's because they don't think you understand them," Rafia said.

"I don't understand them," he said simply.

After the witch's tit incident at the dinner table, Khalid told Rashid that it would be his job to help his Daada-ji with his nightly vocabulary questions. Rashid's protest was not unexpected. "Can't he just look stuff up in a dictionary?" he whined.

"It's good for you too," Khalid told his son. "It'll give you a chance to define things in your own words."

"I already have to do that for school," he said now.

"Even better," Khalid said. "More practice."

Rashid groaned and stormed away but later that night Khalid could hear his son patiently going through his grandfather's list and for a long while there seemed almost a sense of harmony in the household.

His father had indeed been joining him at work—Khalid had even put together a desk for him—but the man did little more than wander around the factory floor, hands behind his back, nodding and occasionally standing beside one of the workers and watching as he or she did some part of the assembly process and then wandering away once more, continuing along what had developed into a worn path, up one row of assembly benches and down the next and so on until he had made it through the whole area and returned to start it all over again. Khalid had continued to assume that his father would, at some point, finally offer his judgment of the business—for what Khalid had at first dreaded he now, of course, craved more than anything—but his father seemed perfectly content with his shuffling daily walk and his little notebook. It was, to say the least, perplexing.

Rafia too had begun to feel similarly, not toward her father-in-law but toward Khalid's mother. She had taken the woman on a shopping trip to Columbus one afternoon while Saroya and Rashid were still in school and that evening, in the bedroom, she related to Khalid her opinion that her mother-in-law seemed deflated.

"Deflated?" Khalid said from the bed. "That's a strange way to put it."

"It's true, though," she said, standing in the doorway now, the bathroom light streaming past her and into the room. "She just seems off somehow. There was one thing—I went to try something on and when I came back your mother was holding a shoe and staring at it and when I called to her the look on her face—well, it was like she thought she had done something wrong."

"You should have bought her the shoes," Khalid said.

"I tried," Rafia said. "She wouldn't let me. She kept saying, 'No, no, I don't really like them. Just looking.' That's all.'"

"So what did she buy?"

"She didn't buy anything," Rafia said.

"Well, it could be that she just hasn't figured things out here yet," Khalid said. "It's like you said a few weeks ago: It's all pretty overwhelming at first. Maybe she's homesick."

"I don't know," she said. "Maybe you're right."

"You know I am," he said. "Anyway, I'm glad you're getting along."

In the mornings he would sometimes find his parents side by side in front of the big window that faced the street, the two of them peering out at the falling snow, even for Khalid a kind of miracle each time it came. How bright it was. How lovely. How different from Lahore, its lowest winter temperature that of a spring Ohio afternoon, its summers blistering well over a hundred degrees for days and days and days on end. This place, this American place, was an unending oasis of loveliness. Had it been difficult? At times. Had he felt isolated? Had Rafia? At times. But they had adjusted and had been successful and was that not what America was?

But then came a night in late January when Rashid appeared in the doorway of the living room, a look of excitement shining in his eyes.

"Abu-ji," his son had said. There was a sense of breathlessness in his son's tone, a breathlessness that drew his father's attention away from CNN and toward his son's figure in the doorway.

"What is it?" Khalid asked him.

"It's Daada-ji," he said.

"What about him?" Khalid said, leaning forward to sit up in the big recliner. "Is he not well?"

"He's fine," Rashid said. "You know that little book, where he writes down things people say?"

"Of course," Khalid said now. "You're still working with him, right? That's your job, you know."

"Yes, yes, Abu-ji, of course I am."

"Well, what is it then?"

He thought Rashid might become irritated at him now, as his son sometimes did—more his mother than himself, Khalid had sometimes thought—but instead he looked about the room rather sheepishly, his eyes seeming to drift over the objects there. Then he turned and stepped forward into the room, Khalid's father appearing just behind. "Tell him, Daada-ji," Rashid said. "Tell him what word you wanted defined."

"What's the problem?" his father said in Urdu. The little book was in his hand, his thumb holding his place, and he lifted it now, held it open before his eyes, reading glasses perched on the very tip of his nose.

"Tell him," Rashid said again.

"Is it something bad?"

"Just tell him, Daada-ji. Please."

"Yes, yes," Rashid's grandfather said. He looked at the book again. "Sand nigger," he said firmly in his musically accented English. Then Urdu again: "I looked it up in the dictionary but it doesn't really make sense to me. Now I think it's something very bad to say. Am I correct?"

"Who?" Khalid said quietly. He could feel a sinking in his chest.

"What are you asking?"

"You heard this at the factory? Who said it?"

"I don't know," his father said.

"Think about it, Abu-ji," Khalid said. "It's important."

"It's an insult?"

"It's a racial slur," Khalid said in Urdu. "Do you understand what I mean?"

"But about whom?"

For a long moment, no one spoke. Then Rashid said in English, "It's terrible. It's a terrible thing to say. And it's about us. Us Pakis."

"Is it?" the older man said.

"What are you going to do about it?" Rashid said to his father.

"I don't know."

"You've got to do something. You can't let them say things like that. You're the boss."

"I'm well aware that I'm the boss, Rashid," Khalid said coolly.

"Well then," Rashid said. "What are you going to do?"

Khalid had not risen from the recliner but continued to sit on its edge, staring up at the twin figures of his father and his son. How similar they looked. And he between them. He had thought, for so many years, that his workers at the factory accepted him, that whatever division existed between himself and his employees was based more on economics than the color of his skin, than his birthplace. And he knew they likely complained about things, even about him, for had he not done the same thing when he had been a laborer, standing around with his fellow workers and griping about the boss, his fancy car, his fancy house. But he had not and would not have ever used such terms. Sand nigger. The thought that his workers used that term to describe him or his father or—lahol!—his wife, staggered him in some deep place inside his chest.

On the television, just across the room, the president waved his hands in the air, as if to cast a spell upon the people, upon the land.

"Father?" Rashid said. "What are you going to do?"

"Stop asking," Khalid said now. "I'll take care of it." But in all honesty he had no idea what he would do.

MARY LOU

She did not think she had ever been as drunk as she now was, the room tilting and sliding, her chest heaving with laughter and with tears and with laughter again, Tom Bailey telling her some story about he and Sam Simmons on a fishing trip years before, the canoe capsizing and Sam in a panic, as if some underwater creature was about to pull him under, Tom Bailey's voice rising and falling with the drama of the tale: "'It's got me! It's got me!' Sam's yelling, and I'm trying to dogpaddle around the canoe and there's our stuff floating all over the place, beer and the cooler and an oar and I'm pushing all that shit out of the way and here's Sam finally, wide-eyed and staring at me, coughing up water and I'm like, 'Sam! Sam! Calm the hell down!' and he's like, 'It's pulling me under!' and finally I'm like, 'Sam! You know what?' and he's like, 'What?' and I'm like, 'The water's only three feet deep!' And then I stand up and show him and he looks at me like I had just saved his ass from the fire." Tom Bailey laughing then, laughing at his own little story and Mary Lou laughing along with him.

She could not remember the last time she had laughed. It might well have been years and years, perhaps even so many that she had been a child when last she had felt that rolling of joy deep in her chest, the beer flowing and Tom Bailey comfortable there, not only at the bar—where people knew him and he knew them—but comfortable with her being with him, as if she was just a friend and they had stopped off for a quick drink after work and despite this being more or less the reality she still felt as if she was somehow in a kind of stage play or movie where at any moment the curtain would be pulled back or the credits would roll and everything would reset, the pins lined up for the ball to knock them down yet again. Tom Bailey would return to his life. And she would once more be alone.

And as if to confirm her thoughts, her fears, he looked at his watch. "Shit," he said. "Shit shit shit."

"Time to go?" she said.

"Yeah, time to go," he mumbled.

She thought he would rise then and that they would pay their bill and make their way outside to his pickup and that he would drive her home and drop her off but he did not move. She thought of asking him what he was thinking but she did not want the evening to end. She only wanted a few more minutes before reentering a life that had come to feel like some long barren emptiness. The car had been towed to a local mechanic in town so that, at least, was over for now.

"You probably gotta get home too," he said.

"I guess so. Gotta dig my mom's car out of the garage."

"Dig it out how?"

"The moving company just piled her stuff all around the car, on the hood and everywhere, so it'll take a while to dig it out. I don't even know if the thing will start."

"Well, you just text me in the morning and I'll swing by and pick you up."

"You don't have time to do that."

"Shit, Mary Lou, if I can't make time then what kind of a friend am I?"

These words, simple though they were, brought a hard lump to Mary Lou's throat.

"Speaking of—what's happening with your mom these days?"

"She's at the assisted living place out on the highway."

"I'll bet that's a relief."

"Sort of. I still feel kinda guilty about it."

"You can't do everything."

She nodded.

"Well, let's go then," Tom said.

There was a long moment before she answered. When she did at last her voice was very quiet. "I don't want to do that," she said. "Can we just, you know, maybe sit here for a little while longer. Just, maybe, a few more minutes."

She thought he might give her that same look she had seen many times before from doctors and therapists and dietitians, a look of pained sympathy which was, Mary Lou knew, also a kind of relief, as if the doctors and therapists and dietitians were actually saying, Thank God this is not me or my life. Thank God I am thin and healthy and feel good about myself. Thank God I am not Mary Lou Miller. But instead Tom smiled at her and nodded. "That sounds pretty good to me," he said. "I don't much want to go home just now either."

"You don't?"

"Not so much," Tom Bailey said. "I feel bad saying it but it's true."

"I'm sure it's still pretty hard," she said. "The baby and all."

"Yeah. And Sarah's just—I don't know, Mary Lou—she's in bed all the time. I mean all day. All day. Every day."

"She's trying to get well," Mary Lou said.

"I know," he said. "I do. I know that. But I sometimes just want to go home and have things the way they were before. You know? Like walking into the house and having people be happy you're there."

"I'm sure people are happy you're there."

"They don't much show it."

"You've been through a lot. All of you have."

"And now she's going to doctors that aren't even in the network so it's all out of pocket. My bank account's so down in the negative numbers that sometimes I look at it and forget the negative sign is there and think, 'Whoa! I'm doing all right!' and then I realize that no, you idiot, you're totally fucking broke."

"Jeez, maybe we should take up a collection at work or something."

"God, no," Tom said. "Absolutely do not do that, Mary Lou. Do not."

"Why not? Your friends will help you."

He shook his head. "Just—just don't. My friends don't have any money either. You know how much we all get paid. You do the payroll."

"Mrs. Marwat does it now."

"Well, it's not like we all got raises since then," Tom said.

"Does Mr. Marwat know?"

He chuckled softly. "I guess he can look at the same payroll any time he wants."

"But does he know you're having a hard time. I mean right now."

"He already gave me some money. At the funeral."

"That's good at least," she said. "He's a good man, you know."

"Is he?" Tom said, his eyes directly on her own now.

"He cares about people."

"Maybe he could show it by paying us a little better than he does."

"You don't know how thin the profit margin is."

"No I don't," he said. "But I also know that he drives a new car and I drive a thirty-year-old pickup."

"The money stuff will work out. It always does, doesn't it?"

"I guess," Tom said.

"And Sarah," Mary Lou said. "I think maybe she just needs more time than you did."

"That's exactly what I keep telling myself but it's hard." After the brandy, they had both switched to MGD and he sipped at his bottle now, setting it down amidst the empties that littered the little table. "It's like she's gone away, even though she's right there. You know?"

"That's pretty much the same with my mom," Mary Lou said. "Although really with her I don't think I want her back."

"No?"

"She was mostly pretty awful to me," Mary Lou said.

"Awful how?"

"Just picking on me all the time. I know how I look. My weight, you know. I'm not proud of it, you know. But my mom just—she's just pretty hard to live with."

"You don't have siblings that could take care of her?"

"My older brother died years ago when I was a kid."

"And your dad?"

"Jeez, my dad," she said. "He left before that even. I can hardly remember him."

"Shit, Mary Lou," Tom said. He sat looking at her, staring across at her, their eyes meeting over all those empty bottles. "I swear you're one of the best people I know."

"Maybe you don't know many people."

"True, but seriously. I've never heard you say a single bad thing about anyone."

"Except the tow truck guys."

"Well yeah OK so you broke that streak pretty good tonight. Still, though, you deserve all the good stuff. You know?"

"We all do."

He nodded. "I know I've said it before but you really oughta come out to league night. Join up with one of the teams."

"Oh," Mary Lou said softly. "I don't really think they'd want me there."

"Who wouldn't?"

"I don't think anyone at the factory likes me very much. I'm not complaining. I'm just telling the truth."

"They like you," Tom said, his forehead wrinkled. "Everyone likes you. What makes you say a thing like that?"

"They don't dislike me. But that's not the same thing as liking someone."

"Well maybe they just don't know you very well."

"I've worked there for almost ten years," she said. "Whose fault is it if they don't know me?"

"Street runs both ways."

"Does it?"

"You could stop and sit at the table with Sam and me sometime," Tom said. "Take up smoking."

"Oh come on," Mary Lou said, a blaze of surprising anger rising up in her all at once. "Sam's going to be happy with me hanging out with you two?"

"He's not so bad. He'd get used to it."

"He's not said more than ten words to me in however long he's worked there. Five or six years."

"Well, yeah, sure," Tom said now. "OK, so yeah, he can be an asshole."

"He is an asshole."

"Now don't start dogging on my friends, Mary Lou." He brought the now empty bottle to his lips and then set it down once more. "OK, sure, you're right, he's an asshole. But a funny asshole."

"Not good enough," Mary Lou said. "I already have my mom so that's one asshole too many."

For a long while Tom Bailey simply looked at her and then they both broke out in laughter. "Jeez first the tow truck guys and now Sam. I'm gonna have to revise my opinion of you."

"I'm not so great after all."

"You're even better," Tom said. "I like this version of you."

"What does that mean?"

"This one," Tom said, waving his hands at her. "The one we don't get much at work."

"Maybe I'll try to be drunk more often," she said.

"Probably terrible advice for both of us."

They sat looking at each other for a long moment, the jukebox spinning up some country tune she did not recognize. "You're a good man, Tom Bailey," she said.

"Don't I wish," he said now, shaking his head, the smile draining out of him all at once. "I'm not a good man, though. Not really. I thought I was but now I just don't know."

"You are a good man," she said again and when he looked at her she nodded. "You are."

"I've made some pretty bad mistakes," he said. "Some of them just the other night."

"Everyone's made mistakes."

"Not like this," he said.

"Well, I'm sure it'll be fine."

"When did everything get to be so fucking hard?"

"When we were born," she said.

"Christ, Mary Lou," he said. "Kick a guy when he's down." And now the smile was back, bright and clean and clear and he was still smiling as he rose from the chair, smiling as he told her it was time to go and still smiling when he held the door for her and she climbed into the passenger seat of the old pickup. He scraped the new snow off the windshield and they sat in the cab shivering and waiting for the engine's heat to come. "We should've stayed inside," Tom Bailey said to her.

She could not answer him for the tears that stood in her eyes. All she wanted was to be back in the bar with him, a friend for this one long evening, midnight never to come so that she would not have to change back into what she was when they were both sober, so that she would not once again have to look into the mirror and see herself staring back from that infinite shining glass.

ANTHONY SHAW

They talked of movies they had or had not seen and finally he pulled to a stop on the dark street in front of a house that might have been anyone's, anyone's at all, and said something like, "OK then, Jane-Jane," but she was so close, not by the door ready to exit but right there next to him and they were magnets drawn together, slowly at first, their lips touching and then their mouths open and then it was all hands and tongues, her hands on his stomach and chest, his on hers, under the shirt, the bare skin rippling to gooseflesh. She said, "Oh oh oh," into his ear. His cock already hard against his pants, painful. How he wanted all of her and yet he said, "Wait," and she stopped all at once, her eyes so close to his, her wet mouth, her skin. A brief moment of trembling heat before they came together once more, not as frantic this time and yet not quite gentle. He was surprised, not at the force of his own hunger, but of hers, of how she pressed against his lips and how her hands pulled at his torso, finding his bare flesh, her palms cool but not cold. He reached for her again, his own hands finding her small, taut nipples, her breath catching, and all the while some part of him shouting, What are you doing? You fool. You goddamn fool.

But then she pulled back from him, her eyes down, her breath in gasps. "OK, OK, OK," she said, tapping his chest with her palms.

"Yeah," he said, an exhale.

And then: "Bye." She opened the door, that cold blast flooding in all at once, but then turned back and kissed him one last time, quickly, before leaping out of the car, the door swinging closed behind her. He would remember the image of her fleeing toward the house forever: a windblown sprite flying nightward. The house door opened. The house door closed. She did not look back.

Later he would lie awake in his auntie's spare room. She had sent him a text: goodnight and a red heart. And then the phone was silent. He clamped his headphones over his ears but the wash of guitars, the guttural incomprehensible voices carried with them a quality that felt more absurd than brutal. A terrifying wail against what life? What experience? She had felt like the sun. Her breasts soft and warm. Her mouth a searching wetness.

goodnight ♥

"Jesus," he said now, a whisper. He set the phone aside and lay back on the mattress. He had already masturbated three times and despite his soreness he stirred to the thought of her yet again. The cross on the wall cast a strange blue shadow. From outside and as if from a long way off came the sound of raised voices: the family across the street once more entering the violence of their relationship, its sonic apex just loud enough to draw his ear so that he found he could not help but listen for its return. Here was the music.

His aunt asleep in her room on the other side of the house. He hoped her slumber was undisturbed, although he suspected she lay listening. That family behind its Confederate flag. A chaos. Sometimes, when Anthony returned from his shift at the factory, the man who lived there, the man who hung that flag, would be stationed on his dilapidated porch, smoking, thin and hard, tattooed. Sometimes the man would say something innocuous: "Howdy?" or "How goes?" or something similar, as if they were simply neighbors, and Anthony would answer in kind, all the while the man standing framed by that flag. How could the world in which they both lived be the same? And yet here they were, across from each other, even now, what heaven identical above them all.

A crescendo of volume now. And the banging of the front door. And the woman's voice yelling something into the night and then the man's response, the latter as clear as if it had been spoken inside his aunt's home: "You fucking cunt," he said. To Anthony's relief he heard the grind of their car starting and then the sound of it peeling away, and the sobbing he heard, just for a moment, was her voice on the porch of that bleak ruined house, a sobbing that quieted and was gone in the darkness.

He nearly reached for his phone to text her, to text Jane, what had happened, stopping only when he saw the red heart once more. And what he thought now was a question: What was wrong with him? A white girl in a small town, a teenager. God. What possible ending could such a story have?

Outside the night was very quiet. He listened for his aunt's car, the sound of the engine, but then remembered that she was already here, already in the house with him. And yet he continued to listen for the engine, the muffled thunk of the driver's door closing, the key rattling in the lock, her quiet step into the entryway. Like a shadow of his heart. He was still listening when sleep claimed him. The window's shadowed pane slid open and out he poured like a flood, across those quiet streets into a world that was bright and clean and warm and in which there was nothing to be afraid of anywhere at all and never would be.

PART 3

RASHID

Columbus, Ohio. Boys sheened with sweat. Oh how they move, spinning and turning and racing from one end of the court to the other, a grace born of practice and power, of muscle and bone. And of desire. Their soles squeak the gymnasium's polished floor. Even through the cheers and groans and applause: that bright, stinging sound. An audience of electric blood, our bodies wired to the court so that when the ball bounces off the hoop there comes a collective sigh of frustration, then the rebound, the spin, and a pale, tall boy tosses the ball in a lazy arc that swooshes down through the net, a gasp, then a great brief yelp of celebration. But courtside there is no time to celebrate, for the ball is already in play again and now they jog in a scattered group across the half-court line and the ball moves, is moving, from player to player, bouncing, firing in an orange streak, the hollow sound of fingers on inflated leather muffled by the audience's gasp and exhale.

Last year they met in this very hall and our boys returned home with platitudes. We played well. We'll get 'em next year. And now next year has arrived and it seems as if the whole town has come, in cars and trucks and school busses, a community united in enthusiasm and rage, calling out by number, by name, their boys, our boys, in the struggle against an enemy who might appear as a mirror—tall and young sweated through with exertion—but for the color of the uniform and the unspoken and unacknowledged fact of their Blackness. The audience too, the other side, a cacophony of difference.

The body a brainstem. They have studied and practiced and pushed to the point of exhaustion night after night, their schoolwork secondary to the fluidity of motion, the drills wearing their bodies into a groove so tight and sharp that their motion is no longer conscious. Were you to ask any one of them what they were doing or why there would be no answer. The body moves as it does because it has tuned itself to the ball, the court, the other players, four of whom are brothers, five the enemy. Thirty-two minutes of play spread over an hour and a half that might well be eternity itself, whole and entire, or no time at all, but a blink and gone, gone again. The ball in the air. A ricochet and the suspended breath. The score clicking upward on both sides, three points in difference, and the clock's temporal constancy dragging them toward an ending that will come regardless of effort, devotion, belief, or doubt.

"Gotta pee," Rashid said, yelled, and, beside him, Tony Mellott nodded in reply.

He wove his way down the stands, the play continuing below him, the audience rising momentarily en masse so that he had to stop his progress to avoid being crushed. Another point, or two, or three. He was not much interested in basketball but everyone from school was at the game and so he had taken one of the packed school busses with Tony and a few other friends and now was mostly enjoying himself. The team was, for the second year in a row, in the state tournament for their division. He had been an eighth grader the previous year and had hardly been cognizant of the high school except as a place his sister attended and which he, Rashid, anticipated with some mingling of fear and excitement. Now that it was here, now that he was a freshman, he mostly found it a continuation of the same familiar educational experience he had been accustomed to since first grade, the only difference being moving from classroom to classroom, teacher to teacher, across the days, and the variety of activities one could, if one chose, participate in: clubs and bands and sports. Rashid had joined the biology club and the chess club and played mellophone in the high school orchestra, as a result of which he knew most of the members of the pep band arrayed in the low center of their side of the bleachers.

Safety in numbers. A lie we tell ourselves.

T.K. Simmons sat in the front row, so close to the walkway that he could easily have reached out to touch Rashid as he passed. Much to his relief he was left alone. He did not even know if the great brute had seen him. He hoped not. Already he was thinking of ways in which he might return to his seat by some other route, some route by which he would not need pass before his tormentor.

He still could not understand why T.K. Simmons had taken such an interest in tormenting him after having ignored his presence for all of that school year. T.K. was a senior and Rashid a freshman and they shared no classes, although Rashid's presence in Mr. Kavanaugh's geometry course indeed put him in at least one classroom with seniors and juniors. In fact, Rashid had made it all the way to the start of high school without experiencing any instance of bullying to speak of, a subject so oft in social media and on television that it had come to feel as if the entire country had defined it as an inevitable terror of childhood and adolescence, an occurrence so commonplace that no child could possibly be spared; and yet, somehow, Rashid had come through unscathed, at least until a month previous, early February, when, out of nowhere,

T.K. Simmons entered his life, a senior with whom Rashid had never exchanged a single word and while Rashid knew who T.K. was, he also had every reason to believe that T.K. could not possibly have known who he, Rashid, was. The freshmen knew the seniors but this rule was hardly true when reversed. Rashid fared slightly better than average by dint of his sister's level of popularity amongst her peers in the senior class, although most of her friends would hardly deign acknowledge him when passing in a busy hallway. They were not cruel by any means; they were merely seniors and he a freshman.

The first act of violence had occurred between second and third periods in a hallway crowded with other students. Rashid had been blithely moving toward his next class when he was pushed from behind with such force that he crashed forward onto the dirty checkerboard flooring, his books and materials scattering in all directions. Around him, various students scattered, their shoes squeaking around his head.

It was his classmate Tony Mellott who told him the identity of his assailant.

"T.K. Simmons?" Rashid said. He was embarrassed to find tears rising to his eyes, not because he was injured in any way but because what had happened had been so sudden, so unprecedented, and he had been so helpless to avoid it.

"Yeah," Mellott said. "Guy's always been a dickhole. Here's your math book."

He had taken his books and had hidden in a bathroom stall until well after the bell had rung, clutching his book bag to his chest and trying to stop the flood of tears that threatened to burst through him like a waterfall, managing to do so, to calm himself, only with great effort.

He had thought, or perhaps hoped, that it had been random but something in Rashid had apparently piqued T.K.'s interest in cruelty for, from that day forward, and on a near-daily basis, the man—for Rashid could only see not a boy but a man—managed all manner of subtle and constant assault: bumping into him in the hall with enough force to send Rashid careening into the drinking fountain, toppling his textbooks from his hands, jerking his book bag from his shoulder, tripping him in the lunchroom so that his tray went flying. Each time T.K. would offer some casual comment, always loud enough for others to hear: "Hey, little man, be careful would ya?" as if it had all been some kind of accident.

"You should talk to the principal," Tony Mellott told him in the cafeteria one afternoon.

"What can they do?" Rashid asked.

"They'll bring his parents in," Mellott said now.

"He's right," another at the table said. "There's no tolerance for bullies these days."

"Right," Rashid responded, but he was not so sure telling the principal, involving T.K.'s parents and his own, would do anything more than to bring T.K.'s interest in tormenting him to a sharpness Rashid would rather avoid, for despite Rashid's rising fear of the giant man, T.K. had kept his abuse to a state that was both public and petty. So Rashid would have to pick his books up off the floor again. He could think of worse things. And T.K. was, after all, a senior and so at the end of this year—four months hence—the giant would graduate and Rashid would be free to continue his high school years in much the same state as when the academic year had started: without that low level of fear that seemed now to grip Rashid the moment his mother woke him each morning for school, his first thought being to wonder what torments would face him in the hours to come.

Even his older sister took notice, knocking on his bedroom door one evening as he was doing his history homework. She did not often talk with him, their sibling friendship of early childhood having faded with the bloom of her teenage years, but now here she was in his doorway. "Hey," she said to him. "Can I come in?"

"I'm doing my homework," he said.

She ignored this, closing the door behind her and leaning against the edge of the dresser. "So, are you, like, OK?" she said to him.

"Fine," he said, shrugging. "Why? Do I seem not OK?"

"It's just that I saw what T.K. did the other day. In the cafeteria. You know."

"Yeah I'm fine."

"It's not all right," Saroya said. "What he did. It's not. He's an asshole."

"It's fine," Rashid said. "I'm fine."

"Is he bullying you? Because I've heard maybe he is."

"What?" Rashid said. "No, he's not. Why would anyone say that?" and even as he heard the words, his own words, his own lie, some part of him wondered why he would say such a thing, such a falsehood. And yet he did not want his sister to know what was happening to him, that he could not, that he had never been able to, take care of himself. He was afraid. That was the truth of it; that was why he wanted it kept secret: he was profoundly and totally afraid.

There were times, deep in the well of his own self-pity and cowardice, that he thought of his grandfather, his daada-ji. Rashid had been raised on stories of the man's rise to prominence, the narrative of Wasim Marwat having become, for him and, he knew, for his sister Saroya as well, a major part of the family legend: starting from nothing and rising to a respectable position of management at one of the most important chemical plants in Pakistan. Of course the man who had actually arrived from Lahore that autumn hardly matched the grand patriarch of the family stories, nor did he even much resemble the grandfather of Rashid's distant memory. When Rashid was seven—the age he had been when he and Saroya and their mother had left Lahore for Ohio—his grandfather had been an imposing figure; the most detailed image Rashid held in his memory was of the great man standing reflected in the polished sheen of his home's marble-floored entryway. The feeble figure who had actually come to their home from the airport in Cleveland did not seem the same man at all.

Rashid had therefore hardly been pleased when his father had asked him—told him, really—to help his daada-ji with his English vocabulary. For many weeks Rashid had done so only begrudgingly, sitting at the kitchen table beside the old man long after everyone else had fled the room, and carefully explaining the words his grandfather had written down, his notebook filled with phrases overheard at the factory or on television. Later there were sentences from newspaper articles, these often-concerning economic realities and political conspiracies that Rashid did not entirely understand so that the conversation sometimes moved in both directions at once, Rashid stumbling through an explanation one moment and his grandfather building on that explanation in the next.

"What is this Pizzagate?" and Rashid would try his best to explain, often by reading, or trying to read, whatever article his grandfather had been studying, very often articles he, Rashid, hardly understood. "But why gate?" his grandfather would say. "Why is there a gate?" Rashid did not know.

Their conversations were not always about vocabulary or language or even current events but very often were about Rashid himself, a subject that he was, at first, uncomfortable discussing. When his father asked such questions, Rashid always felt as if there was some fault-finding mission underway. He knew, of course, that his father loved him but he sometimes wished the man would simply leave him alone. Rashid did not possess his sister's academic aptitude, a fact which was obvious to all without his father there to remind him of his own lack. But his grandfather was less interested in his grades than in his life, what it was like growing up in America, going to American schools, having American friends, doing whatever young people did in this country. He even wanted to hear the music Rashid was listening to while he studied, or at least wanted to until Rashid actually handed him his headphones.

"This is Black people music," his grandfather said after a few moments, his voice slightly louder with the earbuds dangling from his ears.

Rashid shrugged. "Hip-hop," he said. "Everyone listens to it."

"And what is the name of this musical group?"

"MF Doom," Rashid said.

His grandfather removed the headphones now. "I can hear the rhymes," he said, "but the words are too fast."

Rashid thought this was probably something of a godsend, given that he did not think his grandfather would much approve of the lyrical content, although the song that had just begun, its sound tinny and distant through the tiny speakers that rested now upon the tabletop, reflected a narrative which, Rashid thought, his grandfather could indeed relate to. "I only play the games that I win at," MF Doom sang. "And stay the same with more rhymes than there's ways to skin cats." Rashid almost quoted the line to his daada-ji but he knew that in doing so he would need explicate that English language phrase related to cat-skinning, a phrase he was not even sure he could adequately explain, even to himself, and so he did not reference the lyrics but did ask his grandfather what would be the first of many questions about his early years in business in Pakistan, what challenges there had been and how he had worked his way through them—dogged determination, mostly, as it turned out. His grandfather, it seemed, would simply not be swayed.

"I wish I had your courage," Rashid said to his grandfather one evening after they had, together, parsed out the various meanings of the word "bent," a word Rashid had defined quickly and had tried to move on from until his daada-ji had produced the newspaper article in which he had encountered the word, an article describing a political faction bent on abolishing the current health-care system. "English has too many words that look the same but mean different things," Rashid's grandfather had said to him and Rashid could not help but agree.

"No one knows if they have courage until they need to know," his grandfather said now.

Rashid looked up at him. He could feel a kind of nervous buzzing in his chest as if a hive of bees had come alive there.

"You asked about when I first got the job at the chemical plant," his grandfather said now. "When I was picked for promotion—do you remember what I told you?"

"That you had recalculated the heat rate," Rashid said.

"Yes and what would have happened had that failed?"

"You wouldn't have gotten the promotion."

"Worse than that," his grandfather said. "I would have been fired. In fact, I didn't know it worked until I got the promotion."

Rashid watched his face, his grandfather's great brown eyes staring back at his own. "Weren't you afraid?"

"Of failure? Of course I was. But I am a man. And so are you." His grandfather's eyes returned to the magazine upon the table. For the briefest moment, Rashid thought he saw the flicker of some great, silent anguish pass across the man's face, there and just as quickly gone. He turned a page. "Let me find the next," his daada-ji said now. "I circled something here. Where is it?"

Rashid watched him for a moment longer and then both were staring at the magazine once more, the language of their lives together, rising in columns, page after page.

Bent was the word that stuck with him, a word which he associated from that day forth with his grandfather, a man who was, as it had turned out, not fearless but fixed in purpose to the extent that his fear was overcome, not just once but over and over again, like a Pakistani MF Doom, a feature of his grandfather's personality that Rashid thought he himself might yet be able to locate within his own obscure and troubled heart. And indeed for a time Rashid wondered if this new feeling might have somehow manifested itself outwardly, for T.K. left him completely alone for nearly two weeks, enough time that Rashid found that the hot wire of anticipatory shame with which he walked the hallways of the school had become disentangled from him, at least to the extent that he no longer feared turning a corner lest he run into the lumbering shape of his giant tormenter. Even Tony Mellott commented that T.K. had apparently forgotten all about him. What could Rashid feel but relief?

And so his passing of T.K. Simmons upon the sweat-soaked shores of the Columbus basketball arena gave him but a momentary pause. Best to avoid contact when possible, lest he draw the beast's attention once more.

The bathroom was mostly empty, the game having entered its final quarter. He entered a stall and latched the door behind him and pissed down into the bowl. It was not until he was done and reached his foot out to press his heel against the plunging handle that he could sense that something in the room had changed. A quiet had descended, a quiet that felt not empty but full. He flushed and turned and breathed and opened the metal stall door.

He did not think of his grandfather now. He did not think of anything. "Wait," is what he said, although he would remember this only later as he ran the brief encounter over and over in his mind, imagining what he might have done differently, although he knew in his heart that there was no way to change who he was, to make himself stronger or faster or bigger. There stood T.K. Simmons, flanked by two other equally huge senior boys in letterman jackets, the bathroom otherwise totally empty. He loathed them all and yet what he loathed the most was the fact that he could do nothing, that he was so helpless that the sum total of his action was to wait for what was to come. "Why?" he said. Only that. Then T.K.'s fist pounded into his gut. He doubled over, all the air rushing from him so that he ended on his hands and knees, a line of drool stringing from his lips to the polished tiles. He gasped. Gasped again, his own desperation crawling into his throat and for a long trembling moment he wondered if would ever breathe again.

"I'm gonna fucking kill you," T.K. said, his voice quiet and thick. He had knelt and his hand had gone to Rashid's back, the touch almost gentle, warm.

One of the other giants: "That's good enough. Come on."

At last a rattling inrush of air pulled into Rashid's collapsed lungs, his mouth a great terrible circle. "Why?" he gasped again. Already tears stung his eyes.

He waited for another blow to come, for the killing stroke, since that was what T.K. had promised, but instead there came the sound of a door opening. Rashid tilted his face toward that sound to find T.K. standing in the doorway, looking back at him. "Ask your raghead dad," T.K. said, his voice a deep reverberant echo against the tiles.

Then the briefest shift of light, a brief glimpse of the fluorescent hallway beyond, and Rashid was alone.

CHARLIE

Winter was technically over but the great, heart-shaped state of Ohio remained suspended between frozen desolation and the bright green promise of spring yet to come, the snow still holding in patches of gray shadow, its surfaces dingy with dust and soil and exhaust. Nights brought freezing temperatures but the daylight hours were filled mostly with shifts of lemon sunlight broken by occasional rainstorms so that what snow remained became heavy and solid and unbreakable and between which appeared soil increasingly stubbled with the luminous green of new grass. There would come a time soon enough in which every oak and maple and elm would erupt in bright new buds, the landscape transforming from sodden wasteland to verdant paradise in the span of a few weeks, but that time had not yet arrived and it felt, to Charlie, like it never would. This was the part of the year that he hated. Fall brought its shocking blaze of glistening foliage; winter the silent sparkling of snow. Spring, too, had its perfection—except for school, of course—and once they were released from that bondage: summer—a time of skateboarding in the thick heat. But this period between winter and spring had the texture of wet cardboard and smelled of mold and rust and rot. Everything wet, the earth swimming under the soles of his sodden canvas shoes. Too wet to skate, too wet to do much of anything, really, but sulk and smoke and throw shade at the institution that was the school.

It felt to him, the whole gap between seasons, not unlike the after-effects of the OxyContin he had, at Kent's insistence, stolen from his mother a month previous and which, just the day before, he and Kent had decided, based on instructions Kent had found on the internet, to smoke, setting the pill on a piece of tinfoil and burning it from underneath with a lighter, following the black path of that pill around and around with the cylinder of a broken ballpoint pen as a pipe stem until what they were left with was a silver sheet traced with angular black lines. The vague numbness that pervaded Charlie proved difficult to shake and he felt slow and tired for the rest of that day and not much better in the morning. His classes endless and pointless. He might have called home to see if he could convince his mother that he was sick enough to return there except that it was Wednesday and he knew Kent, especially Kent but also the children and Mrs. Simmons too, would be looking forward to storytime.

They had appeared six times and the simple show they put on—Kent's hyper-emotive readings and Charlie acting out the story like a crazed mime—was something that gave him no small measure of pride. The children burst into applause when they walked into the room, so excited were they by the promise of what the two boys would bring. Kent had even begun to volunteer at the after-school program on other days, a fact which Charlie had learned not from Kent but rather from Mrs. Simmons.

"Is that, like, a regular thing?" Charlie asked him out on the street later that night.

"I don't know," Kent said. "Sorta, I guess."

"How often do you come?"

"Few times a week. When I can."

"How come you didn't say?"

"I don't know," Kent said again. "Just a thing. It's not like it's important."

"I could come and help out too maybe."

"Yeah, I guess," Kent said. "I mean, you know, if you want."

Charlie did come a few times to help but it was Kent who wanted to be there and Charlie found little to occupy himself. Kent, it seemed, was perfectly happy on the floor, driving trucks around with a horde of boys and girls, but Charlie was less interested and found himself stopping by the room only to find out if Kent wanted to join him in some other activity. "Yeah for sure," Kent might say in response. "Just let me finish up here." But what he meant was that he would stay for those hours until the parents arrived and the room was closed and the night outside had mantled over the town.

A few weeks earlier, ambling home alone from the church, Charlie had inadvertently surprised his sister in front of the coffeeshop. He had seen Janey and her new friend several times by then, had seen them walking around town and once or twice had spotted them seated at a table inside the coffeeshop itself, so it was not as if his sister's friend was, at least to Charlie, some kind of secret, and yet Janey acted as if she had been caught in the midst of a crime.

"Hey, uh, OK, so, hi, this is my brother," she stammered.

"Hey, I'm Anthony," the boy said.

Charlie said his name and Anthony held out his hand and they shook like adults.

"OK, well, so, let's go," Janey said to the air.

"All right," Anthony said. "Nice to meet you, Charlie."

"You too," Charlie said.

He watched them as they walked off, their bodies not touching but that hardly meant anything.

Later that night, at home, Charlie had asked her about her boyfriend and Janey hissed at him to be quiet and pulled him into her room and closed the door. "Do not tell Mom and Dad," she said. "You hear me? If you do I'll kill you!"

"Whoa. Jeez, OK."

"I'm serious, Charlie. And he's not my boyfriend anyway."

"Seems like he is."

"You don't know."

"I've seen you with him lots of times."

"Where?"

He shrugged. "Walking around."

She was silent for a moment. Charlie thought she might burst into tears. Or punch him. He was not sure which.

"He seems cool," Charlie said.

"Yeah, he is."

"How old is he anyway?" Charlie asked her.

"Twenty. After my birthday it'll only be two years difference. Anyway, he's not my boyfriend. I already told you that."

"OK, OK," Charlie said. "I get it. He's not your boyfriend. Jeez."

"And seriously don't tell Mom and Dad."

"Don't tell them that you're friends with someone who isn't your boyfriend?"

"You know why," she said.

"Because he's Black?"

She stood there, looking at him.

"It's Mom and Dad. They're not, like, racists or anything."

"Just don't, Charlie. OK?"

"Yeah, yeah," he said. "OK. Sure. I won't tell them."

And he did not tell them, not because he held it as any great secret but because he did not think it was anything to tell. If he was to believe his sister, and he did not think she would lie to him, then all she had done was make a friend. It seemed a petty thing to tell his parents, like something he might have done when he was but a child and sought some way to get his elder sibling in trouble, especially if he only had to tell the truth to do so.

He knew Kent was not in the after-school room the moment he walked through the door. Some of the children noticed him and a couple yelled his name but Kent was not present and the children seemed to sense or know that it was Kent, not Charlie, who was important to their afternoon's entertainment; Charlie's job was to act out the story but without Kent there would be no story to tell.

"He's not here?" Charlie said when Mrs. Simmons appeared before him.

"Not yet," Amy said. "Is he coming?"

"I don't know," Charlie said. "I thought he'd already be here. I didn't see him after school."

"Hopefully he shows up. The kids miss him."

"Doesn't he come all the time?"

"He did for a while but he hasn't been here since you two read for the kids last week."

"He's been at school," Charlie said. What he did not say was how quiet and reserved his friend had been, how wrapped in silence.

"Well, maybe he's just got other stuff to do," Amy said. "It's not like we're paying you guys or anything. I wish we could. He's super great with the kids. You too, kiddo."

"I can't really do—you know—our thing without him. Storytime, I mean."

"I know," Amy said.

"I'm gonna go see if he's home."

"You tell him I said hey."

"Yeah, OK," Charlie said. "I will."

"Thank you, honey," Amy said.

He pushed through the door and down the hall and returned to the chill afternoon. The sky bright but for the brackish limbs that bisected it into triangles and rough uneven rectangles and shapes too complex for Charlie's mind to manage. His left foot was already soaked through, the sock bunching in a soggy, cold mess around his toes. He skirted a puddle in which the sky glowed silver blue but, with the next step, plunged the toe of his dry foot into a small river that ran down the edge of the street. For a moment he thought he might have pulled his foot out in time but then came the slow seeping cold and from that point on the walk was miserable. He looked in the direction of Kent's house, knowing that it was likely fruitless, that even were he there he would probably be on what Kent called "house arrest" and would be unable to leave. Charlie's own home was of about equal distance now and for a time he wondered which route to take, thought too that had he his skateboard he might have at least skated through or around the puddles and might have been more dry than he now was, in the end deciding to continue toward Kent's if only, perhaps, to show his friend that he had not been somehow abandoned, although it was also true that it was Kent who had left him waiting after school and not the other way around.

When at last he reached that stub-like street, he wondered if it might have been useful to stop and wring his socks out on the curb. The house was quiet and Charlie crept around the side to Kent's window and tapped on the glass. When there was no answer he tapped again. And then, through the drawn curtain and the inch gap in the open window: the faintest whisper: "Go away."

"Are you OK?" Charlie whispered in return.

Weakly, the reply: "Go away, Charlie. Just go away." After a moment the window's tiny gap closed with a dull click. Charlie thought of tapping the glass again but he was afraid Kent's father might hear and come to investigate and Charlie did not know what kind of trouble his friend would be in were that to occur. That it would not be Kent's fault did not seem to matter.

He scuttled toward the front of the house again, back toward the wet asphalt. The mountain of snow at the end of the road was a misshapen mound, slick with ice and peppered with sticks and dirt and dripping streams of filthy water.

The sound of the voice, when it came, chilled him as if those streams had run down the ridge of his spine: "What you doing there, kid?"

He did not stop moving until he was at the street. Only then did he stop and look toward the porch to where Kent's father stood, leaning forward in a puffy vest, hands on the broken porch rail, his bare, tattooed arms so thin that the veins were like tiny snakes writhing under his skin.

"Nothin'," Charlie said.

"Nothin'?" Mr. Westin said. "You were on my property. You had to have been doing something."

"Just seeing if Kent was around," Charlie said, hoping this did not get his friend in any trouble.

"And?"

"He said he was busy."

Mr. Westin smiled grimly and nodded. "You didn't think of coming to knock on the door?"

Charlie did not answer, the man's eyes were like flints there, sharp and black, cold chips yet sparking with heat.

"Come on up here on the porch," Mr. Westin said. "Want to talk to you a minute." He smiled again and his gapped, yellow teeth shone in the afternoon's light. His bare arms twisting with snakelike veins.

"I gotta get home," Charlie said.

"Come on now," Mr. Westin said. "Ain't gonna bite. Not much anyway." He laughed once, a brief hard sound.

"I gotta get home," Charlie said again and now, much to his embarrassment, a sob wracked his voice. There were no tears, not yet, but his heart was racing. And what was worst of all: He did not know why. In the years of his friendship with Kent, Charlie had hardly seen the man who stood before him on the porch and what brief interactions they had had in the past had been unmemorable. The man was simply a dad, like his own. But something had changed. Somehow the sight of him on the porch, framed by the long X of the Confederate flag, was terrifying. All Charlie could think was that he had to get away and yet his feet would not move.

"Charlie Bailey."

Behind him, on the sidewalk by her car, stood Paula in her work clothes.

"You know your mamma's waiting for you," she said.

"We're about to have us a powwow," Mr. Westin called.

"His mother's waiting on him," Paula said. And then, to Charlie, "Come on now. I'll drive you." She pointed to the car and he moved in its direction.

"Maybe you oughta mind your own business," Mr. Westin said.

"That's exactly what I'm doing."

They had reached the car and Charlie opened the door. Mr. Westin continued to watch in silence. In some way he could not define, Charlie wanted him to say something, as if in doing so he might defuse the ticking that had risen, bright and crisp, into the air.

But then the door closed and Paula turned the key. The interior of the car was still warm. She pulled away from the curb and into the street and Charlie turned to watch Kent's father on the porch. He had come down the rotten steps and stood in the dead, frozen lawn, watching them.

"You OK?" Paula said.

"Yeah," Charlie said.

"You didn't plan on sticking around there, I guess?"

"No," Charlie said.

"Good."

"That's Kent's dad."

"Yeah," Paula said. "Maybe best to keep clear of that for a bit."

"Why?"

"Same reason I'm driving you home," Paul said. "You gotta tell me where I'm going here," Paula said.

"This is fine," Charlie said and to his horror he realized he was on the verge of tears. "You can drop me right here."

"I'll take you all the way home."

"You don't have to."

"I know I don't have to," Paula said. "I want to."

He caught his breath, slowed, looked out at the street, the sharp points of the trees reaching toward a sky of dazzling blue. "Turn here," he said.

MARY LOU

Much to her daughter's surprise, Ginger Lou Miller thrived at the assisted living center, although of course she would in no way acknowledge that Mary Lou had made the correct decision in moving her to that place. And yet the entertainment coordinator told Mary Lou how much he enjoyed her mother's presence in the community. Mary Lou had gawked at him. "My mother?" she said.

"Ginger's amazing," he told her. "She's so funny. Such a biting wit, you know?"

In fact, she did not know. Her mother had a bite, that much was true, but a wit? That seemed one stop too far. But of course Mary Lou agreed and nodded and wandered back to her car, perplexed and silent.

The following week, Mary Lou visited at an hour well outside her normal routine and happened to spy her mother from a distance. Ginger was in a high-backed chair in a circle of other women, all of them chattering and laughing and smiling. She could not recall the last time she had seen her mother smile; certainly it had been a very long while since the woman had smiled at her and yet here she was with a group of women Mary Lou did not know, expressing what Mary Lou could only have called joy.

That night, a Tuesday night, Mary Lou had gone to the bowling alley for the first time. In her fear and trepidation she nearly turned the car back into the street and drove home but the thought of facing that cold, empty house filled her with loneliness and a sense of powerful and directionless longing which, at last, bade her shift her mother's sedan into park and step outside into the sharp frozen air. It was Sam Simmons she wanted to avoid most of all and had Tom Bailey not happened to have been crossing right in front of the doors in the moment she came through them she still might well have turned back but Tom was there and the look upon his face was, to her relief and jubilation, one of happy surprise. "Well, lookie who's here," he said, smiling broadly. "Perfect timing. We're just racking up the first round."

"I think I told you, I'm a terrible bowler," she said.

"So's everyone else," he said.

"No, I mean, I'm just awful."

"Come on then," he said. "Let's see how awful you are."

He led her past the racks of balls to where the team clustered about their lane. "Our salvation has arrived," he announced. Sam Simmons did not seem to be present and after a time she realized that she was bowling as his replacement; if this was a one-time absence or something more permanent she did not know and hesitated to ask.

Over the course of the next few hours, Tom and the other members of his team, Betty Lucero and Cheryl Briggs, both of them from the factory, coached her on technique and approach. She thought at first that they might well have been making fun of her, although in truth there was no reason to think so other than the fact that her life had been filled with people having their fun at her expense, and yet this felt different somehow and at last she released herself to the possibility that they might actually be trying to help. She did not much know Betty or Cheryl, although she had worked in the same building with both of them for several years, and now she found them to be open and funny. It was Betty who showed her how to hold the ball and how to roll it so it did not crack hard against the lane's waxed wood and how to aim for that line of black target arrows just past the foul line. Her only thought was to avoid the gutters, please God, no gutter balls, and in this she succeeded, managing, in her fear of the gutters that lined the lane, to run ball after ball directly down the middle and when she accidentally bowled her first strike everyone, all down the lanes, burst into applause.

"Holy shit, Mary Lou!" Tom Bailey hollered. "You're a natural!"

"We call dibs," someone down the lanes cried out.

"We found her first," Betty yelled.

"We need someone since Vince quit."

"Sorry, Pete," Tom yelled in response. "She's ours. We gotta replace Sam."

"Ain't he coming back?"

"Don't look like it," Tom said.

Her relief at hearing this news was palpable.

Tom turned and winked at her. "You're stuck now," he said. "There's no escape from the Bowl-O-Rama."

"Vince and Sam escaped," Mary Lou said. "Apparently."

Betty burst out with a great snort of laughter.

"Well, they tried to escape anyway," Cheryl said. "It's a very sad story. Isn't that right, Betty?"

"It's true," Betty said sadly. "We had to eat them both."

"Jesus, Betty," Tom Bailey said, laughing now.

"I swear I gained thirty pounds from that," Betty said. "I mean look at me. Does this ass make my jeans look fat?"

Cheryl snorted with laugher.

"Good Lord," Tom said. "You'll have to excuse Betty. She's trash."

"Quality trash," Betty said. "And for that remark you're buying the next round."

Mary Lou could hardly believe what was happening, the looseness of it all, the flirty joy, and among people she knew, many from work, many from about town, some she had even gone to high school with, although she doubted they remembered her from those days. And here they all were, gathered together in the muted light of the Bowl-O-Rama, drinking and laughing, knowing all the while that the next day would bring a return to what had always been: the normalcy of work, of home, of whatever families they had or did not have, a thought which brought her back to her mother in that nursing home. The look upon Ginger Lou Miller's face had been happiness, but why then had Mary Lou so seldom seen that look before? When her mother looked at her, at Mary Lou, at her own daughter, why was her expression always disappointment?

Another round of beer descended and Betty handed her a cup. "You're up, princess," she said and winked. "Make us proud." Mary Lou turned to set the cup down upon the little table beside the row of chairs, hoping that none of them could see the tears that had risen to her eyes.

KHALID

His father came in from the living room in his slacks and button shirt, hair neatly combed and coffee cup in hand. Khalid occupied his customary seat at the kitchen bar, a location of such novelty when they had first purchased the house—a bar in one's own home—that he had made it a habit to have his toast and coffee there each morning, time spent looking over the local newspaper. Today the front page was split between the high school basketball team's recent tournament win, putting them one step closer to the state championship, and news of a group of "concerned citizens" who had taken it upon themselves to mount a protest of the library over texts they deemed unsuitable for local children, these headlines secondary to the alarming news of the president's strange pseudothreats against Kim Jong-un, ruler of North Korea. The thought that North Korea's president might be the more stable of the two was little comfort. He knew his neighbors and most of his employees had likely voted for the man who currently occupied the Oval Office, a continued source of troubled puzzlement as the man, to Khalid, seemed increasingly frightening and unhinged.

His father had said something and now Khalid looked up at him. "What was that, Abu-ji?"

"Is this another American holiday?" his father said.

"No, just another Friday. We'll leave for Columbus around ten thirty."

"Why all the streamers then?"

"There aren't any streamers," Khalid said now. He sipped at his coffee, looked down at the paper again, and then set his cup upon the counter next to the empty plate that had held his toast and looked up, once more, to his father. "What do you mean streamers?" he said.

From the other room came the voice of his daughter, something between a cry of anguish and a howl of rage: "Oh! Oh! Oh!"

He heard the front door open and was already up and stepping across the tiles in his socks, his father following. From elsewhere in the house, his wife's voice: "What is it?" and then the rustle of his mother as she too descended. Even when he had turned into the living room, to where the front door hung open upon a rush of cold morning light, he still did not understand what it was he was seeing, the crisscrossing lines of white paper seeming, to him, in that moment of confusion, not unlike his father's question, as if someone had placed a haphazard series of streamers across the front hedges and into the trees, the latter of which draped in tattered strips from the lowest branches. He could see Saroya through the window, coatless, peering into those same branches, one hand upon the red heart-shaped logo that spanned her chest, the other shielding her eyes against the morning's bright cold sun, her breath a cloud of steam above her.

Then he understood, just a moment before she said it, first into the black branches of the great elm and then, repeated, to where Khalid and, behind him, his father and Rashid and Rafia, all stood in the open door: "We've been TP'ed!"

"What does this mean?" his father said in Urdu from behind him.

"Hang on," Khalid said.

"What's happened?" Rafia said.

"Hang on, hang on," Khalid said again. His house shoes were there by the door, in line with many others, and he slipped them on with some difficulty and headed into the yard.

"This is just awful," his daughter said.

"We'll clean it up," he said.

"But who would do this?"

"Some kids, I'd guess."

"But who?"

They had strung toilet paper through the branches of the big elm and over all of the hedges and around the mailbox. "We'll see if the yard service will help," he said. "It'll all be gone before you get home."

"They threw eggs too," Saroya said. She shivered.

"Go in and finish getting ready for school," he said to her. "You're going to freeze out here."

"So will you," she said.

"I'll be fine. I'm old and cranky."

"I'm young and cranky," she said. "Anyway, I hate this."

"It's all right," he said. "Kids having fun. That's all."

"What's fun about it?"

He told her he did not know and at last she returned to the warm interior. When he looked once more toward the house he could see Rashid staring at him through the front windows. He waved a hand and Rashid waved back, his expression inscrutable. How strange it was to be a father, Khalid thought, to know someone as well as it was possible to know another human being and also to understand that you did not know this person at all, his son a full and complete self with his own mesh of desires and fears and needs and wants. What was he thinking right now, Khalid wondered. What drove him? What drove any of them?

Saroya had said something about eggs and now he saw their evidence:

gobs of viscous goo slickening the exterior of his car—his wife's having been safely nestled in the garage for the evening—and the mailbox and the trees. He supposed they did not throw eggs at the house so as to avoid waking them and having their fun interrupted.

The car could be hosed off, which would at least enable him to drive to the car wash without drawing too much attention. The chill of the morning cut through his thin shirt. He would have to change his clothes first; perhaps Rafia could call the yard service while he hosed things down.

As he passed the Honda he happened to glance inside and saw what he at first thought to be a reflection of something on the opposite window: a gobbet of egg matter and some fragments of shell. But of course it was not a reflection, a realization he had almost in the same moment, pulling open the unlocked door and witnessing the whole of the car's interior—carpets, dash, steering wheel, leather seats, the felt ceiling, all of it—so thoroughly coated in raw broken eggs that there was hardly a square inch anywhere his eyes rested that did not display some sense of the indignity. Eggs had been broken into the heater and defrost vents and splattered into the instrument panel so that the recessed cups of the gauges pooled with slime.

"Son of a bitch," he muttered under his breath. And then, as if mimicking his daughter's words: "Who would do this?"

He looked to the big front window again. His son continued to stand there, staring out at the mess of the yard. There was, Khalid thought, something new in Rashid's expression now. It almost, Khalid thought, looked like rage.

JANEY

At first there had only been confusion. In the days just after he had kissed her, or she him, she had entered a period of frantic and befuddled wheeling, the aphelion of which somehow kept itself in parallel, as if her singular focus were, itself, pressing away not only the solution but the question, not because of the kiss but because of how distant he had become immediately after, his text responses so brief as to seem flippant, cursory, or, even worse, dismissive. And so she had gone through the events of that night as if conducting an autopsy the end result of which was not knowledge but confoundment so that she could not decide or determine to which condition she had failed. Perhaps it was the act itself, that she should not have kissed him at all, or let him kiss her, or whatever it had been, and of course she should not have let him put his hands up under her shirt, although she wanted that touch even now; but in some other way, and perhaps this the actual fulcrum upon which her thoughts tipped, she also wondered why she had left the car at all, why she had fled across the dark, frozen grass, why she had disappeared into her house when all she wanted was to remain in the car, kissing him, touching his face, his skin warm and his hair thick and woolen upon her palms. She was in that car whenever she closed her eyes, the idea of it so present that she sometimes felt as if she had remained there after all, time made crystalline and perfect.

Except that it was not perfect because she had texted him the day after and he had not responded for an hour and when his response at last arrived it had only been hey sry working and when she asked if she would see him later at the Perk his response had been similarly brief: cant 2night. The entire relationship—friendship, she told herself, or tried to—had begun only six weeks before that night and yet how quickly and totally had it entered her life, her mornings beginning with a few innocuous texts, a quick cup at the Perk which she had come to look forward to with breathless anticipation, the monotony of school, and then, just a few minutes after five each evening, the bright, shining bell of her phone and his text, the confirmation that they would meet and get their mochas and walk the bright cold streets of the town.

She talked to none of her friends about any of it, not even Shannon, and they asked no questions about her quietude, assuming, she thought, that it was yet the ongoing aftereffects of the tragedy of the winter before, and perhaps that was part of it too, the whole of that time a great weight that had come to hang about her neck, the only release of which was, had been, Anthony; she had come to depend on seeing him, that promise of momentary deliverance, waiting through the interminable hours in which he was too busy at work and she with classes for their text conversation to continue, the clouds low over the endlessness of each gray afternoon, clock hands crawling around their distal point at a pace that felt, at times, as if it they scuttled slowly and secretly backward.

She had typed out some variety of whats wrong several times but each time had deleted it. She had let him kiss her—or rather she had kissed him and he had kissed her back—had let him touch her breasts, something she had never let anyone do, and in response he had—there was no other way to put it—ghosted her.

And then, finally, after three days, her phone's digital bell rang in brightness, not in the late hours at all but just after dinner:

hey

hey back

perk tomorrow?

sure

5:30?

Thumbs-up.

cool cu

And then an hour, two, wherein she did nothing more than lie on the bed clutching her phone to her chest.

The school day endless, but all of them were. When she arrived at the Perk she ordered a peppermint mocha and sat sipping it in the front window booth. Two hours before he would arrive and she went through her homework and tried to focus on her reading but concentration was impossible. Her fellow high school students had mostly disappeared and the people who passed the glass were exhausted-looking men and women who had completed their shifts in whatever industry still operated in the county, the factory in which Anthony—and her father—worked among them. Another mocha. And then another.

By the time she saw Anthony's aunt's car, she felt like she was crawling through her own skin. Her jaw ached. And then, there he was through the fog-smoked window: a figure in an olive-colored coat, hood pulled up, breath a white cloud. How beautiful he looked. These are the things we remember. For all her life she would think of him the way he looked in that moment, a beautiful young man moving through the pools of light that marked the sidewalk, coming to her across the asphalt and concrete, coming to her. She wanted to shout, felt a wordless cry in her chest, a trembling that was terror and love and caffeine all at once.

"Jane-Jane," he said when he had come through the glass door.

"Hey," she said. She did not want to smile, was angry at him for the three days in which he had been vacant from her life, and yet she could not help her expression. "Where have you been?"

"Around. What'd you get?"

She handed him the drink and he smelled it and handed it back. "You and your candy canes," he said, smiling. He looked at her only briefly.

He ordered and paid and then they were outside, returning to the street wordlessly and beginning their slow ambulation. When they turned into the battered neighborhoods that surrounded the town's main street, she sometimes wrapped her arm through Anthony's, that act pulling her close enough to him that she could feel the heat of his body through all those layers of clothing. Now she could not do it, could only move beside him in the cold.

"How's things?" he said now, their bodies side by side down the town's main thoroughfare, old storefronts, many empty and shuttered, others open but few customers within. A car on the street, its tires shushing the asphalt.

"Things are fine."

"School?"

"Long," she said. "I thought I'd never get out of there." And she wondered now if it was to be just as it always had been, as if nothing was wrong at all. He had been busy. That was it. Nothing more.

"Yeah that's kinda how it is," Anthony said. "You get out of school and then you get a job where you're pretty much just watching the clock anyway."

"At least you get paid."

"True," he said. "I do get paid."

And then a long silence. They continued to walk, Anthony sipping at his coffee from time to time. Confusion again, the faint heat of her long wonderment beginning to shift into something else, a kind of fluttering, a breath that felt hot and sharp in her chest. "Is something . . . I mean," she started, stopped. "Is something wrong? Is it because, you know, in the car. I didn't mean . . . I mean . . ." God she wanted more than anything to wrap her hand into the crook of his arm, but still the act felt impossible to her. How had she ever done that before?

"I think it's all on me," Anthony said. "I mean yeah it is. It is all on me."

"What is?"

"This," he said.

"Because of, you know, in the car?"

"Because of that, yeah. Mostly that, I guess."

"You didn't like it?" She was on the verge of tears now. She was seventeen and yet had so little experience with boys. What did she know about anything?

"Oh you know I liked it," he said. "That's maybe the problem."

"What do you mean?"

"I don't know. Just like maybe we shouldn't be texting each other late at night. You know?"

"Why not?"

"You know why not. It's just starting to feel like something else. And you know, if your dad found out—"

"I thought you liked my dad. Anyway, I can tell him we're friends. It's not a big deal."

"Is that how you think of me, Jane? As your friend? Because the other night it seemed like something else was going on."

"Yeah," she said. "I don't know. Friends with, I guess, benefits? Or whatever?"

"Friends with benefits?"

They were making their way across the street now. A Subaru was held by the light and Janey could feel the driver's eyes on her, on them both, as they passed. She was embarrassed, mortified, and already tears had come to her eyes. Oh Anthony, she wanted to say. Please don't. Please don't say it. Please. And he did not say it, did not say anything until well after they had reached the opposite sidewalk and had turned toward the homes that stood in their rows under the bare black branches of the trees.

"It's on me anyway. I think maybe I led you on some. I didn't mean to. Or maybe I did. I don't know."

"Led me on how?"

"I don't know," he said. "Texting you late at night. That kind of thing."

"We're just friends," she said, although in her chest was a kind of terrible heat, a tearing, a rending. "And we don't have to, you know, do that anymore. Kiss or whatever. We can just go back to how it was before."

"I don't know about that."

"Why not?"

"Look, I just think that we need to take a break. You know? Just to make sure we know where we stand."

"I don't want that," she said simply.

"That's why we should stop," he said. "That's why we need to stop."

"For how long?"

"I don't know," he said. "Let's see how we feel in a few months."

"But we can still text, right?"

"No," he said, his head moving slowly from side to side. "No texting. Definitely no texting."

She was a flame inside her jacket, as if she might, at any moment, burn right through her clothes and rise into the air like smoke.

"Look, I just don't know what this is," he said at last. They had reached the end of the next block and he had stopped walking, his hands in the pockets of his coat.

"Yeah, OK," she said. "So you kiss me and feel me up or whatever and then you don't want to talk to me anymore?"

"It's not that," he said.

But it was that, of course, for what else could it have been? She called him an asshole before turning and walking back along the street in the direction of home, the whole of that nightscape an aquatic blur through her tears. That this had come into her life right when she needed it most, only to blow her to pieces in the next instant. Had he appeared before her on the street she would have burned him alive with the power of her rage. And she would have fallen into his arms.

What pain the human heart can bring unto itself. One moment a hot muscle overspilling with blood and the next a dry well into which pours salt and sand and bad dreams. And sometimes both at once. This is Janey Stephanie Bailey. Jane. See her now upon her bed in the little room. Muffled television voices through the wall. So tired and yet homework remains. A book open upon the bed. Physics. How does the frequency and wavelength of a wave source change when it moves toward an observer? And a page upon which she writes the answers to the chapter quiz, a list of letters spelling a word of no extant tongue but which is also a description of his brown eyes. The softness of his lips. His warmth. His weight. And his voice. His voice saying her name.

TOM BAILEY

Marwat had fired Sam soon after the start of the new year and Tom had done his best in the weeks that followed to commiserate with and support his friend, although in truth Sam had not made it easy, his sense of betrayal and outrage manifesting as an endless stream of racial epithets and promises of violent retribution, the latter of which Tom knew, or hoped, would never come to fruition. This was further complicated by Sam's ever-increasing interest in the various conspiracies propounded and amplified by the president's strangest supporters. Tom had voted for Trump, of course, but he was also profoundly embarrassed by the man's utter buffoonery.

"You don't actually believe that shit, do you?" he had asked his friend.

"I know what it sounds like," came the response, "but there's evidence. You just follow the emails and it leads to all kinds of stuff. There's even a video of Hillary drinking blood."

"Oh come on, Sam."

"Seriously. It's because of the adrenochrome. Makes it so they can live forever. George Soros. Obama. All those guys. Fucking Satanists. I'm telling you. Read up on it for yourself."

"Where?"

"I'm send you some links. It goes deep."

"I'm sure," Tom said.

And so he felt himself caught between being a friend and wanting simply to flee out of earshot. The message that Sam hated the Marwats had been delivered with utter clarity—Tom could even understand his feelings, to some extent—but to talk, even in jest, about, in the most colorful phase of Sam's range, skull fucking the boss's wife and throwing her corpse into the river was, for Tom Bailey, a bridge too far. He was relieved that league nights were over until the start of February and when they started up again he was relieved once more, relieved and disappointed, to find that Sam was not present. He asked Cheryl and Betty if they had heard from their errant team member and neither had.

"I just don't need to stand around being goddamn friendly with a bunch of assholes who turned on me," Sam told Tom later that night when Tom stopped by the Simmonses' double-wide on the edge of town.

"No one turned on you," Tom said.

"Someone must've."

"How do you figure?"

"Someone told that raghead lies about me."

"Someone told him that you called him a raghead, Sam," Tom said.

"Yeah? So? It's not like I was telling a lie."

"Jesus Christ. If Marwat hadn't bought that factory and kept it open none of us would have had jobs to begin with."

"Yeah well if he wasn't a raghead I'd still have a job, right?"

There was no getting through to him, not even to help him understand that he had been fired for the very thing Tom had, for five years, been telling Sam not to do, not at work, not at the bowling alley, not anywhere, talking about their boss and their boss's family as if no one would dare tell Marwat what they might well have, at any point, easily overheard, Sam's voice being louder than Sam ever seemed to understand or notice. And all the while he had thought, assumed, Sam's comments to be the kind of casual epithets that everyone used from time to time, not actual racism but rather a shorthand for frustration, disappointment, and the ongoing feeling that some had simply been born luckier than others. Lately though Tom had begun to wonder who exactly his friend actually was.

There had been an acerbic wit with Sam, and in that Tom had felt a kinship, as if Sam could, wryly and perhaps even unthinkingly, rattle off what was, to Tom, unspoken. And yet that sense of irony had been replaced, slowly and over many years, with an acid bitterness that was no longer a vehicle for humor or even for release but was instead merely an expression of increasing frustration and anger directed toward an ever-expanding host of real and imagined opponents: Democrats, government systems, foreign powers, coworkers, and, of course, Marwat himself. For seven or eight years he and Sam had been not only coworkers but fishing buddies and drinking buddies and bowling partners and had talked over every subject they could, from parenting to marriage to politics, the latter of which had centered on the foibles of the party they both called the dummycrats, a moniker Tom, at least, thought of as jokey statement underscoring their own shared conservative values. In truth, he had liked Obama just fine, although he, Tom, had not voted for him, instead casting his ballot for John McCain, a man who, to Tom, embodied something of the America he longed for. In truth, he did not see much difference from president to president, his position and finances effectively the same across the eight years of the Obama presidency. He wished McCain had been available to run again but alas this was not to be. They had given the nation the choice of Trump or Hillary, which was not a choice at all. And so their man had been voted into office.

He had not even thought, considered, that the strange grasping conspiracies of the election cycle would not only continue but grow, nor that Sam would so wholly embrace them. Hillary's emails were one thing—a potential breach of national security—but the idea of some Satanic child-trafficking cult operating out of the basement of a Washington pizza parlor was quite another. They agreed that the Clintons were corrupt—everyone knew this as a fact—but to Tom that meant boardroom deals and big money, not actual Satanism. And yet Sam was convinced, by material he had read on the internet, that all the dots connected. George Soros. The Clintons. Anthony Weiner. Bill Gates. There was a secret cabal running the world. Tom's response was casual interest. Of course there was a cabal running the world. There was no secret in that at all.

He had been called into Marwat's office the morning of Sam's termination. In the midst of the terrible sinking feeling that followed, he asked for an explanation. "I'm sure you know he uses language unfit for the workplace," Marwat had said.

"I can talk to him about that," Tom answered.

"I'm afraid it's too late for that now."

Tom said nothing more, only nodding. When Sam was brought up to the office a few minutes later, Tom stood by the desk. "Aren't you gonna say anything?" Sam had said, nearly shouting, his face red with emotion.

"I don't think there's anything to say, buddy," Tom said.

"Thanks a fucking lot," Sam said. "And fuck you and this whole fucking place. Bunch of goddamn camel jockeys. Fuck you."

That he left the factory floor without punching Marwat or destroying anything, apart from a small plastic garbage can he had kicked on the way out the door, was itself something of a miracle, although the fear that he might yet do so persisted, Sam's idle threats including talk of alternately lighting the building on fire or somehow blowing it up with an improvised explosive of some kind.

"You couldn't build a bomb if you wanted to," Tom had said.

"You can find anything you want on the internet," Sam had responded and Tom had felt himself shiver at the sound of his friend's voice. Not for the first time did he wonder what connections Sam had made along the internet's distant fringe.

Things might have been better had Sam been able to step into a new job quickly but the new year had come and gone and winter had faded into the earliest days of spring. What Sam discovered was what they all feared, that apart from the small factory with its twenty or so employees there were really no jobs to be had in the town at all. The best one could do was make the commute to Mansfield for Walmart or some similar big-box retailer and Tom knew Sam would never accept such employment, that somehow it was below his dignity.

"What are you gonna do then?" Tom asked him after bowling one night, when Tom had finally made the return drive over to the Simmonses' double-wide in their little grass lot at the edge of town, a sweep of scraggly and impenetrable forestland bursting forth just behind and from which, when Tom had pulled his pickup in behind Sam's equally rundown Ford, four deer had sprang, a young buck with a small rack of horns and three does, their white tails upright and twitching as they sprinted off across the road, disappearing into black night.

"Hell if I know," Sam told him.

They sat in the little living room, the television on but the sound turned down. From the little crawlspace above them came the skittering of tiny feet.

"You got mice?" Tom asked.

"Rats," Sam said simply.

"I might have some d-CON in the garage."

Sam waved a hand. "Least of my worries," he said. He lifted his beer and drank it down to empty. "I think it's whiskey time. Don't you?"

"None for me," he said. "I gotta get home at some point."

"Oh come on," Sam said. "Just one."

"Beer's fine," Tom said. "I'm off the hard stuff."

"Why?"

"Just felt like it was time for a break."

"Jesus," Sam said, "I don't understand any of it."

"You don't have to," Tom said. "It's just a decision I made."

"Ah well, I don't like to deny myself any of life's little pleasures."

"Oh, I know," Tom said.

"There are few enough of them without crossing any off the list."

The room flickered with reflected blue light and then with a turning of brighter white as a vehicle pulled in front.

"There's Amy," Sam said.

"She's coming in late."

"She's been taking extra hours."

"That's good," Tom said.

"It's embarrassing is what it is."

"Naw," Tom said, "it's a team, right?"

"Yeah, like you'd know," Sam said.

Tom felt himself bristle at the words but the door swung inward now and Amy appeared in the doorway, her glasses fogging as she stepped into the room. "Hey Tom," she said. Her purse thumped to the thin floor as she pulled her arms from her coat and hung it over the great heap of garments already hanging on hooks by the door.

He stood and embraced her, still thinking about what Sam had said to him a moment before, wanting to round on him, at least to tell him that he was an asshole to say such a thing.

"Glad you came by," Amy said. She was a fierce match for her husband. Tom knew that she and Sam sometimes fought with such passion that the police had made visits to their home and once, to Tom's knowledge, Amy had ended up in the hospital with a broken arm. Now, though, she looked utterly spent.

"Well," Tom said, "if I don't come by I never see him."

"You don't invite me over," Sam said sullenly from the chair.

"Christ, you don't need an invitation and you know it."

"Still," Sam said, "I don't want to intrude on your marital bliss."

And now Tom stopped and turned and looked at him. "Now that's the second time tonight you said something that pissed me off."

He thought Sam might say something to make things worse. In truth, Tom almost wanted him to; it would give him reason enough to walk out the door. Sam would cool off at some point, Tom knew, and they could resume their easy friendship, although standing next to Amy in their home's drafty, slightly tilting living room, he wondered if he and Sam would continue to be friends the way they had been before, their daily cigarettes and lunch breaks at work and the bowling league being the activities that, these days, constituted the whole of their friendship.

"All right, all right," Sam said. "I know. I'm an asshole."

"You think?" Tom said.

"I said all right already. You don't gotta bust my balls over it."

"No one's busting anyone's balls," Tom said simply. "Are you done?"

"I guess, but now you gotta have a whiskey with me."

"I told you I'm not gonna do that," he said. He glanced over at Amy, whose eyes met his. They both continued to stand near the door but now

Tom crossed the room and took back his chair. "Maybe you shouldn't do that either, actually," he said.

"Why the fuck not?"

"Maybe we just stick with beer."

"Fuck that," Sam said.

Amy disappeared into the hall now and a moment later Tom heard her bedroom door close.

"She's pissed at me," Sam said.

"Why's that?"

"Thinks I should have a job by now."

"You still out looking?"

"Of course I'm out looking."

"Well," Tom said, "if I hear anything I'll let you know."

"You won't hear anything," Sam said. "There aren't any jobs. You know it and I know it. Unless you're Rachel Denker, the slut."

Tom felt his skin prickle at the name. "What about her?"

"She landed a job at some plant over in Mansfield. Probably fucked her way into it. How else would she have gotten a job like that."

Tom exhaled. "So what are you gonna do?" he said now.

"I don't fucking know."

"Well, you'll figure it out."

"Will I?"

"Sure," Tom said. "You're smart. Just gotta hit it at the right time, maybe."

"Fucking raghead fucker," Sam said.

Sam's son appeared in the hallway now. The boy was larger each time Tom saw him, a great block, solid and heavy, an asset for the high school football team although Tom did not know what such a boy would do next. Sam had told him that his son was not a good enough player to go beyond high school, had told him too that he was dumb as a sack of bricks. This was, Tom knew, Sam's way of expressing his own angry worry although Tom did not know how such words could help any of their situations at all.

"How's it going there, T.K.?" Tom said.

T.K. shrugged, moved to the refrigerator, opened it, removed from its lit interior a carton of milk, and finally disappeared down the hall once more.

"He's a bundle o' joy," Tom said.

"It's not like we're having a party here," Sam said.

"Right." Tom finished the beer, rose to drop the empty bottle in the trash bin by the sink, and then brushed his hands on his jeans. "Time for me to head home," he said. "Kids are probably burning the house down by now."

"OK then," Sam said.

"You'll get back on your feet."

"Sure."

"You will, Sam."

"OK then," Sam said again.

Tom nodded, looked once more around the dingy, dimly lit interior of the trailer, and then pressed the metal door open onto the frozen clear nightscape beyond.

He had just started the pickup when the double-wide's door opened again, a brief flash of rectangular light streaming outside. He thought it might be Sam, perhaps coming to apologize for the nonsense he had said, but the figure that appeared was Amy, her coat wrapped around her like a robe, sleeves flopping empty as she descended the steps and came to the truck's window. He cranked it down and she stood for a moment out of breath.

"You all right?" he asked her.

"Not really," she said. "I don't . . ." She paused. Then said, "You're just . . . well, you're his only friend."

"He's got lots of friends, Amy."

"You're the only one who's come by," she said. There had been a brief wobble in her voice but she had mastered it now. "I don't know what to do with him," she said.

"He'll find a job."

"He's not even looking," she said. "OK? He's not looking, like, at all. He just sits around here all day watching the TV and looking at crazy stuff on the internet. And drinking. God he drinks all day."

"What do you want me to do, Amy?"

She looked up at the trailer for a moment, perhaps scanning the windows. "I told him I was getting something out of my car," she said. "He'll wonder why I'm not back inside."

"Why didn't you just tell him you wanted to talk to me."

"He wouldn't like that."

He studied her face, the way her eyes darted from his to the night to the trailer, back to the night again. "What's going on?" he said.

"Nothing," she said now, quickly. "I shouldn't have come out here. Sorry."

Then she turned and moved to her car and opened the door and entered it and closed the door again. Tom watched her there, curious. Then he levered the truck into gear and backed into the turnaround and finally swung the truck onto the road. The trailer, framed in the mirror: a dark shape cut by oaks, rotating briefly and then gone.

RAFIA

She had backed out of the garage and now shifted into drive and brought the car onto the black stripe of the road. Sunday. The house had been cleaned of its toilet paper and eggs and looked, now that its exterior walls and concrete had been pressure washed by their yard man, as if a new home entirely, so clean and bright in the late morning's sunlight that it positively glowed, the sense of its lambency increased, no doubt, by the continued desolation of that ever-lengthening space between winter and spring, a temporal gap that increasingly felt like a held breath that might never be exhaled.

Her mother-in-law sat next to her in her habitual hijab and ankle-length shalwar kameez, some variety of which she wore every day, most in muted earth tones and some, like that which she now wore, with a brief tangle of color about the throat. When her mother-in-law had first appeared at the kitchen counter, ready for their departure, Rafia had noted the slightest looseness in her hijab, a faint strip of hair visible across her forehead, a change minor enough that it seemed petty to comment upon and yet Rafia could not help but wonder if it indicated a faint relaxation in the rigor of Misbah Marwat's faith: first the loosening of the hijab and then, perhaps later, a dupatta scarf in its stead. Rafia had not much worn a hijab even back home in Lahore but she had worn a dupatta for several years in the United States before discarding it entirely, although seeing her mother-in-law on a daily basis—devout in her hijab—sometimes brought feelings of guilt that manifested as a niggling annoyance she tried hard to ignore.

"Your hijab looks very beautiful today, Ami-ji," she said now.

"Thank you," her mother-in-law answered.

And then, because she simply could not help herself: "You're wearing it a bit looser than you generally do. It looks very nice that way."

Her mother-in-law did not respond and Rafia did not glance over to see what her reaction might have been, instead keeping her eyes on the road as it turned through the abandoned hills and forestlands which, in the spring and summer, still produced a certain verdant magic in Rafia's imagination and had, at least when they had been small, seized the children's imaginations as well, those dark-shadowed trees holding aloft a leafy splendor toward a sun that was, shockingly enough, the very same that had followed its path across the city of her own childhood. In the winter, when the snows came, that forest was transformed yet again into a frozen paradise, the bare branches of the elms and maples and oaks and the shaggy spruce and pines all holding upon their frames the sparkling frozen light of winter. So silent became the world. As if it was created anew.

But then the town. In the earliest years of their time here, she had often wished for some other locale, a place in which, at the very least, she would not be the only woman wearing a dupatta, or who spoke English with an accent, or who had come here from Pakistan. There were such places in America, some even within driving distance—Columbus, Cleveland—but instead they had landed in this quaint, broken hamlet and what she had come to understand was that this was a place striving not for improvement but for a variety of arrested decay, as if to do so, to stop time itself, would be a vindication of its own unflagging belief, its rightness, its righteousness, and as if in concert to the thought: a sky-blue pickup, its running boards rusted, an American flag flapping violently upon a pole strapped or bolted or welded to the cab. Fictions built upon ever-diminishing and distant fictions. And yet this was the town in which she lived and in which her children were being raised. In some future she could hardly imagine, they would think of this town as home, their memories as rich as that of her own childhood, a thought that troubled her although she could not quite define how or why. Perhaps Rashid and Saroya would move to some cosmopolitan area—New York or Los Angeles or someplace else—and they would not feel as she often did: as if a woman in a bottle afloat in the sea. There would come a time in which her children would be grown and would move into their own lives. Her mother-in-law would die. Her father-in-law. And then where would she be but alone?

"It's a nice day," her mother-in-law said now.

"It is indeed," Rafia said. She hoped that her voice did not betray the trembling that had come into her chest.

"I just remembered—father has asked for biryani," her mother-in-law said now. "Do you think we could find the ingredients at the market?"

"I think so," Rafia said. "If they don't have it here, we can drive out to Columbus another day."

"He married me for my biryani. It's still his favorite."

"One of Khalid's favorites as well," Rafia said, smiling.

"Oh but my recipe is special."

"It's your recipe I make him. Don't you remember? You gave it to me when we were first married."

Her mother-in-law said nothing for a long while. They had passed through most of the town, past its dingy signage and its gapped patches of dirty snow, and had turned now onto a spur-road that connected the outskirts to that region where the interstate ran as a hard divider between the town and the farm fields and wilderness beyond. The tenor of the place changed, was changing as they drove, the hills flattening as if in response to the influence of the interstate and its line of gas stations and fast-food restaurants. Unlikely that any of the ingredients could be found at the local grocery. They did not even sell lamb. Biryani she had not made in many, many months, and in truth she did not much savor her mother-in-law's recipe, although that was, indeed, the recipe she used when she prepared that dish. What her husband enjoyed most of all was spaghetti with meatballs and a thick slice of garlic bread, a meal she had made for the whole family several times since the arrival of her in-laws, each time at her husband's insistence although she knew that neither her mother-in-law nor her father-in-law much enjoyed the meal, or rather did not enjoy it half as much as they had enjoyed the lamb curry she had prepared upon their arrival, all the ingredients from the specialty market in Columbus.

In truth, Rafia had never particularly prided herself on being a homemaker, although, of course, she had done as well as she could. Before her in-laws' arrival, the family would have been perfectly happy having a pizza delivered or going out for Chinese but lately she awoke wondering, as if she were a new bride trying to impress her husband, what she would prepare for dinner that evening, what ingredients they had or did not have, what meal might impress upon her in-laws her own capabilities as a wife and mother, roles she had not much scrutinized before their coming but which now felt unavoidable. Her mother-in-law's stealth, though likely unintended, had brought that condition to a sharpness; the woman would drift, nearly unseen, from room to room so that Rafia would often be surprised to find her, wrapped in her shalwar kameez and covered by her hijab, not where she had last seen her but in some other location: on the sofa in the living room or in the kitchen at the little tiled bar or in the otherwise unused breakfast nook, as if the woman were trying out various attitudes of repose in all possible locations within the domicile. Rafia had come to feel that she was being watched by the very fact that she was not, her mother-in-law's eyes so often elsewhere that it had come to feel a strange game of cat and mouse with Rafia playing both roles.

And yet her mother-in-law's criticisms, quiet though they were, could not be denied. The chicken tikka was too dry, naan too crumbly, korma too spicy or not spicy enough. Rafia had expressed her frustration to her husband but all Khalid would do in response was apologize for his mother and express his fervent desire that all get along. "We're in this together," he said to her. She was glad it was dark enough that he could not see her roll her eyes.

The other problem was one of money. When it had become clear that the senior Marwats would be making the trip to Ohio and that such a trip would amount to a permanent relocation, Khalid had spoken with his father about making the downstairs—currently a kind of rumpus room for the children, now mostly disused—into an apartment with its own kitchenette and a full bathroom. This way, they had reasoned, his parents might have the comfort of their own space while still being an active part of the family home. Khalid had expressed this idea to his father and, when asked if he could contribute to the construction costs, his father had readily agreed. But now that her in-laws had actually arrived, all talk of such a project had fallen away to silence. This might not have been particularly important except in the mornings, as the two bathrooms split between Rashid and Saroya were now also shared by their grandparents, the doors opening and closing and opening and closing again, Rashid knocking and then Saroya knocking and then their grandfather knocking, their grandmother all the while calling through the door for patience.

"Something must be done," Rafia had told her husband the previous week.

"I know, I know," Khalid said in response. "I'll talk with father about it."

"When?" she asked him.

"Soon," was his response. "When the time's right."

"They've been here five months. Nearly half a year. Right under our feet." She paused. "And I love them. You know I do. But this isn't how it was supposed to be."

"All right, all right," Khalid said. "I'll talk with him."

"When?"

"Tomorrow."

"Tomorrow?"

"Yes, tomorrow. What do you want me to do—go wake him up and ask him about it right now?"

"Tomorrow, then," Rafia said to him.

"Yes, can you not hear me? Tomorrow, I said. I'll talk with him tomorrow."

But of course tomorrow came and went and when she asked him about it that night he feigned sleep, of all things, the coward.

And so when she had asked her mother-in-law if she would accompany her to Kroger it was in part to get the woman out of the house for a time. The men were watching a cricket match on television—India vs. Australia—and the children were busy with their own concerns. What she wanted was a moment in which to speak to her mother-in-law—two women married to stubborn husbands—about the issues of the house and how they might easily fix them with a bit of construction dust and a small financial investment in their own mutual happiness. And yet now that they were in the car together she felt it an odd subject to bring up and so they were nearly to the grocery store parking lot before she finally screwed up the courage to speak.

"You know, I've been thinking about our mornings," she said at last. "The children in the bathroom in the hall and all that chaos. You know."

"The mornings are indeed busy," her mother-in-law said.

"Well, yes," Rafia said. "More than that, though. I meant that perhaps the two bathrooms aren't quite enough for how many need to use them."

"There's one in your room."

"Of course, but that's not exactly convenient."

"True."

Rafia was relieved that this was already going so well. She hated to think such a thing but also, in some ways, reveled in it: Her husband was a coward. She, on the other hand: a lioness. "I thought you and I could talk about some possible solutions," she said.

"Like a schedule of some kind?"

"Well, certainly that would work, I guess, but I was thinking of something a bit more substantial."

Rafia waited for a response but her mother-in-law had once again lapsed into silence. Rafia glanced over to her in the passenger seat but she continued to peer out the front window. The Kroger sign red and shining.

"You know, Khalid and Abu-ji talked about turning the downstairs into a kind of apartment for you."

"An apartment? Why would we need an apartment when we're perfectly happy where we are?"

"No, I don't think you understand what I mean. I mean we'd make the downstairs complete with its own kitchen and its own big bathroom with a tub and everything. Wouldn't it be nice to have a big bathroom all your own and not have to share it with the children?"

"That sounds very expensive. Does my son have enough money to embark on such a project?"

"Well, no," Rafia said. "We thought that Abu-ji would help pay for it since it would really be for the two of you." They had pulled into a space now and she levered the car into park and turned off the ignition. "It would really be quite nice, I think, and you'd be able to have more of your things shipped over from Lahore. It could be just the way you want it. And you'd still be totally welcome upstairs whenever you wanted to come up. Every day, all day, if you wanted to, but you'd also have your own space to do with as you pleased. And privacy. Doesn't that sound like it would be worthwhile?"

"It sounds like a lot of trouble," her mother-in-law said. Already her hand was clawing for the door handle and then the door was open and a bright wash of cold rushed into the interior.

Rafia followed her outside. "I don't think it will be so much trouble," she said across the top of the car. "We hardly use the downstairs now at all. It might be loud as they do the construction but we've survived worse in Lahore, haven't we?"

Her mother-in-law's hand came up and waved at her, her head moving back and forth in a motion that seemed, to Rafia, involuntary, like a tic or a twitch. "This is for the men to discuss," she said.

"Is it?" Rafia said. "I've been talking with Khalid about it but I think he's afraid to bring it up with his father." Her mother-in-law was moving briskly toward the entrance and Rafia was surprised to find that she had to struggle to keep up. "I don't know if he's embarrassed he can't pay for it all on his own or what the issue is but he still hasn't talked to Abu-ji about it."

Her mother-in-law stopped now, just before the automatic doors, the carts collapsed together in their shiny rows. The look upon her face was one that Rafia could not recall ever having seen before, a mixture of pain and anger that seemed utterly out of keeping with the woman she knew. "What is it?" Rafia said. "Are you all right? Ami-ji, please, what is it?"

And then the moment was over. "Nothing," her mother-in-law said. "Let's get the grocery shopping done and get home." Then she turned and pulled a cart roughly from the line and pushed on through the sliding doors, Rafia nearly jogging to keep up with her.

The aisles silent in their luminous florescence, the two women moving through them as if separate, as if they were each strangers to the other, Rafia wondering, all the while, what had happened, what line she had crossed. Perhaps it was simply that her mother-in-law thought of money matters as the province of men, that Rafia had put her in the position of thinking about subjects that she still felt, even now, here in America—in Kroger, of all places—were not hers to contemplate, this boundary a vestige of the more conservative household in which her mother-in-law had been raised.

The alternative of course was too painful to consider, although its textures flashed through Rafia's mind, here amongst the brightly lit vegetables, her mother-in-law staring absently about her as if she had suddenly lost all interest in the subject matter before her.

"Did you want to pick out the ingredients for the biryani?" Rafia asked her and when no response came: "Ami-ji?"

"What is it?" her mother-in-law said now, peering at Rafia as if she had been in full charge of all her faculties all the while.

"I asked if you wanted to pick out the ingredients for the biryani."

"Oh," her mother-in-law said. "No, I guess we can do that some other day."

"Come, come," Rafia said. "Just pick what you want and put it in the cart. I've got Khalid's checkbook, you know." She lifted an eggplant from its damp cold rack and held it in one hand and then looked over to her mother-in-law, the dark blue hijab framing her face.

Her mother-in-law's eyes skidded away. "I think another day," she said. "Maybe we just get the essentials and head back."

"Why are you in such a hurry to head back?" Rafia said. "You're in the house all day every day. Don't you want to get out and see things?"

"I'm just a little tired. That's all."

"Tired? Did you not sleep well?"

"When you're my age, you'll understand. You get tired for no reason."

"Maybe you should see a doctor."

"I don't need to see a doctor," her mother-in-law said now, her voice hard and sharp.

"What is it?" Rafia said. "What's going on with you two? If you'd tell me I know we could help."

And then, just behind her, a voice barking so close it was nearly in her ear: "Well, I hope you're happy."

She turned now and faced a woman she could not remember ever having seen before. "I'm sorry?" she said.

"I hope you are," the woman said. She was thickset and dressed in a sweatshirt, hair dyed a somewhat unnatural shade of red, and just behind her came a second woman, this one familiar to Rafia, a Black woman who had worked in the grocery for a good many years. And then Rafia realized that the woman who stood before her, the one who had spoken, was familiar to her after all. She, too, worked here, at Kroger, although now she wore street clothes rather than the familiar red apron.

"Amy," the other woman said. "Come on, now."

The first woman, Amy, turned to look, huffing at the approach, and then returned briefly to Rafia and her mother. "You people," she whispered under her breath.

Then she was gone, swinging past them all and moving toward the exit. The other woman stopped beside them, her eyes on the glass doors and then they were all three staring out beyond the racks of lettuce heads and carrots and broccoli stalks and the pyramidal heaps of apples and bananas and onions and the great bin of potatoes, the light beyond shifting uneasily through the glass. "I'm sorry about that, folks," the woman said, not looking at them.

"What was that even about?" Rafia asked.

"It was her last day," the woman said.

And then, before Rafia was able to ask any additional questions, the woman nodded in the direction of the exit and then walked off toward the line of registers that fronted the store.

"Do you know those women?" her mother-in-law said now in Urdu.

"I don't know either of them except here at the grocery."

"The first sounded very angry."

"I think she was."

"What was she angry about?"

"I don't know."

"But what did she say?"

"She said 'I hope you're happy.'"

Rafia's mother-in-law looked at her curiously. "I hope you're happy about what?"

She shook her head. "I don't know," she said. "Let's get to our list. We've barely started."

They shopped for the next half hour in relative silence, exchanging occasional phrases and sentences, Rafia's mother-in-law speaking in Urdu and Rafia answering her most often in English, a policy she had been employing at home as well in hopes that it might help her mother-in-law's language facility improve. Rafia sometimes asked her ami-ji to answer in English, especially if the response could be handled in a word or two but her mother-in-law had thus far refused to do so, speaking strictly in Urdu with occasional Punjabi words mixed in, yet more remnants of her village childhood.

She paid the grocery bill with her debit card, the bagger glancing a few times at her mother-in-law's hijab. Then the parking lot, her mother-in-law a step behind her. Rafia found herself wondering what life would be like for the old woman here in Ohio, her shalwar kameez a sign that screamed out her own foreignness so loudly that even a passing car on the road that fronted the parking lot could recognize that she, Misbah Marwat, was not from this place, not from this town, not from this county, not from this state, not from this country at all, a country of blue jeans and T-shirts bearing funny sayings and cartoon characters, and upon her head the clear declaration of her faith in a region where one simply did not put such things on display, a church on every corner and all of them, to the last, Christian, Christian, Christian. Rafia had struggled with this fact and she knew that her husband had as well and that it was a struggle, too, for the children, but they had adjusted and adapted and they still, all of them, performed their ablutions and evening prayer and Khalid still made the drive each and every Friday to Columbus—now with his father in the passenger seat—to attend the service at the mosque there, that effort, they both hoped, making up for what they otherwise lacked in spiritual fortitude. Such thoughts she rarely had now and it frustrated her that her mother-in-law's presence had stirred them up anew.

They reached the car and she clicked the unlock button and her mother-in-law disappeared inside as Rafia loaded the groceries into the trunk and closed the lid and came around to the driver's seat. She turned the key and the engine hummed into life but when she put her hand to the shift lever her mother-in-law's hand came to meet hers, a touch that stilled her.

"What is it?" Rafia said.

"Wait," her mother-in-law said.

She took her hand off the lever. Her mother-in-law's gaze was unwavering. "What is it, Ami-ji?" Rafia said.

"Your father and Khalid talked of this apartment," she said.

"Yes, Ami-ji. Over the phone when you were first talking about coming to live here."

"But your home is quite large enough now. Is it not?"

"Of course, Ami-ji. Of course it is."

And now the old woman looked away, out through the front window, out toward the long slope of the parking lot, those endless spaces, the street, the gas station across the way. "There's no money," she said simply. "It's all gone."

"What do you mean?"

"We could hardly afford to buy the plane tickets."

"Oh Ami-ji," Rafia said, gripping her hand. "I'm sure that's not true. Don't you still have things in Lahore? The house and the furniture? Those could be sold if you needed money. Of course you know that you can rely on Khalid and I. We're happy to have you with us."

"The house is gone. The furniture is gone."

Her mother-in-law was silent now, a trail of black mascara tracing down the flat plane of her cheek.

"I don't understand," Rafia said. "All of it? How is that possible?"

"Bad investments. Some gambling. Wasim doesn't talk about it much. The house was sold. The furniture with it."

"So there's nothing?"

"You can't tell Khalid that I told you," she said now.

"I have to. You know that. You know I have to."

"Please, daughter." Just that.

"Maybe Khalid can help—I'm sure he can." Rafia reached for her, placing a hand on the elder woman's shoulder. A tremble at that touch. She looked a solid woman in her dress and headscarf but Rafia could feel the thinness of her bones through the fabric. "Everything will be all right," Rafia said.

"This wasn't how it was supposed to be," her mother-in-law said.

"I'm sorry, Ami-ji. I'm so sorry."

They waited there in the car, the cold asphalt of the parking lot stretching out all around them like some gray and impenetrable sea. The windows were increasingly fogged by the condensation of their mingling breath so that the occasional vehicles and pedestrians that passed through their view seemed visitors from some other world, perhaps one better than this, a world filled with grace, a world filled with mercy.

PAULA

The evening before the girl knocked on her door, Paula had been called into Tim Smithers's office and was told that she would not be made the store's night manager despite the fact that she had seniority over all the other store employees. She might have lost her temper—it would have been well within her rights to do so—but was able, somehow, to commute her rage, asking, through teeth alternately clenched and held apart in an attitude of bafflement, who would get the promotion.

"No one," Smithers told her. "There's a new fella, John Forna, coming out from Cleveland. He'll be taking up the evening management duties."

"This Forna's been with the company a long time?"

Tim shrugged. He was thickset, jowly around the throat, his polo shirt pulling against the shape of his chest. "I don't know, Paula," he said. "It's corporate."

"I'm already managing," she said now. "You know that. I'm the one people come to if there's problems."

"Well, hopefully this new guy will take that pressure off."

"I don't want the pressure taken off, Tim," she said. "I want to get paid for the work I've been doing."

"I'm sorry," he said simply. "Corporate's got its ideas."

"I'm sure," she said. "Everyone does."

She left the office in an absolute fury, her mouth set in a sharp hard line, crossing down the cereal aisle and out the sliding doors to her car. At the corner that would lead her home, she rolled straight and then turned away from town and into the clear starry countryside beyond, southwest for no reason other than that this was the direction the road took her. Somewhere in the new darkness amidst the black stubble of cornfields and in sight of a towering grain silo, its floodlit shape a bleak and luminous monolith in the night, she pulled into the gravel and pounded her hands against the steering wheel and dashboard and screamed out everything she had ever wanted to say, not just to Tim Smithers but to all of them, to everyone, and even to herself, for the foolish notion that there had even been a chance she might have been promoted to a position of authority.

The following day was her scheduled night off, although she also recognized the possibility that she might not have a job at all anymore, given that she walked out the night before without a word and had not since called in to explain or apologize or justify. She did not think Tim Smithers would fire her over this single occurrence but she also knew that she did not trust him, did not, in fact, trust any of them.

She had slept in and spent most of that next day watching television from the sagging sofa. Had she planned better, she might have gone to a movie or to the mall in Columbus, might have gone somewhere to fill the hours of the day, but Anthony had taken her car to work and so she was more or less housebound. Most nights he would have returned by now but earlier she had received a text that he had been offered an extra shift and would not be home for another two hours. She texted back and then set the leftover beef stew onto the stove and lit the burner.

When the girl knocked, Paula almost did not come to the door to answer its call. No one knocked on the door much, especially after dark on a weekday, and her thought was that it was likely some kind of religious fanatic out gathering early-evening souls. And yet there was something in the tone of that knock, a quietness, a tentative quality that brought her to the door. She opened it upon a thin, lank-haired girl, her cheeks pink and flushed from the cold, arms tight about her.

"I'm sorry, honey," Paula said. "I just don't have the energy for whatever you're selling. Good luck, though."

She moved to close the door again but the girl said, "Uh . . . I'm sorry . . . I'm looking for Anthony. Is he home?"

"And who are you now?"

"I'm Janey Bailey," she said.

"Oh, Janey Bailey," Paula said. "I didn't recognize you. You all grown up."

"I guess," she said, a faint hint of smile flitting across her features.

"Your momma know you're out here?"

"She knows I'm out," Janey said, "but not exactly where."

"What about your daddy?"

"He's bowling," she said.

"Huh," Paula said. "Well, now, Anthony's still at work."

"Oh," Janey said.

Paula stood looking at her. "What are you doing looking for my nephew anyhow?"

"We're friends," she said.

"How's that work?"

"I don't know," she said. "I met him at the Perk. And we, you know—we're friends."

"Friends," Paula said. She could not help shaking her head at the idea that her nephew was friends—only friends—with this skinny doe-eyed white girl. If it were true, would Janey Bailey be standing in her doorway right now? Would a mere friend walk across half the town in the frozen night for no reason but to say hello to her friend in person? She thought it unlikely. Christ almighty, Anthony, she thought—almost saying it aloud. What on earth have you gotten yourself into now?

Behind the girl, the neighbor's door across the street opened and the lean, hard figure of Billy Westin appeared in silhouette, the red pinpoint of a cigarette in his hand. She could not see the shape of him once the door closed again but could feel his gaze as it cut through the freezing night, its line like a steel wire between his house and her own.

"You cold?" she said to the girl.

Janey nodded.

"Come on in here then," Paula said. "No good standing out there."

The girl stepped forward quietly and tentatively as if she might, at any moment, bolt back into the night, her eyes wide even as Paula closed the door behind her, glancing once more in the direction of the Westins', unable to stop herself from doing so, the house across the street dark but for the lit cross of stars in the window, that shape now partially obscured by the silhouette of the man who stood before it.

"I've got some stew on the stove. You hungry?"

"No, I think I'm all right. Thank you. Do you know when Anthony's going to be home?"

"Can't you text him to find out?" Paula said. She had returned to the kitchen and stirred the pot and turned the burner off and when there was no answer she leaned to look back toward the entryway and the door and found the girl there weeping, her hands covering her face.

"Oh no," Paula said, to herself, to the girl, to anyone who might listen. "Come here now," she said. She reached out a hand and took the girl by the forearm and pulled her into the kitchen and sat her at the little table there, a table upon which she had eaten meal after meal alone but for the presence of the television; now Sarah Bailey's pale, forlorn daughter sat with her elbows upon its surface, weeping.

"I'm sorry. I'm sorry," she said.

"Oh I've had my heart broken a few times," Paula said. She waited for the girl to calm, for her sniffling to slow and her hands to come down from her face once more and as she waited she ladled two bowls full of the stew and set one before the girl and then a spoon next to it and a napkin and a glass of water, all the same for herself. Then she sat in the chair that was, when they ate together, Anthony's, and lifted a spoonful and blew her breath across its surface. "Go ahead and eat," she said to the girl before putting the spoon into her own mouth.

The girl lifted her own spoon and blew on it in much the same way and took a bite and then another.

"You're hungry," Paula said.

"I guess so," the girl said.

"Look," Paula said, "it's none of my business what's going on between you and my nephew but he's old enough to know better so if he's done something he shouldn't have—"

"He didn't," the girl said.

She began to tear up again and Paula watched her. What was this? What had Anthony done to this girl to get himself so entangled in her heart? That boy. All boys. "Look, Janey," Paula said. "Boys don't know what they doing. They just don't. They're stupid about that stuff."

The girl sat with the spoon in her hand, not looking up but certainly listening.

"Anyway, what're you doing hanging around with a twenty-year-old man anyhow."

"I'm only two years younger."

"You eighteen now?"

"Almost."

"Right. And you're over here crying when you should be home having dinner with your family."

"I'll go," she said and the spoon clattered to the table.

The action was so fast that Paula almost did not have time to react, the girl like a deer, frozen one moment and springing away the next, but Paula's hand was out and once more it found the girl's forearm and that touch seemed to still her. "Now hold on, hold on," Paula said. "What's going on now?"

"I don't know," Janey said. "I just miss him."

"You got your heart broken," Paula said. "That's the boy's fault. Not yours."

"It is my fault. He said we were only friends. He said that lots of times."

"How is that your fault then?"

"It just is."

Paula watched her. There was something unspoken here, an omission that was almost a lie, but Paula did not think she wanted to know what it was. Some things were better left alone. "Maybe it's good to take a break then," she said.

"No it's not," the girl said now and there was heat, fire. "He's just afraid."

"Afraid for who?" Paula said. She almost smiled for how she could remember that feeling, that heat, that fire, but her own had been different from this girl's. In Janey was the sense that she might, in the crucible of her own passion, remake the world into some shape that better fit her own heart. But Paula knew she herself had never felt that way. Her own fire had been relegated, even when she had been but a girl, to an understanding that the world into which she had been born had been wrought of a metal too cold and hard and dark for any child from Kinsman to scratch, let alone reshape. "You think he's afraid for himself? That boy grew up a survivor. He's not thinking of himself."

"He's afraid for me?"

"Honey, I don't know if he's afraid at all," Paula said, "but if he is it sure isn't for himself."

"OK," Janey said. "I'm sorry—you probably think I'm just, like, some kind of maniac coming over here."

"Like I said, I had my heart broken a few times myself."

"Tell me," Janey said.

She was surprised at this response, surprised, indeed, at Janey Bailey herself, a girl who seemed meek but then not meek, quiet and then filled with fire, the question not a question at all but a statement, a command. Tell me. She looked over at the girl and her eyes were filled with such longing, such desire, that Paula found herself drawn into them, drawn forward, almost out of herself. "My husband, Anthony's uncle," she began, "he and I moved out here because he got a job at a lab."

"What kind of lab?"

"Medical stuff. He had a degree in biochemistry, of all things."

"Smart," she said.

"Smart as all heck," Paula said and she could not help but smile, marveling, even as she did so, that such a thing were possible after all these years, that she had clawed her way through it and had reached this place, at this table, telling the story to a teenaged girl. "And he knew it too. Knew that coming out here was only a stepping stone. You know?"

"What happened?"

"Hard to say," Paula told her. "I've been thinking about it for almost twenty years now. But I still don't really know. He worked all the time, never home. We talked about having kids but it never happened. Not for lack of trying, you know." She looked over at the girl and, to her relief, saw her blush. "And then one day I come home from work and he's moved out. Left me an envelope with some cash in it and nothing else."

"No letter or anything?"

"Not a word. I didn't hear from him for four months and then the phone rings and he tells me he's in Washington, DC and has a new job and is doing fine. And even after what he'd done to me, leaving me here, I was hoping he'd say, Come on and join me. You know? But he didn't say that. You know what he said? He said that he was calling to let me know that the divorce papers would be delivered by courier the next day and that it would a great help if I could make sure I was home when they got here."

"Fuck," Janey said. She clapped her hands to her mouth in embarrassment.

"No, that's right," Paula said, smiling now.

"That's awful," the girl said.

"Yeah, well, I wasn't too happy about it neither," Paula said. "He left and I was stuck here in this town. I mean no offense, honey, but this ain't the place for a woman like me."

"Why'd you stay then?"

"I ask myself that about every day. And I don't got an answer. I truly don't. I guess I just didn't want to go back home feeling like I lost my husband. I was ashamed."

"But you didn't do anything. He left. You didn't."

"I know that now. But back then—I just felt like I wasn't good enough to hold on to him."

"How old were you?"

"Nineteen," she said. "He was twenty-four. I tell you what: that about broke me all the way down to the dirt. It really did." She set her hands on the table, pressed her fingertips against the wood as if she were holding that surface to the earth. "But you survive it. You don't think you can but you do. You go on. With the good Lord's grace, you go on."

The girl was quiet now, eating and then not eating and she looked, to Paula, as if she might crumble right to the floor.

"I don't know what Anthony did to get you all tangled up in him like this," she said now, "but you gotta know that's not going to work."

"Because he's Black," the girl said, her voice deadpan.

"No, honey," Paula said now. "Because you're white. And you're seventeen."

The girl gazed at her with those giant, doe-like eyes, blue and wet and shining. "Thanks for dinner," she said.

"I can drive you home."

"It's OK. I'll walk."

"You sure? It's cold out there."

"Yeah, I'm sure. I guess I'd better go before Anthony gets here."

"That might be best," Paula said.

She rose from the chair and got her coat and hat and scarf and gloves. At the door the girl thanked her again and Paula opened it and was relieved that the house across the street was quiet, the door closed, the porch empty. "You be careful now," she said. "I don't much like you walking at night."

"I do it all the time," the girl told her.

"I'm not gonna stop you."

"You wouldn't be able to anyway," the girl said. That spark again.

The door closed and Paula was alone in the house once more. She had enjoyed the girl's company. There was something there that made her believe the girl might well survive in the world into which she was headed. She did not know if her nephew had such a trait, if he could stand up to the real pressures that were undoubtedly headed his way, but she thought that the girl, that Janey Bailey, likely could and in thinking this she knew that the statements she had made in the end were for the girl's benefit and not for her nephew's. He had something to lose, this much was true, but she might well lose everything. There would be heartbreak and turmoil and fear and rage, not only from quarters expected but from people she knew and loved. They would break her heart. They would break it again and again and while that was likely true even without Anthony's presence in her life, was there any sense in pushing such a girl closer to a fire the heat of which she could not possibly understand?

Anthony arrived home nearly two hours later, his eyes haggard from his day, stomach grumbling with hunger. She emptied the remaining stew into the pot and heated it up, trying to make small talk but he was very quiet. It occurred to her now that he had been quiet for several weeks, a fact that she had not noticed much on account of her own situation at work, not just yesterday but in all the days leading up to it. She had lived most of her life alone in this town and the highest level to which she could set her sights was night manager at the Kroger and she would not even attain that.

"Anthony," she said now, lowering herself into the chair that the girl had sat in just a few hours before.

He did not look at her, staring instead into the bowl, ladling the stew into his waiting mouth, but he made a sound, a kind of grunt.

"You all right?" she asked him.

"I'm fine," he said simply.

"You don't seem fine. You seem, I don't know, broke up about something."

"I got some stuff on my mind."

She wondered now if she should just remain quiet about her, the girl, being here, but one thing she had learned in her life was that secrets ruined people. All those weeks she had wondered where her husband had gone, had wondered if he was in trouble, if he was dead in a ditch somewhere, and the sense of it, secret and rotten and terrible, was what had hurt her the most. Even now it felt to her like a dull file running under her skin.

"Some of that stuff was sitting at this table here couple hours ago," she said.

He looked up at her. "What does that mean?"

"Janey Bailey was here," she said.

The look in his eyes was like nothing she had ever seen from him, a level of anguish that made her suck in her breath in alarm. "Jane was here?" he said.

"How come you never told me you was running around with some white girl?" Paula said.

But Anthony did not answer this, instead asking a question of his own: "What did she want?"

"I guess she wanted to see you. I gave her some of that stew you're eating up."

"What'd she say?"

"Said you told her that you two needed to take a break."

"What'd you tell her?"

"I told her I thought that was a good idea."

"Why?"

"You don't gotta ask me that. You know that's not gonna work. Not in this town. Maybe not in any town."

"Did you tell her that?"

"What did you want me to say?"

"Did you?"

"Don't raise your voice to me," she said now. "You're sitting in my home at my table."

He looked, to her, nearly crazed with anger and pain and frustration and when he spoke again, even though his voice was quiet, the edge that ran through it sent a shiver through her: "Did you tell her that?"

"Of course I did," she said.

The spoon clanged into the bowl. He was already on his feet, reaching for his coat. "I gotta go," he said.

"Just wait a minute," she said.

"No, no, no," he said, the syllable bouncing out of him like a rubber ball against concrete.

She stood now too, moving between him and the door. "Don't be foolish now," she said. "You told her you wanted to take a break. She told me that. And that's a good thing, right? You don't want to lead her on. You can't be toying with a girl like Janey Bailey, not in a town this small."

"I'm not," he said and now there was a raggedness to his voice.

"Look at me," she said.

He told her no, his head down, his body moving to dress himself, moving to avoid her hands upon his shoulders, upon his arms but at last she got a hold of him and pulled his chin up so that he faced her at last, his eyes brimming over with tears.

"You're gonna charge on over there?" Paula said. "Disturb those good people in their home?"

"I don't know what I'm gonna do," he said.

God the anguish. A hot wire. "She's a seventeen-year-old white girl," she said. "How you think that's gonna work?"

"I don't know," he said, his voice rising in volume again, not in anger now but in pain. "I don't know what else to do. Let me go, Auntie. Let me go." He shook his head as if he could not believe what he was saying, as if his mouth had somehow separated from his body, from his mind, and what came from him now was from some other version of himself that he could not recognize or control and maybe this was the truth of it after all for had she not felt the same way so very long ago and did she not wish she could feel that way again one day. Here was her nephew, sweet and kind, his heart breaking in his chest right there in her doorway.

"Just wait, honey. Wait until tomorrow. Another day. Can you do that?"

She stood clutching his collar and his hot, fevered, exhausted eyes met her own. "No," he said. "I need to tell her."

"Tell her what?"

"Everything."

MARY LOU

Her game improved over the weeks that followed, in large part because she listened closely to Tom and Cheryl and Betty and John Hardiman and others and tried hard to put their advice into practice, even watching instructional bowling videos on the internet in the evenings when she was home alone. Sometimes this backfired and she bowled much worse than she might have had she simply slung the ball down the center of the lane, but she persevered, not only with her mind, her concentration, but with her body as well and she found, much to her surprise, that she had come to feel a kind of fluidity in bones and muscles she had mostly forgotten existed. At first her right arm and shoulder ached so powerfully in the days afterward she spent each night collapsed onto the sofa with a package of frozen peas melting against the pain. But that too faded and it occurred to her at some point that she must have been getting stronger, at least in that one arm, to be able to throw the heavy ball down the lane again and again without the pain that had once followed.

Her team made her want to do better, to be better, not in a way that felt like shame but instead like care, perhaps even love. They were happy to see her when she came into the cavernous space from the cold black slate of the parking lot. "Hey hey, Mary Lou," Betty might say. "How're things with your mom?"

"Oh jeez," Mary Lou might say in return. And she would tell them, tell the lot of them, about her troubles there, about her mother's anger toward her but then also of spying the woman smiling and laughing with her geriatric peers, gathered around a television or engaged in some arcane card game. During the months in which her mother had lived in her home, Mary Lou had asked her many times if she wanted to play a game with her or watch television together but her mother would only bark out some irritated response. And yet in those instances when Mary Lou saw her at the retirement home, especially at a distance, from across the room, her mother was often watching something they might well have enjoyed together on the sofa, her mood casual and flirty and funny in ways that Mary Lou could barely remember from her own distant childhood and which brought a hard lump of disappointment to her throat.

But none of this concerned her as much as the crushing reality that, with the end of March, the league schedule had reached its conclusion. It felt as if she had finally attained something worthwhile; that it was bowling of all things was more surprise than embarrassment. Bowling had saved her. Tom and Cheryl and Betty and even John Hardiman and all the rest of them, the competition fierce and friendly and boozy all at once. She could not have articulated what had been lacking in her life but this had filled it and now it was ending, or had already ended but for what Tom Bailey called Awards Night. She thought this meant that the league's winning team would get a trophy or something and that they would all applaud and raise their plastic beer cups toward the ceiling but after the bowling was over—a significantly boozier night than their normal league games—she found there was a fair amount more merriment and whimsy to the awards than she had anticipated. The big trophy for the winning team went to the Lickety Splits, a team composed of line welders from the factory and to which they all applauded with abandon. John Hardiman received a special award for his perfect game and then a second award for being the player with the most strikes. But there were others too. When they called out that they would give an award to the bowler with the lowest score, Mary Lou felt her heart begin to sink. She must have betrayed her feeling because Tom Bailey leaned over to her and put his hand on her shoulder. "Watch Bart over there," he said.

She found the man he meant, a squat, pale figure with a ridiculous mustache like some villain from a silent movie. When the award was announced, Bart Rich named as its recipient, he leapt to his feet, threw his ball cap in the air and crowed like a rooster, hands up like he had just won the lottery.

Tom Bailey laughed. They all did. Betty and Cheryl clapped and one of them handed Mary Lou another beer.

Dick Anderson, the Bowl-O-Rama's owner, was almost done with the awards but Mary Lou did not want the night to end. There would be a brief respite between this run of games and the beginning of the next, but she wondered if they would want her back. She did not know how to tell them how much these nights meant to her and did not want to admit that they had had such meaning, that bowling had saved her from a loneliness so deeply rooted in her soul that she had ceased to think of it as something that could change but instead had come to understand that it was the very center of her, that she would always feel this way, that she would always be alone.

"Well, there's just one more award here at the end," Dick Anderson was saying now. He swept his hand through his hair and looked out at the gathered bowlers, twenty or so of them in all. Tom Bailey sat forward now and when Mary Lou glanced over at him he winked at her.

"We've got one nice lady who has earned our treasured pin for most improved bowler this time through and that lady is a member of the Flamin' Cheeseballs over there in the back."

The fact that this was her team, hers and Tom's and Cheryl's and Betty's, did not sink in at first, Dick Anderson's voice continuing: "She came in here not knowing how to bowl much at all and this session her score improved by nearly forty points on average. Forty points, people. Take note. Dedication and perseverance pays off. Come and get your pin, Mary Lou Miller."

Her team erupted in wild applause. Indeed it sounded as if the whole hall had joined in that raucous celebration, Mary Lou looking toward the front of the room and then to Tom and Betty and Cheryl and back to the front again. "Well, Mary Lou," Tom said, "better get up there before Hardiman steals it from you."

She was smiling, smiling so broadly she wondered if she looked crazed, her face, her whole body, suffused with sudden heat as she made her way to the front and was presented with a wooden bowling pin signed by the members of her team. Someone had drawn a wedge of cheese with flames coming off it at the base and had written the team's name in bright red letters through that fire. Betty's signature. Cheryl's. Tom Bailey's. She returned to her seat with Dick Anderson's voice echoing out somewhere behind her, telling everyone in the room to rack up one more set on the house and that the bar would be open until people decided to get on home.

"You got an award," Tom Bailey said to her as she returned to their little cluster of chairs on lane 8.

"As if you didn't know," Mary Lou said. "You guys could've warned me."

"Where's the fun in that?" Betty said.

"It's all about the surprise," Cheryl said.

"Gonna be hard to beat your handicap when we start up again next week," Betty said.

She looked at the three of them, Tom nursing a beer, the others smiling, Cheryl looking off down the lane at the pins in their tight triangle. Mary Lou tried to hold back her tears, taking in a great breath of air and holding it and then exhaling, slowly. "The teams are all the same?" she said.

"Mostly," Tom said. "You're coming back, right?"

"Can I?" she said and then held her breath once more.

"Oh you can't escape now," Betty said.

"She's right," Cheryl said. "There's no escaping the Flamin' Cheeseballs."

"It's pretty much a cult," Betty said.

"It's true," Cheryl said. "We're like broke-ass Scientologists."

"You're freaking me out," Tom Bailey said. "Maybe I should see if I can slip on over to the Pinheads."

"Don't even think about it, buster," Betty said.

"Yeah, we've killed for less," Cheryl said.

They all laughed then, Mary Lou too.

"Well, Mary Lou," Tom Bailey said now. "What do you say? Still a Flamin' Cheeseball?"

"My choices are being murdered or being a Cheeseball?"

"Sounds about right," Tom said.

"I guess I'll have to think about it," Mary Lou said smiling.

And she was still smiling when she returned home, and still smiling when she checked her messages on the landline, the recorded voice at first failing to make any sense at all, although just at the end, just before she pressed the button to repeat the message, there came into her a feeling of falling, as if the floor of the house had given way and she was tumbling down some dark pit in the earth, the message starting over again, listening now, listening and understanding that it was the voice of one of the attendants at her mother's nursing home.

When she arrived at the hospital a half hour later it was to be told that her mother was dead.

ANTHONY SHAW

He did not take his auntie's car but instead ran the black streets, ran them like a madman, knowing all the while that his urgency was wholly out of proportion to the situation. He could call her. Or text. Or simply wait until he next saw her at the Perk or elsewhere, might let the burning of his heart cool to some warm ember. Even as he ran he wondered at what he was doing and why. What would he say when he arrived at the door and knocked and stood there as it opened and revealed, not Jane, not Jane herself for that would be too easy, but Jane's father, Tom Bailey? For already had come the strip of broken concrete that led to the door, that path demarcating some interminable distance he could hardly fathom, his mind continuing to waffle between incredulity and the strange sense he had of being some creature other than himself, possessed, that is, of a surety that could not possibly be his own for he was not sure, not about this, not about anything, and yet he was sure nonetheless, certain, his feet taking him across the cracked concrete to the wooden stairs and finally to the landing, his knocking accompanied by the thought again that Jane's father would look at him in confusion and wonderment the moment he opened the door.

But it was not Tom Bailey who appeared, nor Jane herself, nor even Jane's little brother, whose meeting had led Anthony, for reasons that now seemed utterly absurd, to wonder at the whole of the relationship, the boy's presence there in front of the coffeeshop those weeks before seeming to break whatever enchantment Anthony had woven for himself, their meetings, his and Jane's, sequestered, as they had been, upon quiet and public town streets, not really alone but at the same time totally and completely separate from any influence but that of each other. And even though each day he saw Jane's father at the factory, most days even sharing those few moments of their cigarette break on the windswept bench under the old oak, it was Charlie's presence in front of the coffeeshop that finally broke what had come to feel as a secret hymn, not because the boy was more important than the father but because he had appeared at the beginning of their joint solitude, not intruding upon it but simply there, present, and thus reminding him that the world through which they walked was real and filled with the same set of rules and prohibitions and expectations that had always governed it back through to God's creation.

Then there had been the kiss, the kissing, the frantic groping in the front seat of his auntie's car, this too added to the weight of it, the feeling that he had been indentured to some situation that had grown quickly out of his control until it had become the sole and complete purpose of his being, a relationship that he wanted, craved, needed, needed more than he could ever remember needing anything, although that was untrue for it felt in some way the mirror and opposite of the desolation that had come in the wake of Rudy's death, the great vacancy that had manifested itself not in the moment of the death, the killing, but in the days and weeks and months afterward when he, Anthony, would think of texting his friend, each time experiencing anew that vacancy and each time knowing that it was growing within him, within and without because it had passed through his flesh, no longer contained by him at all but containing him wholly and entirely. This was what, how, Jane had come to mean to him, not the vacancy but its reverse, the apotheosis of which was, had to be, that moment in the car. If he could have somehow pressed her body into his flesh, he would have done so, not sexually—although he had thought of nothing else even before that night—but in terms of his soul or spirit or whatever else came between his mind and his heart, his mind telling him that all of it, in the most basic of terms, was wrong, the repercussions of which would not only excoriate Jane but might put him in mortal danger for had the police not already picked him up once for the simple act of walking? (And yet he had run through the night like a fugitive.) But his heart wanted to text her, to talk to her, to walk with her at his side all night, every night, every day too. The space between was the whole of it, inarticulate and magnificent, a location where words failed because it was no location at all and never had been. God if only Rudy was here to talk to about this. He would not even supply a solution but instead would just listen and say something like, "Damn," and that would be enough.

The woman at the door must have been Jane's mother, a figure wrapped in a thick bathrobe with a blanket over her shoulders. Her eyes were Jane's eyes: wide open and dazzlingly blue. "Hello, Mrs. Bailey," he said. He had pulled a sock hat on over the bristle of his hair but he removed it now and held it before him in his hands. He was out of breath, panting. "My name's Anthony. Anthony Shaw," he said. "I'm sorry to bother you at night like this but I was hoping to speak with Jane."

"You want to speak with Janey?" she said, her head dipping slightly as if to make the request fit in her thoughts.

"Yes, ma'am," Anthony said.

"And who are you again?"

He told her and she asked him what his business was and he told her he and Jane—Janey—were friends.

"From school?" her mother said.

"No, I . . . uh . . . already graduated," Anthony said. He wrung the hat between his hands like it was something he might crush to pieces there. "I actually work with your husband at the factory."

"You work with Tom?"

"Yeah. Is he home?"

"He's bowling," she said.

"Right," he said. "It's Tuesday. They crazy about bowling over there." He smiled. Then said, "They are, I mean. Crazy."

"Hang on," she said now. She stepped away from the door, leaving it open, and when he did not come through it she called back to him, "Come on in. It's too cold to stand out there. Come in and have a seat."

She moved through the house into some hallway that was, from where Anthony stood, a kind of cave. Off to his right, the television murmured, someone laughing through the speaker. He stepped forward into the room and pulled the door closed. The house looked like anyone's: a worn sofa with a few sagging pillows, a thick armchair, its cushion pressed flat, knickknacks on a little shelf above the television, the screen itself showing some white people in an apartment somewhere, one of them gesticulating wildly while the others looked on, eyes wide. He wondered what he looked like there as he lowered himself to the sofa.

He did not hear her approach from the hall. It seemed to him as if she had simply materialized out of his own desire. "What are you doing here?" she said. And he was on his feet, the hat once more clenched in his hands.

"Hi," he said.

She said his name and then asked him again why he was there and he looked at her and there was nothing he could say, his words emptying out of him all at once like a flood and he was left mute and impossible.

"Is everything OK?" she said.

"I just . . ." he mumbled. "I just . . . you know . . . I just wanted to see you."

"I thought you didn't want to see me."

"No," he said, "I mean yes, that's what I said but . . . look, can we sit down for a minute?"

She watched him, unmoving, for a long moment, and then finally nodded. He lowered himself to the sofa once more and she beside him, a full cushion between them.

"My auntie said you came by," he said then.

"I did. Why are you sweaty?"

"I ran here."

"Why?"

"Just . . . just . . ." He breathed. "My auntie . . . she told you that us two taking a break was a good idea."

"She told me a lot more than that," she said.

He nodded. "She's looking out for me," he said.

"She's looking out for me," Jane said now.

Again he nodded, more emphatically, his head bobbing hard as if on a string. "That's right, that's right," he said.

"Why are you here, Anthony?"

"I guess I thought . . . maybe . . . that I'd made a mistake. I thought maybe if I didn't see you or talk to you or anything that you'd just, you know—I mean, I'd stop, I guess, wanting to see you and talk to you."

He glanced up at her briefly and she was looking away, toward the window, that black glass plane reflecting back the room in which they sat as if it were a veil of ghosts.

"You know, like, when we were texting and all, it was like, you were the last thing I thought about every night and, you know, I started to—well, I guess it was, you know, I don't know, I mean—I know we said we were just friends and all but, I don't know, I just thought maybe that I shouldn't be thinking about you regular like that. Every night before I sleep, I mean. But it doesn't matter if I get that text or not. I still do. Think about you, I mean. You know?"

She was quiet but when he looked up from the sock hat he continued to knead between his hands he saw that her eyes were turned toward his own now, blue and wide like some sea he could not imagine. That this was her, that this was the girl to whom his heart had run felt a wonder to him. But here she was.

"I don't know what else to say," he said now. His eyes jumped from her face to the window to his hat to her face again, her gaze so intent that to stare back was to send a heat through him.

"I don't really know what you're saying," she said now.

"OK, OK," he said, shaking his head. "What I'm saying . . . I mean, what I'm trying to say, really . . ." He felt himself shaking inside, a quick trembling that seemed to come from somewhere behind his lungs and felt like it was rising all through him at once like wings and not like wings, like himself bursting all at once into feathers. "What I'm trying to say, Jane . . ." he began again and inside, in that feathered self, came a brightness, a courage that was also a kind of loss for what could he do but tell her the truth of it, beyond which there was only a return to what had been before, that sense that he had lost something so precious that it could never be regained. "What I'm trying to say, Jane," he said at last, "is that I think—I like you. I mean, you know, like I really like you. Like a lot."

There was a brief sound from the hallway, something like a muffled squeak. Jane sat motionless, her eyes on his own, and then drifting down toward the carpet. He did not know what he should do now, if he should rise to leave or sit there with his hands still clutching the sock hat, his body beginning to perspire under all the layers of his clothes. Speak to me, he wanted to say now. Please, Jane. Just say something. But he could not speak, his mouth dry and his heart thumping slow and steady in his chest.

When her voice came at last it was so quiet that he almost did not believe it had sounded at all. "I missed you," she said.

"I missed you too, Jane," he said. "I missed you too." And when he reached for her hand she took it and its warmth, its pressure, pulled him to her side and she leaned into him, his coat crunching against her weight, his arms around her as if they had been there all the while. Their lips met only briefly. She placed a hand on his cheek.

They were still holding each other like that when Charlie crossed through the living room, hardly glancing at the two of them there on the sofa. "Hey," he said simply.

"Hey," Anthony said in response. He had loosed his hold on Jane the moment there had been movement in the room. "OK so I should go. But I'm going to text you."

"Yes," she said, and when they embraced and their eyes locked, he leaned forward and kissed her again, a kiss dry and soft and warm and which seemed to run all the through his body as if he had been plucked like a harp string and now vibrated everywhere at once. "Bye," she whispered to him.

He said the same and then stood and moved to the door. When he turned one last time to look at her his eyes caught the shape of her mother in the hall. She stood just beyond the edge of the light, tucked into the shadow, still in her robe with the blanket hanging over her. How long she had stood there he did not know but when his eyes met hers she raised a brief hand to him. "Goodnight," she said.

"Goodnight," he said in response.

Then he opened the door and blew out into the cold night. Already his phone rang with the arrival of a text.

hi, she wrote.

And he: hi.

Is this not all that need be said?

RASHID

For most of that week he had thought about the egging and the toilet paper, how his steely, brave older sister had, after returning from the cold, besmirched lawn, gone into the bathroom and wept for the better part of an hour. His sister's reaction had troubled him not because he had never seen her cry—as his brother, he had seen her cry too many times to count—but because she seemed to view the occurrence as a personal attack, as if someone had chosen their house because of a vendetta against her, personally, and the fact that she could think such a thing meant, to Rashid, that she harbored this possibility as a deep and enduring fear. She was, not only to Rashid but, he thought, to most of the students at the high school, considered one of the popular girls, so the notion that she might be at the receiving end of such a banal indignity as having her home egged and TP'ed felt, at least to Rashid himself, a totally foreign and unwarranted idea.

His father had taken the car to a detailing shop and the yard service pulled all the toilet paper from the trees and hedges and power sprayed the front of the house, after which the house and front yard and the car were returned, once more, to normal. And yet something in Rashid himself had broken that morning. His father had continued to mumble out his wonderment that someone, anyone, would do such a thing but of course Rashid knew who had done it, although he still did not know why, not until he overheard his mother and father talking soon after the yard service had finished their work.

"What about that Sam Simmons?" his mother had said.

"He's a grown man," his father had answered. "He wouldn't stand in someone's front yard in the middle of the night throwing toilet paper into a tree. It just doesn't make any sense."

And yet, of course, it made perfect sense to Rashid. He did not know Sam Simmons, of course, but it took little effort to put the last names together.

He had been terrified of T.K. Simmons ever since that terrible encounter in the bathroom at the basketball tournament, had gone to great lengths to avoid being caught alone, but after the long day that had begun with discovering the toilet paper and eggs, his feelings about T.K. had changed. It was not that he was no longer afraid, for in many ways he felt just as afraid as he ever had, but rather that what was happening to him went far beyond the pettiness of some schoolyard bully but could affect, had already effected, his mother and father and his sister and even his grandparents and indeed had actually started with his grandfather's overhearing that terrible terrible phrase, the two words that, when they had first escaped his grandfather's lips, made Rashid nearly shout in protest. And now here was that same terrible man's terrible son taking out his own misplaced anger, not on his own racist father but on the son of the man who had fired him.

He did not know what he would do upon seeing T.K. again, although there had been moments in which he thought he could crush T.K. Simmons with his bare hands. And yet for all that week there was no trace of him. It was as if his tormentor had, just after the indignity of the attack on Rashid's family home, vanished.

So when that voice came shouting at him across the parking lot he did not really expect to find that hulking figure, instead assuming that a teacher had spotted him. "Hey!" the voice had come. Just that. Only that. And Rashid turned. Across the lot, toward the entrance to the science building, he thought he caught a glimpse of a figure, someone by the stairs, but then his eye fixed on T.K.'s great, looming shape, cutting through parked cars like an icebreaker through frozen seas. A week earlier, he might have run. Now he stood and watched. I am bent, he thought. I am bent against you. He opened his mouth, his voice coming at first in an almost silent wheeze. He sucked in a breath and when he shouted again he was surprised at its volume: "You threw eggs at my house!" he yelled, his mouth going dry even as he spat the words, the next word collapsing in volume but still audible. "Asshole."

T.K. had arrived now and stood before him, his great lumbering shape so large that Rashid's eyes were hardly at the level of the man's sternum. "I'm an asshole?" T.K. said, his voice booming. "You people ruined my life."

"You ruined your own life," Rashid said. He was shaking now but hoped T.K. did not notice.

"All you raghead fuckers should just go back to fucking Iraq."

"Pakistan," Rashid said.

"Fuck you, Pakistan," T.K. said.

"No fuck you," Rashid said. He took a step forward, his feet moving without conscious thought, and to his surprise T.K. actually took a step back at his approach. "You came to my house when my grandparents are sleeping and think it's funny to throw eggs into my father's car. You should be ashamed of yourself."

"You people ruined my life," T.K. said. "You know that? We're moving. My senior fucking year and we're moving. Today's my last day at school."

"Good," Rashid said. "I hope you have a terrible life."

In a way, he had been waiting for T.K. to make his move, knowing that once that happened their transaction would be over, for Rashid knew that he would not be able to stop any kind of physical altercation. It would roll over him like a wave. He steeled himself for the blow, sucking in his stomach and trying to hold fast to some sense of pride. His grandfather was Wasim Marwat, a man who had come from nothing and had risen to prominence through fortitude, strength, and, yes, courage. And how could Rashid quail in the face of this mindless idiot with that great lineage at his back? He closed his eyes. Waited.

"What the fuck are you doing?" T.K.'s voice said in the blackness.

"Go ahead," Rashid said.

"Go ahead and what?"

"Hit me."

"Hit you?"

Rashid waited.

"Fucking raghead fuck," T.K. said.

He waited. There was nothing. The wind in the trees, the street, the more distant sounds of his peers on the grounds of the school. He opened his eyes slowly, the light a tentative slit at first and then the whole of the parking lot flashing into being before him. A few dozen yards away, T.K.'s back pushed through the cars toward the outer edge of the parking lot and finally disappeared from view.

For a long while he could not move, the fear overtaking the rage now so that his whole body trembled, the force of it so strong that it felt as if his skeleton was trying to escape from his flesh. He wanted to shout, to scream, to do anything, but instead he merely stood there, partially leaning against the rear fender of a car he did not know or recognize. From somewhere very far away, the school bell sent up its long peal into the sky.

CHARLIE

They had smoked at the edge of the parking lot many times, sometimes cigarettes, sometimes the mediocre bud they managed to buy from fellow students, their hideout a small patch of concrete half under the stairwell that exited the science building. Most of it did little more than produce a lethargy and vague headache but the weed that Kent now produced from a plastic sandwich bag was like nothing Charlie had ever seen: pale green and sticky with resin and emitting an odor so strong and sweet that Charlie immediately craned his head about to make sure there was no one in sight.

"Holy shit," he said. "Where'd you get that?"

"My dad," Kent said simply.

"Does he know you took it?"

"Hell no," Kent said. "And if he finds out he'll go nuts."

"Maybe you should put it back."

"I found his stash," Kent said. "There's like twenty times this much. And a bunch of other shit too."

"Like what?"

"Check it out," Kent said. From his backpack he produced a small baggy filled with a pale tan powder.

"What is it?"

"You don't know?"

He shook his head. "Is that—is that heroin?"

Kent shrugged.

"Jeez," Charlie said. "Why do you have that?"

"I don't know," he said. "Just took it."

"Shit, isn't he gonna flip when he finds out?"

"He won't even notice," Kent said. "There's, like, a whole big stash of all kinds of shit there."

"Jeez, man," Charlie said now. "I didn't know that was going on."

"Yeah you did," Kent said simply.

He returned the baggie to his backpack and packed the bowl of his little glass pipe and now lit the bud and pulled his thumb off the tiny carburetor hole and sucked in the smoke and then handed the pipe to Charlie, who sucked its end quickly so as to avoid relighting the bowl. They both held their breath and then exhaled, coughing faintly.

"There's that asshole T.K.," Kent said now, looking out past the stone stairwell to where T.K. Simmons was thumping across the parking lot, his letterman jacket appearing a size too small for his giant frame. "I wish I had something I could throw at him."

"He'd crush you like a can," Charlie said.

"Only if he caught me," Kent said. He made his hand into the shape of a gun and pointed it to where T.K. walked, mimicking cocking back the hammer and pulling the trigger. "Fuck you," he said absently, quietly, and then, in a singsong voice: "You suck my balls. You eat my dick. You eat my dick's balls."

They watched the whole thing unfold. When Rashid did not immediately run, Charlie could feel his heart draining out of his chest. "Aw no, man," Kent whispered. The pipe had gone out and now a small plume of delicate smoke rose into the air beside him. "Don't stop walking. Don't stop, man. Run. Run, you idiot. Run."

That the small brown figure had stood his ground against the great white whale seemed impossible and yet this was what happened, like David standing before Goliath, only there was no sling nor stone in Rashid Marwat's hand. Kent was so excited by the unfolding occurrence in the parking lot that he began hopping up and down, his thin wiry frame like that of a gangly puppet being jerked about on a string, returning to stasis only when it was over and T.K. had stomped off across the parking lot, leaving Rashid whole and intact.

"Holy Christ," Charlie said. "That was nuts. 'I hope you have a terrible life.' Man, that Rashid. He's kind of a badass, right?"

"T.K.," Kent said. "Did he say . . . he said he was moving?"

"Yeah, something like that," Charlie said. And then, in a deep, lumbering voice: "Today's my last day at school." He laughed but when his eyes found Kent again he saw that his friend's face had gone the color of ash. "What?" he said. "You buggin'?"

"I gotta go," he said.

"Go where?"

Kent stood up and the pipe was in his pocket. "Church," he said.

"Now? Why?"

"I gotta go," he said again. And then he stepped through the gap in the foliage and strode out into the wet parking lot.

For a long moment, Charlie merely watched him, unsure of what to do, Kent's loose frame seeming possessed of a will and purpose Charlie had seldom seen, his book bag flapping against his back with each hard rhythmic step. At last he sprinted to follow, charging through the cars at a diagonal that took him away from where Rashid continued to stand as if dazed.

"What are you doing?" he said when he had once more reached his friend.

"They're moving," he said.

"Yeah, so what?"

Kent looked at him now and Charlie was shocked to see that his friend's eyes were red, his cheeks wet.

"What's going on?" Charlie said.

"They're moving," Kent said again, a wobble in his voice.

They did not speak after that, continuing their walk down the block to the great brick shape of the church, Charlie starting to untangle what T.K.'s words might have meant to his friend but still not really understanding why Kent would have such a reaction. He hit the doors to the church hard, their shapes flying open with a bang, and came down the hall walking so quickly that Charlie had to jog to keep up with him.

Charlie did not know if there would yet be anyone at all in the afterschool room as it was only noon but when Kent opened the door they found three or four children within and the other teacher, Mrs. Schmidt, tidying up a stack of stuffed animals in the corner. "Hi boys," she said when they came into the room. "You're early."

"Where's Mrs. Simmons?" Kent said.

"Oh," she said, "I guess you didn't hear, honey. Amy's not working here anymore."

"Why not?"

"Her and her family are moving to Cincinnati," she said.

"Why?"

"Work. Her husband got some kind of job out there. Whole family's moving."

"Will she be back?"

"Here? No, she cleaned out her stuff a few days ago."

Charlie could not see Kent's face but something in it brought Mrs. Schmidt forward. "I'm sorry, honey," she said. "I'm sure she wanted to see you before she left."

But Kent was already moving again, out into the hallway, Charlie running to keep up. "Do you know where they live?" Kent said, still moving forward.

"I think so," Charlie said. "Out on the edge of town."

"Show me," Kent said.

"It's a long ways," Charlie said.

"Will you show me or not?" There was an edge in his voice now, a fierce, wild desperation.

"Yeah, yeah, OK," Charlie said.

He led them out away from school, away from their own homes and across streets they knew but did not much travel since there was no location on the far side of those locales, no store or park or river to set as a lodestone, the streets there the same as any other in their town: great bare trees hunched grayly over houses battered by winter after winter, their walls streaked with water stains, roofs patched with old plywood and windows occasionally blocked by torn cardboard roughly duct-taped in place. An occasional car moved up the center of the asphalt and they would step to the broken sidewalk for its passing before returning to the road once more.

It took nearly an hour to reach the Simmonses' and Charlie was relieved when they finally did, relieved because the long silent walk was now over and relieved too because he was not entirely sure he would be able to find the place at all. His father had brought him there a few times when he had been younger but that had been a long time ago now and beyond those places he and Kent had skated or walked his map of the town was hazy at best. But there was the home, a double-wide trailer, with its little wooden foundation and the gravel parking area nettled with clumps of wet grass and upon which stood an old brown Oldsmobile Charlie thought he had seen parked at the church.

"This is it," he said.

Kent nodded and climbed the short run of stairs to the landing and knocked three times on the door. Charlie stood below, watching, but when Mrs. Simmons opened the door he moved slowly up the stairs to stand just behind his friend.

"Boys," she said. "Why aren't you in school?"

"They said you're moving," Kent said, his voice breathless. "They said you're not coming back."

"I kept hoping I'd see you," she said. "You haven't been by in a while."

"My dad," he said. "He makes me come home."

"I know, honey," she said. "I know." She paused, looking at him. "You'd better come in for a little while," she said now. "Sam's off getting more boxes. But you can visit until he gets back."

They entered the trailer. The front room, Charlie saw, was composed almost entirely of boxes. They lined the walls and rose in stacks along the counter. The furniture remained in place but seemed utterly useless now, as if a kind of afterthought, as if the whole purpose of the space was only to store boxes and nothing else.

"Does my mom know?" Charlie said.

"Of course, Charlie," Mrs. Simmons said.

"When are you leaving?"

"Couple days," she said. "Just finishing up and we'll be on the road."

It was silent for a moment, the room dead around them, as if no one had ever lived here at all.

"I don't have any pop. You want some water?"

"Cincinnati?" Kent said at last.

"That's right, honey," Mrs. Simmons said. "Cincinnati. You ever been?"

He shook his head. Charlie did too, although Mrs. Simmons was not looking at him now, only at Kent.

"Funny thing is, I've never been either," she said.

"Do you want to?" Kent said.

"Move? Not at all."

"Then why are you?"

"Well, you have to go where there's work. We can't live here on just my income."

"Don't they pay you at church?"

"It's not enough. Plus Sam can't just sit around at home while I go to work. Men just aren't really cut out to do that."

"But can't you—I mean maybe if we helped or—couldn't he do something at church or something?"

"You're a sweetheart, Kent Westin," she said. "You really are. It's not that easy."

Silence again. Charlie shuffled his feet. He did not know what this was, what he was supposed to do or say, wondered too why he had come inside at all.

"What am I supposed to do?" Kent said, his voice continuing to wobble.

"Oh honey," Mrs. Simmons said and to Charlie's horror he realized that Kent had begun to sob, his shoulders hunched forward and breath coming in ragged terrible gasps. Mrs. Simmons's arms went around him, his frame collapsing under her so that her smaller, thicker body enveloped him as he continued to weep.

She shushed him and held him and stroked his hair and finally pulled a chair from under the table and led him to it and then another for herself and she sat close enough that their knees touched and his hands were in hers. "Honey," she said, "you're gonna be all right."

"I don't think I am," he said and Charlie's flesh prickled at the sound of those words, the anguish they held, the fear.

"You will be," she said. "You've got a friend who'll stand by you for one thing. Isn't that right, Charlie?"

"Yeah," Charlie said quickly.

"That's no small thing," Mrs. Simmons said. "And you got the church. Don't forget that."

"But you're leaving," he said.

"You don't come to help out at church because of me," she said now. "Those kids love you. They do, Kent. They love you. And you just bring such a joy to them. It's a gift you have. You know that? It's a gift. You remember that. Don't give up on that. Those kids need you. And you need them. You hear me?"

"OK," he said.

"You'll keep on with your work there?"

"Yes."

"Promise me."

"I promise."

"The Lord walks with you, honey. He does. He carries you when it feels like you can't carry yourself. You just gotta let him. And I know you got troubles at home. I know that. But you gotta have faith that things'll get better. And they will. I promise you. It's not always gonna be like this."

And now there were tears in Mrs. Simmons's eyes too, Charlie looking back and forth between them, wondering if he should simply move to the door and disappear outside but also not knowing how to do so or even if it was what he should do. He would stand by his friend. That much was true and certain. And so for the moment he literally did just that.

"You're a good boy, Kent Westin," she said now. "You're one of the best people I know. You hear me?"

"Yes."

"Do you believe me?"

"I don't know."

"Do you think I would lie to you?"

"No."

"Then I must be telling you the truth," she said, and now she smiled through her tears and through his.

From outside came the sound of crunching gravel and the low hum of a car coming to a stop.

"There's my husband," she said. "You gonna be OK?"

"I think so."

"Well, I guess that's the best any of us can do," she said. "You'll keep helping the kids?"

"Yeah," he said. His tears had lessened now and he wiped at his face. From outside: the low thunk of a car door closing.

"Charlie," she said now, "your friend might need some extra help for a while. You can do that, right?"

"Sure," he said.

"Don't forget that," Mrs. Simmons said. "Either of you. That's one thing you have no matter what."

"OK," Charlie said.

"All right then," Mrs. Simmons said. She released Kent's hands and stood, Kent following a moment after, his hair swinging across his face so that Charlie could not see his eyes. They moved toward the door together as if by some common desire to flee. And perhaps that was exactly how it felt. "You boys be good," she said.

"OK, Mrs. Simmons," Charlie said.

"Bye-bye, honey," she said, pulling the door open. A flood of bright light poured into the room.

Kent said nothing more, stepping onto the wooden platform and moving down the stairs without another word and without looking back. Mr. Simmons stood in the bed of his pickup, throwing flat boxes off to the side and into the gravel, pausing for a moment as Kent passed and then continued with his work.

"He gonna be all right?" Mrs. Simmons asked Charlie in the doorway.

"I don't know," he said. "His dad has drugs. All kinds of stuff. There's heroin or whatever. I don't know."

"That so?"

He nodded. "Don't tell anyone," he said then and in truth he wished he had not opened his mouth at all for what would Mr. Westin do to him if he discovered he had been spreading their secrets.

"I won't," she said. "Cross my heart."

And then he was gone down the stairs, his feet through the gravel and out onto the street, Kent's shadow dancing behind him against the long strip of the road.

MARY LOU

Her mother had died not, as it turned out, as a result of her rapidly advancing Alzheimer's but from a brain aneurism that may have been secretly threatening her life for many years. Mary Lou took the rest of the week off of work, intending to return on Monday but when that morning came she found she could not manage to climb out of bed. She could feel all her weight, the heaviness of her bones, the rolls of flesh, thick around muscle, could feel it as a solid mass all around her. That afternoon she ate a gallon of ice cream and when she was done she felt sick enough to vomit, although she did not vomit but only lay there, no longer weeping but thinking of the smile she had seen on her mother's face from across the room, that bright arc of joy. And why not for her? Why not ever, in her life, for her? "I understand," Mr. Marwat said to her, the accent in his voice feeling, in that moment, like some warm lifeline to which she could almost hold fast. "You take as much time as you need. Really."

On Wednesday night the phone rang and she lifted it from the receiver and offered a weary hello, expecting it to be the nursing home or the insurance or the funeral director, but the voice that came to her was Tom Bailey's. He said her name and she said his and then he told her that he had heard what had happened, that her mother had passed, and he wanted to know if she was all right.

"I'm fine," she said. "I'm just, you know, a little overwhelmed."

"You've got some help there?"

"Help for what?"

"I don't know—cooking dinner? Doing the dishes? You know—that kind of stuff."

"No, I'm fine, Tom," she said.

"You got family around here?"

"No," she said. "Cousins in Indiana somewhere."

"You're doing this alone?"

"I'll be all right," she said, but now her voice wobbled.

For a moment there was silence on the phone. She could hear the sound of a television through the tiny speaker, the sound reminding her of her mother yet again, of how the BarcaLounger still occupied its position in front of the TV in the spare room. "Hang on a minute," Tom Bailey said. She could hear a brief, muffled discussion; then he returned to the phone. "I'm coming over there," he said.

"Oh you don't have to do that," Mary Lou said, although the thought of it, of someone coming, anyone, made her heart race.

"Have you eaten?" he asked her.

"Tom," Mary Lou said.

"Have you eaten, Mary Lou?"

"No," she admitted. "Why?"

"Because I'm gonna come over there and make you dinner. Don't get excited—it's gonna be frozen pizza, 'cause that's what I've got, but we'll eat and then we can watch TV or something."

She was crying now, sobbing and she could not stop when Tom said her name again, asked her if it was all right that he was coming over, although he also said that he did not care if it was all right or not, that he was coming over anyway because that was what friends did and he was her friend.

He hung up and she lurched out of the bed and dressed and tried to control the great mass of tangles that her hair had become, tried to do something with her face, her swollen eyes, her puffy cheeks, her lips gone pale. "Fuck it," she said to herself. And then giggled at the sound of it, giggled even through her tears.

Tom arrived a few minutes later, his very bearing, his self, changing the color of the room all at once. "Well, heck, Mary Lou," he said in the doorway, a grocery bag in one hand and a six pack of beer under his arm. "I thought you'd look like hell on a bagel. But you look just fine. You're not trying to play me with some sob story just to get some free frozen pizza, are you?"

"Oh you," she said, smiling, already smiling, but also tears coming to her eyes. "I'm glad you're here."

"Hey, don't start," he said. "We've got all kinds of pepperoni to deal with first."

"OK," she said.

He turned the oven on and unwrapped the pizzas and put one and then another on the racks and set a timer. They sat at the kitchen table then and Tom uncapped a beer for himself and one for her. "Look," he said, "when the baby . . . you know . . . back at the end of October, well, people were super weird about it. I was super weird about it too, I guess. I didn't know if I wanted to talk about it or wanted not to talk about it." He sipped at his beer. She did the same. Then he said, "So we can talk about your mom if you want. Or we won't. It's up to you. And you can change your mind if you want. We can talk about something else and then if you want to talk about your mom we can do that too. I mean there's no rules. It's just, like, friends hanging out eating shitty pizza."

"I don't know what I want to talk about," she said. "Maybe we don't have to talk about anything?"

"That works too," he said. They sat in the silence of the kitchen now, nursing their beers. "Maybe we watch some TV?" he asked her.

"It's in my mom's room," Mary Lou said. "Or what used to be her room."

"Is that where you want it? The TV, I mean?"

"No, I guess not," she said. "I moved it in there for her. It used to be right there." She motioned through the doorway to the empty spot on a sideboard in the living room.

"You want me to move it back out here?"

"I can do that," she said. Then she looked at the empty space again. "No, yeah, OK. That would be great. If you could. Do that, I mean."

He set the bottle down without another word and rose and there came, from the bedroom that had been her mother's for nearly a year, sounds of motion and then Tom appeared again with the television in his arms. "There's a big chair in there," he said as he set the television in its former position on the sideboard. "That's probably from out here too, right?"

"Yeah," she said.

"Heavy?"

"Too heavy for me."

"Well, let me see what I can do about it."

It took them both to get the chair down the hall. Tom was concerned that they would scratch the floor but Mary Lou was well beyond such thoughts now. Part of her wanted to wrestle the chair all the way out the door and to throw it into the yard, perhaps soak it with lighter fluid. She and Tom could eat their pizza out on the soggy, frozen and refrozen lawn, watching the chair go to bright ruin in the night. But when they finally got the thing back into its former location it already seemed like a return to some reality she had held before her mother's arrival, before, that is, her mother had so painfully reminded her of all her own personal failings, her weight, her loneliness, her lack of real friends. She hated to think bad thoughts about people but there was, deep within her, a great wide sense of utter and total relief that her mother was dead. Even thinking such a thing brought tears to her eyes.

"Oh Mary Lou," Tom said.

As if in response to his saying her name the oven's timer went off with a bright bing.

"I'm a bad person," Mary Lou said.

"You know that's not true."

"I am, though," she said. "I'm a bad daughter, anyway."

"You had your mom live with you for a year. I don't think a bad daughter would have done that. Do you? You got to share that time with her at the end. That's something."

"Oh I wish it were that," Mary Lou said. "I feel bad saying this but really, my mother wasn't very nice to me."

He exhaled. "Well," he said, "that's more evidence that you're not a bad daughter. Taking care of a woman who doesn't treat you the way you deserve to be treated. That's something to feel good about."

"Is it?"

"Sure," Tom said. "Anyway, we don't get to pick our parents."

"That's the truth."

Tom pulled the pizzas from the oven, using a spatula and a fork to slide them back onto the tops of their own cardboard boxes. They smelled, to Mary Lou, simply amazing, like life itself wrought in bubbling cheese and pepperoni and crisp-edged crust and although she was ready, as she always was, for the disappointment to come, she was pleased to find that the taste was much the same as the smell.

"This is the best pizza I've ever had," she said when she had finished the first slice and had started in on the second.

Tom Bailey smiled. "You've lost your mind, Mary Lou," he said.

"I'm serious," she said, lifting another slice from the box lid. "I could eat ten of these right now." Her eyes flicked up to him then. "I guess I shouldn't say that," she said.

"Why not?"

"Well, you know, it's not like I'm skinny."

"Nope," Tom Bailey said. "You're not."

She felt a warmth of heat in her face. "It's embarrassing," she said.

"What is?"

"How much I eat."

"I didn't come here to starve you."

She looked down at her plate. The orange smears of grease. The flakes of crust. "How many pieces did you have so far?" she said.

"Four."

"Would you think I was gross if I told you I could eat all the rest by myself?"

"Go ahead," he said, smiling.

"No, you're not hearing me."

"I am hearing you. Would it make you feel better to eat the rest of the pizza?"

Her eyes were tearing up again now. "I don't know," she said. "Yes. I guess so."

"Well good," Tom Bailey said. "We're gonna need to order more. I guess I'll call Sal's. They deliver."

"Look at me," she said.

"I am looking at you, Mary Lou. I am."

"What are you doing?"

He shrugged. "I'm just trying to make you feel better," he said.

"By filling me up full of pizza?"

"Not all of it's for you," he said.

"But it's too much," she said. "Isn't it too much?"

"What?"

"Me eating and eating and eating. I try to stop, Tom. I've done WeightWatchers and all that. Jenny Craig. I can't stop."

"Why do you want to stop?"

"Because I'm a fat ass," she said. Now the tears really were coming.

"Who told you that?" Tom Bailey said and when Mary Lou did not respond he said, "Who called you that?"

"My whole life," she said simply.

"Well, it's bullshit."

"I'm fat," she said.

"So what?"

"I don't want to be."

"Why not?"

"Because I don't, all right. I don't want to be a fat person. I hate being fat. I hate how I am."

"Well, I don't think about you like that."

"What about Sam?"

"What about Sam?"

"He did, I'll bet."

"Sam's an asshole. Plus it wasn't like he was some skinny guy anyway."

"You know . . ." she said slowly, "I'm the one who told Mr. Marwat about, you know, the kinds of things he said."

Tom sat for a minute, chewing his pizza, drinking his beer. Then he said, "Well, it's not like you were saying something that wasn't true. You know? I always told Sam he had it coming."

"He wasn't a good person," Mary Lou said.

"Well, I wouldn't say that exactly," Tom said. "He just wanted to stop the clock."

"What do you mean?"

"Change," Tom said then. "He just couldn't stand it. Needed things to be the way they were when we was kids."

"I can understand that, in a way," Mary Lou said.

"Easy to find reasons to hate the boss even when he's not from Pakistan. But if he's a brown-skinned guy, it's even easier, you know?"

"Mr. Marwat's a good man," she said simply.

"I believe you."

For a time they sat in silence again, sipping at their beers and eating until the pizzas were gone. Tom leaned back in his chair. "Well, I'd better get these pizzas ordered," he said.

"You're just saying that to make me feel better."

"Might be," he said smiling. "Can't have the team go hungry. What's your favorite? Anchovies and artichokes? I'm kidding—no one likes that shit."

"I don't know. Maybe just, like, a combination?"

"Combo it is," he said, reaching into his pocket for his phone, scrolling through screens until he found the number and then pressing the call button. He asked some questions of the employee who had answered the phone and then ordered two large pizzas and gave the address.

"We can't eat that much," Mary Lou whispered.

"For the other Cheeseballs," he whispered back.

She did not understand what this could have meant but before he was done with the call she heard a door thump closed outside.

"They're here," he said, clicking his phone off and slipping it into his pocket once more.

"Who is?"

"Cheryl or Betty. Or both."

"Why are they here?"

"Because they're your team," he said as if this were obvious. "Like we said, you can't escape the Flamin' Cheeseballs."

"Oh my," she said. She felt herself suddenly lightheaded.

When the knock came and Mary Lou did not rise to answer its summons, Tom Bailey did, opening the door and greeting the two women as they entered. Betty carried a bottle of Jack Daniel's, Cheryl a supermarket bouquet wrapped in cellophane. "How you doing, sweetie?" Betty asked her.

And Mary Lou looked at them there, Flamin' Cheeseballs all and herself among them. They had come to her in the night of their own accord with alcohol and flowers of condolence and pizza and concern. And they had come bearing friendship too; this most surprising of all. It had been a long, long time since she had felt the way she felt in that moment, so long that she did not at first understand what that feeling was, what it meant to her, to the people who stood in her home, their figures lit as if from some heat she could almost see but which was yet invisible, pulsing, just out of reach, their hearts beating as one.

"I'm doing all right," she said at last and despite the reason her team had come to gather around her, she smiled. "I'm doing just fine."

KHALID

They had spent the day in Columbus and Rashid was with them, the boy seeming, for several weeks, as if he had entered some deep funk from which he could not clamber of his own accord, although it was also true that recent days had evidenced otherwise. It had been his grandmother, Khalid's mother, who had suggested letting the boy miss school so that he might, as a rare treat, join the men at jumma namaz, the Friday service at the mosque in Columbus that Khalid attended with regularity, his father having joined him ever since coming to live in America. The boy's secular education was an inviolable pact and neither Khalid nor Rafia allowed the boy to miss classes except in instances of illness, and even these were generally confirmed by thermometer; nonetheless, Khalid understood that his mother's suggestion spoke to something profoundly amiss in regards to his son and the fact that Rafia had readily agreed only served to confirm what they all tacitly knew: that Rashid had not been himself. Perhaps getting him out of the house for the day would do the boy some good.

On the other hand, having Rashid with them also meant that Khalid would not have opportunity to talk with his father in private, for Rafia had told him what his mother had said, that his father had lost everything. Khalid still could hardly believe such a thing could be true. They had had so much money in Lahore, not to extravagance but certainly to a level of comfort: a housekeeper and a cook, a car and driver, good tutors for Khalid when he had been a child, an entire world that spoke of economic security. How could all of that be gone?

Of course they were in the car together each morning and afternoon and even without that time Khalid could well have met with his father in his office, door closed, but he had not. In some ways he wondered if his mother had misinterpreted their financial situation. He wanted to hear the facts from the man himself and yet each time he was in a situation in which it might have been possible to broach the subject, he could not find the words. And to think that he had been afraid that his father would take over his beloved factory in some way, when what had actually occurred had been just the opposite, a turning away from all business dealings such that Khalid could not talk to his father about the factory at all. Khalid had come to realize that he had been, in some ways—in many ways—looking forward to having his father at hand, even beyond his own trepidation and nervousness at the man's power of will, had even imagined long discussions about the intricacies of the business. But the man who had stepped off the plane at Cleveland Hopkins seemed a sad, quiet ghost occupying his father's aged flesh.

The car ride to Columbus might have been silent had Rashid not been there. From the back seat, the boy had initiated a conversation about the mosque his grandparents had attended in Lahore, a conversation which elided into various aspects of his grandfather's professional life, a good many of which Khalid himself was unfamiliar. But even more than that, he realized, listening to them, that a comfortable familiarity had developed between the two, a relationship that surprised him. Khalid wondered where he fit into such an equation. Before his father had arrived in Ohio, Khalid might have claimed that he knew the man quite well, perhaps as well as any man can know another and yet, now that the old man was here, he did not think he knew him at all. And of Rashid: How little of his son's heart and soul he really understood. When he thought of him, he still thought of a boy sitting at the kitchen counter with his infernal laptop open playing some terrible film or pointless videogame. And yet there might well have been a whole world inside of his son. Khalid realized he did not even know the names of those terrible films or pointless videogames or what drew his son to them. At one point in the car, Rashid had given his grandfather his earbuds and pressed play. "Check this out, Daada-ji," he had said.

Khalid sat tense behind the wheel, wondering what it was that his son had foisted upon his aged elder. In the rearview mirror, the boy was smiling broadly, his eyes bright, brows raised.

"What is this?" Rashid's grandfather said. "They're speaking in Urdu?"

"That's right, Daada-ji," Rashid said. "They're from Karachi."

The old man listened for a time, staring out at the road. "Oh," he said, holding a brief hand to his forehead. "The language is so profane. It's terrible."

"You gave your Daada-ji something profane to listen to?" Khalid said.

But Rashid's grandfather waved a hand to quiet him. "So angry," he said. "Why are all these people so angry?"

"They're talking about—"

"What?"

Rashid fiddled with the controls, the song apparently pausing. "They're talking about life on the streets, Daada-ji. It's a serious topic."

"Why don't they just get jobs and work to improve themselves?"

"I don't know," Rashid said. "Maybe it's not that easy."

Khalid thought his father might counter this with something to indicate that it was, in fact, easy enough if one put his shoulder into it, but instead the old man nodded. "Well, that's true enough. What does this person call himself?"

"The Young Stunners," Rashid said. "It's a group."

His grandfather sighed. "Press play again then," he said.

For a long while no one spoke, the old man listening. Khalid sometimes glancing into the mirror to catch sight of his son. "Real talk, no comic," the boy's grandfather said at one point. "What does that mean?"

"He means he's telling the truth," Rashid said, smiling.

"But is he? How do we know?"

"I guess we don't," Rashid said.

When the song was apparently over, his grandfather returned the headphones. "It's still terrible," he said simply. "There's no musicians. It's just talking over a drumbeat."

"It's the music of the streets," Rashid said.

"The streets?" his grandfather said in response. "I grew up on the streets and it didn't sound anything like that."

Khalid tensed at the note that had entered his father's voice, a note that he had heard many times growing up. Disapproval. Perhaps even disappointment. The sound of it still felt as a sharp point pressing against his heart. And yet, Rashid either did not notice or did not care. "I'm going to make you into a fan, Daada-ji," he said, wrapping the headphone cable around his fingers and slipping the apparatus into the pocket of his coat. "You wait and see. One day you're complaining and the next you're listening to Jay-Z."

"Jay-Z. That's not even a name. Those are just letters. Even I know that."

"That is his name," Rashid said. "He's married to Beyoncé."

"Beyoncé," his grandfather said. "These people don't even bother identifying themselves as part of a family. It's like they just dropped to earth out of an egg." And then, to Khalid's surprise, and to Rashid's immense enjoyment, the old man reached his hand toward the back seat.

"What?" Rashid said.

"What else is there? Why did you take the headphones away?"

"You want to hear another song?"

"I won't lower myself to call that a song but yes play me something else. Something that sounds like music this time. And in English please. I already know Urdu. And Punjabi and Pashto and several others besides. It is English I wish to work on."

It went on like that, Rashid cueing up a new track and his grandfather listening and then commenting, until Khalid suggested they plug the player directly into the vehicle, at which point Rashid assailed the car with a constant stream of sonic noise. Khalid had been in America long enough to have heard rap and hip-hop and all the rest and he still did not understand the appeal of such music but of course he recalled many things from his own childhood that provided only a sense of confusion for his parents. Perhaps this was but the same for his son's generation. Jay-Z and Beyoncé and all the rest.

"We're almost there," he said at one point during a brief lull between tracks. But it felt as if neither his father nor his son were listening to him at all.

After the prayer service, they ate lunch together in Columbus and shopped at the specialty market for spices and foodstuffs Rafia had listed, ingredients, she had told him, to prepare his father's favorite dish from back home in Lahore. When they were done with the shopping it was nearly three and they did not reach the factory until well after four, the day's work nearly at its end. Tom Bailey met them as they came through the door and relayed the numbers they had reached, the orders they had filled and the orders they had yet to complete. Khalid's father listened with his head cocked to the side like some querulous bird.

He had a few phone calls to make to update customers on their orders, although in truth most of those he called at that late hour had already gone home, their businesses closed for the weekend. Mary Lou was back in the office, much to his surprise, and he offered his condolences at the loss of her mother. He could feel Rashid watching him closely as he spoke to her, as if trying to imagine himself into the scene that was playing out before him.

He made a final phone call close to five and that customer, the representative of an electronics company out of Chicago, wanted to discuss the technical specifications of his order and by the time that call was complete the factory was silent. He exited his office to find his father sitting at the bare surface of the desk Khalid had installed for him.

"Where's Rashid?" Khalid said.

"Downstairs listening to his music."

"You're very kind to him," Khalid said.

"He's a good boy," his father said.

"Takes after his daada-ji."

"I wasn't quite so . . ." He hunted for the word. Then he said, "Bent."

"Bent?"

"Am I not using that word correctly?"

"I don't think so," Khalid said. He thought for a moment, then said, "Do you mean weird?"

His father looked aghast. "Weird?" he said. "Does it mean that too?"

"I guess it could. Like you could call someone bent in a weird way. Bent out of shape is the phrase. But that doesn't really mean weird, actually; that means, like, irritated. Is that what you mean? That Rashid seems irritated?"

"No, no," his father said. "There's another—it's something like being aimed at a target."

"A target? Like a gun target?"

He shook his head again, obviously frustrated. "Bent for a purpose," he said.

Khalid thought about this phrase: bent for a purpose. "Right, right," he said now. "Like 'bent on destruction' or something."

"Bent on destruction? That's where your mind goes? No wonder Rashid listens to such music."

Khalid said nothing now, the old prickle beginning to run through him again: that he had failed his father somehow, that he had disappointed the man who had given him life itself. "All right then," he said simply. "Let's go."

But his father did not move from his seat at the desk. "Wait," he said. "I didn't mean it like that."

"Like what?"

"I didn't mean to upset you."

"You haven't," Khalid said. "Let's go."

"I have though," he said. "And I have no right to."

Khalid had been swiveling back and forth between the little office and the door that led down to the assembly floor but now he turned and faced his father. "You have every right to say whatever you want, Abu-ji," he said.

His father looked up at him from the desk, his eyes wide and wet and dark. "Khalid," he said, "there's something I want to tell you."

Ah, Khalid thought, here it comes. He thought he would be relieved once it was all brought out into the open but now that the moment had come he realized he did not want to hear this confession at all, wanted instead to simply walk away and let the old man hold his secret forever. But instead he said, "I'm listening." Only that.

For a long while the old man did not speak, continuing to sit there at the desk his son had placed in the office for his sole use but which he had never once sat at until this night, his eyes not on Khalid now but out across the room, empty but for the two of them. Then his father nodded as if relegated to what he was about to say. But when he spoke at last there was no great confession, or at least no confession of financial disaster. "I wanted you to know," his father said simply, "that I think you're doing a fine job."

Khalid waited. He had not even really heard his father's sentence, steeled as he was for the confession that had not come. When his father said nothing more he finally cleared his throat. "All right," he said. "Thank you."

"You know," his father said now, "I tried very hard to make something of myself."

"And you did."

"Yes, I did," his father said, "and it took a great deal of time. So much time. But you know how that is, running a business of your own."

"Certainly," Khalid said. "It takes a great deal of time."

"It felt like I never had enough time, really. But then one day you find out that you've become an old man and . . ."

"You're still a young man," Khalid said.

"No, no," his father said, waving a hand toward him, "that's not what I mean. I'm not looking for a compliment."

"I'm not trying to give you a compliment, Abu-ji," Khalid said. "Just stating the truth."

His father shook his head. "Let me finish," he said. He looked up at him and Khalid nodded and then his father said, "When you're old you suddenly have all the time in the world. So much time. And there's nothing to do with it but think. So you find yourself thinking back over what you made of your life."

"You need not be idle, Abu-ji. I've been asking you to help me here at the factory. Right there at that desk you're sitting at."

"You misunderstand," his father said. "It's not that I don't want to help you, Khalid. It's that you don't need my help."

"Of course I do."

"No," his father said.

"Why would you say such a thing?"

"Because I'd just make a mess of it," his father said. "You took this place and made it what it is. And it's doing well. I can see that. If there was some way I might be of help I'd be glad to. But you're doing a good job, Khalid. And not only with this but with Rashid and Saroya. You're a good husband to Rafia." He paused a moment. "And you're a good son," he said.

"You're an excellent father."

"You know that's not true," the old man said and in his voice was a roughness, a fullness that sounded, to Khalid's ears, like sandpaper across the grain of a board. "Khalid," he said, "listen to me."

"I am listening," Khalid said. He could hear his son's footsteps in the stairwell that led up from the assembly floor, the dull knock of his tennis shoes against the risers.

"Really really listen."

"I am listening, Abu-ji. I am. I promise you. I am."

"I'm proud of you," his father said.

And now Khalid did hear, at last, what his father was trying to impart to him, not some grand confession of misdeeds in a country which was, even in that moment, ten full hours in the future, seven thousand miles away across an ocean and through political boundaries untold.

He did not know what he would have done if his son had not come bursting into the room in that moment, his father saying simply, "There he is," and rising from his seat behind the desk and coming around to Khalid's side. His hand gentle upon his elbow. "We should get home," he said.

"Yes, yes," Khalid said, his vision wobbling so that the whole office felt, for a moment, as if it had slipped underwater.

"Are you all right, Abu?" Rashid said.

"Yes, I'm fine," Khalid said. He reached out and touched his son's shoulder.

"What's all this?" Rashid said. "Are we going or not? It feels like we've been here for days and days."

"Lead the way," the boy's grandfather said.

Khalid followed in a kind of daze. He felt utterly exhausted, as if he had traveled the length and width of the state, but also strangely exhilarated, as if in completing such travel he had somehow accomplished a task he did not know he had been working toward. His feet on the stairs felt heavy but in some part of him he floated, weightless and alive.

And from just ahead, his father's voice, grandfather to grandson, in English: "Look at what your father has built."

Khalid paused there beside them under the harsh fluorescent lights. There ran the cavernous assembly floor with its rows of benches and machines, small welding apparatuses and hanging tubes for air hammers and racks of testing equipment and supplies, all of it orderly and organized. It was hard to imagine, now, in the quiet of the early evening, that this room was, during the daylight hours, a blaze of industry. And yet twenty-one souls worked here, welding and screwing and hammering together hundreds of electronic transformers to customer specifications that varied along every conceivable line. Khalid had known so little about such things when he had first come to purchase the place but now the factory occupied a part of his soul. What if it was gone? How could he ever pull back that empty piece of him that had been burned away?

"Yes, it's very good," his son said.

And then his father: "Khuda ussay khush rakhay."

That glimmer a kind of light now. Khalid could feel it coming in through the steel walls of the factory, a brightness from elsewhere, the light of some star from across a thousand fields and farms, from across one ocean and another, cities and deserts and people uncountable.

"I'm starving," Rashid said. "Let's go."

They stepped into the new darkness, first Rashid and then his grandfather. "Maybe we should bring home something to eat so they don't need to cook," the old man said.

Khalid set the alarm and looked back one final time at the expanse of the factory floor, the far lights going out and the next and next in series so that it felt as if a wave of darkness rushing in from some horizon he could not see.

"What would you like for dinner then, Daada-ji?" his son said as Khalid pulled the door closed on that darkness.

"You know I am partial to the sushi." He held up a finger. "Dragon roll," he said.

Rashid laughed.

Khalid was a step behind and he slowed to watch them, adrift under the luminous firmament of wheeling stars. There stood the picnic table around which his workers smoked their cigarettes, the oak above it a massive shape twisting into that dark sparkling sky. The silent parking lot. And beyond that the hills rising away in all directions, the continent around them, sea to shining sea.

And there they were at the heart of it all: himself and, just ahead, his father and his son, the two of them laughing, talking lightly about dinner now, about their day in Columbus. Khalid knew he would remember this moment all his life and he wondered if Rashid too would recall it one day, perhaps when he was Khalid's age and had children of his own, time wheeling on and the people who ran upon that wheel plucking an occasional moment from its turning like a pearl stolen from the sea. That he had once been Rashid's age was difficult to fathom. That his father had was impossible. And yet here they were, the cloth of their own imaginings, the old man into whose shape both Khalid and Rashid would one day find themselves and the boy from which Khalid and his father had come.

"So it's to be sushi?" he called from behind.

Rashid turned to him and smiled. How beautiful his son looked. How beautiful was his life.

PART 4

SARAH

See the town.

Steeples and storefronts and homes shining in Sunday morning light. The three downtown traffic signals rotate through their colors regardless of the empty streets, their sidewalks gapped by emptiness—boarded windows, padlocked doors—but a few scrappy survivors hold fast to the heart: two bars, a diner, the coffeeshop, a variety of small retailers abide by means unknown through an economy pitted wholly against them. And all the while the political signs in the windows and on the lawns promise a return to better days. Is this not all of us together? When will they come? Oh Lord when will they come?

From the churches come the townspeople. All winter huddling through the glacial cold and now at last they emerge to find Ohio in the spring. This is what was promised in the shifting stained-glass interior, their souls anointed by Christ: grasses viridescent in the cool brightness of the late-morning sun, greens of emerald and hunter, greens beyond description, and scattered among them tufts of buttercup and trillium, the ghostly purple of wild geranium, pale flecks of foam flower and white baneberry and shooting star, and through which travel the slow shadows of rainclouds, their shapes heavy against the blue.

Sarah could name nearly all of her fellow congregants and was there not some sense of comfort in that fact? Her shoulders ached, her back, but she tried not to wince. There had been moments, over the past months, in which her joints felt as if some iron claw were crushing the bone, the sinew, but the doctors continued to act as if it were all in her head. She did not understand how it was possible to charge her for the visit even when they could do nothing. Would a mechanic do such a thing? Would a plumber, if they were unable to repair the leaky pipe? What she wondered was when she would fall to pieces all over again. This hour? This day? This week? Surely it would come, but when? Her body had become a great and secret betrayer. And yet she also reveled in the light, the spring morning, her friends at the church, the pastor's familiar voice, the way he had, on the first Sunday of her return, stood at the pulpit and welcomed her back, Tom's hand squeezing hers gently as she smiled and the voices of the church murmured her name. She almost burst into tears from the force of it, the understanding that she had not been forgotten, that she still lived in a world of people and those people knew her, even if her body had gone to pieces, even if her sweet baby James was in the heaven of children.

Beside her, Tom stood with Janey's boyfriend, awkwardly introducing him to the various congregants who milled about outside, Janey herself smiling and nodding but saying very little. Between conversations she looked, to Sarah, like a frightened rabbit, nervous at this public event. At least her father had come around, although that was Anthony's own doing more than her own. She had tried, after his initial outburst, to soften the news by telling him what she had overheard, that she had not intended to eavesdrop but had only lingered there because when she had first entered her daughter's room and had said that boy's name—and this she had left out of her telling—Janey's face had gone pale. And so Sarah remained in the hall and listened. When Charlie appeared from his own room, he did not say a word to her in the hall but only passed in silence. She expected him to be surprised at the boy's presence but he only offered an impassive, "Hey," and the boy, Anthony, did much the same, a familiarity there that Sarah wondered at even as she continued to stand in that dark hall, listening as the boy unpacked his heart on their sofa, unpacked it for Janey to do with what she wanted and when Anthony had told her, at last, that he loved her, that he loved Janey, his fumbling words telling her, telling Sarah, just how young he was, how young they both were—I like you. I mean, you know, like I really like you. Like a lot—the effect so stunningly complete, complete and incomplete, formed and unformed, that she, Sarah, had emitted a small brief yelp, a response so wholly involuntary that she clapped her hands over her mouth in surprise.

She spoke with Janey after the boy left and spoke with Tom about it the following evening, thinking, perhaps naively, that he would adjust to the news with some semblance of grace but his reaction had been one of instantaneous and bewildered rage.

"I'm just telling you," she said, "so that when Janey tells you, or Anthony does, or you find out some other way, you won't be surprised."

"Surprised? I'm gonna kick his teeth in."

Then had come the stomping around the room, the ranting, the waving about of his hands, his reaction, at least at first, simply that of a father worried for his daughter's safety, a worry perhaps shaded by the proximity of the threat, not someone from the high school, a figure he could understand, but instead someone from Tom's own circle, an employee with whom he had spoken many times. But there also had been, Sarah thought, a deeper level to his distress, his anger. Nothing he said spoke to the color of Anthony Shaw's flesh. She did not think he had ever heard her husband use the word, not the actual word, and he did not do so now, and yet his reaction was itself a variety of occupancy, as if slipping into a role he had not known he needed or wanted but which was there, had always been there, since before his own birth, an outraged baffled white man insensate at the news that his daughter had been violated by a man, no, a creature not quite human at all, none of this articulated, not in words, but present nonetheless in the swinging arms, the fist against his palm, the way his eyes moved about the space without end.

"Just stop it," she said at last. "No more. He's just a boy."

"He's twenty."

"Fine, he's twenty. I wish he were younger but he's not."

"Are they . . . you know . . . are they . . . ?"

"Having sex. I have no idea."

"Jesus fucking Christ. I think I'm gonna puke. That's my baby girl."

"She's growing up."

"We'll just ground her."

"That's a terrible idea."

"Is it? Is it? Well I don't hear any solutions coming from you."

In the end, she had at least elicited a promise from her husband that he would not talk to Janey about it until he had calmed down some, and hoped, too, that he would not talk with Anthony either. When she asked Tom about Anthony's presence at work the next day, her husband admitted that he had avoided the boy entirely. He continued to do so all week, much to Sarah's relief.

Then, on Sunday afternoon, there had been a knock on the door. Charlie opened it and Sarah, from the kitchen, was not entirely surprised to find Anthony Shaw standing there, sock hat once more clutched in his hands.

"I'll go get her," Charlie said to him.

"I'm here to see your folks, actually," he said.

"OK," Charlie said simply. Already he had stepped to the side and waved Anthony into their home.

She and Tom stood in the kitchen and Sarah could feel her husband harden beside her. "What are you doing here?" he said.

"I just wanted to talk to you and your wife," Anthony said, the sock hat twisting in his hands.

Sarah touched Tom's arm but there was no reaction from him at all.

"Come in, Anthony," she said. "Sit down."

"Thank you, Mrs. Bailey."

"Sarah."

He nodded but did not move.

"I'm going out," Tom said suddenly.

"No you're not."

"Yes I am."

"Tom Bailey you are not going anywhere," she said. "Go sit down."

And then Anthony from across the room: "I should go. I didn't mean to ruin your afternoon."

"You're not the one ruining the afternoon," Sarah said.

Tom did not seem to know what to look at, his eyes darting about as if searching for a solution he could not, as of yet, locate or identify. "Fine," he said at last. "But I'm gonna need a beer." Then he glanced at the boy, man, still standing just inside the door. "You want one?"

"No thank you," Anthony Shaw said.

He talked to them for nearly an hour, telling them about his childhood in Cleveland, about what had happened to his friend there, and why he had come to their town to live with his aunt, a woman Sarah had known for many years at work, and that he had not intended to fall in love with Janey. Those were the actual words he had used, "fall in love," and Tom, for all his bluster and his protectiveness and his fear, seemed to melt at those words, his clipped diction falling away until there came a moment, midway through that hour, when he had cracked a joke of some kind; Sarah could no longer remember what it had been, but she had felt, in that moment, a wave of relief for she knew that it meant that her husband's mood had changed, slipping from that fear, that protectiveness, into something else, something that felt like acceptance, however grudging.

Jane returned home only after Anthony had left, a passing that, Sarah thought, must have been orchestrated. She ate dinner with them and they did not speak of Anthony's visit, did not speak of much of anything, until Charlie rose to clear the plates. "Hang on there, buddy," Tom said.

The boy looked confused but returned to his chair.

"So I hear you've got a boyfriend," Tom said to his daughter.

"Yeah, so?"

"Well, I just want to make sure you're OK and all that. I'm your dad and I get concerned about these things."

"Yeah," she said. "I don't know. It's just kind of like a thing that happened."

"Most things are," he said. "I wish he was a bit younger."

"He's . . ."

"I know, I know. He's just two years older. I know. I'm just old fashioned, I guess. I didn't know you got so grown up. And, you know, I don't know, he's Black."

"Yeah," she said. "I noticed that. Are we gonna be racist now?"

"No," Tom said. "No, I just, you know, I mean, your mom and I . . ." He glanced at her. "It's just that it's gonna be hard for you. For both of you."

"Yeah well maybe let's not start that here."

"You know what I mean. People around here . . ."

"They're racist assholes."

"Well, sometimes, yeah."

"I know."

"OK," he said. "I just wanted to get all that out in the open. Anyone have anything else to say about it? Charlie?"

Charlie shrugged. "I don't know. Seems cool." He shrugged again.

That had been more than a month ago now. Time and its passing. Now Tom stood in conversation with Anthony and Pastor Mitchell. John Hardiman was there too and she could see his eyes flashing back and forth between Anthony and Tom, as if unsure what to make of their proximity, as if it was one thing to see them talking at the smoker's table at the factory but quite another to find them here on a Sunday in front of the church. Janey had sat next to Anthony all through the service but Sarah noticed that they had not shown any public displays of affection; she did not know if this was a planned calculation on their part or an instinctual behavior, but she did not disapprove. It had taken them some weeks to adjust fully to the idea of this twenty-year-old Black man dating their daughter and so it made sense to her that the congregation might need some time to adjust to the notion as well. This was a world beyond their understanding in many ways and she knew that, like she and Tom, many looked upon Sarah as the young girl she had been just a few scant years before, those moments between girl and woman so quick that they had passed by Sarah's eyes without her noticing, a blink, a flicker, and here she was, a woman, graduating high school in just a few weeks and off to college, thankfully on scholarship, and close enough that she could still live at home, at least until she decided to do otherwise. Sarah did not know how much of that decision lay in her relationship with her new boyfriend but her mother would take it. She was not ready to watch her daughter fly fully into the great world beyond, although she knew, hoped, that Janey was ready for whatever was to come next. Sarah wished she herself could say the same.

The congregation drifted apart, the knots of conversation lessening and splitting up, people calling to their neighbors and friends that final goodbye as they went on to whatever errands they had yet to accomplish on that Sunday afternoon.

"Hey, we're gonna skate," Charlie called to her from where he stood with Kent.

"OK," she said. "I think your dad and I are gonna go out for a while so we might not be home."

"Out where?" Charlie said.

"I don't know."

"K," he said. "I'll text you."

They clambered into the car only after Sarah and Anthony had wandered off together.

"Jeez I'm glad that's over," Tom said beside her. "I felt like a cruise director or something. Interracial *Love Boat*."

He turned the key and the car rumbled to life.

"You're a good cruise director."

"Love . . ." he sang. "Exciting and new . . ."

She had told Janey the same thing she had told Charlie, that they would not be home for a time, and as they drove she wondered if it would sound, to her daughter, like an invitation to have sex in their house, although also understanding at some basic level that, if they indeed were having sex, she would rather they do it at home then somewhere less safe. What a thought to have about her baby girl. She wondered if there was a way to talk about such things with her daughter but of course she also knew that the only way to have such conversations was to have them or not have them, that nothing about parenting was ever easy and most of it was near impossible and that this, a conversation, was merely awkward. That she could have such a conversation, that it was possible to do so, was itself a blessing to her, for God knew she had been through much worse.

The grave, when they reached it, was covered in the same bright swell of spring grass that they had seen all about the church grounds that morning. The flowers they had left the previous week were brown and Tom scooped them away and held them in his hand, their sad weeping buds leaning downward toward the earth. JAMES WILSON BAILEY, the stone read. The dates just six months apart. How small he had been. Good God. She had held him and now he was gone. Even now it felt as if a hammer had struck the diamond of her heart and had shattered it to pieces all over again.

"There he is," she said quietly at Tom's side. "Our baby."

"Oh," he said, more a sound than a word. A hitch in his throat. His arm moved around her. She knew he hated to come here, that for him it was a terrible reminder of everything that had happened to them, his heart to gray ash all over again. That he came with her, that he did not complain of it even though she knew how he felt, was itself a kind of blessing.

"I can still feel him," she said.

"So can I."

"Sometimes I wake up and reach for him and he's not there."

"I know," he said.

"I want him back."

He had been quiet the previous times they had come there together, had come to stand before the stone, but this time something had changed and the sob that escaped him was terrible to hear, breaking through him like a wave and when she looked to his face it was caught in a rictus of agony like she had never seen before.

"Oh, honey," she said to him now, her tiny form wrapping into his. "I'm sorry. I'm sorry I brought you here."

"Shit, shit," he said. "I'm sorry. I just wish it wasn't always so hard."

"It'll get better. I'll get better. We'll make it. We will."

"Will we?"

"Sure," she said. "We always do."

And there they were, these two, clinging together as we all do in times of terror and heartbreak and sadness. And in love. The unbearable days cresting on into others until we know that they were not so unbearable after all for here we stand, still and ever, you and I, our hearts beating in our chests and our lives wild in the face of it.

ACKNOWLEDGMENTS

For their knowledge, care, friendship, intelligence, and patience, especially in relation to specific details of geography, character, culture, artifact, sound, language, and/or idiom: Andrew Beckner, Cassandra Brown, JaNay Brown-Wood, Kristina Esfandiari, Maura Grady, Tim Johnson, Kaelin Lee, Douglas Manuel, James Plotkin, Sarosh Shahbaz, Sharene Siddiqui, and Dawn Weber. Thank you all, my friends.

My gratitude to those who read manuscript pages, especially to address my worries about possible missteps and/or misuses of culture but also just to help me make this book the best possible version of itself: Saim Arshad, Jane Bauer, Musharraf Ali Farooqi, John Freeman, Dana C. Johnson, Emily Nemens, Muhammad Tahir Shahbaz, and Bilal Tanweer.

Michael Spurgeon and Eleanor Jackson, to whom this book is dedicated: thank you for continuing to believe in me even when I did not.

This book, like all books, is a team effort. Thank you to everyone at Melville House who made this possible: Maya Bradford, Susan Chodakiewicz, Beste M. Doğan, Molly Donovan, Dennis Johnson, Mike Lindgren, Valerie Merians, Ariel Palmer-Collins, Alison Strobel, Janet Joy Wilson, and most of all, my editor, Carl Bromley, who read this book with care and love.

Macie: ever and always. And my boys. And of course Vivian, who lived.

Finally, the music of the late Jason Molina played a significant part in this writing of this book. You are forever missed, my friend. I leave the reader with your words, rather than my own:

It'll get so quiet when this record ends
You can hear the first hour of the world

ABOUT THE AUTHOR

Christian Kiefer has a PhD in American literature from the University of California–Davis and directs the low-residency MFA at Ashland University. He is the author of three prior novels: *The Infinite Tides, The Animals,* and most recently *Phantoms,* which was one of *Kirkus Reviews* and BBC's Best Books of 2019. He lives with his family in Placer County, California.